BAKER CITY

C.J. PETIT

TABLE OF CONTENTS

BAKER CITY 1
PROLOGUE 4
CHAPTER 1 14
CHAPTER 2 40
CHAPTER 3 55
CHAPTER 4 84
CHAPTER 5 112
CHAPTER 6 147
CHAPTER 7 192
CHAPTER 8 226
CHAPTER 9 268
CHAPTER 10 323
CHAPTER 11 378
CHAPTER 12 413
CHAPTER 13 439
CHAPTER 14 459
CHAPTER 15 479
EPILOGUE 501

PROLOGUE

May 12, 1867
Along the Oregon Trail
Idaho Territory

It was just a rock. It wasn't anything special. It wasn't big, and it surely wasn't valuable, but it was there, and it was about to become the instigator of disaster.

The other wagons had already passed the rock, and not one of the drivers or anyone else had paid it any mind as they climbed the Oregon trail up toward the pass.

The oxen team pulling the Orson wagon was under the whip as the last wagon creaked its way up the trail's incline. While the rock was ignored, what no one could have seen even if they had looked, was the crack in the yoke connecting the team to the wagon.

It had been there when it had been built back in St. Joseph, Missouri just eight months earlier. The wagon builder hadn't been negligent in his construction, the wood had looked good, but that crack was there deep below the surface of the six-inch thick oak. As the wagon trundled along through Nebraska and then Wyoming Territory, the crack grew. Each time the yoke was torqued, the split widened and lengthened. It only grew by hair widths most of the time, but the yoke itself was severely weakened as the wagon made the long climb up the grade.

To the right of the wagon was an ominous falloff of almost a thousand feet, ending in a distant river and narrow valley. It was nothing new to the travelers who took the Oregon Trail in search of a new life. They'd climbed and descended dozens of passes and normally frightening plunges off to the side of the trail were no longer frightening or even noteworthy. They were just routine.

Rebecca Orson, on first seeing the drop, had switched places with her husband Bob so she could be on the side of the seat away from the chasm. She didn't want to even look down there. Bob thought it was funny that she would still be spooked by the thought of tumbling into the steep decline.

Even the children in the back of the wagon wouldn't have paid attention to the long drop if they could see it.

Bob Orson, like all of the preceding drivers, ignored the eight-inch tall flat rock off to the side of the trail, and when the wagon's right front wheel met the rock, the wheel hopped up and began to roll over its rounded granite surface. As the wheel started to rise, the front axle began to increase torque on the weakened yoke and just before that wheel reached the full eight inches above the ground, the strain on the yoke became too great.

With a resounding crack, the yoke snapped with the sound of a small cannon blast, and after the yoke separated from the axle, the wagon broke loose and the oxen, freed from the onerous weight they were pulling, started jogging up the incline.

Rebecca was thrown from her perch on the left side of the driver's seat, tumbled to the dirt, landed on her left elbow and rolled three times before coming to a stop in the middle of the trail, stunned by her sudden ejection.

Her husband was yanked from the seat when the reins he had wrapped around wrists were suddenly snapped taut by the trotting oxen. He slammed to the dirt on his stomach, then found himself rolling to the right and began sliding toward the edge of the trail, then slid into the steep decline, screaming as he began to be pummeled by the rocks, but continued to hang onto the reins knowing the consequences if he let go.

The wagon yoke's demise left the front axle in a moderate right turn, and after the wagon lost its forward momentum, even as Bob screamed and Rebecca was tumbling to the ground, gravity exerted its pull and the wagon began to roll backwards, not having very far to go.

Inside the wagon, Andy and Addie had been chatting when the yoke snapped, and the loud crack and the sudden chaos startled them both, but they took a few seconds to wonder what was happening. By the time they began to crawl to the front of the wagon to find out what had happened, they felt the sickening sensation of the wagon's backward movement.

As the wagon began to tilt, Addie screamed, "Mama!"

The tilt didn't last long as the heavily loaded wagon accelerated, made its slight turn, then left the trail and plunged into the chasm, rolling over as it picked up more speed. As it tumbled, parts began to snap from the wagon, beginning with the right front wheel, then its contents began flying away as it gained momentum, beginning with the water and flour casks on the outside of the wagon.

Bob was still rolling and sliding as he was being pulled along by the oxen. The animals finally stopped, and Bob's momentum carried him into a heavy rock outcrop, but he had already slowed considerably, and the rocks acted as a hard brake to his forward movement, bruising but not breaking anything. Once the dust had settled, he groaned, took a deep breath and used the reins as a lifeline, pulling himself back onto the trail, collapsing onto the flat ground when he reached safety.

Rebecca had quickly scrambled to her feet even as the wagon rolled backward and tipped over the edge. She had heard Addie's scream, and despite her damaged elbow, ran in a panic to the spot where the wagon had disappeared. When she looked over, she witnessed the heart-stopping sight as the wagon continued its long, tumbling drop to the bottom of the chasm and could only watch helplessly with horrified eyes as the wagon plummeted down the long drop flipping over as it fell. *Her children were in that wagon!*

She stared in complete terror as boxes and furniture were being ejected from the wagon. The water barrel exploded, creating a rain cloud hovering overhead as the flour barrel burst making a white fog that followed the disappearing wagon. She began to scream as other members of the wagon train came running to see what had happened, knowing there was nothing anyone could do.

She had stopped screaming and covered her open mouth with both hands as she stared in disbelief as the distant wagon continued its awkward journey to the bottom of the abyss, spewing fewer contents now, the canvas top nothing but a ragged flag signaling the wagon's expiration.

From the moment the wheel struck that rock until the wagon reached its final resting place had taken less than a minute. Far below at the bottom of the chasm, the remains of the wagon lay still, the flour dust cloud still hanging in the air. There was no sign of life from her children who had been peacefully sleeping just minutes earlier.

Rebecca was so devastated that she hadn't even thought about her husband. She had only been married to Bob Orson for a little more than a year, but the children were hers. She thought she saw something moving, but it was so far away, she couldn't identify it behind the white cloud of flour.

Rebecca continued to stare, ignoring all of the other members of the wagon train nearby, and finally seeing no more sign of movement, Rebecca closed her eyes, and just stood there frozen as she wept. She was unaware of the other women who tried to console her. She had just lost all that mattered to her…her beloved children.

She continued to cry quietly for five minutes, before finally opening her eyes, drying them with her skirt, then turned to find out what had become of her husband. She assumed he was all right because she knew he hadn't fallen down into that chasm. She finally found him surrounded by other men, and slowly walked toward him.

Bob spotted her, his eyes narrowed, then he stood and as the others watched, stalked angrily in her direction.

"Come to see if you were a widow yet, Rebecca? Or hoping you were?" he growled when they were ten feet apart.

Rebecca was stunned by his attack. *Didn't he even care that the children had gone over with the wagon?*

"Bob, the children! They went over with the wagon and may be dead! Don't you even care?" she pleaded loudly.

"Why should I? They were yours, not mine. That wagon had everything we owned in it. Son of a bitch! Don't you understand? All we have left are those damned oxen and the money in the lead wagon box."

Rebecca's anger flared as she said through clenched teeth, "Yes, Bob, they *are* my children, not were. I know that they're still alive, and I'm going to go and find them!"

Bob sneered and shouted, “Well, you go and do that, you silly, stupid woman! I’m gonna see about finding a ride because I’m going to Oregon. If you wanna climb down that cliff or walk back to Missouri, go ahead, I don’t care. I’m going west. If you finally get a lick of sense in that tiny brain of yours and you want to ride, come and find me.”

He turned and stormed away, his anger still evident as witnessed in his tight jaw and his clenched fists.

The crowd of onlookers were in various levels of shock at Bob’s reaction, but they still began to disperse back to their wagons. They thought he was probably just upset from his near-death battering and surely didn’t mean those horrible things he had said.

Tragedy wasn’t uncommon on the long trail and they were reaching the end of their long journey cross the western half of the United States. They needed to go on but would support Bob and Rebecca as best they could.

After Bob had gone, and the others began filtering away, Rebecca stood there totally numb. She knew Bob meant every vitriolic, heartless word he had uttered. *How could she go on when in her heart of hearts, she knew her children were alive at the bottom of that gorge?* She forgot about her husband for the time being because she needed to know if there was anything that could be done to rescue her injured children. She desperately looked among the remaining crowd.

She spotted Leo Crandall, the wagon master, hurried to him and said desperately, “Leo, my children are down there! We need to go and see if they are alive. We need to hurry! They’re probably hurt!”

Leo looked down at his feet for a few seconds, then looked back at Rebecca and said, “Ma’am, there’s no way they could have survived that fall, and we couldn't get down there anyway. I'm sorry, but those are just the facts. You go and see your husband now. I reckon the widow Murphy or Emily Amber would be able to put you up."

She began to cry again, hearing what she knew was probably the truth, but believed that if her children had died, she would have felt it in her soul. And then, there was that movement far down below that prompted that tiny hope that they were still alive. Her mind was tortured with logic that said they were dead and a mother's desperate hope that they were alive at the bottom of the chasm.

———

At the bottom of that gorge, the only wheel that was still round rotated slowly on its axle. There were creaks and groans from the wagon announcing its demise as the wood settled, but there were other, human groans as well.

Andy Orson was lying on the ground near the wagon, out of sight from far above. He had been thrown free early and had slid and tumbled alongside the wagon, his fall hidden by the flour cloud. He had hit a few rocks along the way and had hurt his knee and shoulder. He was hurting, but he was alive.

He was still dazed by the event. One minute he was in the back, teasing Addie about her hair and then the world turned upside down. He tried to get up, but was still dizzy, so he plopped back down to the hard ground, turned and looked at the crushed wagon and knew his sister was dead. He began to cry for his mama and Addie. They'll come and get him, he thought, and then he passed out.

———

The wagon train families were all pitching in to cope with the disaster. Bob found a spot on the widow Murphy's wagon and the Orson oxen were hitched behind the Wheeler's wagon, and twenty minutes after the disaster, they were moving up toward the pass again.

Rebecca needed to talk to someone, and the last person she wanted to talk to was Bob Orson, so she walked to Florence Johnson's wagon.

Florence was the first woman to rush to Rebecca as she had stood staring over the edge of the chasm, watching the wagon and her children meet their ends. She had heard Bob's rant and expected to have Rebecca show up at her wagon rather than ride with her husband, so when Rebecca did arrive, she wordlessly assisted her onto her driver's seat.

Rebecca and Florence had met in St. Joseph and had struck an instant friendship. Their husbands hadn't gotten along all that well, but she still had spent a lot of time with Florence and now needed her support.

The wagon train crossed the hump of the pass and began its downward trek thirty minutes later and had ten more miles to go before they would make camp.

As they drove, Rebecca didn't say a word, and Florence just began talking about inane subjects to try and take her friend's mind off of her loss and what Bob had said. She knew that it was impossible, but it was the best she could do.

Andy slowly opened his eyes. His shoulder and knee were throbbing as he carefully sat up and looked around. Nothing had changed. He turned and looked up the wall to the top where the wagons were and didn't see any of those canvas tops that should be there. *They were gone! They had left him here! How could his mama allow that to happen?*

He slowly tried to stand, giving himself some support by keeping his left hand on a nearby rock. His knee hurt, but he finally stood and began hobbling over to the wagon. He needed to find Addie. He knew she was probably dead, but he had to make sure. He suddenly felt bad for teasing her. If only he had known what was going to happen, he would have been hugging her instead. If by some miracle he found her alive, he told God he would never tease her again, and he'd give her a big hug, too.

He reached the back of the wagon, or what used to be the back before it rolled over a few dozen times. Now, it was nothing more than some broken slats of lumber.

"Addie! Addie! Are you in there?" he shouted.

Then he stopped moving and listened for a response. He thought he heard something move but wasn't sure. Maybe something just fell.

"Addie! This is Andy. Are you okay?" he shouted again, hoping for an answer.

Then, to his incredible relief he received one.

A weak, "Andy?" emanated from somewhere in the wagon, but it was barely above a whisper.

Andy was both elated and afraid. His sister was alive but didn't sound good. He began to pull things out of the way furiously. He couldn't identify some of the things he tossed aside. It was just a mess inside.

"Addie! Say something so I can find you," Andy shouted.

"Over here, Andy," she said, her voice sounding stronger.

Andy, focused on her voice, and despite his shoulder pain began throwing things out of his way faster. He had heard her voice to his left. The wagon had come to rest on its right side, where the water cask had been, so she would be at the bottom of the wagon. He continued to burrow to his sister and was almost there. Just a few more things were in the way and suddenly, he could see the top of her blonde head and a grin crossed his face.

"Addie! I can see you. I've got to get a few more things out of your way," he said excitedly.

"Okay."

He finally saw why Addie had survived. She was sandwiched between the floor of the wagon and the mattress that she slept on. He just moved the still intact items, so he had more room. Finally, he saw her face.

"Hello, Addie," he said as he smiled at his little sister, "Are you hurt anywhere?"

"My leg hurts, Andy. Where's mama?"

"We're at the bottom of a giant hill, Addie. I don't think mama knows we're here. They're gone, Addie."

Addie began to sob. Andy felt bad for making her cry, but she had to know. She was only seven, and he had to be brave now. He had to protect his little sister.

CHAPTER 1

Just a couple of hours after the crash, and eight miles northeast of the destroyed wagon, Hugh McGinnis felt like an idiot. He'd been followed for three days by those pesky Cheyenne, and even after he picked off three of them, the other five kept coming. He should have just avoided them entirely. He had seen them with his field glasses from half a mile away, but figured he'd just pull off into the trees and let them pass in front of him. But then the wind changed, and their horses had picked up his horse or his mule's scent they were alerted to his presence.

As soon as he had seen their rapid change to his direction, he had quickly ridden in the opposite direction. He set his mare to a fast trot down the side of the Oregon Trail that he had been following and into the uncharted wilderness of Idaho. They chased but were leery of getting too close until they ascertained how much firepower the white man had with him. They found out soon enough that he had quite a lot, but the long manhunt was on.

During the past three days, it had been a game of cat and mouse, and he was the mouse, but at least he was a mouse with sharp teeth. He had used the Sharps for all three of the dead Cheyenne but had to be careful. He only had another eighteen rounds for the big gun, but still had plenty for his Henry. He would just rather they didn't get that close. If they got within a hundred yards, he'd have a real fight on his hands.

Yesterday, they had circled around the night before and almost drygulched him. He had caught a reflection off one of the three Springfield muskets carried by his pursuers, and that had saved his hide. He stopped and reversed his direction, much to the chagrin of his antagonists, as they had to remount and resume the chase. Hugh used that to his advantage and set up his own ambush, picking off one more. While they waited to see if he'd shoot again, he made his break. He changed his direction again and headed west. He wanted to stay roughly oriented toward the Oregon Trail. He would like to start riding west again to Oregon, but with his hair intact.

His last trick had been the old follow the stream routine, but it really wasn't very effective as a deception. It might slow them down just enough for him to find a good place for another ambush, though.

He knew they were after his supplies more than his scalp, but he needed those supplies now more than ever. He was a good week from the nearest settlement, and that was behind him and didn't like to go over ground he had already passed.

His current path had curved widely, and he knew he was now traveling due west again, but his many turns to avoid the Cheyenne had put him a few miles from the Trail. He'd leave the stream and turn more southwest toward the trail, not wanting to get too far away. He had a compass and a good pocket watch, so at least he knew where he was and when he was there. He wasn't sure it was necessarily an advantage, though. Knowing where and when you might die doesn't make it any more pleasant.

After crossing two miles of open ground with no sign of the Cheyenne, he came to a genuine river and figured it must be the Sweetwater, which ran mostly west to east and paralleled the Trail. He decided to cross the river and see if they'd follow. They may not want to risk being caught in the river with him hiding on the other side with his rifles.

He led the mule to the bank to prepare to cross. His horse didn't mind crossing rivers, but that mule surely didn't care for it.

"Too bad, mule," Hugh thought, "we need to cross that cold water."

He walked the horse into the water and the unhappy mule followed but didn't complain. Three minutes later, they were across and heading west again with the river on their right. He paused occasionally to see if the Cheyenne were behind him, couldn't see them, but that didn't count for much.

He led the mule up the opposite riverbank and then crossed over a rocky area. He had to walk the animal slowly to avoid injuring their ankles and debated about finding a good place for setting up an ambush. Only three of the remaining Cheyenne were armed with guns and they had a limited amount of ammunition. They were always short on ammo for an obvious reason…they had to steal it. He had also discovered that Indians were generally poor shots with white man's weapons. They often broke off the sights finding them annoying. They had a lot of misfires with the old muzzle loaders like those carried by his friends behind him. A shootout might be best after all. He was tired of running but rode for another hour without any sign of his pursuers.

That was because his Cheyenne followers had stopped and were having an argument. They were low on food and were no closer to the white man than they were two days ago. White Antelope was their leader, and even he had doubts about whether to keep up the chase or not. They needed the guns and ammunition that the white eyes had with him, but they had already lost four of their party to his long gun. Their Springfields could match it for distance but they were well aware of their inaccuracy at long range. Plus, they only had seven percussion caps between them, and one of their guns wasn't even working any longer and was carried just for show.

White Antelope listened to his warriors discuss the possible abandonment of the chase and finally told them of his decision. They would hunt for food then wait and see if the white man returned to the trail for three days, but no more.

Hugh, of course, was unaware of the decision. What was worse, he knew they had chased him into Crow territory and he'd rather face the Cheyenne than the Crow. The Cheyenne seemed like good old pals compared to the Crow.

———

Andy had finally managed to free Addie from under the mattress. He thought her left leg was broken, although he wasn't sure. She was just happy to be out from under the tangle of debris.

She sat next to Andy as he held her, having given her the hug he had promised God he would give her if he found her alive.

"Andy, will Mama come back for us?" she asked plaintively.

"I don't think so, Addie. We have to take care of ourselves now."

"Andy, you're only nine!" she protested.

"I know. But I'll be ten soon. I can do things to help us."

"Andy, I'm thirsty."

"Me, too. I'll go get us some water. We have plenty of water with the river so close. You sit right here, okay?"

"Okay," she replied as Andy smiled at her.

Andy reached into a pile of things he had gathered that he thought they could use and pulled out a tin cup. He hobbled down to the river, dipped it into the cold water, drank a full cup and then filled it again for Addie. He limped back and gave her the cup.

"Andy, what's wrong with your leg? Is it broke?" she asked after drinking some of her water.

"No, Addie. I think I twisted my knee when I fell down that giant hill."

"Does it hurt?"

"Some. But it'll be okay. Drink the rest of your water and I'll see if I can get us something to eat."

"Okay," she said as she emptied the tin cup, then set it down on a nearby rock.

Andy began weeding through the jumble that was still in the back of the wagon looking for something edible. The problem, he soon discovered, was that the food they carried almost all required preparation. He found raw beans, some sugar, some bacon, potatoes, onions, and finally, some dried beef. He took two pieces of dried meat and brought them down to Addie.

"Addie, do you remember how mama used to cook?" he asked hopefully as he handed her one of the jerky strips. She was a girl, after all, and girls knew how to cook. He knew he didn't because he was a boy.

"No. She did it so fast, I just waited for it to be cooked."

A deflated Andy said, “Me neither. I’ll figure something out. Don’t worry.”

But Addie had seen his reaction to her answer and worrying was no longer an option.

Three miles east, Hugh was plodding along. He was still debating about re-crossing the river and was giving it a good looking over when he saw some odd things floating by. He watched intently as he first saw what looked like a chest of drawers, but in pieces, with clothing scattered among the wood. The chest itself didn’t surprise him, but no one throws clothing out when they’re ridding a wagon of excess weight.

Then he spotted larger pieces of wood and a child’s doll. If it had been just the dresser, he’d figure that some overloaded wagon owner had decided to divest himself of some weight, but the clothes and doll, along with the broken boards indicated a full wagon had crashed down from the trail above.

He had been following the Oregon trail for three months now and was just a couple of weeks from his ranch in Oregon, a ranch he had never seen. He knew the trail was nearby, and he intended to pick it back up after the whole Cheyenne situation resolved itself, one way or the other. He had gone far afield in the chase and only recently had begun to circle back toward the trail. If the wagon had been on the trail, it could have tumbled off on one of the approaches to a pass. Looking at the condition of the debris, it wouldn’t be too far ahead. But it would be on the other side of the river. That settled the argument. Free supplies would be worth the risk.

He led his horse into the cold water again. This time the mule didn’t suffer the cold water without complaint. As soon as he hit the water, he let his opinion be known and Hugh didn’t know why he let that Missouri liveryman talk him into getting the mule instead of a second horse. They were being swept downriver as they made the crossing, so he watched upriver for any more debris. Another sizeable piece of furniture could spell disaster.

The horse touched bottom on the opposite bank after two minutes of swimming and the mule followed, complaining as always.

He let them stand for a few minutes to rest and let their legs warmer. After five minutes, he turned upriver and had them moving, hoping to find the damaged wagon and its wealth of supplies.

———

The wagon train was almost back on level ground again after its long downward trek from the pass. The wagon master had been this way before and knew of a good campsite another four or five miles away.

Ella Murphy had offered the Orsons a ride in her wagon. Ella was a little younger than Rebecca, but not as pretty. She wasn't bad looking, but she wasn't in Rebecca's class. But to Bob Orson, her best feature was that she didn't have any children. Ella's husband, Ian, had died almost six weeks earlier when they were crossing a ford. The water had been swift and deep, Ian had slipped and hit the water hard. He was gone before anyone could react. In just seconds, Ella Murphy had become a widow.

Bob had told Ella that Rebecca was with Florence and would be over shortly. Until then, he spent time talking with Ella.

———

Florence had stopped the inane chatter and tried to console Rebecca, but it was pointless so soon after the accident. The train had suffered other losses on the journey. The Amber family had been taken ill with dysentery in Nebraska and only Emily Amber had survived. A snakebite from a water moccasin had killed young Ben Crowley and Ian Murphy had died in the river crossing. There were now two new widows among their number.

All Rebecca seemed to be thinking about were her children, and Florence understood her situation. She had been a widow herself and her seven-year-old son Charles was hers, but not her husband's. She had married Cliff Johnson just before the trip, but Rebecca had married Bob Orson a little more than a year before. At least, she thought, Rebecca seemed to have had better luck with husbands. Bob wasn't the best-looking man on the train, but he seemed to treat Rebecca and her two youngsters better than Cliff treated her and Charles.

———

Andy and Addie were sleeping. Andy had pulled a blanket from the wagon along with Addie's mattress. It had taken him a while to do it and a lot of pain, but he felt it was the best thing for her because they both needed some rest.

Suddenly, Andy's eyes popped open when he thought that he had heard something. *What was it?* His greatest fear was Indians, followed closely by bears. He scrambled to the wrecked wagon and found his stepfather's big rifle. He didn't really know how to shoot it but he knew enough to pull back the heavy hammer, then aimed it where he heard the noise. Maybe he could scare away the Indians, but if it was a bear, he knew they'd be in trouble.

He watched the edge of the trees and waited, his arms getting tired holding the heavy barrel toward the trees. Then he saw the nose of a horse and knew that the Indians were here. He pulled the trigger, and the hammer fell with a loud snap, but nothing else happened.

Hugh cleared the trees, having already seen the wagon wreck ahead, but caught sudden movement to his left and was stunned to see what looked like a young boy aiming a Spencer rifle at him. When he heard it click, he was grateful it wasn't loaded as even an amateur could do some serious damage with that carbine.

"Whoa, there, son! I'm not wearing any war paint!" he shouted as he held up his hand.

Andy was horrified when he saw Hugh sitting high on the horse. *He almost shot a white man!* Addie had stirred and saw the big man and his horse, too, and stayed under the blanket.

Andy shouted, "I'm sorry, Mister I thought you were Indians coming to scalp us."

Hugh had to laugh. That little man had sand. He continued to walk his horse and mule until he was close to the destroyed wagon.

"Nope. It's just me, my horse and that ornery mule behind me. Mind if I come over to your camp and set?"

"You mean sit down?"

"Set means step down from the horse. You don't step down unless you're given permission. It's just not polite."

"Oh. Then you can set. We had an accident."

"I can see that," Hugh replied as he stepped down.

He led the horse and mule to a nearby shrub and tied off the horse then walked up to the boy, knelt on one knee and asked, "What happened, son?"

"I don't know, sir. We were inside and suddenly we were crashing down from up there," he replied as he pointed up the steep slope.

"When did this happen?"

"This morning. I don't know what time, though."

"Are you or your sister hurt?"

"My shoulder and knee hurt, and I think Addie broke her leg."

"What's your name, son?"

"I'm Andy Orson, but that's my new name on account of my mother marrying Mister Orson. Me and Addie both were Hobsons first, though."

"Well, Andy and Addie, my name is Hugh. Hugh McGinnis. It looks like you both could use some help. First, I'd better take a look at your injuries to see if I can help. Okay?"

"Okay. Could you look at Addie's first?"

Hugh smiled and tapped Andy on the top of his head, saying "You're a good big brother, Andy. I'll go and see to your sister's injuries first."

As he turned to Addie, he found her blue eyes examining him as he looked at her.

"Hello, Addie. Can I see if your leg is broken? I'll try not to hurt you. Okay?"

Addie finally spoke, replying, “Okay.”

Hugh lifted the blanket and looked at her left leg. If it was broken, it wasn’t displaced at all.

“Okay, Addie. Point to where it hurts.”

Addie pointed to the outside of her leg, about halfway down the calf.

“Okay, I think I know what that is. The good news is that it’s not too bad, even if it is broken. So, I’m going to push on the front of your leg. You tell me if it really hurts, okay? Not if it hurts where you just pointed.”

Huge began slowly working his way down her tibia, watching for any signs of distress. Addie watched as he pushed and gritted her teeth but didn’t cry out. Finally, he reached the ankle.

“That’s good, Addie. You’re a very brave young lady. Can you wiggle your foot for me?”

She did. It hurt, but not as badly as she had expected.

“Very good. What I think you have is a broken fibula, Addie. See, there are two long bones in that part of your leg. The tibia, which is the big bone, the same one I was pushing on, and the fibula, the skinny long bone that you broke. Now, when you walk, the tibia does most of the work. The skinny one just kind of follows along and keeps the big one from doing stupid things like twisting the wrong way. So, I’ll make you a splint for the bone and you’ll be able to walk a little bit. It’ll hurt, but it’ll heal soon because you’re so young. Old folks like me take longer.”

“Why?” she asked, tilting her head.

"Because you youngsters are still growing. If you break a bone, Mother Nature says no problem, we'll just grow right around it. When we stop growing like I did, Mother Nature is not happy and has to stop what she's doing somewhere else to fix it."

"Oh."

"Now, come over here, Andy, and I'll look at your injuries."

Andy stepped over and Hugh put his large hand over Andy's shoulder, then rotated his arm as he left his hand in place.

"Good news, Andy. I think that it's just a bruise. It'll be better in a few days. Let's check out your knee."

Andy stood still as Hugh examined his knee. Then he had him sit down and pressed on the outside, then the inside. He put one hand behind the knee and bent it slowly. Andy grimaced as it bent.

"I think you wrenched that knee pretty good, Andy. It's gonna be sore for some time, maybe two or three weeks. We'll need to keep you off it as much as we can, so try to take it easy."

"Are you a doctor?" asked Andy.

"I was going to be one but went to fight in the War Between the States and never got back to it, but I should have. It's a bad thing to waste education."

"Why did you have to go to war?" Andy asked.

"I didn't really have to, but when my brother died, I thought I should."

"Oh."

"Now, would you both like something to eat?"

In a chorus, they answered, "Yes, please!"

Hugh smiled. They were great kids and he always had a soft spot for kids and dogs.

"Okay. You two just relax. I've got to get the horse unsaddled and the mule unpacked. Andy, you keep an eye out for Indians."

"Are there Indians around here?"

"I had a party of Cheyenne behind me for three days. They may have given up, though. They should have caught up with me at the river right after I crossed. I checked an hour later, and they weren't there, so it's possible that they're gone."

"Did you have to fight 'em?" Andy asked excitedly.

"A few times. I shot four of them and that could be one of the reasons that they might have gone."

"That's good."

"Good that they left. Not so good that I had to shoot them."

"Why not? They were Indians."

"Now, Andy. You seem like a smart boy. Why should I shoot them because they're Indians?"

"Cause they're bad."

"No, I had to shoot them because they were shooting at me. If they didn't do that, I would have just let them go. Indians aren't good or bad. They're just folks like us with different ways, that's all. I've met a lot of white men that are worse than any Indian I've met, and I've met a lot of fine white folks, too. When you look at a man, look at his eyes. If they're honest eyes, he's a good man. If not, he's a bad man. Don't look to see if he's wearing feathers or a top hat. You follow all that?"

"Yes, sir. I'm sorry."

"It's not your fault, Andy. It's what a lot of folks are taught. Now, I'll get moving."

Hugh unsaddled his black mare first. He called her Middie, which was short for 'Midnight', and thought it sounded more feminine, too. After he had Middie settled, he unloaded the pack mule. By the looks of things, he might be here for a while until the children could travel, and how they traveled would take some modification of his saddles.

Once the animals were cleared, Hugh began setting up a regular camp. He had a two-man tent, but first, he built a fire and set up his cooking grid. He didn't have any milk for the youngsters, but he'd figure out something.

He set his frypan on the fire and sliced up some bacon. While it was sizzling, he started setting up his tent. He had to go back and flip the bacon once but managed to get the tent up in short order. He'd pitched the tent so often, he could do it quickly. He went back to the bacon and took out the four strips he had fried, glancing up at the anxious small faces who were staring at the fried pork strips. Then he cut up some bacon into chunks and tossed them into the frypan, which started them shrinking into tasty meat. He snatched the four cooked strips of bacon and handed Andy and Addie two strips of bacon each.

He knew they were very hungry, but still, each said, “Thank you, sir,” when they accepted the meat before they took a bite, then they practically inhaled the bacon.

He smiled at them, then returned to his frypan and added two cans of beans. He couldn’t go through his supplies like this for very long. He’d have to see what the wagon held in the way of food.

When his bean and bacon mix had cooked, he scooped it out and filled two plates. There was enough in the frypan for him, so he pulled it off the fire. He put his coffee pot full of water on the grid and brought the food and two spoons over to the children.

“These are still hot, so you might want to put them on the ground nearby. Now, I don’t have any milk for children with me, so do you want water with your food?”

“Water is good,” replied Andy.

“Coming right up,” Hugh said with a big smile as he snatched two tin cups and walked to the river.

The children were already digging in when Hugh returned with the two cups of water. He gave one to each child and returned to the fire to add coffee to the boiling water in the coffeepot, then took his remaining cup and sat down. He began eating out of the frypan and then filled his cup with steaming black coffee.

“Mister Hugh, how did you get here?” asked Addie as she paused between bites.

He smiled at her. The sound of her voice alone created the smile, and her angelic round face and bright blue eyes added to the effect of incredible cuteness.

"Well, sweetie, that's kind of interesting. You see, I was in Michigan, studying to be a doctor. The war was going on and my brother, who had a ranch in Oregon, joined the army three years ago, but died a year later. He had sent me a letter telling me that the ranch would be mine if anything bad happened to him. So, when he died, and it wasn't even in a battle, you know, he died from being sick. When he died, I felt somehow that I needed to help other soldiers. I left school and joined the army. Anyway, I got out a year and a half ago, and thought about going back to school, but after the war, it didn't seem to matter much. So, I decided to go and see the ranch. I had a horse, and I bought the mule in Missouri. We've been heading west ever since. I followed the Oregon trail because it made sense.

"Now, how I got here directly, was because I ran into those Cheyenne three days ago. They chased me off the trail and I ran around all over the place trying to shake them. I saw some of your things floating down the river, so I came up here to investigate and I found you and Andy. That's the whole story."

"Aren't you lonely?" Addie asked.

"Sometimes. I can always yell at the mule, though."

She giggled as she looked at the mule who was staring at Hugh as if he knew that he was the subject of Addie's merriment.

They had finished eating and Hugh collected their plates and cups and took everything down to the river for a good cleaning.

After he returned to the children, he said, "Addie, I'm going to make a splint for you now to keep your leg from getting hurt any more than what it is now. I'll make it as comfortable as I can. Okay?"

"Okay, Mister Hugh," she said as she smiled at him.

Hugh searched the wagon and found a small, thin board. It looked like it used to be part of a piece of furniture, but what kind, he had no idea. He then found a man's shirt and took them both outside. He stepped over to his packs, found his hatchet, then took the board over to a log and split the board lengthwise with the hatchet and then chopped it at the base to shorten it even more. He took the board over to a large rock and began rubbing the rough edge until it was smooth. Once he was pleased with the support, he took the shirt, pulled out his knife and cut the shirt into wide strips. The strips were about three feet long and six inches wide. He carried his splint makings back to Addie and set them down next to her.

"Okay, young lady, here's your new splint. This is to keep it from twisting and making it break a little more."

Addie nodded.

First, Hugh removed her shoe. He took one of the shirt sleeves and slid it up her leg to prevent the splint from rubbing on raw skin. Then he placed the splint on the inside of the leg and wrapped one of the strips around her leg, just below the knee. He then ripped the strip at the end and tied it off. He repeated it at the ankle end then he put her shoe back on.

"Okay, Addie. If you want to try to walk, you can. It'll feel funny, but it shouldn't hurt so much."

"Alright."

Addie rolled over, stood up, and gingerly put her injured leg down, took a step and then two more.

She looked up at Hugh and grinned as she said, "It only hurts a little. Thank you, Mister Hugh!"

"You're welcome, Addie."

"Mister Hugh, what are we going to do?" asked Andy.

"Well, Andy. I think we take a couple of days to figure out what we can take with us and then we head back and pick up the trail. Then, once we get on the trail again and go find your mama and papa."

Andy's eyes lit up. "*We're gonna go find my mama?"*

"Of course, we are. She's probably already missing you both something terrible. We'll be a few days behind them, but even if we're only walking the horse and mule, they won't gain on us. Once I figure out seating, we can ride and gain on them much faster. I think we should catch up with them in a week or so. Is that okay?"

Addie was clapping, as she exclaimed, "We're gonna see our mama!"

———

Their mama was finally talking to Florence.

"Flo, I'm sure I saw movement down there. My children may be alive and lost. Is there any way we can go back? I can take one of our oxen and head back. It would only take me a day or so."

Florence was struggling to bring Rebecca back to reality.

"Becky, you know that the children couldn't have survived that fall. What you saw was probably the wind blowing a piece of canvas or something. You need to let it go. Now, we'll be pulling over shortly and you need to go with Bob. He's up front with Ella Murphy."

Becky nodded. She was ashamed to admit that all she cared about was her children. If she hadn't needed to provide for them, she never would have married Bob Orson, and she never would have agreed to take them halfway across the country to Oregon. The truth was she hated Bob Orson now. He had caused her children to fall, maybe to their deaths, and he didn't care. She knew it wasn't his fault, but if he hadn't insisted on dragging them away from their Missouri home, her babies would still be with her. She would still be able to hold them and hear them laugh, but never again.

Bob Orson hadn't thought one bit about the missing children. All of his plans were gone. They still had their seed money in the community wagon, but it didn't matter. He didn't care about the children. They were excess baggage anyway. He needed a wife to cook and take care of the house he would build in Oregon. Rebecca Hobson was good-looking and well-formed, and she could really cook, too. The kids were just a nuisance, and she doted on them. It became downright irritating to tell the truth. And now this. Everything was gone, and it wasn't his fault.

He was wondering how much Ella Murphy had in the chest in the community wagon and knew she had a full wagon, too. He smiled at Ella and told her he didn't know why Rebecca was taking so long. Ella said it was alright, and she enjoyed having him there anyway. Bob was thinking there might be a way out of this loss, but that wife of his would be a problem.

Leo Crandall saw the camping location he wanted to use a mile ahead, then rode over to the lead wagon and pointed it out to John Cruikshank. They'd make camp soon.

———

Hugh was checking the inventory of what was available. A big bag of dry beans wasn't even broken open. He found some sugar, salt and coffee, all good. There was a little flour, but not much. He found some tin plates and cups and utensils. Good. Potatoes and onions. Both good. He found a box of ammunition for the Spencer. Very good. He wondered if Andy could use the gun, if not, he'd show him.

He found some clothes for the children, which was very necessary, but it wasn't much and in a sad state. He could see many repairs, so their mother was trying, but they needed new clothes.

He added some blankets and pillows to keep them warm and comfortable, and that was about it. There was nothing else worth taking. He thought about bringing some of their mama's clothes to her, but they weren't much and not in good condition either. He noticed that the man's clothing was in much better condition and there was more of it. He was a smaller man, a much smaller man, so the clothing was of no use to him, and he wasn't about to bring clothes back to some bastard who shortchanged his wife and children in their needs but not his own.

After he'd finished his scavenging, he said, "Andy and Addie, this looks like all we're going to get out of the wagon. Do you have anything in there that you want?"

"Is Maggie inside?" asked Addie.

"Who's Maggie?" asked Hugh, startled that he may have missed someone.

"She's my best friend."

Before Hugh could panic, Andy said, "Maggie is her doll."

Hugh blew out his breath and said, “Honey, I’m afraid that Maggie went for a swim. I saw her floating down the river. If I knew she was important to you, I would have dived in and saved her.”

Addie’s eyes saddened at the loss of Maggie, but said, “I understand, Mister Hugh. I wouldn’t want you to drown to save her.”

Hugh looked down at the cherubic face and crouched down.

“When we get to Oregon, I’m going to find you a new doll, Addie. Okay?”

Addie’s eyes widened and she replied, “You will? Really? Thank you so much, Mister Hugh.”

She beamed at him and said, “Mister Orson didn’t like us to have toys. He said they cost too much money. But mama got me Maggie anyway.”

“I thought Mister Orson was your papa.”

“He’s not our papa. Our papa died and mama had to marry Mister Orson ‘cause we were poor. Mister Orson doesn’t even like us.”

“Now how could anyone not like two such smart and wonderful young youngsters like you and Andy?”

“I don’t know, but he doesn’t.”

“Well, maybe I’ll have a little talk with Mister Orson when we catch up to them.”

“You can do that?” Addie asked.

"I can, and I will. Until then, we need to start getting organized. It's getting dark soon, so we'll set up camp. Tomorrow, we'll stay here and get everything balanced and ready to get loaded. Then we'll leave the day after. How does that sound Andy?"

"Real good, Mister Hugh."

Hugh stood up to his full six feet and four inches and stretched.

"Mister Hugh, are you a giant?" asked Addie.

Hugh laughed. *Lord! Was she a cutie!*

"No, sweetie, I'm just taller than most men. My brother was tall, too."

"I wish I were tall," said Andy.

"You still have a lot of growing to do, Andy. How old are you?"

"I'll be ten in October."

"How about you, Addie?"

"I'm seven. I just had my birthday. Mama made me a cake, too."

"It sounds like you have a very nice mama."

"Oh, she is! She's the prettiest lady anywhere and everybody likes her."

"What's your mama's name?"

"Rebecca."

"Well, in week or so, I think that you'll be making her the happiest mama in the world."

They both grinned at the thought of making their mama happy. She hadn't been happy after marrying Mister Orson and they weren't happy with him either.

The wagons were set up for camp and Rebecca was helped down from the wagon by Cliff Johnson. He smiled at her and seemed to hold onto her hand too long. Rebecca didn't like Cliff at all and knew that he wasn't kind to Florence or Charles. She had suspicions that he hit her when they were in the wagon and no one could see what he did.

She knew she had to see Bob sooner or later, so she took in a deep breath and began to walk to Ella Murphy's wagon. She was carrying a loaner dress from Florence. She hadn't had much of a wardrobe before, but now she only had two dresses, including the dirty and torn one she was wearing. At least her elbow was already feeling better.

As she approached, she was a bit surprised to hear Ella giggling. *Bob had made Ella giggle?* They were still on the driver's seat in animated conversation as Rebecca rounded the back of the wagon. Bob caught sight of her, and the chatter and giggling stopped instantly. Bob knew he had to be civil to Rebecca in front of Ella because he wanted Ella to view him as the victim.

Bob said loudly, "I'm glad to see that you're better, Rebecca. Ella has graciously offered us the use of her wagon for the remainder of the journey."

He was hoping Rebecca would say no but didn't get his wish.

"Thank you, Ella. You're very kind. I don't have anything else to wear, but Florence Johnson has loaned me a dress. Could you show me where to store it?" she asked.

Ella was a bit disappointed as well when she had accepted the offer but tried not to show it.

"Certainly, come around back."

Bob was much more than disappointed and didn't hide it very well at all.

Rebecca walked to the back of the wagon and Ella showed her where to put her borrowed dress, and then they began removing food for supper. Once that was done, Rebecca told Ella she needed some time to herself.

Rebecca walked to the edge of camp and as soon as she found herself alone in the dwindling light, she folded her arms across her chest, closed her eyes and began to cry. Not because Bob treated her as he had because it was nothing new. She was letting her tears flow because she had finally come to join the common belief that her children were lost to her.

She almost considered walking out of camp and just keep on going into the wilderness. *Why was God doing this to her?* Her first husband, John Hobson, wasn't great, but he wasn't mean. He was bland, but he treated the children well. It was her children who were her life. Now, they were gone. She was only thirty and could have more children. *But could she? Did she even want any more?* Surely not with Bob. He had treated her like a pariah when it came to that part of their relationship. He indulged his husbandly prerogatives only when he knew it wouldn't make her pregnant, which suited her fine. She did her wifely duty and nothing more and even those memories repulsed her. She felt totally lost and overwhelmed. After almost a half an hour, she turned and walked back to the Murphy wagon with a heavy heart and red eyes.

———

Hugh had set up camp and had put the mattress into the tent. It was a tight squeeze, but he managed it. Then he laid down one of the blankets on top of the mattress. Even though it was late spring, he knew it would get pretty chilly at night at this altitude and latitude.

Andy was moving a little better and Addie had adjusted to her splint and was hobbling around quite easily. Hugh was impressed with both children. They were bright and well-mannered, and he attributed that to their beloved mama who had done a good job raising them. It was their mother who was the prime topic of most of their conversations with him.

Hugh had showed them where they could go if nature called, and just before putting them to sleep, he put some water in a pot he found in the wagon and heated the water until it was just warm and not hot. He had found a few bars of soap in the wagon, which augmented his own short supply, and let them wash up in the warm water before tucking them in. He watched as they said their prayers, thanking God for Mister Hugh and asking Him to watch over their mama until they could see her again.

Hugh set his bedroll outside the tent and placed his two Colt New Army pistols on either side for quick retrieval. The Colts were readily available after the war, as was the Sharps. The only gun that cost him was the Henry. It was worth every dime, too. He had plenty of .44 cartridges for it, and a good amount of powder, ball and percussion caps for the Colts. The Spencer would be a welcome addition to the arsenal. He hoped he wouldn't have to use any of them now that he had the children to protect, but it was dangerous territory. One thing he knew for certain, he would get them back to their mother. They needed her, and he was sure that she missed them both terribly, and probably thought they were dead.

CHAPTER 2

The wagon train was moving just after breakfast. Rebecca made it a point to sit as far away from Bob as possible on the driver's seat. He was acting as if she didn't exist and probably would act the same way if she was sitting on his lap.

Ella sat closer to Bob on the other side, but having Rebecca there made her uncomfortable. Rebecca had told her she wanted to sit on the outside to keep checking if her children were being returned. Ella thought she was losing her mind and felt even more uncomfortable, but she felt bad, too. But not for Rebecca or even the children. She felt bad for Bob.

After about thirty minutes, Rebecca thought she may as well walk for a while, so she clambered down from the seat and was soon just stepping along beside the wagon. It was fairly common to see people walking beside the wagons. It lessened the load on the oxen or mules, and it built the stamina they would need when they reached their destination in Oregon.

Hugh hadn't woken the children early, letting them get the sleep they needed. He took care of his own personal needs, including shaving, and had heated some water for that. He never could adjust to shaving in cold water and considered it a fault. During the war, he was just about the only man he knew that didn't shave in cold water. At least among those that shaved at all, but he was in the medical corps, so he wasn't harassed about it as he would have been if he'd been an enlisted man.

He was preparing breakfast when the first sounds of movement came from the tent. Andy was the first to awaken and soon crawled out of the tent.

"Good morning, Andy."

"Good morning, Mister Hugh. I gotta go pee," he announced as he hobble-sprinted for the spot that Hugh had shown him.

He returned a minute later, relieved.

"How do you feel this morning, Andy. A bit stiffer, I'd imagine."

"Yes, sir. But it doesn't hurt as much in my shoulder."

"No, that should be all right soon. Your knee will take a little longer, but it should be fine in two weeks. Andy, do you know how to shoot that Spencer carbine?"

"No. I just was doing what I saw Mister Orson did."

"Would you like to learn? I think you're big enough to handle it."

"Can I? Really?"

"Sure. I'll show you some today and more as we travel. You'll need to understand how to use guns before you shoot one, though. Like when I first showed up and you broke a big rule about using guns."

"I did? What rule? I didn't even know there were rules."

"You were going to shoot without knowing what you were shooting. You thought I was an Indian, but what if the gun had been loaded? You would have shot me, then who would be taking you back to your mama?"

The thought shocked Andy, who replied, “I understand. I won’t do that again.”

“Good. I’ll teach you more later. Now breakfast is almost ready. We’ll eat, and I’ll save some for Addie.”

Then he heard from the tent, “I’m awake now. I can eat, too.”

Hugh smiled and said loudly, “Well come on out, Addie. Unless you want to visit the private place.”

“I think I need to do that first, Mister Hugh.”

Addie crawled out of the tent and limped over to the private place, and two minutes later came back, gimping quickly, then awkwardly plopped near the fire. It was still chilly, but Hugh had found their jackets, such as they were. They were worn and should have been replaced, and Hugh made a mental note to add that to the list to discuss with Mister Orson. Hugh was already growing a distinct disgust for the man.

The children finished eating and Hugh cleaned up before returning to the dying fire.

“Now, folks, I need to know if there is anything left in the wagon that you want to take with us tomorrow. I have to start arranging the packs in a little while. Andy, have you been through the wagon since I pulled out all of the food and your clothes?”

“Not all of it. Did you want me to go now?”

“Go ahead. Nothing really heavy, mind you. It’s stable, but don’t pull anything down on top of yourself.”

"Okay," Andy replied, then stood and gimped his way to the crumbled wagon.

He climbed inside and began rummaging through the remaining things, then found his mother's trunk and opened it. Her clothes were there, so he pulled them out and found a tintype. He took it out and looked at the image. It was of his mama and another man that he thought might be his real father but wasn't really sure. The picture was old, and he hadn't seen his father for a long time. He put it aside and kept looking then soon found a fancy pin that he seemed to remember his mother wearing a long time ago. It was almost black with a face on it that was looking away. He put it onto the picture and resumed his search. There was nothing else in the small trunk, so he closed it, then kept looking and found his hat, and pulled it onto his head. He didn't find anything else worth taking, so he picked up the pin and the tintype and left the wagon.

He hobbled back to Hugh and said, "I found my hat, and these were in mama's trunk".

He handed Hugh the tintype and the pin.

"Is this your mama?" Hugh asked as he looked at the photograph.

"Uh-uh. That must be our real papa. I don't remember him very well."

"Your mama is a very pretty lady. No wonder you both are so handsome. Did you want to hold this, Addie?"

She nodded, and Hugh handed her the tintype.

She stared at it and quietly said, "Mama."

"What's this, Mister Hugh? I found it in Mama's trunk, too," Andy asked as he handed him the pin.

"This, Andy, is called a cameo. I think maybe your mother got it from her mother. That would make it very special to your her. Where do you want to keep it?"

"Can you hold it for her? I might lose it."

"Okay. I'll put it in my saddlebag. Is that alright?"

"That's good."

"I'll wrap it up, too, so it can't get scratched."

He wrapped the cameo in some scrap cloth and slid it into his saddlebags. Addie handed him back the tintype, then he wrapped them both in a heavy cloth before sliding them into his saddlebags.

Then Hugh went about the business of balancing the new load. It took a while. He didn't want to leave any of the food behind, not with two hungry children to feed.

Once he was happy with the packing job, he weighed the panniers and other canvas bags. He guessed that he had about a hundred and eighty pounds of gear. He knew he weighed just at two hundred and twenty pounds. His two rifles and saddlebags with ammunition added another thirty pounds. So, he'd have two hundred and fifty pounds on the horse and a hundred and eighty pounds on the mule. Andy probably weighed around seventy pounds and Addie weighed no more than fifty.

"Andy, running the weight numbers, I think you'll be riding the mule and Addie will be with me. I'll try to make a place on the top of the supplies that you can use as a seat. Do you think you can handle that?"

"Yes, sir."

"Good. Now, Addie, tomorrow when we start riding to the Oregon Trail to catch up to your mama, you'll be riding with me. I'll put a blanket across the front of the saddle for you. If either of you starts getting sore or something hurts, I need you to tell me right away. I can adjust things, so it'll feel better. We won't seem to be going fast, but that wagon train is only going as fast as I can walk, so we'll start catching up with them as soon as we get back on the Trail."

The thought of going and seeing their mama again cheered them both up.

After lunch, Hugh took out the Spencer and checked it over, and wasn't pleased. The weapon needed a serious cleaning. There was already some mild corrosion in the barrel and Hugh was annoyed for a man who mistreated weapons almost as he would be with one who kicked a dog.

Andy watched as Hugh cleaned the gun.

There was nothing he could do about the corrosion, but he was concerned about the ability of the carbine to fire and not explode.

"Andy, I'm going to have to rig up something to fire this weapon from far enough away so if it explodes no one will be hurt."

"Why would it explode, Mister Hugh?"

"Because Mister Orson didn't take care of the gun. He fired it and never cleaned it. That means the metal will start to go bad. Bad metal means bad things happen when you pull the trigger. I want to make sure that won't happen. This will take a while. So, you both relax while I build this contraption."

While Hugh was building his makeshift remote firing mechanism, he thought he heard something in the brush. He slowly lowered his construction and easily pulled out his Colt. He pulled back the hammer, locking it into place and stared into the shrubbery before he heard it again. It wasn't human, and it wasn't a bear. It was smaller, so he thought maybe it was a fox or badger.

He walked to the shrubbery and when he got within six feet, he saw a pair of eyes, but they weren't angry eyes.

He released his Colt's hammer, slid it back into its holster, then crouched down, sat on his heels and said, "Come here, boy."

The eyes emerged and were followed by a very thin, black and white dog. Hugh put out his left hand to let the dog smell it. The dog timidly stepped forward and sniffed his hand, then licked it and his tail began to wag. Hugh reached over and scratched the dog behind the ear as his tail wagged more vigorously.

"Come here, boy. Let's get you something to eat."

The two children watched with pie eyes while the dog trotted behind Hugh as he walked to the panniers. He found some jerky and offered one to the dog. Hugh was expecting it to almost take his hand off to get to the dried meat, but he was pleasantly surprised when he just took the meat carefully but then quickly inhaled the meat after he had the jerky in its mouth. Hugh gave him the second piece and the skinny dog followed the same polite acceptance then a rapid chew and swallow. Then the dog ran around in circles before sitting down and looking eagerly at Hugh.

"Well, Andy and Addie, looks like we have another mouth to feed."

"Are we gonna keep him?" asked Andy.

"It's not so much that we're going to keep him, Andy. I don't think he's going to let us go anywhere without him."

"What's his name?" Addie wanted to know.

"I think you two should give him a good name. Let me know what you come up with."

The two children huddled, and Hugh smiled as he heard all sorts of names being bandied about. Some bordered on absurdly funny, but they were kids and they were entitled to it.

Hugh went back to making his contraption as the dog sat and watched him while the children were still discussing names.

Hugh had the setup done, then took the Spencer and set it on the v-shaped limb. The stock's butt he set into the bag of beans. He tied a string around another stick and ran it past the trigger and wedged it behind some rocks at the far end. He tested it out without ammo and was rewarded with a solid click as the hammer dropped. He set it all up again and put in a round. Then he moved the children and the dog on the other side of a big boulder. The horse and mule were behind some trees. When everyone was safe, he returned to the carbine and cocked the hammer. Then he trotted back to the rock. And again, after making sure everyone was safe, yanked the cord, and was relieved to hear the gun fire normally. The dog and the children were startled by the roar of the large caliber carbine.

He looked at them and said, “Well? What name did you come up for him?”

Andy declared, “We want to call him Chester.”

Hugh smiled and said, “Well, I, for one, am astonished at you two. That is an outstanding name for a dog. He even looks like a Chester.”

Both children were beaming that their naming was so well received by Mister Hugh.

“Can we pet him?” asked Addie.

“Go ahead and let him smell your hand first.”

Addie put her hand in front of Chester. He sniffed it and then licked her hand as Addie giggled.

Andy did the same and had exactly the same reaction.

Hugh stood as both children took to petting and scratching the dog. Hugh guessed it had come from a passing wagon train some months back, if not longer. He was so skinny because he had to compete with more skilled predators and scavengers and wouldn’t have lasted much longer.

Hugh walked to the Spencer and picked it up from the ground where it had fallen after the test firing. He opened the breech and examined it closely. It looked clean, and he was satisfied that the gun was safe to fire.

Four miles away, White Antelope heard the report. The white man must be hunting, which was a foolish thing to do with them so close. They would continue to wait, knowing that he must come this way to return to the trail.

Andy hobbled around the rock toward Hugh as he asked, "Did it work, Mister Hugh?"

"Yep. It worked fine. Now, have a seat on those beans right there. I'll tell you some rules about using guns. Okay?"

"Yes, sir," Andy answered seriously as he sat.

"The most important rule is to never point a gun at anything you don't intend to kill. It's not a toy. It's a very dangerous tool. Second, assume every gun is loaded and will fire until you have looked inside and made sure it is empty. Don't let someone else tell you it's empty. You need to look yourself. If you do point that gun at someone, you must want them dead. You can't shoot it at someone and hope that they'll only be wounded. Now, those are the most important rules. There are other rules, too. One of those is always clean your gun after you shoot it. Mister Orson didn't do that. That's why I had to try that odd way of testing it. Do you understand the rules?"

"Yes, sir."

"Tell me."

"Never point a gun at anything you don't want to kill. A gun is loaded until I look myself. If I shoot at someone they will die. Clean the gun after shooting."

"Very good, Andy. You are one smart young man. I'll bet you did really well in school."

"I never went to school, Mister Hugh. I'm sorry."

"Now, why are you sorry, Andy. Is it your fault?"

"No, sir."

"Then don't apologize. You only apologize if you did something wrong that hurt someone. It's like telling a lie. Never lie. Lies always hurt someone. Most of the time it hurts the person telling the lie, and even one lie can change your life. You can go your whole life always telling the truth, then you tell just one lie, and no one believes you anymore. So, tell me, how come you never went to school?"

"When my papa died, my mama had to move to a place that was too far away. I never learned to read or write. Mama said she'd show me, but she was always busy working and then she'd fall asleep after feeding us dinner. Mister Orson said schooling was for sissies."

"Well, Mister Orson is going to have a hard time convincing this big old sissy that it's true. Wouldn't you think so, Andy?"

Andy started laughing as he looked at a grinning Addie.

"Well, I'll tell you what. While we're riding to meet your mama, why don't I start to show you how to read and write a little bit? Addie can join us."

"Can you do that? Mama would be really proud of us."

"I think your mama is already proud of both of you, and rightfully so. Now, while Addie is playing with Chester, let me go through the basics of loading and firing the Spencer."

Rebecca was walking with Florence next to her wagon while her husband Cliff drove.

"You've got to let it go, Becky. Your place is with Bob now."

"I know. I'm a terrible person, Flo. All I can think about is Andy and Addie. They were my whole life. Everyone says to get over it, but I can't."

"I know how it is with you and Bob. He's kind of remote, isn't he?"

"I wish he had been remote. He really seemed to resent that I had the children at all. He just wanted a free cook and housekeeper. Why does it have to be this way, Flo? Why do women always seem to get the short end of the stick? You're in worse shape than I am."

Florence sighed and said, "I know. Cliff wanted a whore more than a wife. Now that he's used to me, he's looking elsewhere for his dalliances."

"I can tell. He keeps looking at Emily Amber like she's a steak dinner. Bob seems taken by Ella Murphy, so maybe I'll just let him enjoy himself and walk to Oregon."

"What will you do when we get there if Bob leaves you?"

"I don't think he will. He'll put up with me now that the children are gone. I just don't know what to do."

"We have two more weeks before we get there. Maybe something will work out."

"I don't know why God would suddenly start liking me. He sure has hated me so far."

Andy had just fired his first round and had almost been thrown back by rifle's kick. Hugh knew he'd be surprised but had to let him feel the kick.

"That gun fires a big cartridge, Andy. Don't try to fight it. Let it push your shoulder back. Want to try another one?"

"Okay."

Hugh handed him another round. He wanted Andy to load the carbine and lever in the shot. Andy loaded the cartridge into the tube and slid the tube home. Once it was secured, he levered the round into position and cocked the hammer. This time, he sighted and squeezed the trigger. The carbine bucked, and Andy held his ground. Impressively, Andy had struck the thick tree trunk fifty yards away. Hugh knew the carbine's range was much further, but Andy needed something to show for his hard work.

"Great job, Andy! You'll be a marksman shortly. I don't want you to fire too much, though. That kick will play havoc with your young shoulder."

Andy grinned at the praise as it was a new experience for him. The only praise he had received before was from his mother and that didn't count.

After they finished, he let Andy clean the gun while he watched. Chester and Addie were watching, too, with Addie constantly petting their new friend as they stared at Hugh and Andy.

"Now, tomorrow, Andy, we're going to load seven rounds into the Spencer and you're going to carry it with you. I'll make you a sling to keep it on the mule, so you'll be able to slide it out and use it if I tell you to get ready. Okay?"

"Yes, sir."

"Good. Now, before we eat supper, we have a couple of hours of free time. So, do you know what we're going to do, Andy and Addie?"

They shook their heads.

"School will begin in five minutes. You two are going to learn to read and write. That will surprise your mama almost as much as your return from the dead like Lazarus in the Bible."

They seemed almost as happy about that as they had been when they got to name Chester.

So, their first lesson began. It helped that they were both very bright children and wanted desperately to learn. Hugh injected humor into the lessons that made them seem fun. He had scrawled the letters of the alphabet on the ground on the riverbank and had them reciting the alphabet by the end of the first lesson. They were both proud of themselves, as was their teacher.

He had not only had them memorize the letters, but had explained the importance of the vowels over the consonants and gave each letter a humorous personality and how it could be used in silly words.

They were so pleased with their progress, that after dinner, they begged Hugh to continue. He was gratified to hear their insistence and showed them how each letter worked in making a word. Their first word, naturally, was 'mama'. Their second was 'dog'.

They asked him how to spell his name and he told them that his name would cause trouble because it had a disappearing letter. They were curious, but he held them off and finished the lesson by showing them how to spell their own names. It helped that they were so similar. He could show the sounds as he wrote the letters to their names in the sand. Soon, the children were happily spelling their names and singing the alphabet. It was a good start, and it would keep their minds busy on the long journey ahead.

He tucked the children in and set up outside. Tomorrow they would begin their way back to the Oregon Trail, hopefully free of those Cheyenne, but he wouldn't be surprised if they were still waiting for him. He knew that if they were there, then the gunfire would have confirmed his presence. He'd find out tomorrow and his primary concern now was to protect the children.

———

White Antelope and his three fellow warriors had heard the two shots and were curious. *What was the white eyes doing?* They resented the use of the ammunition but at least they knew he was still there. He would come back soon because the only other way out was into Crow land and they knew the white man wouldn't want to go that way.

———

Bob and Ella were getting along famously, while Rebecca had taken to walking most of the time but would spend a few hours a day in the wagon. It was a real mood dampener for Ella and Bob when she did show up, but Rebecca had no other choice. She had nothing. The money was all Bob's, even though she had put what little she had into the marriage. First there was Hobson and now Orson. Men could just go to hell as far as Rebecca was concerned. They never did her a lick of good.

CHAPTER 3

Hugh woke earlier than usual to saddle the horse and pack the mule. He had shaved and cleaned up the camp except for the tent. He pulled back the flap, looked at the two innocent faces and smiled. He'd get them to their mama as soon as he could and couldn't wait to witness the reunion.

He walked down to the fire and started it burning again, using pieces of the wagon for fuel. As dry as it was, it burned quickly and hot. He soon had his coffee going and set the frypan on the grate and sliced some bacon. He tossed four strips into the frypan as Chester watched with anxious eyes. When they were cooked, Hugh pulled off the first four strips and then added four more. When he thought they were cool enough, he offered one to Chester who swallowed it almost without chewing. A minute later, he heard Andy leave the tent and was soon followed by a yawning Addie. Andy made it out of their private place just as Addie entered.

When he was close, Hugh smiled at him and said, "Good morning, Andy."

"Hello, Mister Hugh."

"Grab a strip of bacon before Chester eats them all."

Andy smiled and snatched one from the tin plate and Chester followed it with his pleading eyes all the way into Andy's mouth. Andy naturally only ate half and gave the other half to Chester.

Addie hobbled down, and Hugh offered her a strip of bacon. She glanced down at Chester and broke off a piece and gave it to him before eating hers.

"You two are going to turn Chester in to a fat puppy."

They giggled at the thought of Chester being fat.

After they had eaten, Hugh removed the bedding and collapsed the tent. He left the mattress as there was no room for such extravagance. After he had packed the tent and cooking gear, Hugh set up making a seat for Andy on the mule. He used a six-foot length of rope, then slid it through the front loop on the pack saddle and tied it off so Andy could use it for a handhold. Then he folded a blanket and set it on top. Andy's little butt would fit nicely in the gap between the panniers. He slipped the Spencer between two lashings, then tested it to make sure it wasn't going anywhere. It was reasonably tight and he should still able to slide it free if necessary, and he hoped it wouldn't be.

His last act was to set a blanket on the front of his saddle for Addie and folded it twice to make a thick pad.

"Okay, Andy. You're up first. Come on over."

Andy had a grin on his face as Hugh picked him up and sat him on his mule throne.

"Now, his is your handhold," he said as he handed him the rope, "You won't be steering or anything, but you'll be able to ride like you are. The Spencer is right here. Leave it there until I tell you to take it. Okay?"

"Yes, Mister Hugh."

"Comfortable?"

"Yes, sir"

Hugh nodded and walked over to Addie.

"Addie, you're next. You'll have a different way of mounting. Are you ready?"

"Yes, Mister Hugh."

Hugh smiled and scooped her up, causing another Addie giggle as she wrapped her arms around his neck. He walked over to his horse and stepped up easily into the stirrup with Addie still holding onto his neck while he held her in his right arm. He stepped into his saddle and then set Addie down on the blanket.

"Comfortable, Addie?"

"Yes, Mister Hugh. This is very nice."

"You can hold onto my waist if you feel like you might fall. Okay?"

She already was holding onto him as she replied "Okay."

"Good. Let's go find your mama."

Hugh turned along the river and set off, with both children smiling broadly as they moved. Mister Hugh was taking them back to their mama.

Rebecca still walked most days. Sometimes other women would walk with her and talk for a while, but she wasn't a very good conversationalist. She really wanted to be alone. She was miserable and wanted no part of anyone. Her children were gone and nothing else mattered.

———

Hugh walked Middie and the mule with their precious cargoes across the rocky ground and talked to the children as he scanned the landscape for potential enemies, furred and human, but mostly Cheyenne.

———

The children were both singing their alphabet song when White Antelope heard the high-pitched singing. *He knew they were white children, but where had they come from?* It must have been from that wagon train that had passed three days ago. The white man would be at a big disadvantage now. He'd have to protect the children at the cost of his own life.

He told his warriors to prepare for the ambush. He had the other warrior with a working musket load it and get ready to fire. His was already loaded, but still needed one of the precious firing caps. He put the small metal cap on the gun's nipple but didn't cock the hammer yet.

They were in position on a low ridge and caught sight of the approaching white man and the two children when he was less than a mile away as he came around a bend in the river.

Oblivious to the danger, Hugh was spelling different words for the children, diverting his attention as they drew within eighty yards of the Cheyenne. White Antelope was a better shot than Walking Bear, so he cocked his hammer and sighted on the big white man, then pulled the trigger. The musket bellowed fire and smoke, sending the massive .58 caliber round flying toward the target.

Hugh heard the giant report at the same time as the bullet tore through his left sleeve and creased his bicep. He didn't waste any time before picked up Addie and lowered her quickly to the ground, ignoring the pain.

"Lie down on your tummy, Addie! Now!" he shouted.

She did as she was told, terrified by the sudden thunder of gunfire. Chester hovered nearby, alternating between running and curling up in a ball.

"Get down and grab that Spencer, Andy!" he shouted as he grabbed the Henry. It should have a round in the chamber, so he just cocked it and fired at the smoke. Walking Bear fired his musket and Hugh heard the round ricochet off a nearby rock.

He levered a new round and fired directly at the second cloud of smoke. The .44 caliber rifled round slammed into Walking Bear's left upper chest, ripping through arteries, resulting in a massive loss of blood that quickly pooled in his lung. He'd die in less than two minutes.

Hugh dropped down quickly to protect Addie as Middie walked twenty feet to his left, taking the mule with her.

Hugh felt Andy sidle up beside him, but he kept his eyes on the Cheyenne as he said, "We have lousy cover here, Andy. I think I got one, maybe two of them, though."

Walking Bear was dead. White Antelope had taken Hugh's first round in his upper thigh. It wasn't fatal, but he knew he couldn't run or walk. That left two able warriors. He called over Still Water and gave him his unloaded musket and told him to move to the right and shoot the white eyes. Still Water stood to load the musket and that turned out to be a fatal mistake.

Hugh spotted the sudden movement behind some trees ahead, then aimed where he had seen it and squeezed off a shot.

Still Water was ramming the new round into the musket's bore and was suddenly thrown back. The Henry's report followed immediately, and White Antelope cursed the gods. This white man was a devil with that weapon and knew it would be foolish to continue the fight. He called over to his remaining warrior and signed that they would leave. White Antelope knew that he would face shame for what had happened, but he could not lose more men.

He trotted over, bent low to keep from drawing more fire, then they gathered all the horses, six of them now empty and left the site of the skirmish.

It took Hugh another ten minutes to realize that they had gone, but he wanted to be sure.

"Andy, I think our friends have gone. I'm going to go up there and be sure. Before I go, I'm going to take you and Addie over to those boulders over there. Okay?"

"Okay, Mister Hugh. Do I take the rifle with me?"

"Yes. And Andy?"

"Yes, sir?"

"That's a carbine, not a rifle. I'll explain later."

He smiled at the boy and scooped up Addie, then trotted to a clump of boulders twenty yards from the river. Once they were in a safe position, Hugh jogged back up to where the Indians had launched their ambush. When he got there, he found two more dead Cheyenne and blood where he had fired his first shot. That left only one healthy warrior and one wounded one. No wonder they didn't stay. He was eternally grateful they didn't have better weapons. A Spencer, Sharps or Henry would have done them all in. He had to be more careful.

Hugh walked back to his young charges and said, "Okay, Andy and Addie. It's safe now. They're gone."

The children walked from their temporary fortress and approached Hugh.

"Let's ride for a while until we get hungry. We still have a way to go before the trail. We should get there by early afternoon, though."

He took the Spencer from Andy and let him climb aboard his makeshift saddle. Hugh slid the Spencer back into position. Then he picked up Addie and set her on his saddle before climbing aboard. They resumed their journey to the Oregon Trail.

When they were riding, Addie saw Hugh's torn sleeve and asked, "Mister Hugh, were you shot?"

"Almost, Addie. The bullet went through my shirt and I felt the bullet go past and scrape my skin, but it didn't even bleed. It's a bit sore, but it'll heal faster than your brother's shoulder did."

"Okay, Mister Hugh," she replied.

They rode for three more hours when Hugh first spotted the Trail.

"There's the Oregon Trail, my young friends," he announced loudly so Andy could hear.

Ten minutes later, he turned west onto the Oregon Trail and began the serious pursuit of their mother. As they rode, he taught them letters and sometimes diverted into numbers. Numbers weren't as abstract as letters because they made sense: ten fingers, ten toes, one nose, two eyes and two ears. He had them singing different memory songs for letters and numbers as they rode along. They were having a good time learning and Hugh was astonished by how quickly they were picking it up.

Chester wasn't about to let his meal tickets get away and trotted along behind them.

When they stopped for lunch after mid-day, Hugh simply stepped down with Addie attached, and after they were safely on the ground, helped Andy to the ground and let the children rest while he made a quick meal of beans and bacon.

He let the horse and mule graze after they drank at a stream that was little more than a trickle.

Hugh let Chester have the leftovers from lunch, which he gratefully accepted. With the children back in place, they began riding west again. Hugh began spelling words and having each child in turn say the word. He would see if they could write some words when they stopped for camp that night.

He was glancing back at Andy when he saw movement in the distance behind them. He didn't want to alarm them, so he just would take the occasional backward glance to get a better idea who was back there. He soon estimated there were four horses and was reasonably sure that they were Cheyenne. They didn't seem to be a war party, though, as it was too small. It was in the wrong place for a hunting party, too. They're on the Oregon Trail, and there was no game on the Trail itself.

He finally reached behind him, opened his left saddlebag and took out his field glasses. He usually avoided using them until he had to, but they could obviously see him. He stopped Middie, pulled up the glasses and looked. There were four Indians, but two were women, which wasn't too odd, but what was different was that neither of the men had rifles. They didn't have a lot of food with them, either. The more he looked, he began to think they weren't Cheyenne after all.

He started them riding again, maintained their previous pace and kept talking to the children, leaving the field glasses hanging around his neck. He waited for one of them to ask, as he knew they would because both had turned to look while he was watching with his field glasses.

"Mister Hugh, who is that behind us?" asked Andy.

"I don't know, Andy. They're Indians, but I don't think they're Cheyenne. We're too far south to be in Crow territory. They could be Nez Perce, though, and if they are, they're out of their territory, too. They're too far east. But they seem harmless because they're traveling with two women and they aren't armed with rifles."

Hugh intentionally began slowing down to allow them to get closer to make sure they weren't a threat but was almost positive that they weren't. Soon they were within a mile, and Hugh looked at them again through his glasses. He still couldn't make them out, but as he was looking, he saw another band of Indians further behind them. There were six in that band who were definitely Cheyenne and they were moving faster than the group closer to him. As he watched, the first group began to run from the Cheyenne. They were coming right at him and the children and had closed the gap to a half a mile.

Hugh stopped the horses and lowered Addie to the ground.

"Stay right there, Addie. Andy, grab that Spencer."

Hugh pulled out the Sharps but left the Henry in its scabbard. If he needed its faster rate of fire, he could grab it quickly. He then took out six of his precious Sharps cartridges, put them in his pocket, flipped up the ladder sight on the Sharps and adjusted it for five hundred yards. Then he brought the rifle level and just waited.

As he watched, the Cheyenne were within fifty yards of the other Indians and knew he couldn't wait any longer. Hugh let out his breath and squeezed the trigger. The big gun bellowed, and Hugh quickly opened the breech, extracted the hot brass, pulled a fresh cartridge from his pocket, slid it into the breech, and snapped it closed. When he looked downrange again, he was gratified to see that his first round had taken out the leading Cheyenne warrior. He picked out a second target quickly, fired and wasn't sure if he hit the warrior or his horse as the animal and rider both smashed into the dirt, raising a large dust cloud.

He quickly reloaded his Sharps and sighted a third Cheyenne.

The Cheyenne knew where the shots were coming from but couldn't do anything about it as none of their rifles had percussion caps in place. Hugh's third shot took out another warrior, leaving them with three. They must have realized how tenuous their situation was and quickly turned and raced away from the scene.

Hugh blew out the corrosive smoke from the gunpowder. He loaded another round, then returned the Sharps and its remaining cartridges to Middie. He should have used the Spencer, but he wasn't sure of its accuracy and he was comfortable with the Sharps. He just hated to use the ammunition.

He slid the Henry from its scabbard and let the muzzle drop toward the ground as the four unknown Indians approached. They were hesitant but saw the rifle's angle and came forward.

Hugh was finally able to identify them as Nez Perce. He held up his hand in the almost universal sign of peace, and it was returned by the older man. Hugh saw that the older man was about forty, the younger in his mid-twenties. The two women were very young, upper teens maybe.

Hugh couldn't speak any languages other than English, Latin and some Greek. A lot of good they did now.

"You are Nez Perce?" asked Hugh, hoping one could speak English.

"We are Nez Perce," said the older man, who then asked, "Why did you kill the Cheyenne? It was not your fight."

"It was not a fight at all. They had rifles. You did not. You had two women with you, and they were all young warriors. I had a rifle, so it helped to balance the scales."

The Nez Perce smiled and said, "I thank you for balancing the scales, then. I am Red Owl. This is Long Wolf. Our women were taken by two Cheyenne four days ago, and we went to take them back. They are my daughters. My younger daughter is pledged to Long Wolf. We caught up with the Cheyenne and killed them, then started back. You saw the rest."

"Yes."

"You have young ones with you. They are yours?"

"No. I found them three days ago. Their wagon had fallen down the mountain. I am returning them to their mother who travels ahead. She does not know they live, and it will bring her great happiness to see them. The little girl is Addie. The boy is called Andy."

Red Owl nodded and said, "As a father, I know the loss of children wounds the heart, and you are doing a good thing to bring them back. My daughters are Pale Dawn and Blue Flower."

"You and their mother must be proud to have such beautiful daughters, Red Owl. I am Hugh McGinnis."

Then he turned to the children and said, "Andy and Addie, I'd like you to meet Red Owl and Long Wolf. The two young ladies are Pale Dawn and Blue Flower."

Both children waved and said, "Hello."

Hugh then said, "I noticed that you have no food with you. Perhaps you would join us in camp. I have sufficient food."

Red Owl turned to Long Wolf and said something to him, then looked back at Hugh and nodded.

"We will join you. I see the young one has a rifle."

"Why do you not have any rifles? The Cheyenne have guns."

"We have so few that I did not want to leave our camp without protection."

Hugh walked over to Andy, put out his hand and Andy gave him the Spencer. Andy walked to the pack horse and pulled out the box of ammunition for the Spencer, then walked to Long Wolf and handed him the Spencer and the cartridges.

“Why are you doing this?” Red Owl asked, shocked that a white man would arm any Indian.

“No man should be asked to protect his women without a good weapon. You are both good men, Red Owl. Any man who would risk himself to protect women is a good man. Keep the weapon and ammunition.”

Red Owl translated to Long Wolf, and when he finished, Long Wolf reached out with his right hand. Hugh did the same and they clasped each other’s forearm, almost in Roman fashion.

“Let us go and find a place to camp before the Cheyenne return. They may come back with more warriors this time,” Hugh said.

Red Owl agreed, and Hugh picked up Addie, mounted his black mare and the enlarged group began riding west.

They continued along the trail until Long Wolf pointed and said something to Red Owl. Hugh didn’t need an interpreter to tell him that he had spied a good campsite.

Hugh turned in the direction he had indicated and moved off the trail about a quarter of a mile. It was a good place to spend the night. There was a stream nearby and plenty of fallen wood scattered around for a fire as well as grass for the horses.

Hugh dropped Addie to the ground, dismounted and then helped Andy down when he saw Pale Dawn fall from her horse as she tried to dismount.

Long Wolf rushed to her side and knelt beside her as Hugh watched with concern. She hadn’t fallen because of a misstep.

Red Owl said to Hugh, “Pale Dawn is not well. For two days, she has had troubles with her belly. Now she is with fever. It will pass.”

“Red Owl, I am not sure it will pass. Is her belly pain here?” he asked, pointing at his lower right abdomen.

“Yes. She says it causes her much pain to touch it.”

“Red Owl, Pale Dawn has appendicitis. Have you heard of this?”

“No. That is a word I have not heard.”

“At the bottom of the large bowel. You know ‘bowel’?”

“Yes.”

“At the bottom of the large bowel is a small, thin pouch called the appendix. It has no function at all. It does nothing. But it can become swollen and cause much pain. When it does, it can then burst, causing death. The only way to stop this is to cut out the appendix.”

Red Owl digested this news. He loved his younger daughter. She was his favorite and the thought of her dying was almost too painful. *But could he trust this white man?*

He turned to her betrothed, Long Wolf, and spoke to him. Long Wolf’s eyes grew dark as he listened to his future father-in-law tell him what Hugh had described.

Then his eyes grew wide and he shook his head and said something firmly in protest.

Red Owl turned to Hugh and said, “Long Wolf asks why we should trust Pale Dawn to you? I have the same question.”

"Red Owl, you have no reason to trust me. I could have said nothing and let Pale Dawn die. You both would have been greatly troubled, and no blame would be placed on me. But I cannot allow people to suffer. The cutting out of the appendix is a very simple thing. I would make a cut across here," he showed the location and the length, "then I would reach in and pull the bowel forward and tie off the end. I then cut the appendix off and sew the end closed. Then I sew the opening. She will be sore for a week or two, but her fever should be gone by morning, and she will live. I do not demand that this be done. It is your choice. I am simply offering my services."

Red Owl translated Hugh's words to Long Wolf. They talked briefly and then Red Owl asked, "How long will this cutting take?"

"From the time I make the first cut until I finish sewing the cut, less than one hour. But we must decide soon. We will lose the light in two hours."

Red Owl walked to Pale Dawn and spoke to her. She looked at Hugh and then at Long Wolf. Hugh could see the sweat on her face. She acquiesced to their requests and stepped forward. Hugh smiled at her. She tried to smile back, but a wave of pain caused her to grimace.

"Let us start, Hugh McGinnis," said Red Owl.

"We need to find someplace that is elevated."

He looked around and saw where the bank of the stream had cut away and he'd be able to stand with his back to the stream.

"Over there, by the stream. I'll get blankets. But before I start, I want Pale Dawn to be removed from pain. I have a bottle of whiskey in my pack that I use for wounds. Doctors don't understand how it works, but if you pour it on a wound, it keeps infection away. I need her to drink a cup of whiskey. It will make her pass out and then I can work without causing her any pain."

Hugh trotted to his pack horse and pulled out the whiskey and a cup. He poured a half cup of whiskey and handed it to Red Owl, who explained to Pale Dawn why she needed to drink the whiskey and she began to sip it, making a sour face after the first taste. By the time she had finished half of what was in the cup, she was already lightheaded.

Meanwhile, Hugh began taking out what he would need. The only sharp instrument he had was his razor, which he sharpened. He took out his sewing kit and threaded a needle. It wasn't going to be ideal, but considering the alternative, it would suffice.

He laid a blanket on the ground near the edge of the riverbank and they laid Pale Dawn on her back. She had already passed out, so Hugh told Red Owl that he needed to have her abdomen exposed. Red Owl told Blue Flower to pull Pale Dawn's deerskin dress away from her belly and cover her from the waist down with another blanket.

Hugh rolled up his sleeves and took the bottle of whiskey, his razor and the sewing kit over to Pale Dawn.

As all this was going on, Andy, Addie and Chester sat in silence near the horses watching. Andy had picked up what was happening and had told Addie that Mister Hugh was going to have to save the Indian lady by cutting open her tummy, and they needed to stay back. They stayed far enough away so they couldn't see too much, and Hugh was grateful for Andy's cool head.

Hugh splashed some whiskey on Pale Dawn's stomach and then on the razor and the needle in his sewing kit. Finally, he splashed some on his hands. He was ready.

The three Nez Perce watched as Hugh began. No one said a word. It was as if the entire world had grown silent. The only noise was from the burbling stream behind him and the buzzing of insects.

Hugh worked swiftly but surely. He had done two appendectomies in his last year of training before he left, and three more while he was in the army. He actually found this easier because of the increased light. Once he had opened her viscera, he found the appendix almost ready to burst. He tied it off at the base and removed it, tossing it into the stream behind him. Then he sutured the end and returned the bowel to its normal position. Finally, after fifteen minutes closing the cut, he splashed more whiskey on the wound to prevent infection. Even in her unconscious state, Pale Dawn flinched.

Hugh stood and stretched his back, then looked at Red Owl and smiled as he said, "Pale Dawn will be smiling again by tomorrow, Red Owl."

Long Wolf needed no translator. He had seen the swollen, ugly appendix that Hugh had removed and knew that it would have killed his future bride. He whooped and swept Blue Flower into an impromptu dance.

"Red Owl, I'll go and get a cloth we can wrap around Pale Dawn's abdomen to protect the wound. In ten days, those threads across her belly will need to be removed. Just cut each thread and pull it out. It won't hurt much at all."

"This will be done, Hugh McGinnis. I saw that which you removed. It was death. You have done well, and I cannot thank you enough for the gift of my daughter's life."

Hugh nodded and turned to the stream to clean his razor. When he had done that, he returned to where the children sat with Chester.

“Are you two hungry?” he asked.

“Is the lady going to be all right now?” asked Andy.

Hugh noted the absence of the adjective ‘Indian’ and smiled. Andy was growing up.

“She’s going to be fine. Her tummy will be sore for a few days, but she should be smiling again by tomorrow.”

“You saved her, Mister Hugh,” said Addie.

“She was sick, Addie, and I knew how to fix it. I’m glad I was here to do that. God must be looking out for Pale Dawn.”

“I hope God is looking out for our mama,” added Andy.

———

Sixty miles further down the Oregon Trail, the wagon train had pulled over for the night. There was a big fire going and food was being prepared, but Rebecca was away from the fire, past the last wagon. She was sitting and staring back down the trail to the east.

Bob was sitting with Ella Murphy and Rebecca couldn’t care less.

She didn’t want to eat. *Why bother?* She hadn’t eaten all day because it just didn’t matter anymore. As she stared into the darkness, the same questions that had haunted her since the accident continued to plague her mind.

"Why?", she kept asking herself. *Why was God punishing her so? What egregious sin had she committed that would bring such wrath down upon her?*

She reviewed her life and couldn't find it. She reviewed the Ten Commandments one by one and didn't see any transgressions that could warrant such punishment. *If she had sinned so badly, why had God punished her now rather than simply condemning her to eternal damnation after she died? And why punish her innocent children for her undiscovered sin?*

She went to her knees and asked God directly. *Why have You done this? Why have You taken my precious children? Do You love them more than I could and took them for Yourself? Are you a selfish God?* The questions kept coming and she became more and more intense in her pleadings. Then she simply fell forward, collapsing onto her face in the grass.

As she lay there, she asked one last time, aloud this time, "Why?"

Then she heard a voice from deep inside her.

"Your children are not with me. They will be returned to you. Have faith."

Rebecca was startled. She quickly sat up and looked around quickly. No one was near, yet the voice had said her children would be returned to her. She had to have faith. If it took faith, then she would have faith…lots and lots of faith.

Rebecca stood and brushed off her dress, then lifted her skirt and ran back to the fire. She looked around and found Florence sitting with her son. Cliff was nowhere to be seen. She stopped by the fire, took a spoon and plate and filled it with stew, then hurriedly walked to where Florence was sitting and sat with a beatific smile on her face.

Florence looked at the complete transformation in her friend and asked, "Becky? Are you all right?"

Becky took a big bite and after she swallowed, turned to Florence and said, "It's going to be fine now, Flo. God told me that my children were alive and were going to be returned to me."

Florence was taken aback. She knew that Rebecca wasn't one of the religious zealots that were scattered among the wagons and asked, "God talked to you?"

"Yes. It was a voice deep within me. My children are coming back, Florence. I don't have to be afraid anymore."

Florence didn't know what to make of this. She was happy that Rebecca was no longer so morose, but worried that she might be losing her mind. Her children were dead. This was just her mind playing tricks with her to ease her pain. Rebecca wanted her children alive so much, her mind had finally told her what she wanted to believe. Florence finally decided that a happy, delusional Rebecca was better than the almost suicidal Rebecca that she had been.

"I'm happy for you, Rebecca," was all she said.

Rebecca was still gushing about her revelation when the camp was pierced by a loud scream. Florence and Rebecca, like everyone else, felt the chill run down their necks. They looked to the east for the source and soon Emily Amber ran into camp. Her dress was partially torn, and she was bleeding from a cut on her face. She was quickly surrounded by women who all suspected what had either almost happened or had happened.

Rebecca and Florence drifted over to Emily and could hear her sobbing and talking.

"...to go and needed privacy. He...he came from behind. He grabbed me. He had a knife. He was going to...."

She was interrupted by Maddie Porter who asked the question they all wanted answered.

"Who was it, Emily? Who did this?" Maddie asked loudly.

"It was Cliff...Cliff Johnson," Emily replied as she sobbed.

Florence felt her stomach plummet. She knew Cliff was tired of her and was looking elsewhere, but to do this!

She had barely begun to deal with that horrible thought when there was a further scuffle from the same direction. Two of the men had Cliff between them and were roughly marching him back to the fire. He was struggling to get away, but one of the men holding him was the blacksmith and Cliff wasn't going anywhere.

"We found him trying to sneak back into his wagon. He's got some blood on his shirt," said Jason Morris, the blacksmith.

Leo Crandall said firmly, "Bring him over here."

As they brought the still-fighting Cliff to the fire, the entire population of the wagon train gathered in a circle around him.

"I don't think we need to have a formal trial for this crime," announced Leo.

There was a murmuring of consent that confirmed his statement. It was a jury of his peers, and the verdict was unanimous. Cliff Johnson was guilty as charged.

Leo glared at Cliff Johnson and said, “Cliff Johnson, you will be given one week’s rations and a rifle with three rounds of ammunition. You will be banned from coming within a mile of the wagon train. If you are seen, any member of the train can shoot you on sight. The money you have in the community wagon will be given to your wife. You should be hanged, but that is beyond our authority.”

He looked at the men holding Cliff and said, “Now, prepare this piece of manure for his sentence.”

The finality of the judgment pronounced, they dragged a more docile Cliff Johnson, who had expected to be hanged, to his wagon. They picked out his rifle, three rounds of ammunition and packed a bag with enough food for a week or so. They gave him a canteen with water and then marched him outside the boundary under gunpoint and tossed him into the tall grass.

Cliff scrambled to his feet, turned, scowled at them, and yelled, “You ain’t heard the last of me!”, before he turned away and disappeared into the night.

———

Hugh had the pot of stew bubbling. It had canned beef, potatoes, and onions, flavored with salt and pepper. He had apologized for the lack of fresh meat as he hadn’t been hunting. His Nez Perce guests still appreciated the hot food, and Pale Dawn was resting comfortably, her fever already diminishing.

"So, where will you go after leaving the children with their mother and father," asked Red Owl.

"I'm going to my ranch in Oregon. It was my brother's, but he died, leaving it to me."

"You could not save your brother?"

"No, he died far away."

Blue Flower had been studying Hugh. She was a beautiful young maiden, and many young warriors had wanted to be her husband, but she had not chosen yet. Her younger sister, Pale Dawn, had already chosen Long Wolf, but Blue Flower was more particular in her choice. She had watched Hugh save her sister's life, after saving all four of them from the Cheyenne, and was taken by the tall white man. She couldn't understand a word he said, but his voice sounded so gentle and kind. He was the tallest man she had ever seen and was very handsome. She wondered if he had a woman but was sure that he had. Maybe he was returning to her in the west.

The children were huddled next to Hugh with Chester. The dog had enjoyed the meal as well, even the onions. There would be hell to pay for anyone close to Chester later, though. He was already gaining some weight and was looking less like a starved cur.

Long Wolf felt a special debt to Hugh. The big white man had saved his Pale Dawn, but he didn't know how he could satisfy such an enormous debt. Then there was the incredible gift of the rifle and ammunition.

"How much further to your village, Red Owl?" Hugh asked.

"Just another day's ride. To the northwest after the next pass. Will Pale Dawn be able to ride?"

"She will be weak, and you should probably go more slowly than usual, but she should be all right. In our hospitals, we keep patients who have had this operation for a week, but that is mainly to make sure it does not become infected. I believe the whiskey will keep the infection away."

"So, we will travel together tomorrow for the morning and then we will leave you after the pass. You have been a good friend, Hugh McGinnis."

"I am proud to have you, Long Wolf, and your daughters as my friends. But now, I need to prepare the children for sleep."

He stood and began setting up the tent. Without the mattress, Hugh unrolled his bedroll inside.

"Andy, you and Addie will need to sleep in the bedroll from now on. I tossed the mattress because it was too big, but the bedroll should be big enough for you both."

"But, Mister Hugh, where will you sleep?" asked Addie.

"I'll be on a blanket out here. Don't you worry. I'll be fine."

"Alright."

Hugh got them clean and then Addie slid in first with her splint before Andy slipped inside. They smiled at Hugh and said their prayers as before, asking God to protect their mama and that He look after Mister Hugh.

Hugh walked back to the fire as Chester sat in front of the tent watching over his young friends.

"They are good children," said Red Owl.

"I think that was because of their mother. Their father died when they were very young. They don't even remember him. Their mother had no money, so she married another man who was taking them to Oregon. The children tell me that he did not like them. They love their mother very much. She is why they are so polite and good."

"You have not met the mother?"

"No, I just happened to find them. I was being followed by some Cheyenne. I had to leave the trail and they followed me for three days. They attacked again earlier today. Of the eight that began to follow, only two returned to their camp."

"Your god protects the children. You are their guardian warrior."

Hugh didn't know what to make of his new title.

He said, "I know that in just three days, I have come to see them as my own children. They are very special, and it will be hard to leave them."

"It is the way of life."

"I know, but it doesn't make it any easier."

Red Owl nodded.

Blue Flower said something to Red Owl, then after he looked at her for a few seconds, he turned to Hugh and asked, "My daughter asks if you have a woman."

"No, not yet. I spent many years in school and then the war. After that, I have been traveling."

Red Owl translated for Blue Flower, who then smiled at Hugh. Hugh smiled back, but knew he was on dangerous ground and it was time to shift the topic.

"Red Owl, can you ask Long Wolf if he has ever shot a Spencer carbine before?"

Red Owl looked at Long Wolf, asked, then turned back to Hugh and replied, "He has not. He said that they are all the same."

"Tell Long Wolf that there are many different models of rifles. They can be very different. I'll show him how to load and fire the Spencer, if he'd like."

After Red Owl told Long Wolf, he nodded his agreement who then walked to his horse and brought the carbine back to the fire.

Hugh took the gun and removed the feed tube. That opened Long Wolf's eyes. As he ran through the loading procedure, Red Owl translated, and Long Wolf studied intently. Hugh showed him that the lever only ejected the used cartridge and loaded a new one. He'd still have to cock the hammer manually. He let Long Wolf go through the actions with the empty carbine. Once he was satisfied, Hugh looked at Long Wolf and just nodded as Long Wolf grinned. He had learned a valuable lesson.

Rather than risk any possible interface with Blue Flower, Hugh said he'd take the first watch. With his two pistols and the Henry, he felt ready for any problems, so he walked off from the fire and climbed a one-man sized boulder as security.

He stayed on the boulder until his butt grew numb and guessed he'd been up there for three or four hours. He finally slid down and stretched his back. There was a three-quarters moon high in the sky, so everything was well lit. He looked at the tent with the children and their sleeping canine friend out front and wondered why Chester hadn't reacted at all to the presence of the Nez Perce. Maybe it had to do with their lack of hostility. *Did it make a difference in the scent to a dog?*

Speaking of the Nez Perce, he looked over and saw that Pale Dawn was sleeping peacefully with her sister sleeping next to her. Red Owl and Long Wolf slept on the opposite side of Blue Flower and Hugh felt safer. After she had asked her question about his having a woman, he had seen the danger signs. He could understand, too, as he had saved her sister and probably all four of them. She probably thought he had great magic, and after Red Owl had said he was a guardian warrior, he was beginning to wonder himself after that near miss by that Cheyenne bullet.

He wasn't tired at all, even at this late hour and that surprised him. It must be two or three o'clock in the morning. It also wasn't as cold as it normally would be, so he thought he may as well stay up for the rest of the night, which wouldn't be much longer at this time of year, especially at this latitude.

Hugh began running through the timetable for finding the wagon train. He guessed that they were at the roughly the same spot where the wagon went over. He had seen the rise ahead and the chasm. From this distance, the wide trail looked like a footpath on the side of a mountain. That meant they were about sixty miles or so behind, maybe less. The train moved at a walking pace. Oxen made great towing beasts, but they only walked, unless they were spooked and unhitched, then they could move.

So, as they were moving at double that speed, probably more, they should gain twenty miles a day which meant they could be anywhere from three to five days behind. Not bad at all, unless you considered the downside of all those calculations. He'd be losing the children's company after that and he was already saddened by the thought.

Then he began playing through various return scenarios. He really would like to give the children private time with their beloved mother, but he couldn't arrange that. So, he thought that if he gave the wagon train a warning that they were approaching, maybe their mother would see her children and leave the wagon. He'd see what happened when it happened, but he already knew one thing, he'd have to move on right away. Once the children were reunited with their mother, he'd have to leave quickly. The longer he stayed, the more difficult it would be.

He spent another hour walking along quietly, thinking of what he'd do when he got to the ranch. *Would he stay or return and finish his schooling at the University of Michigan?* He only needed another year, and that was all practical work. He'd learned much more in his time with the medical corps. So much of his future depended on what he would find in Oregon.

As he continued his meditation, he noticed the sky brightening with the pre-dawn. Everyone was still sleeping, so he walked back toward the trail. It was empty, as it should be, but he watched for a little while longer until he heard footsteps behind him. He could tell they were a man's, so he didn't turn around.

"You didn't wake us for a watch, Hugh McInnis."

"No, Red Owl, I enjoyed the peace of the night."

"I understand why you sought this peace. You are wise beyond your years. You feared Blue Flower."

Hugh laughed, then said, “You do understand, Red Owl. I did not wish to offend or cause disharmony. I felt it safest to stay awake.”

“You can return safely now, Hugh McGinnis. I am awake and will protect you from my daughter,” he said as he laughed.

The two men returned quietly to the camp.

CHAPTER 4

Hugh started a fire and the others began to stir. He walked over to see how Pale Dawn was doing and found her awake and Long Wolf had already explained how the surgery had gone and how bad the appendix was that he had removed. She looked up at Hugh and smiled warmly. Hugh returned her smile and asked Red Owl to ask her how she felt. He talked to her and then turned to Hugh.

“She feels much better and thanks you with all her spirit. She says her belly feels sore, but the awful pain is gone. She asks how you can stand to drink the whiskey.”

He laughed and said, “Tell her that I don’t like it either. I only use it to pour on wounds. I’ll get breakfast going.”

As Red Owl translated to Pale Dawn, Hugh walked to the fire and set his grate on top and began to cook breakfast. Chester was awake and sitting nearby awaiting his share.

Soon, everyone was eating, and the children were animated. Pale Dawn had gotten to her feet with support from Long Wolf and joined them a short time after washing.

After breakfast, Hugh loaded up the packhorse and made Andy’s throne. He saddled Middie and included Addie’s blanket seat, then tied the trail line from the mule and sat Andy onto his seat before he picked up Addie and stepped into the saddle. They were ready for their second full day on the trail.

The Nez Perce were all on their horses. Pale Dawn had mounted hers with assistance from Long Wolf, of course. They returned to the trail and started up the incline to the pass.

As they rode along, Hugh continued his lessons with the children. He had explained to Red Owl that the children wanted to learn to read and write, so they were taking advantage of any free time to do that. Soon, they came to the spot of the accident.

Hugh pointed out the wagon far below, and Red Owl said that their god must surely have been watching for them to allow them to survive that fall.

They left the scene of the accident behind and an hour later, cleared the pass.

The wagon train finally gotten underway as Hugh and his party crossed over the pass. It was a later start than usual, and Rebecca had helped Florence get the team harnessed. Without Cliff around, it was a much more pleasant trip. Florence told Rebecca that they had over five hundred dollars in the community wagon, and even though she didn't know what she'd be doing when they arrived, it was wonderful to be free from Cliff.

Florence was always more spirited than Rebecca. She would always like men, despite Cliff. Once Cliff was gone, Rebecca knew it wouldn't be long before some started giving her an interested look.

There were six unattached males in the wagon train, if you disregarded Leo, the wagon master. Most were teenagers between sixteen and nineteen, but there was that twenty-two-year-old Leroy White. He wasn't the most polished man, but he had a nice shape to him, and Florence had said that she could live without the polish.

Florence was a year younger than Rebecca at twenty-nine, but she still thought of herself as a young girl. She had a good figure and was proud to show it…within bounds, of course.

Rebecca, who had a better figure, didn't care to let anyone know at all. Besides, she thought, it would be a cold day in hell before any man got to see it again, especially Bob Orson.

Three miles behind the wagon train, Cliff Johnson walked along the trail. He would bide his time, and then he would extract his vengeance, beginning with Emily Amber. He had watched her walk away into the night after she had told everyone she had to go and relieve herself, but he knew better. He had been watching her for days and knew that she wanted him. She would look at him and then look away as if she hadn't meant to see him.

When he approached her that night as she was lifting her dress, he knew what she wanted. He had surprised her and pulled her to him to kiss her, and she had slapped him! *That harlot had dared to act like she was offended!*

So, he had pulled his knife to make his intentions clear and ripped away the front of her dress. She tried to run, and he had reached for her, but he had forgotten the knife was in his hand and he had sliced her. That was when she screamed, began running and he stupidly followed. Then he stopped and began to circle around to get to his wagon. Once there, he could claim innocence, but it was too late. That bitch had spilled her guts and named him, so he never got there. Those two bastards had grabbed him, and he'd make them pay, too. They may have only given him three bullets, but he still had his knife.

They'd all pay for what they were doing to him.

Hugh's entourage was on the long downslope after the pass and were making good time. The children were in good spirits and spelling as many words as they could. They began pointing at objects and trying to spell the word. They butchered the long words like 'mountain' and 'eagle' but were either correct or very close with 'bush', 'tree', 'rock' and 'grass'.

The Nez Perce enjoyed the energy of the two children, but sooner than Hugh had expected, Red Owl pointed to a distant spot and told Hugh that was where they would turn northwest. It was about twenty minutes away at their current rate, and Hugh would be sad to see them go as they were good traveling companions, but it did remove the danger of Blue Flower.

She seemed a bit distraught as the time for their separation drew closer, and Hugh momentarily wondered if he was making the right decision. Blue Flower was a very beautiful woman with a lithe, well-formed body, but he couldn't speak to her and didn't know her personality at all. Besides, he might offend some warrior who had his mind set on her. Then there were the children. Everything now revolved around the children. They were his top priority, and he knew he was making the right decision.

When they reached the bottom of the long decline. Red Owl signaled that they would turn here.

He shook Hugh's hand and said, "Hugh McGinnis, word of what you have done for us and especially my daughter, will be told among my people. You will be honored as the best of friends."

"Thank you, Red Owl. I have been honored to know you, Long Wolf and your daughters."

Long Wolf trotted his pony to Hugh and shook his hand and thumped him on the chest, saying simply, "Friend."

Hugh nodded and smiled at Long Wolf.

Then, Pale Dawn drew near, then she leaned over and kissed Hugh on the cheek. He wished she hadn't risked it, but smiled at her and said, "Thank you, Pale Dawn."

Then after Pale Dawn walked her horse to Long Wolf, Blue Flower rode hers close to Hugh. She looked deeply into his eyes and a single tear fell from her left eye. She reached around her neck and took off her beautifully worked necklace, then reached over, took his hand and placed the necklace onto his palm and closed his fingers. She said something to him and rode off. Hugh didn't know what to say.

He looked at Red Oak, who said to him, "Blue Flower said that she will miss you greatly as you have touched her heart. She asked you to give the necklace to the woman that will touch yours."

Hugh blew out his breath and said to Red Owl, "When you think it's the right time, Red Owl, tell Blue Flower that I will always remember her and that she did touch my heart. But fate is one thing that we do not control. Tell her I wish her nothing but the greatest of happiness in her life."

Red Owl smiled at Hugh, waved goodbye, turned his horse and the Nez Perce began their ride to the north.

Hugh and the children began riding west again as he tucked the necklace into his saddlebag. Then to drive away thoughts of Blue Flower, Hugh immediately picked up their schooling lessons.

They stopped for lunch at a small cluster of pines near a good-sized pond where he watered the horse and mule and let them graze. He fed the children and just grabbed a piece of jerky for himself...and one for Chester, of course. You can't resist a dog staring at you while you eat, at least he couldn't.

As he chewed on the dried meat, he thought about Blue Flower, the necklace and what she had told him. *Would he ever meet a woman that would touch his heart?*

They were on the road making good time twenty minutes later and Hugh estimated they were traveling at double the speed of the wagon train at least. So, if the wagon train was making twenty-five miles per day, they were making fifty, maybe a little more. With the Nez Perce gone, Hugh had been able to keep them moving quickly.

"How much longer before we see mama?" asked Addie, as if she had been reading his mind.

"I was just running those numbers in my head, Addie. Now, we crossed the pass that they crossed three days ago. They have probably gone sixty miles since then. We've already gone twenty miles today and will probably do another twenty before we stop for the night. With the distance they traveled today, that means they are at the most about forty miles ahead of us, probably less. So, we should catch up to them in two more days."

That excited Addie, who shouted, "Andy! Mister Hugh says we will see mama in two days!"

Andy was excited at the news as much as his sister. Just two more days before they saw their beloved mama. But then

Andy realized the bad side of reaching the wagon train. Mister Hugh would leave them, and he really liked Mister Hugh. Mister Hugh was nice and was helping them to read and write, and he was much better than Mister Orson. He would ask Mister Hugh about it tonight.

As they trotted along, Hugh would give them words to spell. Finally, he said, “Okay, you two. It’s time you learned to spell a word that will make your mama cry.”

Addie asked, “Why would we want to make mama cry?”

Hugh smiled at her and replied, “First, when she sees you, she’ll already be crying.”

“She will? Why? I thought she would be happy.”

“When people are really, really happy, they cry. Now, your mama is going to be the happiest lady in the world when she sees you again because she loves you both that much. But do you know what would make her even happier?”

Andy, who had moved the mule close asked, “What?”

“What is your mama’s name?”

“Rebecca,” Addie answered.

“Now, how do you spell Rebecca?”

Addie scrunched up her face as Andy started, “R-E-B-E” then he paused and began to sound out what he had started. Then he brightened up, and finished, spelling, “R-E-B-E-K-A”, with a big grin.

“Andy, I’m really proud of you. If you wrote that out, it sounds just like your mother’s name, but names are tricky.

Your mama's name doesn't have a K. It has the same sound but remember what I told you about the letter C. It can sound hard, like 'cart' or soft like 'face'. Now, in your mama's name, it has two of them in a row to make sure you know it means it's a hard letter. Try it again."

Andy paused for a second and then spelled, "R-E-B-E-C-C-A".

"That's it! Now you and Addie can practice saying that over and over so when you see your mama and after she covers you both with kisses and hugs you to death, you just say, 'Mama, we know your name. It's R-E-B-E-C-C-A.', and she'll be so surprised and happy that she'll start crying all over again. It will tell your mama that you're learning to read and write."

They wasted no time and began chanting the letters to a sing-song tune of their own design as they rode along. It seemed to provide a rhythm to the animals as well.

Anxious to close the gap, Hugh kept them on the trail until almost six o'clock before he finally pulled off the Trail and found a nice spot to set up camp for the night.

After they had eaten dinner and cleaned up, Hugh tucked them into the bedroll inside the tent while Chester was in his accustomed position. As Hugh was getting ready to get his own sleeping arrangements configured, Andy spoke up.

"Mister Hugh, what will you do after you leave us with our mama and Mister Orson?"

Hugh couldn't help but notice his separation of the two adults.

"Oh, I'll probably continue on. The wagon train goes so slowly, and I'd be in the way. So, I'd give you each a big hug and leave you to your mother."

Addie sniffed and asked, "You're gonna leave us?"

"Addie, you belong with your mama and Mister Orson. I'll miss you both, but I don't fit in there. Do you understand?"

"No. Why can't you stay and make Mister Orson leave?"

"Because, sweetheart, he married your mama. The law says that she has to stay with him. And you want to stay with your mama, don't you?"

"Yes, but…" Addie said, and then stopped.

"Now, it'll be all right. You're both very good young people. When we catch up to the wagon train, you'll see your mama again and you'll be very happy."

He stood and walked back to the campfire. He knew it had to happen this way. Nothing much was worse than having an unattached male hanging around a marriage.

He crawled under the blanket and laid there staring up at the darkening sky, which matched his mood. They were getting close enough that he might even lose the children tomorrow.

The wagon train had been pulled over since five o'clock. They were only seventeen miles ahead of Hugh and the children because of the delays caused by Cliff Johnson and a broken axle on the Jefferson's wagon that took almost an hour and a half to repair, even with six men working on it.

Rebecca and Florence were still talking under the wagon where they would sleep as Rebecca didn't want to be near Bob and Ella. Lord only knew what was going on over there.

Florence asked, "Are you disappointed, Rebecca? I saw you as you walked or even as we rode how you kept looking behind us."

"No. God said they would be returned to me. He didn't say it would be today."

"What if he meant twenty years from now?"

"Then I'll be an old lady waiting for her children."

"Maybe tomorrow, then."

"Maybe, but if not, I'm not going to lose faith. I can't."

"For me, I'm just so pleased to be free of Cliff. Did you notice that LeRoy has been looking over at me a few times today?"

"Really, Flo. You're what, seven or eight years older than he is and besides, he's a bit on the crude side, don't you think?"

"I know Emily Amber sure wouldn't mind dragging him into her bed."

"Trust me, Florence. I don't think she has her eye on him."

"Really? So, I have a clear playing field?"

"As clear as you can make it."

"Wonderful," Florence replied as she stared at the bottom of the wagon and dreamed lascivious thoughts of Leroy.

Rebecca stared at the same boards and underpinnings and wondered when her children would be returned. God had promised her.

Early the next morning, Hugh was up before the sun. He shaved and put on a clean shirt. He'd have to wash the other one when he got a chance and repair that tear, too. He restarted last night's fire and soon had everything packed and saddled, waiting on the children.

He started cooking and was immediately joined by Chester. When the sun finally arrived, he had breakfast cooked and Chester had already been given his now-expected share. The children stirred, getting used to the early departures. They knew that if they got up early and rode longer, they'd find their mama sooner. But today, Hugh had given them their clean clothes to put on, anticipating that they might catch up to the wagon train today, but he decided not to tell the children in case he was wrong. He took their dirty clothes and put them in a bag with the rest of their clothes.

He had them fed and all of them mounted by six-thirty. It was an early departure because Hugh wanted to close the gap as soon as possible. He was getting more attached to the children with each passing hour, and that would make their separation even more painful.

An hour down the trail, Andy asked from behind, "Mister Hugh, how do you spell your name? You always said it was spelled different."

"Okay, Andy. Go ahead and try to spell it."

"I've already been thinking. It's H-U-E."

“That would be correct if I was a shade of a color. That’s how you spell ‘hue’, like a hue of green or brown. But my name is spelled, now don’t let this make you crazy, but it’s spelled ‘H-U-G-H.”

Andy tried to pronounce it the way it was spelled and had problems. Finally, he gave up.

“Are there other words like that?”

“A lot of words. It doesn’t make any sense, does it? They make some words easy to spell, and then, you run across words that don’t make any sense at all. Then you have words that sound the same and are spelled differently.”

“Like what?”

“Oh, for example, ‘road’ like a highway and ‘rode’ like in riding a horse.”

“They’re different?”

“Yes, sir. Rode, like on a horse, is ‘R-O-D-E’, but road like a highway, is ‘R-O-A-D’.”

“That makes my head hurt.”

“It does to all of us, Andy.”

Addie had just been looking at him as he explained it, wondering how he knew so much. As she looked at Hugh, she grew saddened by his imminent departure and without a word of warning, reached over and hugged Hugh around the neck and began to cry. Hugh had no idea what had set it off but put his free arm around her and let her have her tears. *Lord! He would miss these two!*

They began climbing a rise to another pass and Hugh guessed it was around ten o'clock or thereabouts, so as soon as they got on the other side, he'd start looking for a place to have lunch. Addie had finally let go and just sat back down and sniffled. She never told Hugh why she had cried so much because she knew she'd cry even more.

———

Cliff Johnson was still about three miles from the wagon train but had stayed off the trail. He didn't want them seeing him but kept them in sight on the horizon.

Rebecca was riding with Florence, who was already openly flaunting her availability. She had the top two buttons of her dress undone, because it was getting warmer, at least that was the excuse she had given to Rebecca.

Leroy White had already ridden by twice to talk to her about one nonsensical thing or another, and Florence had flirted to her heart's content. Rebecca was just happy she wasn't upwind of him.

They broke for lunch and Rebecca decided to walk for a while to get away from the omni-present Leroy White. She stepped down from the wagon and began to walk up the road, her eyes downcast as she worried that she might be losing her all-important faith in her children's return.

———

Hugh and his charges topped the pass just before noon, and before he could even begin to search for a place for lunch, he spotted the wagon train a few miles ahead.

"Andy, Addie. Look ahead, way down in the valley. It's your mama's wagon train."

The children started bouncing in their limited locations.

"I'll tell you what. We're not going to stop for lunch, okay? I'll give you each a piece of jerky to chew on and we'll just press on. We should be able to get their attention in a little while. Let's move quicker. Okay?"

Addie's sadness was washed away. *Her mama was within sight!*

The wagon train had halted in place for nooning, but Rebecca wasn't hungry at all. She walked further away from the covered wagons and started back down the trail, but her eyes were on the ground as she ruminated about her children.

Hugh had the horse and mule moving at a fast trot which was the fastest they'd gone since he'd run into the Cheyenne just last week. The wagon train was getting closer fast, and only then did Hugh realize that the train had stopped for lunch, but he didn't know he'd just passed Cliff Johnson. Cliff was sitting a hundred yards off the trail in the tall grass, nibbling on some venison jerky when he saw them go trotting past and wondered who the hell the guy was, as they quickly passed.

They were less than a mile away now and closing the gap, and even though he'd seen Rebecca walking away from the wagon train, he didn't know who the woman was.

"I think they're close enough now," said Hugh, "Addie, honey, put your fingers in your ears. This gun is really loud."

"Okay," she answered as she put her fingers in her ears as Hugh pulled out the Sharps.

He aimed it to the right of the wagon train, cocked the hammer and pulled the trigger.

Rebecca had just turned back when she heard the loud echoing boom from a big gun behind her. She whirled, thinking that someone had shot at her, then she shaded her eyes in the bright sunlight and looked further down the trail and saw a cloud of smoke in the distance, then spotted a tall rider holding a long gun, not an Indian. He was wearing a hat and trailing a pack horse. She squinted and saw him slide his rifle away and tried to make out more details.

What does he have on the pack horse? she asked herself. It looks like another rider. She squinted harder and began to trot toward the rider, her heartbeat growing faster. *No! It can't be*! *Can it? Is it possible?*

The tall rider came closer. She saw something else in front of the rider. He was so tall she almost missed it. *A child! He had a child on his lap, and she has golden hair like her Addie!*

She pulled up her skirt and began to sprint toward the rider. *It couldn't be! But God had said it would be!*

She dropped her skirt and stopped. She covered her mouth with her hands when they got within a quarter mile. Then she heard it.

"Mama!" first from a little girl's voice immediately echoed by another "Mama!" from a young boy.

It was her children! Her babies!

She almost fainted but began walking almost in a dream…a wonderful, unbelievable dream. She was almost numb with ecstasy and soon they were within a hundred feet. The big rider stepped down and lowered her darling Addie to the ground and then he plucked her dear Andy from his perch and they both ran to her as she ran to them. She was in such a state of euphoria that she doubted if there was a word to describe it. All those days with people telling her that they were dead meant nothing. *Her children were hers again!*

She crouched down as they plowed into her outstretched arms.

Hugh watched with a smile on his face as they kissed her and kept saying "Mama!" over and over again and tears rolled down her joyous face.

She was in a state of numb rapture as she clutched her precious children, felt them holding her and talking excitedly to her. She had her eyes closed and was thanking God as she felt her children hugging her. Her sobbing and the children's jabbering filled her ears and her heart.

Hugh stepped up into the saddle and moved on. He had to leave quickly as he knew he would. His heart was already tearing apart but joyful at the same time. As he and his animals passed the incredible reunion, he looked down and smiled.

She was so wrapped up in her children she failed to notice the passing of the horse, the mule, and the dog. Hugh knew that if he stayed any longer, he would never want to leave. He was so happy for them. He had left the children's bag of clothing on the ground where he had mounted.

Others in the wagon train had heard Hugh's Sharps roar and had looked down the Trail at the source and saw the big rider and his pack mule approaching.

He pressed on and passed the last wagon. They were all empty for the break until he reached Florence's wagon and stopped.

"Excuse me, ma'am," he said.

Florence thought she'd died and gone to heaven. *Where did this piece of manhood come from?*

"Yes?" she asked in her most 'come-hither' voice.

"Could you see that Mrs. Orson gets these. I forgot to give them to her children," he said as he handed her a packet with the tintype and the cameo.

Florence accepted the cloth-wrapped items and smiled as she said, "I will."

Hugh smiled back as he said, "Thank you, ma'am."

Hugh then tipped his hat and rode on, passing the first wagon just three minutes later and then nudged Middie to a medium trot as he left the wagon train behind.

Florence, getting past her initial fluster after meeting Hugh, realized suddenly what he had said. He had said give this to Mrs. Orson and that he had forgotten to give it to her children. She swiveled and looked back down the Trail and saw Rebecca still on her knees with what looked like her children.

Rebecca couldn't believe this had happened. She let her children step back and looked at them. They were so clean and well-fed, then she noticed the splint on Addie's leg.

"Addie, what happened to your leg?"

"I broke my fibbila, but it's okay. It'll be good fast 'cause I'm seven."

"You broke your leg, but it's going to be okay?"

"Uh-uh. Oh, and we have to tell you something."

"What?"

Addie looked at Andy and he nodded.

Together they recited in their own sing song, "R-E-B-E-C-C-A".

Rebecca was flabbergasted. *Since when could they spell?*

She started crying again and hugged them harder. After her tears finally ended, she looked at their faces again and simply absorbed the image. Her children had returned to her.

It was only then that she realized that she had thanked God but hadn't even thanked the man who had saved them. She looked up to thank him only to find him gone. She saw the bag nearby, then stood up and looked inside to find all their clothes. It was a very thoughtful thing to do, *but where was he?*

She looked around and found no one until she spotted the rider in the far distance.

But the important thing was that her children were here.

"Addie, Andy, I've missed you so much. They all told me you were dead, but God said you'd return to me. Come, we must hurry. The wagon train will be moving soon."

She plucked Addie from the ground and took the bag of clothes. Andy walked beside her, and Rebecca was grinning widely as she finally reached Florence's wagon. She debated bringing them to Ella Murphy's wagon and then decided against it. She knew her husband wouldn't want to see them anyway.

She put Addie on the seat and then helped Andy onto the seat as well.

Florence smiled as the children climbed on board and said to Rebecca, “They’re back! You were right all along. I’m so happy for you. They look really healthy for having been alone for a while.”

“They weren’t alone,” Rebecca said as she climbed into the seat.

“I know. I meant until they were rescued. But I need to know, Becky. Who was that gorgeous tall piece of manhood that saved them?”

“I never even saw him. I don’t know his name.”

Florence was astonished and asked, “You never even saw him? The man brings you back your children and you don’t even know his name?”

“I couldn’t help myself. My children are back. I only had eyes for them.”

Addie had been listening and said, “That was Mister Hugh, Mama. I miss Mister Hugh already. I’m never gonna see him again,” then buried her face in her arms and began to sob.

Rebecca didn’t know what to make of this. She was so overjoyed with having her children returned to her, and now her daughter was already crying over the loss of someone she called Mister Hugh. She had never heard anyone with that name before, so she turned to Andy.

“Andy, did Addie get that right? You were rescued by a Mister Hugh?”

Andy clarified, saying, “That’s what we called him. He said it was okay. His last name was McGinnis, I think. His first name was H-U-G-H. So, we called him Mister Hugh.”

"Andy, did Mister Hugh teach you how to spell?"

"Yes, Mama. He made it fun. We would ride along, and he would have us spell words. He showed us numbers, too. But we can't add or subtract yet."

"Was he a schoolteacher?"

"No, Mama. He was a doctor," he answered nonchalantly.

Rebecca was skeptical because there were very few doctors in the West, and they did not ride alone on the Oregon Trail.

"Did he tell you that?"

"Yes, Mama. Kind of," Andy replied.

"Many people claim to be things they aren't just to make themselves sound important."

Andy shook his head and said, "Mister Hugh wouldn't do that, Mama."

"But, Andy, there are almost no doctors out here."

"He said he didn't finish school yet. He went into the army in the war."

"So, he's not a real doctor."

"He said he wasn't, but you should have seen him when he operated on the young lady."

He had a woman with him? Where was she now? And he had 'operated' on her in front of the children? This was sounding like questionable behavior at best. If he hadn't rescued her children, she might give him a good dressing down.

"And what did he do to the young lady?"

"Took out her pendix," Andy replied.

That threw Rebecca. It wasn't the kind of 'operating' she had expected to hear.

"*He took out her appendix? In the middle of nowhere?*" she asked in disbelief.

"Uh-uh. He had to use his razor to cut open her tummy. We didn't see up close, though. He made us sit with the other pretty lady."

Rebecca's astonishment continued as she asked, "*He had two pretty ladies in the camp? And he took out the appendix on one?*"

She turned to Florence in exasperation. These stories were getting stranger by the second.

"Yes, Mama," Andy replied.

"And did he like these young ladies?"

"Yes, Mama."

Florence added, "I'll bet."

Rebecca asked, "I don't suppose you know the pretty ladies' names, do you?"

"Yes, Mama. The one he took out the pendix was Pale Dawn and her sister was Blue Flower."

"*They were Indians? He brought two pretty young Indian women into camp and operated on one?*" she asked, utterly stupefied.

"He didn't bring them into camp, Mama. They came with us on the trail. They were Net Pears. So were Red Owl and Long Wolf."

"There were four Nez Perce Indians in the camp. How did they get there?"

"Cause the Cheyenne were chasing them, and Mister Hugh shot them. The Net Pears were our friends."

She turned to Florence in total disbelief and asked, "How much of this do you think is true?"

"It all sounds kind of far-fetched to me, but if believing it will bring that man back here, then I'm a first-class believer."

Rebecca turned back to her son and asked, "Andy, is this all the truth?"

"Yes, Mama. Mister Hugh said never to tell a lie because it hurts someone, and most of the time it hurts the person telling the lie even more."

First spelling and now this.

"So, where did the Indians go?"

"Back home. Mister Hugh gave them Mister Orson's rifle and some ammunition, and they rode away."

"He armed an Indian? Wasn't he afraid that he'd shoot you all?"

"No, Mama. They were our friends. The first day Mister Hugh found us, I almost shot him with the gun. So, he showed me how to shoot it and follow the rules. But when he told me that he shot three Cheyenne trying to escape and I said 'good', he got sort of mad at me."

"Why would he get mad at you for being pleased that he shot three Indians?"

"Mister Hugh said just because somebody is an Indian it doesn't make him bad. He said he only shot them Cheyenne because they were trying to kill him. He said look a man in the eye and see if he's a good man."

"We'll talk more later. It's our turn to move the wagon. You go in the back and talk to Charles and Addie. I want to talk to your Aunt Flo for a while."

Neither child asked the important question concerning the whereabouts of Mister Orson. They didn't seem to care one bit, and hoped he had fallen off the cliff, too.

Rebecca turned to Florence and said, "Florence, it's only been a few days. Does this all sound possible to you?"

"They both talk about it like it really happened. Maybe he told them stories and they think that they happened while he was with them."

"But the spelling and those things Andy said about not lying or judging people. Those are every bit as extraordinary as the Indians and the surgery. I suppose it doesn't matter. He's gone, and we'll never know. But my children are home and that's all that matters."

"Maybe to you, Rebecca. But you never saw him, and I did."

———

When the wagon train began to move, the rumor of the miraculous return of the Orson children raced through the group and finally reached Ella Murphy's wagon.

"Oh, Bob, you must be so happy!" Ella gushed.

Bob tried to put on a happy face but failed and had to improvise. He looked down, mustering the saddest visage he could manage.

Ella asked, "What's the matter, Bob? Doesn't that make you happy?"

"Ella, I'll be honest with you. Rebecca never cared for me at all. All she used me for was to provide for her and the children, and even denied me my husbandly rights. I put up with this for over a year now, and I thought at least with the children gone, as tragic as it was, maybe it would give us a chance to become a normal husband and wife. But now that they're back, I can't see that ever happening."

He even sighed deeply for effect.

He looked at Ella and saw the concerned look of sympathy in her eyes.

"I would never deny you, Bob," she said quietly.

"I wish it could be so, Ella. I've come to care for you these past few days, but I'm still married to Rebecca, sham marriage that it is."

"You could divorce her for not being a true wife to you."

"I could, but that would be difficult to prove. I need something more substantial, like if she were caught with another man."

Ella produced a genuine sigh as she looked at Bob.

"Well, Bob, I think that problem will resolve over time. Women have needs, too, you know. Take me, for instance, my husband has been gone for only six weeks and my needs haven't been satisfied."

"I'd like to satisfy those needs, Ella. We just need to point some man in Rebecca's direction. Any ideas?"

Ella slid over and put her hand on Bob's thigh and began sliding it back and forth.

"There's always Leroy White. He's a randy one. He's tried working his way into my bed, but I have standards, Bob."

Bob didn't hear very much of what she was saying. He was busy running his hand along her thigh as well.

Finally, he smiled at her and said, "We'll see."

———

Hugh and Chester were already three miles ahead. Now that he had no one else to worry about, he was able to maintain the pace.

No one else to worry about, thought Hugh. Well, at least he still had Chester.

He kept up the fast rate and by the time he set up camp, he was a full ten miles ahead of the wagon train.

He made his dinner and leaned back against a tall Ponderosa pine, rubbing Chester's head. He began humming the children's sing song, "R-E-B-E-C-C-A" and smiled, feeling the saddest happiness or the happiest sadness he had ever experienced.

Rebecca, Florence and the two children as well as Florence's son, Charles, were sitting in the darkened wagon.

Rebecca asked, "So, Andy, how did Mister Hugh find you?"

"He was being chased by some Cheyenne Indians when he saw some of our things floating in the river. He rode up and found us."

"And he fixed you food and took care of you from the very start?"

"Yes, Mama. He told us how good we were, and we must have had a wonderful mama to bring us up that way."

"But, why did he leave? He never even talked to me."

"Because he said you were married to Mister Orson and the law says you have to stay with him."

Then it dawned on Andy, and he asked excitedly, "Where is Mister Orson? Did he fall off the cliff like we did?"

Rebecca shook her head and replied, "No, Andy. He's up front in Mrs. Murphy's wagon."

Andy was disappointed that he was still alive, but then perked up and asked, "Does that mean he won't be back?"

"I don't think so. He's just there because we don't have a wagon anymore."

"Oh," Andy said as the dejection returned but asked, "But if he's there, couldn't Mister Hugh stay with us now?"

"No, Andy. I'm married to Mister Orson. He's my husband. Another man can't stay with you because it isn't allowed. Now, enough of this talk about Mister Hugh staying here. You're both going to have to live with the fact that your Mister Hugh has gone and will never return. But isn't it enough that we have each other now?"

Andy was downcast as he replied, 'Yes, Mama."

Addie was more direct as she said, "Mister Hugh was good to us and liked us. Mister Orson hates us."

Rebecca was getting exasperated, and said, "Mister Hugh took care of you, and I'm grateful for that, but he isn't here."

"But he liked you and said you were really pretty," said Andy.

Rebecca was taken aback and asked, "Why would he say that? He never even saw me until he dropped you off."

"He looked at your picture. I showed him after I found it in the wagon."

Her picture! Her wedding picture and her mother's cameo! She had forgotten about them, *and now the mysterious Mister Hugh had them?*

"And did Mister Hugh take the picture?"

"Yes, Mama. He took the picture and a black round thing with a face on it."

So, he did have the cameo! She was about to get angry when Florence interrupted.

"Hold on. I forgot. He stopped by and gave me something and asked to give it to Mrs. Orson. I was so wrapped up in looking at him, I almost didn't hear what he said."

She went to the seat and pulled the small cloth-wrapped package out of the foot well and handed it to Rebecca.

Rebecca unwrapped it and found the tintype and the cameo. She closed her eyes, held it against her breast and sighed. The only two inanimate objects she wanted. She felt guilty for accusing Mister Hugh for doing something so vile.

Why had she even thought of such a thing? This man saves her children, feeds them, keeps them safe and clean, teaches them, gives them life lessons, protects them and has enough moral courage to leave rather than cause dissension in a marriage that didn't matter. Yet all she had done is think badly of him. She was being unfair, and she knew it.

Beside her, Florence was salivating over him after just seeing him for thirty seconds while she, the one woman who owed him so much, was thinking of him as just another poor excuse for a man, but there was nothing she could do about it.

CHAPTER 5

Hugh was up early again the next day, packed his mule, then saddled his horse and just grabbed some jerky for breakfast and tossed three pieces to the ever-present Chester who then followed him as they regained the Trail. He guessed that three more days on the trail would get him to his destination, which seemed almost pointless now. The children seemed so much more important. In such a short time, they had wormed their way deeply into his heart.

He shook it off and began to ride. By noon he had put another ten miles between him and the wagon train and was going to stop for lunch when he noticed a structure in the distance. It looked like a fort or a settlement. He didn't expect to see one yet, so it must be new.

He skipped lunch and rode the four miles to what turned out to be a trading post. He pulled up in front and hooked Middie's reins over the rail and stepped inside. It was a pretty well-stocked place considering its location. With the children no longer with him, he didn't need a lot, but he wandered down an aisle of canned goods and picked up some more beans and beef. Then he saw some canned peaches and smiled as he thought how much the children would enjoy those, then added two to his growing stack. He carried them up front and set them down on the counter.

He smiled at the proprietor and said, "I've got to add some more stuff. I'll be right back."

He picked up some more coffee and salt and a slab of bacon, a large bag of flour and a tin of baking powder and a bag of sugar. He added thirty eggs to the list. As he was putting them on the counter, he saw a small display of penny candy and knew the children would love those, too, but there was no need.

He headed back down the last aisle to buy another shirt. He picked up two shirts and turned to leave when his eyes fastened on something that he had forgotten...a broken promise. He had never broken a promise before in his life and wasn't about to this time. He reached down and pulled a box off the shelf. Inside was a pretty little girl doll with curly blond hair and blue glass eyes. It reminded him of Addie. She even had a dress on that Addie could change.

But what to do about Andy? He went up front and found his answer when he found a nice pocketknife with two blades. It was a young boy's dream possession until he moved up to those things that went bang.

He took the shirts, knife and the doll up front and added them to the stack. Then, knowing he now had an excuse to visit the children, he bought ten cents worth of penny candy, which was a huge bag of sweets. The proprietor smiled as he saw the doll.

"You're gonna make some little girl very happy."

"That's the idea. She's a real sweetie. And give me one of those twelve-gauge shotguns and two boxes of bird shot and four of the number five buckshot."

He added the total and Hugh paid for the order while the proprietor bagged it all up and gave him the doll separately.

He went back outside and loaded his new purchases on the mule and headed for the diner. He had a good non-Hugh cooked lunch and then walked back outside, untied Middie and the mule, mounted, and headed back east. He stopped to let the animals eat and drink at the first location he could, then continued eastward on the Trail. He was now fifteen miles in front of the wagon train, but this time, the distance was closing rapidly as the two converged.

He didn't care one iota about Mister Orson. He wasn't courting his wife or anything, he was fulfilling a promise he made to Addie. Besides, he still needed to set Mister Orson straight about how he treated his wife and children.

He had Middie moving along at a good pace. The wagon train continued at a leisurely pace, but they were closing at almost ten miles an hour.

———

In the Johnson wagon, Rebecca and Florence sat in the front seat. The children were in back talking about the adventures with Mister Hugh to Florence's son, Charles, as Leroy White rode alongside talking to Florence.

Rebecca had been listening to Andy and Addie tell Mister Hugh stories since the train started moving before seven o'clock, and they never seemed to end. Rebecca was now truly ashamed of herself for thinking ill of the man and even more sorry for not have taken a brief interlude to thank him for what he had done.

Rebecca had been most intrigued by the story about Blue Flower. Andy had said that he thought she really liked Mister Hugh, and when she left, she gave Mister Hugh a necklace that was very pretty which made her feel strangely jealous. *Why should she be jealous?* She had never even met the man. Besides, she was married.

"Was she young, Andy?" Rebecca asked after he had told the Blue Flower story.

"Yes, Mama. She was even younger than Mister Hugh."

That surprised her because she thought, if he was almost a doctor, he'd be older than she was.

She turned to Florence and asked, "How old would you say he was, Florence?"

"Mid-twenties, I'd guess. It doesn't matter to me. He sure looked like prime beef."

Suddenly, Rebecca felt very much thirty, not even twenty-nine. She was what they considered 'mature'. Why it had become something to be concerned about was new to her as well.

The wagon train rolled on another hour after the noon break, and children were in the back taking a nap.

Two miles ahead, Hugh could make out the dust from the oncoming train and felt an elation about seeing Addie and Andy again. He slowed the horse down and set him to a walk, no use making a show about it.

The wagon master saw the rider ahead and wondered what his business was. He had been on the opposite side of the train when Hugh had ridden past going west.

He set his horse into motion and rode out to meet the stranger.

Hugh saw Leo coming and waved to set his mind at ease. Leo pulled up in front of Hugh and both men brought their animals to a stop.

"Howdy. Don't see many folks out here heading east."

"My name's Hugh McGinnis."

"Leo Crandall."

"I was just riding to your wagon to deliver a package to Miss Addie Orson."

"Addie?"

"I made a promise to her a few days ago, and I always keep my promises."

"You're the fella that rescued the children, ain't ya?"

"I found them, but I made a promise to Addie and I need to deliver on it."

"Well, come on. Addie is in the Johnson wagon. That's the ninth one in line. Her husband, Bob, is in the Murphy wagon. It's fifth in line."

"Okay. Thanks," Hugh replied as he wondered why they were in different wagons, thinking that it must have something to do with space allocation, but recalled how Andy and Addie had talked ill of the man and wondered how bad it was between him and their mother.

Leo turned his mount around and headed back.

Hugh started passing wagons and looked at the fifth wagon and saw Bob Orson. Bob had seen him coming and hadn't bothered removing his right hand from Ella's thigh.

Hugh noticed that Bob was obviously in contact with the woman close to him. She wasn't his wife, so he took a second look and was met with a definitely hostile glare from Bob.

Hugh just kept walking his horse. He reached the seventh, then stopped Middie and turned her facing the wagon train, waiting for the ninth to pass.

Rebecca and Florence were engaged in serious conversation when Leroy White saw Hugh waiting and sneered before stopping his mount and then turning and moving on.

Hugh wondered what that was all about. He turned Middie parallel to the train and pulled up alongside the wagon.

"Excuse me, ma'am. You must be Addie's mother," he said loudly.

Rebecca looked up and was startled. It must be the mysterious Mister Hugh, and she immediately knew why Florence was so smitten.

Florence turned at the same time and was re-smitten. She was about to answer when Rebecca replied to Hugh's question.

"Yes, I'm Addie's mother."

"Would it be alright if I spoke to the children for a little bit. I made Addie a promise a while back and I need to fulfill it. Then I'll be out of the way. I don't want to cause any problems."

"No, not at all. You won't cause any problems. I'm so sorry, that I never even got a chance to thank you for bringing my children back to me."

"You're welcome, ma'am, but I have already been rewarded many times by just being in their company. I apologize for my hasty departure, but I didn't want to interrupt or cause any family problems. But if it's alright, I'd like to give something to Addie, and Andy, too."

"Surely," she said and then turned and shook Andy, saying "Andy, can you wake Addie? You have a visitor."

Andy was still a bit cotton-headed, but he shook Addie who sat up and yawned as he said, "Addie, mama says we have a visitor."

Addie understood immediately, and screamed, "Mister Hugh!"

Then it was a mad scramble out front as both children clawed their way to the driver's seat.

Addie practically jumped out of the wagon, shouting, "Mister Hugh! Mister Hugh! You came back!"

Andy stood behind her grinning and waving.

Hugh smiled broadly at them and said, "Addie, I felt bad for not keeping a promise I made to you. So, without any further delay, I am going to fulfill my promise to the prettiest girl I've ever met."

Addie was beaming from the combination of seeing Hugh again and his compliment. She didn't remember the promise he was talking about, though.

He turned to the pack mule that he had pulled to his side and pulled out the box and handed it to Addie. Her eyes kept getting wider as she opened the box and saw the doll.

"Mister Hugh, she's so beautiful! She's much prettier than Maggie. Thank you."

"You're very welcome, sweetheart. She's still nowhere near as pretty as you are, though."

Addie alternated smiling at Hugh and the doll.

Hugh then looked at Andy and said, "Andy, I didn't feel right about bringing a present to Addie and forgetting about you, and I wondered what I could get for my good friend, Andy. I almost bought you a toy gun, but that wouldn't be right, with you being almost ten. So, I found this," he said as he reached into his saddlebag and pulled out the pocketknife and handed to him.

Andy's eyes lit up as he accepted the gift and said, "Thank you, Mister Hugh. My very own pocketknife! Wow! It even has two blades!"

"And I bought this for the family, ma'am, but I want you to use it," He said as he reached over to the pack mule, took out the shotgun and handed it to Rebecca.

"This is very easy to use. Here are some boxes of shells for it," he said as he handed the shells to Florence who passed them to Rebecca.

"I'd like to show you how to use that weapon, but I'm sure Mister Orson can do that. Just make sure he knows that I gave that gun to you and not to him. This is your weapon. Alright?"

Andy answered quickly, "But Mister Orson isn't here right now, Mister Hugh. You can show me."

He knew where Mister Orson was and what he was doing, so he looked at Rebecca and asked, "Ma'am?"

"Andy is correct. I can't call you Mister Hugh. Is it McGinnis?"

Hugh laughed and replied, “Call me Hugh, ma’am. They called me Mister Hugh from the start, and I thought it was cute, so I let it continue.”

“Are you going to be staying around, or are you moving on?”

“I’ll probably just camp near the wagon train tonight. I’ll be honest with you, ma’am. It just wasn’t the promise that drove me back here. I really missed your children. They just lit up my life when they were around.”

Rebecca smiled broadly and said, “They do that for me too, Hugh. And please call me Rebecca.”

“I’ll do that, Rebecca,” he said as he returned her smile.

Hugh continued to ride alongside the wagon until Leo called it time to set up camp.

Hugh said to Rebecca. “I’m not sure he’s aware of it or not, but there’s a trading post about twenty more miles down the trail.”

“There is?”

“There is. And it’s pretty well stocked, too. I’ll be right back.”

He rode to where Leo was setting up the camp and pulled up alongside.

“Leo, just thought I’d let you know that there’s a new trading post about twenty miles further on.”

“I wasn’t aware of that. Is it a good one?”

“A lot better than you might expect out here.”

"Great. I'll pass along the word. Thanks."

Hugh tipped his hat and rode back to see Rebecca and the children. He didn't want to admit to anyone, including himself, how taken he was with Rebecca but should have expected it after listening to the children talk about her and seeing her picture. But seeing her today and those kind, lively eyes with a smoother, more refined face than the younger woman in the tintype was much more revealing of the character within. Hugh McGinnis was mighty taken with Rebecca already, but she was married and tomorrow morning, he'd be moving on. It was better in the long run. He was already attached to the children and didn't need to add their mother to the list.

The wagon train began settling into their positions for the night camp.

Hugh approached and parked his horse and mule near the Johnson wagon, dismounted, walked back to his pack horse and retrieved a large sack. He walked back to where Rebecca and the children were seated next to Florence and her son, then sat down next to Andy.

"Rebecca, would you mind if I indulged myself in a bit of a fantasy of mine?"

She smiled at him and said, "It depends on its nature."

"When I was a beanpole of a lad, I always thought it would be a wonder if someone came up to me and just offered me some penny candy for no reason. Now, that never happened, so I thought it would be just as good if I could be the one doing the offering. I realize that it's close to dinner time, but do you think I could offer each of these three youngsters one piece of candy before dinner?"

Charles, who until this moment felt out of the whole conversation suddenly took note that he had said three youngsters.

Rebecca held back a smile, turned to Florence and said, "I think that would be acceptable. Florence?"

"Whatever you'd like, Hugh," she replied as she batted her eyelashes at him as Rebecca rolled her eyes.

"You heard from your mamas, young folk," Hugh said, "So, each of you gets one piece, and I may try one myself."

He offered the big bag to each child who examined the selection before taking one treat. When they each had one, he offered the bag to Rebecca and asked, "Rebecca?"

"I haven't had one since I was a young girl. But they do look tempting," she said as she took out a peppermint and popped it into her mouth.

"Ma'am?" he said as he offered the bag to Florence.

"Oh, thank you, Hugh. You're so sweet, and please call me Flo. All my close friends call me that."

She took a cherry and made a show licking it and then rubbing it across her lips before putting it in her mouth with an audible moan. Hugh had picked up on Florence right away. It wasn't difficult.

Hugh gave some to each child to share with the other children in the wagon train and they took off, Addie still hobbling and Chester following.

Hugh handed the bag of remaining candy to Rebecca.

"You can dole these out as you see fit."

"You were traveling with a dog?" Rebecca asked.

"No, ma'am. After I found the children, the dog found us. I think he had been abandoned by a previous wagon train. He was very thin before, but he's put on some weight already. The children named him Chester. He's a good dog."

"My children tell me you're a doctor, Hugh. Is that right?"

"Not quite. I left medical school before my final year to go into the army. I should go back and finish, though."

"From what I hear, you did a remarkable job removing an appendix."

"You sure do have some smart children, Rebecca. It was just a routine appendectomy, although I had to use some makeshift tools. Luckily, I got there in time. I don't think she had another twelve hours before it would have burst and then it would have been too late."

Hugh asked, "Rebecca, why is it that you're not riding in the wagon with your husband?"

Rebecca was afraid this would come up.

"It's a matter of space. When you returned my children, it was easier to ride with Florence."

Hugh knew that was a cover story. Her husband was riding in a wagon with just one woman and had been very touchy-feely with her. He could see the embarrassment it caused Rebecca, so he turned to Florence,

"So, are you a widow, Florence?"

Florence replied, “Not exactly. My husband has been cast out because he tried to assault a woman two nights ago.”

“I would have shot him,” Hugh said calmly, startling the two women.

“That’s somewhat of a surprise coming from you, Hugh. Andy told me how you didn’t even want to shoot the Cheyenne who were chasing you,” said Rebecca.

“That was different. Those were warriors, and we were engaged in a running battle. We were on even terms, even though they outnumbered me eight to one. I was much better armed than they were. If they chose to give up the chase, I’d let them go. Now, a man who assaults a woman has no standing at all in my book. He’s as bad as it gets. You’re both women. Do you think life is fair to you?”

They both looked at him as if he hadn’t really expected an answer.

So, Hugh continued, asking, “Who does all the work on the wagon train or at home? The men go to work. What do they do there? Have you ever seen what they do? They’ll do maybe six or seven hours of work in a given day, unless they’re farmers. Now, women, on the other hand, especially if they have children, have to wake up early, make breakfast, dress the children, clean up after breakfast, clean the house, do the laundry, then make lunch, clean up after lunch, churn the butter and other household chores, prepare dinner, take care of the children, clean up after dinner and it never stops. Every single day, including Sundays.

“The husband comes home, takes off his shoes, then sits down and complains about what a hard day he had. The wife dutifully says, ‘Yes, dear’, prepares his dinner and then when she’s on the verge of collapse, must fulfill her other wifely duties if her husband demands that as well. And we all know that too many women, and children as well, fall victim to the husbands that are allowed by the sole virtue of being a man, to be able to beat them.

"Many of those husbands go off to the saloon at night and come home and make more messes for the little wife to clean up. If he decides to have an affair, good for him. He deserves it. He's the breadwinner. But if little wifey decides to add a little excitement in her life, well, that's different. She's called every bad name you can assign to a female. Her husband can chuck her aside with no means of support whatsoever.

"No, ladies, life isn't fair to your sex. And I, for one, am ashamed for mine. When I get married, I will share as much of that burden as I can. I will treat my wife like a queen and my equal, for she surely will be that. And that, ladies, is why I will never tolerate men who abuse women."

Both women stared at Hugh with blank faces.

He saw them smiled, then said, "Sorry. I got carried away. It's my biggest sore point."

Florence finally spoke, asking "So, I take it then that you're not married?"

Hugh replied, "No, ma'am, I'm not married. I'm not engaged, and I have no girlfriends. I never had the time."

"Andy says you're going to your ranch in Oregon," said Rebecca, changing the subject.

"I am. I've never been there, though. My brother left it to me after he died in the war."

Rebecca said, "I'm sorry."

"That's alright. It's been a while. I don't know what to expect when I get there, though. It's only a few days west of here."

"How big is it?"

"Pretty big. It's eight full sections. That's over five thousand acres. He paid the taxes for five years in advance before he left, which is why I could take my time to get there. I could have gone by rail or ship, but I had my reasons for doing it this way. My brother told me that there's lots of timber on the ranch, too. He built a house on the property, but I don't know how big it is or what condition it's in. He said he was thinking of clearing some of the timber. There's a good-sized river running through the property, so it would be easy to move the logs, but I'll decide what to do when I see the place."

"Do you know anything about that?" asked Rebecca.

"Logging? Probably more than I know about medicine. I grew up cutting trees, climbing them, getting them down to the river, breaking up jams. It's a dangerous job. We'd lose two or three workers a year, not to mention lost limbs and broken bones. It got to where they'd call me whenever there was an injury because I was good at it. So, after high school, I went to the University of Michigan to become a doctor."

"That explains your physique anyway," Florence said with a smile.

She didn't bat her eyelashes, but she did wink.

"So, why did you leave school to go to war?" asked Rebecca.

"It was a stupid reason, really. My brother had died of dysentery, and I signed up that week. Even though I didn't have my M.D. yet, they were so short of surgeons, they put me in the Medical Corps. I became very adept at amputations, as we all did. But I learned a lot more about trauma medicine in those two years than I ever did in medical school. That's why I was confident I could do Pale Dawn's surgery in the field."

Rebecca looked at Hugh and asked, "It's a big leap from lumberjack to doctor. What's the full story, Hugh? Does it have something to do with why you're so angry about what happens to women?"

He looked back at her and smiled, "You're very perceptive, Rebecca. Alright, if you can stand a long story, here it is.

"I grew up doing a lot of lumber work. The reason was that my father was in the lumber business in Michigan. He started with a lumber mill then began buying tracts of lumber and kept expanding his operation. When I was young, it was more like a typical household. My mother did all those jobs that women have to do to keep a household running while my father would come home at night and expect the house clean and dinner on the table. He'd eat, relax for a while, and then he'd go out. I was usually asleep when he got home.

"When I was about ten, things changed. My father began getting big contracts, and my mother hired a cook and a maid. We had moved into a big house by then, but their relationship stayed the same. He'd come home, eat, relax, and then disappear. I didn't know why. I thought that's what all fathers did.

"By the time I was a teenager, I began working summers out in the timber. I never told them my name and just did the work. It was hard, dangerous work, and I saw what happened to workers when they were injured. I even made the mistake once of asking my father why he didn't at least take care of the families. It wasn't something I should have asked. But when I was working, I found the other lumberjacks talking about my father. They referred to him as 'the stud of the North Woods', and I found out what he had been doing at night was keeping a lot of women busy, including some of the wives of the workers. The men were either envious of him or they admired him. I thought of my mother and wondered why she put up with it.

"My brother, Brian, was four years older than I was, and I finally asked him about what seemed to be the big family secret. He told me that he had heard our parents argue years earlier when my mother brought up the subject of his infidelity and my father told her that he'd throw her out into a Michigan blizzard naked if she ever said anything about it again. I thought at the time that my father was a vicious man and it turned out that the only difference between him and other men is that he had the money and the power to get away with doing it. That's why so many men admired him.

"Now, my mother wasn't a saint. She wasn't mean or anything, she was just aloof. She was a very beautiful woman and treated me and Brian well, but she had been shut out of any type of affection, and I think she began to resent us for being sired by my father. Anyway, she became more and more isolated and lonely, so she began looking elsewhere. She found it in a sometime visitor to the house, one of my father's foremen. I knew what was going on, as did Brian. That was one of the reasons he didn't come home from school during the summer months after his first year in college.

"Word got back to my father about the affair she was having, and one summer evening after he had gone and the foreman had arrived, my father returned home and just walked upstairs and shot them both. I was in my room studying when I heard the shots."

Hugh paused as the memories of that night flooded his mind, then continued.

"I ran out of my room and heard my father shouting. I ran down to my mother's bedroom and saw my father there with the pistol in his hand with gunsmoke still leaking from the muzzle. He was shouting at my dead mother, not her dead lover. He was calling her a harlot, a whore, and every other name attributed to loose women. I saw my mother naked, lying under the naked foreman, but my father never even noticed I was there.

"I knew she was dead, so I returned to my room and wondered what I should do. This wasn't some act of outrage by my father, it was an assassination. I thought, surely, the law would come and talk to me, but no one ever did. My father never said a word about it. It was like she just went off on vacation or had never existed.

"I found out later that he told the local sheriff about what he had done, and the sheriff told him not to worry. My father had my mother and the foreman buried together in an unmarked grave and I have no idea where it is.

"The odd thing about all of this was that my father always liked me. He still does. He'd get mad at me sometimes, like when I told him I was going to medical school or when I went into the army, but he always liked me, and more than he liked Brian, for some reason. I always thought Brian was a better man than I was.

"He had finished college and moved to Oregon, where he bought the ranch near Baker City. He wanted me to come and work the ranch with him when I finished and even had my name put on the deed to try to get me to come. He had married a wonderful girl before he left, and I was happy for them both. Then she died in childbirth along with their baby girl. He was devastated and left the ranch to join the army. He died, and I signed up the day after I was notified. My father tried to use his influence to get me tossed out of the army, but it didn't work.

"When I mustered out, I knew my father would be looking for me and I decided to go to Oregon, to what was now my ranch. I bought a horse a pack mule and a bunch of supplies. I even told them all that I was going to Arizona in case my father hired Pinkertons to find me. So, I took the long way, the slow way. I would like to believe that he's given up hope of finding me, but I doubt it. I'm not sure he knows about the ranch, though."

Both women just looked at him before Rebecca asked, "Do you think he'll try to harm you?"

"Heck, no. I'm his only son and heir. Besides, he still likes me. No, he'll try to influence me to return to Michigan and take over his empire."

Florence asked, "Then you're telling us that you're really rich."

"No. My father is. I have a healthy amount of money in my bank account from the birthday and Christmas gifts and other cards with some cash inside that he had sent over the years. All the gifts were always money, by the way. He never gave me a gift that showed any thought whatsoever. Do you know what the first real gift I ever received was?"

"No."

"The necklace that I received from Blue Flower."

"Really? What were birthdays like?" asked Rebecca, mesmerized by his tale, as was Florence.

"I'd have a cake and then there'd be an envelope on the table nearby with cash inside, so I could buy what I wanted. For the first few years, I'd put the money in a box under my bed. Then, when I was twelve, it got too full, so I asked my father to open an account for me at the bank. He was enormously proud of me that day. It made no sense to me why he was, but I put the money in the bank and continued to add to it until I moved to Ann Arbor to go to college.

"I opened an account there at a larger bank and moved all my money there. My father was paying for my schooling and giving me spending money to boot, so I never came close to spending that much money and kept tossing it in there. That's why I don't have a problem with money. It's just there. I never had a good enough reason to spend it, but I never received a true gift, one from the heart, until I received Blue Flower's necklace."

"So, it means a lot to you."

"It's more valuable because of what she told me when she gave it to me."

Rebecca asked quietly, "What did she say?"

"I can't say. What she said when she gave it to me can only be shared between the two of us and one other."

"Who is the one other?"

"It may not matter at all. There may never be that other person."

Rebecca almost whispered, "That would be a tragedy, wouldn't it?"

He looked into her eyes and answered just as quietly, "Yes, it would be."

They continued to look into each other's eyes for another ten seconds, and a lot of information passed between them in those ten seconds.

Then they were somewhat startled when they heard a noise behind them as the children returned, with Chester trotting behind.

"Everybody is happy about the candy. They haven't had any in a long time," said Andy, "I even gave one to Harvey Gray. He's the wagon train bully. He was surprised, too."

"Andy, you are turning into one first-class man. I'm really proud of you," said Hugh as he put his big hand on Andy's thin shoulder.

Andy beamed at his mother after hearing the praise, and Rebecca had never seen him so proud. Of course, no man had ever praised him before he met Mister Hugh.

Addie came over and plopped on Hugh's lap.

"I gave candy to all the girls, too, Mister Hugh."

"Of course, you did, Addie. But I'm not surprised at all."

"You're not?"

"Nope. Because you are the sweetest and most generous girl I've ever met."

She gave her mother the same beaming smile, then hopped to her feet, leaned over and gave Hugh a hug and a kiss on the cheek.

"That's for the doll, Mister Hugh."

"Thank you, Addie. Do you have a name for her yet?"

"I'm going to call her Sophie. Is that a good name?"

"That's a very good name. There's another present I need to give you, Addie."

"Really?"

"Come here, sweetheart."

She walked over and Hugh began unwrapping the cloth strips holding the splint in place. Then he removed the splint and tossed it away before having her sit down while he pulled the shirt sleeve off.

"Addie, you just need to keep from jumping around and you'll be fine. How does it feel?"

She smiled and said, "It feels nice!"

She kept her smile and bounded after Andy.

Rebecca smiled at Hugh and said, "You sure seemed to have won them over."

"They make my heart melt whenever they smile. You did a wonderful job raising them, Rebecca. I saw that on the first day, and I knew it was you that had done it, too."

"How did you know that?"

"Because you were all they ever talked about. They said how nice and kind you were and how you were the prettiest lady ever, too."

Rebecca laughed and said, “They’re my children, Hugh. They had to say that.”

“I don’t think so. You had to see their faces and read their eyes. You can tell a lot about someone by looking at their eyes. You can tell if they’re lying or telling the truth, or whether they intend to kill you or hug you. It’s difficult to hide what’s in your mind and heart from your eyes. When they talked of you, Rebecca, their eyes sparkled. They both love you very much.”

Rebecca’s heart melted as she said, “Thank you for saying that, Hugh. I know they do, but it feels good to have someone else tell me that.”

“Besides, I had seen your picture.”

“That was taken more than ten years ago, Hugh.”

“For most women, that would be a bad thing, but not for you. I think you look better now than in the picture. Your face is fuller, and the girlishness is gone. I believe you’re prettier now than then.”

“Now, you’re just telling a big white lie.”

“I never lie, Rebecca.”

“So, they tell me. Andy passed along that morsel.”

Florence finally got a word in, asking, “You’ve never lied?”

“No. There’s nothing to gain in lying. If you’re honest all the time for ten years, but then tell one lie, those ten years have meant nothing because you’ve lost your integrity.”

“So,” she continued, “if I were to ask you if I could entice you into my bed, you’d tell me the truth?”

"I would, but as a true lady, I'm sure you would never ask that question."

Rebecca smiled inside. Hugh had seen the danger in the question and parried it with a disarming answer. She could only ask the question by admitting she wasn't a lady.

"No, of course not. But if some other woman asked that question, would you answer it?"

"Sure. The answer would always be 'no'."

"Always? I find that hard to believe. What if the most beautiful woman in the world were to come and ask you that question? Would you still say no?"

"Of course, I would. Remember earlier when I ranted about the lives of women? At the end, I said when I married, I would treat my wife as an equal. How could I treat her as an equal if I had no respect for her? Respect is the key to marriage. Love is wonderful and friendship highly desirable, but respect must be at the foundation."

"I always heard that if there was fire in the bedroom, the house would be warm," she almost giggled.

"That would last about a month or two. If that was the basis of the marriage, infidelity would occur soon after the marriage was consummated."

Florence sighed and said, "I have to admit that's the way it was with Cliff. He got tired of me so fast."

Rebecca asked, "So, you'll stay with the wagon train now, Hugh?"

"No, I think I'll be leaving in the morning. I've gotten too attached to the children already and I'd just cause more problems if I stayed. I'll be heading to my ranch and see what happens there. It's southeast of Baker City."

"Oh. I'm sorry to hear that you're leaving. Why did you give me the shotgun?"

"Well, when I found them, Andy tried to shoot me with a Spencer. He didn't know how to shoot it, so I cleaned it and showed him how. Then I gave the gun to Long Wolf, so I knew the family would be without protection. I bought the shotgun for a replacement. It has a good kick, probably worse than the Spencer, but he got to handle the kick on that pretty well."

"He fired the Spencer?"

"After I had to clean it extensively. Mister Orson really let that thing go, and I wasn't pleased with its condition. I was afraid it might blow up it was so bad, so I had to rig a test stand and fire it from behind some rocks to make sure it was safe to shoot. Once I knew it was safe, Andy fired two shots with it and did pretty well, too. I thought the shotgun was a better choice for protection, though. That's why I bought it."

"Protection?"

"After looking at the Spencer, I doubted if Mister Orson would provide you or the children with sufficient protection, so when I came back, I gave you the shotgun. That's why I insisted that Mister Orson knows it's your weapon."

Rebecca knew he had that pinpointed as well. Bob didn't care for guns and when they had run into a dangerous situation in Wyoming, he had simply climbed into the back of the wagon and hunkered down. He didn't even worry about her or the children.

"At least we're almost to Oregon."

"Yes, ma'am. Well, I'd better be heading off to set up my camp."

"Good night, and thank you again, Hugh."

"You're welcome, Rebecca," he replied with a smile.

"Good night, Hugh, and don't be a stranger," Florence said with a bigger smile.

"Good night, Florence."

Hugh tipped his hat and headed back to his animals and led the horse and mule to a camping spot a few hundred yards away.

Hugh was setting up his camp and didn't need to pitch the tent. He did make a fire, though, and then sat with his back up against the tree. Rebecca was an incredible woman. She was all those things he had talked about earlier. He respected her immensely and enjoyed talking to her because she challenged his mind. And she was quietly beautiful, if there was such a term. He remembered watching her rapturous joy as she found her children standing before her.

In his life, he had never brought that kind of happiness to anyone. He had delivered babies and saved lives, and there had been grateful thanks, but that face was so incredibly ecstatic, and he knew he'd never see its like again.

He crawled into his bedroll with his thoughts as Chester curled at his feet, already making all those strange dog noises as he dreamt.

A half mile east of the wagon train, Cliff Johnson waited. There were still some awake, and he just needed to pick the right wagon. He could identify Emily Amber's wagon during the day. She usually had the fifth slot in the train, so he'd head for that one and see if it was right.

Hugh realized he wasn't going to sleep for a while, so he slid back out of the bedroll and put on his boots. He walked south for a hundred yards and found a rock to sit on and just stared at the wagon train in the moonlight.

Thirty minutes later, Cliff decided that it was late enough. All the fires were out, so he started walking quietly. He just had his rifle and his knife. Tonight, would be knife work, so he had stashed the rifle, but his three cartridges were in his pocket.

He reached the last wagon, the Porters and thought that this was going to be easier than he expected. They were all sleeping under the wagons, so he just had to make sure he was far enough away to avoid detection. They usually had two guards out, but they tended to be sleepy and would be nodding off by midnight.

He passed the Henderson's rig, then the widow Murphy. If she wasn't so annoying, he'd take her first. Then he saw his wagon, and saw his boring wife, Florence, and Rebecca Orson under the wagon. He thought that Rebecca was a tasty morsel. He had wanted her for a long time, but it would be hard with all those damned kids spread around.

He walked past the Inman wagon, then at last, he found Emily Amber's, and spotted her asleep under the wagon, all by herself. He ought to just kill her quick for what she did, but she sure looked nice under the wagon. As he pulled out his knife, a beam of moonlight glanced off its shiny surface.

Across the way, Hugh was turning back to his bedroll thinking he needed some sleep and was walking toward the wagon train when his eyes caught the glint of polished metal. At first, he thought it was an Indian, but that would be stupid. Indians wouldn't attack a wagon train at night with a single warrior. It must be Florence's husband, the one they banned for attacking a woman, and now he was going to do it again. He knew it wasn't Rebecca's wagon, but it didn't matter. He had to stop this.

It was too late to go back and get his gun, so he just sprinted the sixty yards to where the knife-wielding assailant was standing, planning on using his size to plow into him before he could do anything.

Cliff was leaning back to strike when he heard the rush of feet behind him, turned his head, and before he could raise his knife in defense, Hugh smashed into him and rammed him into the left front wagon wheel. Cliff's blade fell to the ground as he struggled against Hugh's greater size and strength.

Then all hell broke loose. Emily, seeing the fracas three feet in front of her, screamed, and others immediately began waking, including the two sleeping guards. After they all struggled to their feet, they rushed to where Emily was still screaming.

Cliff was desperate and had to get away. He knew they'd hang him this time, so he began groping for his knife, knowing it had to be close and managed to spot it right near his right hand. He lunged the last few inches, grabbed the handle, and thrust at the big man who was trying to hold him down. He felt the blade strike bone before he shoved the man away and sprinted away into the darkness.

Suddenly, the whole camp was alive as the guards finally reached the location and pointed their guns at Hugh, who was still a bit dizzy after hitting his head on the wagon wheel when he had first charged. He knew he had been stabbed, so he ripped open his shirt sleeve to find the location of the wound. With the blood pouring out, it wasn't hard to find. The tip of the blade had struck his left forearm, just below the elbow. It was deep, but not that long, and he needed to get the blood stopped.

A crowd had circled Hugh and the wagon. Most didn't know who the stranger was, and Hugh began scanning the faces looking for assistance to help him repair his wound.

"Looks like you got what you deserved, mister," said Leroy White, one of the sleeping guards, "I saw you checking out them women earlier. Now, you're gonna bleed to death, so make it quick."

Hugh laughed at the absurdity of the man's accusation, as Rebecca made her way through the crowd and saw Hugh leaned against the wagon wheel with blood-soaked shirt with more blood dripping onto the ground, and no one was helping, so she stepped quickly toward him.

He saw her and said, "Rebecca, tell this idiot that I didn't stab myself. Some guy was here with a knife. He was going to hurt that lady and I had to stop him. I need to stop the bleeding now. Please."

Rebecca noticed no one was going to help, so she pushed Leroy out of the way and bent over Hugh, then ripped her dress, took the cloth strip and wrapped it tightly around his arm. The blood flow lessened, so she took more cloth, added a second layer and then a third.

She looked over at Emily and asked loudly, "Emily. What the hell just happened?"

"I don't know," she sniffled, "I woke up and heard them fighting. Then he got stabbed and the other one ran off. I think it was Cliff."

Rebecca fumed and turned to the crowd, "You bunch of idiots! This man is bleeding to death and you're all standing around! Get out of my sight, Leroy, and go take a damned bath!"

She leaned close to Hugh and asked, "Hugh? Can you hear me? I've slowed down the blood, but what do I do next?"

"I need to sew the wound closed. I'll need someone to hold the two parts together while I do it. Get some man to do this, Rebecca. It'll be messy."

"No, I'll do it," she replied, then turned and shouted, "Florence, go get your sewing kit."

Florence raced off to her wagon, plucked up the sewing kit and returned quickly to where Hugh lay.

"What else do you need, Hugh?"

"A canteen of water, whiskey and light. More light."

"Whiskey?" she asked in surprise.

"Yes."

"I need a bottle of whiskey, a canteen of water and get some lamps over here," she shouted to no one in particular.

A bottle was produced before the canteen, which was odd, and Rebecca uncorked it and put the bottle to his lips, but he shook his head.

"Can't stand the stuff. I need it to clean the wound."

Three lamps were brought and set nearby along with two canteens of water.

"Florence, can you thread a needle with some black thread? I know pink would work, but it would clash with my manly image," he said as he smiled.

Florence threaded the needle and handed it to Rebecca who said to Hugh, "The needle and thread is ready."

"Okay, Rebecca. Are you ready?" he asked.

"Yes, Hugh. I'm ready."

"Now, when I tell you to go, take off the bandages you applied. Thank you for that, by the way. More blood will come out, and I'll pour water on it and then the whiskey. Then push the wound together. I'll start sewing, and you may have to move your hands out of the way. Okay?"

"Okay, Hugh. Whenever you're ready."

The crowd watched as Rebecca, her hands already bloody, rapidly unrolled the bandages. The bleeding started again, but not as badly. Hugh uncorked the canteen and washed the blood off his arm.

"Rebecca, give me your hands," he said as he picked up the canteen.

She held out her hands and he poured the remainder of the water on them to rinse off the blood. She dried her hands on her already ripped dress.

He dropped the canteen and poured whiskey from the open bottle into the open wound. Everyone grimaced at the pain it must have caused.

“No wonder I hate this stuff. Now, shove it together, Rebecca.”

She pressed the two edges of the wound together and the wound closed. The crowd watched mesmerized as the skilled hand of Hugh McGinnis began sewing his own arm. Rebecca stared attentively as he progressed across the wound and moved her hands twice as he approached her fingers. Finally, he put in the last suture and poured more whiskey over the top.

“Rebecca, I’m not going to ask you to sacrifice any more of your dress. Just cut off my right sleeve and use that. The shirt is a waste now anyway. I liked this shirt, too,” he said as he smiled.

She was astounded that he kept making light of his situation as she ripped his right sleeve and pulled it off his arm, then wrapped it around his still leaking wound.

“Thank you, Rebecca. You are a remarkable woman.”

“Hugh, can I help you get up?”

“Just let me stay here for a few minutes. I’ll be fine. Everyone can go back now.”

The crowd began filtering back to their wagons, chatting about what they had just witnessed.

Bob and Ella had seen the job Rebecca had done in helping Hugh sew his wound together, but their reactions were totally different.

“I’ve never seen anything like that before, Bob. I couldn’t have done that. Rebecca pushed that wound together and held it there while he sewed it closed. I would have fainted.”

"Maybe he's trying to get into her bed, Ella. A little sympathy goes a long way."

Ella was stunned by his comment. This wasn't the poor, denied husband she had been caring for. Maybe he meant that he suspected the big man as Rebecca's lover.

"That must be it," she thought.

Hugh waited until everyone had dispersed. He knew he had lost some blood, but not too much. He was impressed with Rebecca's cool demeanor, but it was time to return to his camp. He needed to be moving in the morning.

Hugh stood and felt everything sway just a bit. He put his hand on the wagon until it settled, then he walked unsteadily the hundred yards to his camp.

Rebecca watched him as he stumbled past. If anyone didn't know any better, they'd take him for a drunk. She had never had an experience like this before, and didn't know why she had stepped forward, but was glad she did. She felt so alive for actually doing something that mattered. But as he made it to his camp, she began to get angry.

The one decent man in the whole group of them and they act like he had done something wrong. He tried to save Emily from Cliff, gets stabbed in the process, and that idiot Leroy White is telling him that he got what he deserved. She knew she had to go back and talk to the children.

She stepped back to the wagon knowing the dress was lost which left her with one borrowed dress.

She approached the wagon and saw the children staring at her. She tried to smile for them but failed.

Andy asked, "Mama, that Leroy man said that Mister Hugh tried to hurt Miss Emily. He's lying, isn't he? Mister Hugh would never hurt anyone."

Rebecca fumed. *That bastard!*

"Yes, children. Leroy is the biggest liar God put on the planet. Mister Hugh caught Mister Johnson trying to hurt Emily again and tried to stop him. But Mister Johnson had a knife and Mister Hugh didn't have anything to protect himself. Mister Johnson stabbed Mister Hugh and then ran away, and Mister Hugh did the bravest thing I've ever seen."

"What, Mama?" asked Andy.

"He had a big cut in his arm that was bleeding. First, he poured whiskey on it which must have hurt him terribly, but he didn't shout or anything. Then he sewed up his own arm and poured more whiskey on it. All the time he was doing this, he was saying funny things to make it sound as if it didn't hurt. So, if you ever hear anyone say anything bad about Mister Hugh ever again, you tell them they are liars and your mama said so."

"Is Mister Hugh going to be all right?" asked Addie.

"Yes, sweetheart. He will. He's sleeping right now. Right over there by that tree."

"What happened to your dress, Mama?

"I had to rip some cloth off to stop the bleeding from the cut."

"Thank you for helping Mister Hugh, Mama."

Rebecca smiled at her daughter and said, “I had to, sweetie. He saved my children.”

———

A mile to the northeast, Cliff Johnson sat hidden in some deep grass. He’d been so close in both aspects. He had been very close to killing that bitch and then close to getting caught. He’d be more careful the next time.

———

Rebecca as laying on her side under the wagon looking out across the way to the tree wondering what she should do. There was no doubt in her mind that she was taken with Hugh McGinnis. She knew he loved her children, but she was married, and he was leaving. Maybe it was better that he did.

CHAPTER 6

Hugh was up before the dawn despite his late-night escapade and loss of blood. He drank a lot of water before he dressed quickly and packed everything. It was a tough thing to do with only one working arm, but he managed. He had it all done and shared a quick, uncooked breakfast with Chester then walked the horse and mule west as the first light of day were showing on the horizon.

Rebecca was up early as well, but not as early as Hugh. She knew the wagon train would be leaving in a little while, but she didn't know if Hugh could even move with that recent wound. She slid out from under the wagon and walked quietly to Hugh's camp, still wearing her ripped dress and found his camp empty. He had gone as he said he would, and she should have felt some form of relief somewhere, but all she felt was a deep sense of loss.

She turned and walked back to Florence's wagon to change into her borrowed dress and toss this one into the rag bin.

Hugh didn't really push the pace, figuring he'd be at the trading post by noon. Maybe he'd just set up camp nearby and relax for the afternoon. He knew he was only a day or so away from his ranch, but it wasn't going anywhere.

His arm was throbbing, but it wasn't nearly as bad as he had expected. He was pleased with his sutures but knew it would leave a scar.

———

The wagon train was moving by seven and Rebecca was riding with Florence, as usual while Bob was in Ella's wagon.

Ella had overcome last night's misgivings about Bob, but she was beginning to feel guilty. She had seen the fire and passion in Rebecca's eyes as she helped the wounded man. *How could such a woman be less passionate with her husband?*

Bob noticed that Ella wasn't stroking him as she had yesterday and wasn't about to let that get in the way. He smiled at her, rested his hand on her thigh, and she didn't object.

Rebecca had told the children earlier that Hugh had gone on to his ranch. They were upset, as she knew they would be, and she wasn't very far behind, but managed to hide it better. They would be at the trading post soon, not that it mattered to her. She had no money and Bob wouldn't buy her a thing.

———

Hugh arrived at the trading post just before noon, dismounted, tied Middie to the hitchrail and walked inside, leaving Chester outside.

"Howdy. Back so soon?" asked the cheery proprietor.

"Yes, sir. I just needed a few things. You have a wagon train about two or three hours down the Trail coming your way."

"That's good news. Thanks for telling me."

"I'm going to buy some things, but I have no idea what I'm doing. Are you married?"

“Yup. The missus is in back. Why?”

“Do you think she could help me buy some women’s clothes?”

“Sure. Just a second.”

He walked to the back storeroom and called, “Martha? Can you come out front and help this gentleman?”

A round woman of about forty came out of the room, saw Hugh and smiled. “What can I do for you?”

“I need to buy some women’s dresses and those underpinnings that I know nothing about. I’m not sure of the size, but she’s about five feet and a half and I’d guess about a hundred and twenty pounds. I’d like to buy six dresses and anything else you think she might need. She’ll need stockings and shoes and probably needs some good boots, too.

“I need some children’s clothing as well. Four little girl’s dresses and underclothes, socks and shoes. She’s seven. And I’ll need four pairs of boy’s britches and shirts, a belt, underpants, socks, shoes and boots. He’ll be ten shortly, and he’s about five feet and two inches and seventy pounds. Can you pick those things up for me? I’ll be getting some other things on the other side of the store.”

“I’ll do what I can,” she said as she smiled and headed down the clothing aisle.

Hugh walked to the other side and found a hairbrush and comb set and a child’s hairbrush and mirror set. He added four bars of scented soap and four regular bars, three toothbrushes and tooth powder. Then he added a passel of hair ribbons of different colors for the two ladies. He couldn’t think of anything else, so he carried them up front where the proprietor’s wife had already begun making a huge pile of things for the clothing side of the order.

"You're gonna have one happy family, mister," the store owner said as his wife left to get more things.

"They're not even my family. I was riding by my lonesome and came across a crashed Conestoga at the bottom of a ravine a while back and found two children, then I brought them back to their mother. They didn't have much clothing because of the crash, so I figured I'd get these. After I pay for them, I'll leave them with you so when they come in, just give them to her and the children. Her name is Rebecca Orson. Florence Johnson is her friend, so she can take them if she doesn't show up."

He wrote down the names and asked, "Did you want to write a note or anything?"

"No. It's not important. It's only important that they get them."

By then, his wife had brought the last of the order to the counter.

"I found everything. I even picked the prettiest dresses for the lady and the little girl."

"Can you think of anything I missed?"

"No, I see you took care of the other things," she said looking at his other purchases.

"Yes, ma'am. I really do appreciate your help."

"The total is $46.45," the storekeeper said.

Hugh paid the bill, shook the proprietor's hand and walked out the door.

They watched him leave and his wife turned to her husband, saying wistfully, "That young man is in love."

"For that much money, he'd better be," her husband replied.

Hugh walked across the way to the diner where he had a steak with a big helping of mashed potatoes and gravy. Then he had them cook another steak and wrap it up for his canine friend.

As he walked back to his horse and pack mule, he looked to his left and saw a corral behind the livery. There were a few horses inside, and one really attracted his attention, so he sauntered that way.

The liveryman was inside, mucking out one of the stalls when he entered, so he called, "Good afternoon!"

The man turned and smiled as he said, "Afternoon. What can I do for you?"

"Are any of those horses in the back for sale?"

"Sure. Let's go back there."

They walked out to the good-sized corral behind the livery.

"They all saddle broken?" Hugh asked.

"Yep. Some more than others. That big black over there is just green broke."

"They all shod?"

“Yup. Did all of them myself.”

Hugh looked at the horses. They were a mixed bunch. There were two that seemed a bit long in the tooth. There was a small gray gelding that had the look of a Morgan, which he liked. But he really did like that big black stallion.

“What’s the story on the gray?”

“He’s a Morgan. Has a good temper. Personally, he’s the one I like the best.”

“Do you have any saddles?”

“Two. One’s an old army saddle in bad shape. The other is a pretty nice riding saddle.”

“What kind of deal can you give me on the gray, the big black, and the nice saddle.”

“A package deal, huh? All right. I’ll tell you what I’ll do. Both horses and the saddle for a hundred and thirty dollars. I’ll even throw in that old army saddle.”

“Make it one twenty and you’ve got a deal.”

They shook on it, and Hugh asked him to saddle the gray Morgan with the nice saddle because of his wound. He’d put a lead rope on the big black and bring him along, wearing the army saddle loosely.

When the transaction was completed and the horses saddled, Hugh led the two animals over to where Middie and the mule waited. The stallion noticed Middie right away and sidled up next to her.

Hugh patted his neck and said, “Not yet, big boy. We have some traveling in front of us, so you and Middie can get along later. She’s really named Midnight, but I call her Middie. How about if you’re Midnight, too, only I’ll call you Night?”

The black stallion nickered, so Hugh figured he appreciated the moniker.

After tying off the leads from his two new horses to the mule’s pack saddle, he mounted Middie and turned north away from the trading post. He rode about a half a mile and found a nice spot by a clear stream.

After he had unpacked and set up his tent with not as much difficulty he had experienced just this morning, he was pleased by the location’s relative remoteness. It would be difficult to see him if you didn’t know where he was.

When he was settled, he called Chester over and gave him the steak. He had to take care of his only companion. The horses and mule didn’t count.

Chester hunkered down on all fours with the steak under his front paws and began ripping at the meat. He was one happy pooch.

The wagon train came pulling into the trading post two hours after Hugh had set up his camp and had barely stopped when most of the women poured out of the wagons. Rebecca stayed behind as there was no point in leaving as she couldn’t buy anything without begging Bob for the money and she wasn’t about to do that just for another dress.

“I’ll see if I can find something for you, Rebecca,” said Florence before she left for the trading post.

"Don't worry about it, Flo," replied Rebecca to a quickly receding Florence.

She wanted to stay with her children anyway. They were still morose after Mister Hugh's departure, and she wasn't too pleased about it either. He was so pleasant to have around, and he kept the children happy, and to be honest with herself, he made her happy, too. He actually listened to her, and then there were those ten quiet seconds. She closed her eyes and relived them in her mind. Ten long, meaningful seconds that, in the end, meant nothing anymore.

In the trading post, the women were busy buying replacement items for things they had lost and maybe adding a few things while they were there. As they came to the counter to pay, the proprietor asked each woman her name, but none were Rebecca Orson or Florence Johnson.

Finally, Florence arrived to buy herself a new dress. She had paid for the order, and as the proprietor gave her change, he asked if she was either Rebecca Orson or Florence Johnson.

"I'm Florence Johnson. Rebecca is back at my wagon. Why?"

"I have an order for her. My wife can help you carry it to the wagon."

"I need help?" she asked.

The proprietor grinned and replied, "Most assuredly."

He called his wife out front and she began loading part of the order onto Florence outstretched arms, then took the rest and the two women waddled their way through the wagons until Florence reached hers.

As she got close, she called, “Rebecca! Come over here and help!”

Rebecca stumbled out of the back of the wagon and was startled to see Florence with bundles of clothes and bags with an unknown woman walking beside her with just as much.

“My goodness, Florence. You really went crazy in there,” she said as she climbed down from the wagon.

Florence said loudly, “No, I didn’t. These are all yours.”

Rebecca didn’t think she heard correctly and asked, “*What?* That can’t be right.”

Rebecca trotted over to Florence and began helping load the items onto the wagon’s tailgate.

When they had finished, Florence pulled out one dress and said, “This is mine, the rest is yours.”

“But how? Why? Who?” asked a confused Rebecca.

The proprietor’s wife looked at her, smiled and said, “I can understand now,” laughed lightly, then left to go back to the store.

“What did she mean by that?” Rebecca asked.

“I don’t know, Rebecca, but look at all this!”

Rebecca started going through the items. There were six very pretty dresses, and in the right size, too. There were new bloomers, camisoles, and nightdresses. There was a new pair of shoes, a pair of boots, and four pairs of stockings. *And they were all hers?*

Then she found the children's clothes. Four new dresses for Addie, new shoes, socks, underclothes, and there were pants, shirts, underpants and socks and boots for Andy. Then she opened the bag with all the other items, the soap, the hairbrush and comb set for her and the brush and mirror set for Addie. There were even toothbrushes and powder.

The final touch was the bag of hair ribbons, and it was the ribbons that clinched it for her. She knew who had bought all these wonderful and necessary things, and he was on the way to his ranch southeast of Baker City.

"Florence, this is too much. How did all of this show up?" she asked, pretending not to know who had bought them.

"When I got to the counter to pay for my dress, the man just asked my name and told me he had an order for you."

"You don't think Bob is trying to make up, do you?"

She didn't even know why she asked the question. In the year plus that they had been married, he hadn't bought her a single thing.

Florence knew better herself, but replied, "Maybe. Are you going to go over and ask him?"

"I think I should."

Rebecca would have been shocked if Bob had made such a sudden change in his treatment of her. It was so unlike him. She thought he didn't even know how old the children were, much less their sizes. But she had to be sure that everything was really from the man who had returned her children and given her so much more already.

She reached Ella Murphy's wagon, but there was no one on the front, so she went around back, but there was no one inside either. The next stop was the store, but they weren't there. She thought about asking the proprietor, but wasn't sure he'd tell her anyway, so that left the café, the livery, and the butcher's shop. She checked the café next and found them having dinner together.

Bob looked up and saw Rebecca coming towards them and was hoping for a big row to gain Ella's sympathy, but it had to be his wife who had to start it.

"Good afternoon, Rebecca. How are you?" Bob asked with a smile.

"I'm fine, Bob. I just wanted to thank you."

"Thank me? For what?" asked a totally befuddled Bob Orson.

"You know, the clothes and things."

Bob saw a chance to portray himself as a thoughtful and considerate man.

"I'm glad you liked them," he said.

"They must have cost a lot of money."

Bob was somewhat lost now, because he had no idea how much dresses cost but had to keep playing the game.

"It wasn't too bad. I just wanted to keep you well clothed."

Rebecca had known just from the look on his face when she'd asked, but this was getting more obvious and it was time to prove it to herself.

"Well, you should have bought something for the children."

"Oh, I will. I just wanted you to have something first."

"Good. Well, you and Ella have a nice dinner. Good evening, Ella."

Rebecca smiled at Ella and left the diner.

Ella was mortified to be found eating with another woman's husband and not even inviting her to sit and join them.

She looked at Bob and asked, "When did you go to the trading post?"

"I had someone else buy them. He was supposed to buy something for the children, too. I'll have a word with him later."

"Oh. That was very thoughtful, Bob."

"Even though she has treated me horribly, Ella, I always try to keep up with my obligations."

Ella smiled at Bob, who patted her leg under the table. Ella returned the gesture and Bob smiled. He was back on track.

Rebecca walked back to the wagon fuming. She had doubted from the start that Bob had bought them, but to take credit for it just to worm his way into Ella's bed was despicable.

When she reached Florence's wagon she asked, "So, did he buy all that?"

"Of course, not. He tried to take credit for it, so he could win Ella's favor."

“Then, who did?” she asked, just wanting to hear Rebecca admit it.

“Who else? There’s only one person that I know that has that kind of consideration, our elusive Mister Hugh. I knew almost from the start, but I had to be sure. When the children come back from playing, I’ll be sure to give Hugh all the credit he deserves. What’s so extraordinary about this, aside from the generosity, is that he didn’t miss anything. He even remembered toothbrushes.”

Then she laughed and said, “I noticed he only got three. He probably guessed correctly that Bob’s personal hygiene left much to be desired.”

Then she became more serious and said, “Florence, did you notice that all the sizes are correct as well? Even my dresses are perfect. The children’s clothes will all fit perfectly, too. I don’t know what to make of all this. I know he loves the children, but why would he buy all of those clothes for me?”

“Rebecca, if you don’t know, then I can’t explain it to you.”

“Maybe he was grateful for my help with his wound.”

“Personally, I don’t think that made one bit of difference, but if you want to believe that, you go right ahead. It’s easier than admitting the truth.”

Rebecca flushed and said, “I’m not hiding anything!”

“You and Mister Hugh are both hiding the same thing. I understand, too. You’re married, and he knows it. But that doesn’t mean that those feelings you two already are sharing isn’t there. It’s just hidden.”

“Can we just let this go? Please?” Rebecca begged.

"Sure. Let's get all this stuff packed up."

The two women took their time as they examined each item before they stored the order in Florence's wagon.

Leroy White was at the eastern end of the train looking further east. When he was returning to his horse, he thought he saw someone in the grass a few hundred yards away and guessed that it was Cliff Johnson. He looked behind him, and no one was watching because they were all enjoying the trading post's offerings and started walking toward Cliff in the dying light.

Cliff saw the younger man approaching, and knew if he ran, he'd be shot down, so he readied his rifle. If he shot Leroy, he'd have to run, and he'd have to run faster and further, so he just waited.

Leroy got within a hundred feet and said as loudly as he dared, "Hey! Cliff. I need to talk to you."

It was an unexpected twist, so Cliff replied, "About what?"

"Women."

"Come on over, then."

Leroy scampered over like he was under surveillance and crouched down near Cliff who remained hiding in the grass.

Cliff asked, "So, what do you want?"

"Florence. I really want Florence."

"Take her then, she's no use to me. I need food."

"I can get you food, but I really want your wife. She's been talking to me and I think I can have my way with her, but there's that kid and she's always hanging around Orson's wife and kids, too. I don't want any damned kids. Then there's that big guy that you stabbed. He's always there, too. I don't know if he's after Florence or Orson's wife, but it don't matter. I need help to get her outta there, and I'll get you some food."

Cliff thought about it and said, "I really want that Emily Amber. I almost had her once, but damn, that is one tasty little morsel. You can do whatever you want with Florence. How are we gonna do this?"

"I don't know. I can probably lure Emily away. She's kinda sweet on me, but she doesn't have enough meat on her bones to suit me. Now, Florence has more than enough, and in the right places, too. I don't know why you weren't diddlin' her every night."

"She got old, but you'll enjoy her. You say you can get Emily out of there?"

"I think so. How about this? I'll tell her something or other and then just give her a quick tap on the head. Then I'll tell Florence that Emily wants to talk to her. Once I do that, I can talk her into what she thinks might be a little sparking then get her far enough away and then give her a little love tap, too. I have my horse, but I can get another one for you. I'll load up with supplies and we can head north for a while. They won't know where we went. The grass is so thick, they can't track us. Besides, we'll have the only two horses in camp. After that wagon train leaves, we can head into Oregon and avoid 'em altogether."

Cliff was impressed and said, "That's good thinking, Leroy. So, you'll cart Emily to me and then, you'll go get Florence and the horses and food. When do you want to do that?"

"I'll leave the horses with the food about a hundred yards south for you. I'll be on watch tonight. They only have one guard because we're at the trading post. Then I'll bring you Emily and go back and get Florence, then we make our break. We'll head north until we find a good place to hide and wait 'em out."

"Great. I'll see you then."

Leroy went back to the camp to prepare. The second horse he was going to confiscate belonged to the wagon master, and Leroy snickered as he thought of leaving that damned Leo horseless. He doted on that animal.

———

While they were in the grass conspiring, Hugh was taking his bath in the stream a mile north. He didn't think the water was as cold as he had originally anticipated and thought it might be because it was night and the cool air made the difference less noticeable. He used a plain white soap and thought his wound was doing better and even washed it. He washed his hair, dunking his lathered head under the cold water so none of the soap got into his eyes.

He stepped out of the stream and walked back to his camp, dried off and put on his clothes, sauntered over to his bed roll and sat on it for an hour or so, then removed his boots and slid inside, leaving his pistols within reach as he always did.

Hugh stayed awake for a long while, just staring at the sky and marveling at the stars and planets. He was never good at picking out the planets from the stars, despite understanding the differences and what to look for. He did see a couple of shooting stars, though, so that made his viewing more interesting.

Leroy had been busy. He had saddled Leo's horse and led him away, then gathered enough food for two weeks. He had them draped over his horse and walked the two animals out of camp quietly and led them east of the camp about a hundred yards and hitched his horse to a young pine. He saw Cliff nearby in the moonlight and waved. Cliff hopped up and stepped over.

"Okay. You gonna get the women now?" Cliff asked.

"I'll bring you Emily in a little while, then I'll return, grab Florence and we'll ride north."

Cliff was so excited, he just nodded.

Leroy went back to the wagons, walked past Florence's and looked as he passed. She was in there, and on the outside, too which made it a lot easier.

He reached Emily's wagon less than a minute later.

He crawled next to Emily and loud whispered, "Emily! Emily! Mrs. Porter wants to talk to you. She says it's an emergency."

Emily stirred and slowly opened her eyes before asking, "Leroy? What did you say?"

"Mrs. Porter is having some problem or other. She said to come and ask you to help."

Emily was confused. *Why would Alice Porter ask for her help?* They weren't that close. But one doesn't turn down a request for help in a small community.

"Alright. Give me a minute."

Emily tossed back the blanket and put on her shoes while Leroy watched. Maybe he was too hasty in his assessment of her and Cliff would share.

She slid out from under the wagon and started to walk in front of Leroy as he glanced around to be sure no one was watching. When he didn't see anyone, he pulled his pistol and rapped her skull, collapsing her to the ground before she took another step. He picked her up and carried her easily over his shoulder out of the camp, saw the horses in the moonlight and quickly walked that way. He reached Cliff and dropped her into his waiting arms.

"I'll be right back," Leroy said as he turned.

"Go ahead. I'll keep busy while you wait," Cliff said quietly.

As Leroy turned back to the wagon train. Cliff began exploring his new, unconscious possession.

Leroy quickly reached Florence's wagon, then dropped to his knees, bent down very close to Florence's sleeping face and whispered, "Flo! This is Leroy. Flo!"

Flo's eyelids flickered open and she saw Leroy not six inches from her face and whispered back, "Leroy, what are you doing here?"

"I needed to talk to you alone, Flo. It's just been kinda hard, you know."

Florence wasn't quite sure, but it'd been a while since she'd had a man and this one seemed anxious.

She whispered back, "Alright. I'll be right out."

Leroy stepped back, already getting excited, but he knew he'd have to follow the plan.

Florence put on her shoes and slid out from under the blanket. She slipped from underneath the wagon and stood up next to Leroy.

"Where do you want to go, Leroy?"

"How about east of the wagon train? There's lots of open space where we can talk in privacy. Unless you'd like to do more than talk."

Florence simply replied, "Let's go."

She almost was trotting away east and Leroy knew that the danger would come when she saw Cliff and he'd have to put her down before then.

He caught up with her and whispered, "Slow down, Florence. You might step in a gopher hole."

Florence realized he was right and slowed. Then everything went black before Leroy slung her over his shoulder, feeling the added weight of the softer things that he liked. He reached Cliff and found he had already availed himself of an unconscious Emily Avery and thought of doing the same to Florence, but there was no time.

"If you're done, Cliff, let's get out of here."

Cliff hadn't noticed his approach, but he was done, so he stood and pulled up his britches. He picked up the still comatose Emily and put her across his horse, then climbed aboard. Leroy already had Florence loaded and they started riding north.

The sound of the hooves woke Hugh from his semi-sleep. He shook his head and looked at his horses, finding them all there. *What had made the noise?* Then he wondered if the noise was part of a dream.

But then an unreasonable fear struck him. *What if Rebecca and the children had been harmed?* It made no sense at all, but they were all he cared about, so he got out of his bedroll rapidly and pulled on his boots, then strapped on his gunbelt and grabbed his Henry.

He trotted across the trail to Florence's wagon, and when he reached it, looked underneath and blew out his breath in relief when he saw a sleeping Rebecca, with Andy and Addie scrunched together in their bedroll. He had no sooner been relieved when he noticed that Florence wasn't there, but her bedding was and so was her boy.

He leaned down and whispered as loudly as he dared, "Rebecca! Rebecca!"

Rebecca heard Hugh's voice almost as if it were a dream and smiled. Then she realized that it wasn't a dream at all, her eyes snapped open and focused to see Hugh crouched in front of her. *He was back? Where did he come from and why was he here so late?*

"Rebecca, where is Florence?" Hugh asked.

Rebecca suddenly realized that her friend was gone, but her son, Charles, was still sleeping nearby. Then she remembered that she had thought she heard someone talking to Florence. She had never opened her eyes, but she wasn't sure if Florence had gone or not.

"I think someone might have been talking to her. Let me come out of here."

Rebecca slipped from her bedroll and put on her new boots. Then she crouched away from the wagon.

“Hugh, why did you come back to look for Florence?”

“I didn’t. I came to look for you and the children. I was worried. I heard horses running and I had to come and make sure you were safe.”

“I don’t like this at all, Hugh.”

“What was the name of the woman that Cliff abused that night?”

“Emily Amber. Let’s go and make sure she’s all right.”

They hurried down the two hundred feet to Emily Amber’s wagon and found her sleeping place empty.

“This is really bad, Hugh. What do we do?”

“This,” he replied as he raised his Henry to the air and fired three quick shots.

The entire community was awake instantly and poured from under their wagons and everywhere else. Leo came running toward them and saw Hugh standing there with a smoking rifle.

Leo Crandall was furious. He didn’t even have his boots on as he came running to the source of the loud reports.

“What the hell did you do that for, Hugh?”

“Leo, we have a problem. Both Emily Amber and Florence Johnson are missing. I heard horses running about twenty minutes ago. I think they’ve been taken.”

"You sure?"

"Pretty much. Who was on guard tonight?"

"Just Leroy White. Why?"

"Is he here? I would think the guard would have heard those horses running or at the very least responded to the three shots."

Leo turned to the awakened crowd and shouted, "Leroy! Leroy White! Are you here?"

There was no response.

Rebecca said, "He's been hanging around Florence's wagon a lot these past few days, and everyone knows Cliff has been after Emily for a while."

"Well, let's go after them!" shouted Leo.

"Leo, you can't chase them in the dark. It'll just make a mess of things. It'll be dawn in just three or four hours. I'll start getting my horse ready. Who else has a horse that knows what to do?"

Leo answered, "Leroy and I had the only two horses left. We only had a couple of more weeks, so we haven't added any."

"Well, Leo, I didn't hear a horse, I heard more than one. You may want to go see if you still have yours."

Leo's eyes grew wide, and he growled, "That bastard! He'd better not have nicked Lola."

Bob turned to Ella and said, "Looks like my wife has been playing hanky-panky with that big guy. Notice how close they were? And she was the one who wrapped him up. I feel so ashamed. How could this happen after I bought all those things for her?"

Ella tried to console him and said, "Bob, two can play at that game. Let's go back to my wagon. You shouldn't have to feel bad. I'll make you feel better."

"Thank you, Ella."

Bob and Ella returned to her wagon as Leo arrived where he had tied his horse outside the camp to the north but didn't find Lola.

Hugh could hear the string of curses from a hundred yards away.

"Hugh, what are you planning on doing?" asked Rebecca.

"At first light, Leo and I are going to chase them down. What happens when we find them is going to be the big question. I don't know how they're going to react."

"I suppose I should go and tell the children what happened. Charles may be upset."

"You'd better do that. I've got to go and get ready. Tell Charles I'll get his mama back."

"I won't have to. Once I tell them that Mister Hugh is going after her, my children will convince Charles that she'll be back."

She smiled at Hugh then returned to the wagon.

Hugh made the long walk back to his camp as Leo finally returned and trotted behind him.

He saw Hugh going through his armory. He had already set aside the Sharps, his remaining rounds of ammunition, and the Henry with a box of spare .44s. He also had his field glasses.

"Hugh, how are we planning on doing this?"

Hugh heard Leo and stood up from his inspection.

"I'll let you ride my black mare, Middie. What do you have for firepower?"

"I have my Colt New Army pistol and a Spencer rifle."

"I'll take my Sharps, the Henry and my two pistols. I'll bring enough caps, powder and balls for about fifty reloads on the pistols. I'll pack enough food for two days, some water, and two bedrolls, although we'd better not need them. You do have a knife, I hope."

"Of course, I have a knife."

"Just checking. I'll also bring my sewing kit and some whiskey if I have to do any repair work."

"Repair work?"

"Like I did on my arm the other night."

"I can't believe you did that."

"I couldn't trust it to anyone else."

"I'll go get my rifle and we'll get ready to go."

Hugh checked his saddlebags and emptied them of everything but Blue Flower's necklace.

He knew that they needed to catch those men quickly. They were on double mounted horses and would have a five-hour head start by dawn. They should cut into that lead quickly, and they should be back before sundown. The problem was the women's safety.

He started getting the food ready, and when that was done, walked down to the stream and filled all four of his canteens, then returned to the camp and set them down near the saddles.

Then he walked up to the stallion, who was staring at him.

"Night, I need you to be steady for this job. You can be as ornery as you'd like after this but today you need to be like a knight. I need to be able to trust you."

He rubbed the horse's neck and the horse nodded before he said, "I hope you mean that, Night."

Hugh smiled at him, then called Chester over and told him to sit, which he did.

Hugh knelt on one knee and said to him, "You're part of this team, Chester. I'm going to see if you're as smart as I think you are. You are going to help me find Florence and Emily. Okay?"

Chester had watched Hugh intently. When Hugh stood, he walked next to him, lifted his leg and peed on Hugh's right boot.

Hugh looked down and said, "This is not a good way to start, Chester."

Leo saddled Middie and Hugh outfitted Night with his gear, ignoring the pain from his repair job. This was not time to worry about such things. They put the food in the saddlebags, hung the canteens, and then slid the weapons into place. They were ready to go in fifteen minutes.

They mounted the horses and rode back to the wagon train.

When they reached Florence's wagon, Hugh dismounted, then walked over to Rebecca, and the children all watched him approach.

Charles asked loudly, "Are you gonna get my mama back, Mister Hugh?"

Andy turned on him fiercely and said, "I already told you, Charles. When Mister Hugh says he's going to do something, he always does it!"

Rebecca looked at Hugh and smiled as she shrugged her shoulders.

Hugh smiled back at her and said, "Rebecca, I need some article of Florence's clothing. Something that had recently been worn and in close contact with her skin. I'm going to see if Chester can track the scent. It could make our job a lot easier if he can and we can leave sooner."

"Of course, Hugh."

Rebecca climbed into the wagon and rummaged around with a lamp. She found a pair of Florence's bloomers and emerged from the wagon holding them aloft.

"These should work, Hugh," she said as she stepped back down.

Rebecca walked up to Hugh and handed him the bloomers.

"Perfect. We may be able to leave earlier than I thought if this works."

He carried the bloomers to where Leo still sat on Middie and said, "Leo, we may be able to get going here shortly rather than wait for the sun to rise after all. Let's get the animals saddled and ready to go. Then, we'll see if Chester can do some bird-dogging for us."

He knelt down in front of Chester and put them under his nose and kept saying, "Flo. Flo. Flo," every few seconds. Chester sniffed at the bloomers and then stood up straight and barked once.

"I guess he's ready. Let's get going, Leo."

He gave the bloomers back to Rebecca, then put his left foot into the stirrup and mounted Night, hoping he didn't get tossed on his behind before they even started out.

He called to Chester and the two horses and the dog trotted away and soon entered the grass. With the moon still brightly shining overhead, they were easily able to spot the crushed grass location where Leroy and Cliff had met and loaded the women. They went to the spot and Hugh looked down at Chester and pointed in the direction of the tracks and said, "Flo!"

Chester barked once and took off in that direction. He slowed after a quarter mile and began sniffing the ground and the air but kept trotting along.

———

Five miles ahead, Emily was awakening from her forced sleep and found herself on a horse with someone pressed against her, his hand on the small of her back to hold her in place and knew who it was without looking. The smell gave him away. It was Cliff Johnson, and he had taken her from the wagon train. She started running though methods of escape in her mind, but pretended she was still unconscious as she was jostled along. At least there was a blanket under her stomach.

She heard Cliff talking to someone, then remembered. Leroy White had told her to come to help Mrs. Porter, and realized it had to have been him who had hit her in the head. She listened to their conversation to learn of their intentions.

"Ain't nobody coming, Leroy. Do you want to stop for a while and get something to eat and maybe some exercise?" Cliff asked then followed it with a girlish giggle.

"Wait until there's some light. They can't come after us until then, and the only other horses in that place belonged to that guy that brought Mister Orson's kids back. He may not let them use them because we didn't grab her."

"Alright. But I'm getting hungry again, if you know what I mean."

Emily felt his hand rubbing her behind and realized with revulsion that he must have taken her when she was out. *How could she live this down? Did she even want to live anymore? What if he got her pregnant?*

"I know. I could use a nice dish of Florence myself."

Florence came out of her daze and heard the last remark. *Leroy? What had happened? Why was she facing down on a horse and why was he doing this?*

She was about to straighten up and confront him when she heard the unmistakable voice of her husband replying, “You can do anything you want with that bitch. I have what I want right here in front of me.”

They had someone else? She was sure that he must have Emily.

Emily meanwhile had already become aware of the other female present on this trip. When Leroy claimed to have Florence, it all came together. They had been taken.

Florence wasn’t despondent like Emily, but she was surely getting mad…deep, burning mad. She wanted to do something but didn’t know what.

———

Four miles behind now, Chester had a good scent and was following it. There was no breeze to break it up, so when they made a gentle curve to the northeast, Chester followed. Hugh watched Chester, but he also watched the east for any signs of light. He had the field glasses around his neck in case they were close.

“Hugh, that dog is doing a great job. He saved us a few hours at least. We might even catch up with them a bit after dawn.”

“That’s what I’m thinking, Leo.”

———

All the bouncing had left Emily with a serious problem. She had to pee and knew she couldn’t last much longer. She didn’t know that Florence had the same issue and had been worried about it for twenty minutes now. But neither woman had to worry much longer.

"Say, Cliff, I don't mean to be a spoil sport, but I gotta go, man. It's almost dawn anyway. The sky is getting lighter. Let's say we stop at the first place we can."

"Yeah, me, too. I'll find a place."

Leroy spotted it first, off to his left about a quarter mile.

"Hey, Cliff. How about over yonder? See that bunch of pines? That'll make a good hiding spot."

"That'll work. We can get something to eat and maybe have us some fun."

They turned their horses toward the small forest. They had all the time in the world. No one could find them now, not hidden away in those trees.

Maybe no one would if they didn't have a tracking dog. Chester was getting stronger scents now, and Hugh could see it. The dog wasn't going back and forth as often.

"We're getting close, Leo. The sky's getting lighter, too. Dawn is about a half an hour away."

"What'll we do when we find 'em?"

"It depends on how serious they are. They've got to know they're going to hang when we find them. We don't have anything we can offer them unless we tell them we'll let them go if they free the women, but they'd have to be real idiots to buy that. I think this is going to come down to shooting, Leo. How good are you with that Spencer?"

"Honestly? Fair at best. You?"

"Pretty good with the Sharps and Henry. Better than average with the Colts. But if it comes to the Colts, someone is going to die that shouldn't. We might be better taking them at range with the Sharps and your Spencer. Do you know what kind of guns they have?"

"Leroy had an old Dragoon pistol and a Spencer rifle. We sent Cliff off with a Burnside carbine and three rounds of ammunition."

"Leroy's Spencer is the only thing we need to worry about. Was he any good with it?"

"I don't know. I don't think he shot it once on the entire trip. I wound up hunting the game and some of the other men would help. Leroy always stuck around the camp."

"Well, let's hope he isn't very proficient."

———

Leroy and Cliff had pulled their horses to a stop deep in the small group of trees that hadn't earned the title of forest or even woods. No one could see them back there. Of course, the reverse was true as well, they didn't know they were being closely tracked, either.

They stopped, and Leroy was beginning to grab Florence in a strategic location to get her down when she yelled, "Get your hands off me, you son of a bitch!"

Emily took that as a clue to quickly slide to the ground and, even though she was a bit woozy and off-balance, she began running from Cliff. But she was too wobbly, and her legs were stiff, so she didn't get far. Cliff tackled her and dragged her fighting back into the trees.

"Let go of me you bastard!" she screamed, as Cliff just laughed.

Hugh and Leo heard both women clearly. They were less than a mile away.

"It sounds like it came from that bunch of trees over there," said Leo as he pointed.

"That's where Chester is going. I'd better call him back. Chester! Come."

The dog stopped dead in his tracks and after hearing Hugh telling him to come, returned to Hugh.

"That is one hell of a dog," commented Leo.

"He is. He's earned a steak dinner. Let's close in and get those two bastards before they hurt the women."

The sun was up now, but it was still dark inside the small grove. The call of nature overrode any other demands and the men took turns relieving themselves while the women waited impatiently. Finally, they allowed the women to go, while they watched. Emily and Florence had no choice, and Cliff and Leroy started laughing as they lifted their skirts.

The laughing was easy to hear from outside the trees, and Hugh and Leo had dismounted a hundred feet from the tree line. Each had his rifle out and cocked. Hugh had told Chester to stay, so he sat and watched them disappear into the trees.

The women were finished and stepped away from their own pools.

“What do we do first, Leroy? Eat or satisfy those women?”

“I don’t know about you, Cliff, but I’d rather let them ladies enjoy our services before we have breakfast.”

“How do we do this?” he asked.

“You already had Emily. How about if you pull your pistol and point it at Florence while we dally. If she gives me a hard time, then you shoot her in the leg, then I’ll do the same for you. How’s that work?”

“Another good plan, Leroy. Just don’t take too long.”

Florence was terrified as Leroy advanced towards her.

Before entering the trees, Hugh and Leo had set their plan. There would be no negotiations and no warnings. Those two men had exhausted any reason for mercy. This was going to be swift justice. Leo would take out Leroy and Hugh would shoot Cliff.

They could see flashes of movement in the central clearing ahead, and they spread out slightly. Each aiming to take out his target and not hit the women or the horses.

They were in position after another thirty seconds.

Leroy had almost reached Florence when the world exploded. Leroy was hit by the massive .56 caliber round from the Spencer at close range. It knocked him from his feet, and he stumbled eight feet away from Florence before collapsing to the ground in a macabre position.

Cliff was struck with the smaller .44 round from Hugh's Henry at almost the same moment. It may have produced less of a punch, but the round was devastating because of the short range of less than thirty feet. It penetrated the left front side of Cliff's chest but stopped in his right lung, at the level of his shoulder blade. Like LeRoy, it knocked him back, but he only took one sidestep before he did a clumsy pirouette and then fell face first into the dirt. Neither lived long enough to know what had happened.

The roar of the two weapons firing in unison was deafening, and the large cloud of gun smoke filled the small clearing.

Both women were shocked by their sudden deliverance, and neither moved as Leo and Hugh stepped into the clearing.

"Ladies, are you both all right?" asked Hugh.

They slowly turned as if in a trance and faced Hugh, who had closed the gap to less than five feet.

"Florence? Emily? Are you all right? Talk to me," Hugh said.

They both popped out of their silence at the same time and both grabbed Hugh, leaving poor Leo standing there unappreciated. They began to seriously cry, and Hugh indicated that Leo should take Emily, so Leo stepped over and just pulled Emily away from Hugh and she transferred her hug to Leo.

The women continued to cry for almost a minute before they regained control. Hugh was somewhat surprised that it was Emily who returned from her tears first. She went from a blubbering mess to a flaming creature from hell instantly as she released Leo, walked up to Cliff's corpse and began kicking and screaming at the still corpse, using every obscenity imaginable, and some that were beyond imagination. Leo watched and listened in amazement but did nothing to even slow her down.

She had barely started when Florence underwent a similar, but not quite as hellish change. She seemed satisfied with just a series of kicks and some relatively mild name-calling, at least they were mild compared to Emily's extensive use of the black vocabulary.

Hugh looked over at Leo and shrugged.

After three minutes, they seemed exhausted both physically and emotionally. They turned away from the bodies and went back to the two men who had saved them.

"Hugh and Leo, thank you for coming after us so quickly. They were going to take us both, and I was almost numb from fear. Can we go home now? Charles will be worried," asked Florence.

Emily just walked up to Leo, hugged him and kissed him on his lips. Then she walked over to Hugh and did the same.

"Okay, ladies, let's mount up. We're not that far away. Maybe three hours or so. Are either of you hungry? I know I am."

"I'm starved right now," replied Florence.

"Come on. Let's go and get the horses."

Leo took Lola's reins and Hugh took control of Leroy's horse, but no one cared about the two bodies.

The four humans and two horses walked out of the trees and had no sooner cleared the last line when Florence pointed and screamed, "Indians!"

Hugh saw them, smiled and said, “Calm down, Florence. I’ll be right back.”

He handed the reins of Leroy’s horse to Leo and walked toward the party of sixteen or so.

When he was close enough he said loudly, “Hello, Long Wolf!”

Long Wolf smiled and slid down from his horse, then stepped forward and embraced Hugh like the friend that he was.

He knew Long Wolf didn’t speak any English, so Long Wolf gestured to another Nez Perce warrior to come over. He said something to him, and the other warrior nodded and said, “We heard the shooting and came to see who was in our hunting grounds.”

“Tell Long Wolf that two bad men stole these women from our camp and were going to abuse them. We caught them both and they are dead inside the grove of trees. We did not bury them as they were cowards.”

He turned to Long Wolf, told him the story and Long Wolf nodded and replied.

“Long Wolf said it is right. They do not deserve honor. He also said to tell you that he and Pale Dawn are now married.”

Hugh smiled broadly at Long Wolf and shook his hand. Long Wolf grinned back, and then said something else to the interpreter.

“He said to tell you that Blue Flower is going to be the bride of Gray Hawk and she is content. She tells Pale Dawn she always thinks of you and wonders if you ever found the one who touched your heart."

Hugh replied, "Tell Long Wolf to tell Blue Flower that I have found the one, but to remind Blue Flower that she will remain in my heart always."

He spoke to Long Wolf who nodded and put his hands on Hugh's shoulders but said nothing. He finally just nodded, and the band of warriors waited for Long Wolf and the interpreter to climb onto their horses. Long Wolf saluted Hugh before they wheeled and rode away.

Hugh turned and walked back to the small band.

"Let's go and get something to eat and we'll head back," he said.

"Hugh, what was that all about?" asked Florence.

"That was Long Wolf. One of the Nez Perce that I met on the trail. He told me that he and Pale Dawn were now married."

"Oh."

Hugh led them to Night and Middie and took out some smoked meat and ham that he had bought at the trading post. Hugh rewarded Chester with a big piece of ham, before each of them took a canteen and after eating, they mounted their horses and began back.

Leo said, "I had planned on pushing the wagon train on today, but it looks like that plan is dead, because we won't get back until around noon or so. I guess we'll start out tomorrow."

"What are you going to do with Leroy's horse?" Hugh asked.

"I guess I'll just keep him. He's a bit nicer than Lola."

Hugh noticed that Emily was riding close to Leo and kept glancing at him like she had never seen him before, and maybe she really had never seen him as a man before, just a wagon master.

Florence was surprisingly quiet. Hugh had thought she'd be asking him all sorts of questions, but maybe the close encounter with Leroy had put her off men for a while.

The silence was finally broken after twenty minutes, when she rode close to Hugh and asked softly, "Hugh, how can I tell the good ones from the bad ones?"

He smiled at her and replied, "That's a good question, Florence, and a very difficult one. It's a combination of things really. If a man never listens to what you say, ignore him. He's too wrapped up in himself. If a man starts looking at you like you're a fine filet of beef, walk away. He only cares about the wrapping, not what's inside. If a man is volatile and has a quick temper, realize what he'll do when you're together for any length of time.

"He needs to respect you, Florence. That means no flirting or subtle hints of your intentions. Don't play miss demure retiring flower, either, just be yourself. Talk and listen. Say what you mean not what you think he wants to hear. If he doesn't like what you're saying, he has no confidence. You're not a stupid woman, Florence. You have a lot to offer some man. Recognize your value. Don't sell yourself short. You can have a happy life. Find a man that will treat Charles well, and he'll treat you well."

"Like you and Rebecca's children?"

"I love those children as if they were my own and hated to be away from them. It was easy to treat them well."

"You bought all those things for Rebecca and the children, didn't you?"

"She lost everything, Florence. It wasn't right that someone like her shouldn't look nice, and the children's clothes were all in bad condition, too."

"Did you know that her husband Bob took credit for buying them?"

Hugh looked at Florence, shook his head and said, "He should have bought them a long time ago. Whoever gets credit doesn't matter, as long as she and the children have them."

"Doesn't it bother you that he's doing that?"

"Honestly? Of course, it does. I didn't care if I got credit or not, but to have a man who should have been taking care of his wife and children but didn't, suddenly claims to do something nice for them is just plain wrong."

"She knew, by the way. Right away, she knew they came from you."

"It doesn't matter, Florence. I'll be heading out to my ranch soon."

"Her husband is after Ella Murphy, you know."

"Who is Ella Murphy?"

"She's a widow. You probably have seen them together in her wagon."

"Oh. That one. I do remember. I just forgot her name. Why would he do that? She doesn't hold a candle compared to Rebecca, and that's just physically. I doubt if she's even close to Rebecca in any other trait that matters, either."

Florence smiled and asked, "You really are smitten, aren't you, Hugh?"

"Whether I am or not really has no bearing on this anyway, Florence. It doesn't matter."

"Of course, it matters. How do you think Rebecca feels? She won't admit it either and probably for the same reason."

"It's a hell of a reason, Florence."

"I suppose so."

"You're a good friend to have, Florence."

"Thank you, Hugh. You're not too bad yourself."

"Thank you, Florence. What's your middle name, anyway?"

"My middle name? It's Betty, why?"

"Start calling yourself Betty. It suits you better. Florence seems like such a stodgy name. Betty is lively and bright, just like you."

Florence beamed and said, "Thank you, Hugh. I think I'll do that."

Hugh smiled at her and said, "Well, good morning then, Betty."

The newly christened Betty giggled.

An hour later they spotted the camp, picked up the pace and curved around the back of the wagons. Charles had seen them coming and told Rebecca as the entire population of the wagon train poured out and were standing in a large crowd awaiting their arrival.

Rebecca felt a fierce personal pride in watching Hugh escorting the two women and Leo into camp. He had done it again, as she knew he would.

Hugh picked her out of the crowd and waved. She waved back a giant smile on her face as the crowd broke out into applause as they approached.

Addie and Andy were bouncing as Mister Hugh returned. No one noticed Chester as he trotted behind the horses.

The four dismounted, and Hugh called Chester over. Chester ran to Hugh who stretched out his arms, jumped, and Hugh caught him.

Chester started licking Hugh's face as Hugh looked at him and said loudly, "You did it, Chester. You found them and let us get there in time. You are a real hero."

He led Chester down, and he quickly raised his leg and peed on Hugh's other boot.

The crowd roared in laughter, but Hugh didn't care. He'd clean them later.

Leo handed him the reins to Middie, and then Leo took the other two horses' reins and he and Emily walked off toward her wagon. Betty-Florence trotted over to Charles and picked him up, hugged him, then looked back at Hugh and waved.

Hugh smiled and waved back.

Then he turned and led his horses away to his camp, with Chester trotting behind.

Bob and Ella had watched the whole scene.

Bob snarled, “What a show-off. He has to be the center of attention. Always the hero. First, he saves the children, then he stops the knife attack on Emily, now he goes and rescues the women. So, what? I could have done any of those things if I had been in the right place. No one seems to care that he’s an adulterer.”

The recently satisfied Ella didn’t mind what Bob said. She just agreed with him and suggested they return to the wagon.

Florence returned to her wagon with Rebecca and the three children.

“So, tell me, Florence. What happened?” she asked.

“It’s Betty now. I’m going by my middle name, Betty. I like it better, because it suits me. Florence was always such a stodgy name. What do you think?”

“I think you’ve been talking to Hugh.”

She laughed and said, “You’re right, I have. But it does sound better and I like it.”

“Then I’ll just have to get used to calling you Betty.”

Betty then said, “It was horrible, Rebecca. Leroy came to the wagon and told me he wanted to talk to me in private but suggested that more was involved, and I fell for it, Rebecca. If I had a thread of decency in me, I would have told him to go away, but I went. He hit me over the head and the next thing I know, I'm face down on a horse with his hand on my behind.

"Finally, they had to stop so we could all pee. Then, he was going to take me. He said that Cliff had already done Emily once and it was his turn. He was almost there when Hugh and Leo opened fire. The whole place was covered in smoke and they were both gone, just like that. We were both numb for a while, then we broke down.

"When that was over, we walked over and started kicking those dead bastards and screaming at them. You should have heard sweet little Emily. She was using words that I had never heard before. Hugh and Leo just let us go. I was never so happy to see a man as I was to see Hugh."

"He has that effect, Betty," she said as she smiled.

"Then when we were leaving the trees, I saw this whole tribe of Indians. I was terrified and thought we were all dead. But Hugh just walked up to them and talked for a while. They seemed to like him a lot. Hugh said that one of them was the Indian who was going to marry the girl he saved."

"He does get around, our Mister Hugh, doesn't he?"

"Then, on the way back we talked. I asked him how to pick a good man, because I sure seem to be making a mess of it. He made it sound so simple and I think I'll do that, too. Then, I asked if he had bought your things, and he said it didn't matter who bought them as long as you got them. I told him that Bob had taken credit for buying them and he admitted it made him angry. He said that Bob should have been buying you those things all along because you deserved to wear nice things. Then, I said, 'you really are smitten, aren't you?'"

"You didn't!" Rebecca exclaimed with her eyes as big as saucers.

"I did. And he deflected the question by saying it didn't matter if he was or not, because it didn't change the situation. Then he told me that my name didn't fit me, and my middle name did. I'll tell you, Rebecca. I could talk to that man for hours. I never realized that whenever I talk to men, I've always been on edge, like I had to say certain things or behave a certain way. But not with Hugh. I actually got to talk to a man and feel comfortable doing it."

"I know. Did he say what he's going to do?"

"He said he's leaving for his ranch in the morning."

"Oh. Then he'll probably be gone before dawn again."

"Rebecca, don't let that one reason ruin your life. Your husband is probably in Ella Murphy's bed right now. Go over to his camp tonight. Tell him how you feel. Don't let him go."

"I have to let him go. Don't you know why?"

"Not one bit."

"If I go to him tonight, that bastard husband of mine will sue for divorce claiming adultery. If I know him, and I do, he'll try to take the children just to see if he can get something out of me. Maybe he'll try to get Hugh to pay a lot of money. I can't let things like that happen to my children. Hugh wouldn't want that either. Can't you see?"

"Yes, Rebecca. I see now. You're right, of course. Come on in, we've got to get lunch ready for the children."

———

Hugh had unsaddled his horses and brushed them down. They were all contentedly chewing grass near his tent, while Chester was curled up nearby sleeping after his heroic performance.

Hugh was sitting near his saddle and was cleaning his Henry. It had done its job today.

He had planned on an early start in the morning but thought he might want to say goodbye to the children and Rebecca. He wished he didn't have to, but he was convinced after talking to Betty that her husband would try something really shady if he stuck around, but at least he could say goodbye.

CHAPTER 7

Hugh did sleep in somewhat, not sliding out of his bedroll until sunrise. He made his breakfast and gave a good-sized piece of smoked beef to Chester again, then cleaned up the area and packed his mule. He was preparing to saddle Middie for the day's ride to his new ranch, then glanced at the stallion who was staring at him.

He smiled at the big horse and said, "I suppose we've got to get along, Night. You did a good job yesterday and didn't get nasty even once."

He then saddled Night and used Middie and the gray gelding as saddle transports, leaving the displeased mule with all of the supplies. Hugh expected a formal complaint later.

Hugh mounted, then walked the line of animals out of his camp, finding the wagon train was already moving. He assumed that Leo was trying to make up time after yesterday's delay.

Rebecca was on the outside seat of Betty's wagon and knew it would take some time to adjust to her friend's new name, so she'd do the best she could to not slip into calling her Flo. She seemed to relish her new name and the changed personality that went with it. She had to admit that she liked the new Betty a lot more than she had the old Flo.

The Betty-Flo situation wasn't the only thing on her mind and wasn't even taking that much of her mental time. She wasn't in the best of moods and knew why. Hugh was already gone, and she knew she'd never see him again. Soon, they'd get to their destination in the Willamette Valley, and that didn't depress her…it terrified her. *What would Bob do then?* He had control of their money, and if he wanted to stay with Ella Murphy, *then how would he get rid of her? If he succeeded what could she do?* As Hugh had said in his sermon about women, men had all the power.

She was still deep in thought when she almost jumped from her seat when an unexpected voice came from her left.

"Good morning, Rebecca."

She jerked her head to the left and saw Hugh smiling at her. To say her disposition improved would be a marked understatement.

"You didn't leave!" she exclaimed with a big smile.

"Not yet. I couldn't leave without saying goodbye to you and the children."

"Oh. Let me bring them up front," she said, her momentary elation quickly subdued by his stated intention to depart.

She called Addie and Andy to the front of the wagon, and when they popped out of the back, Hugh noticed that both were wearing new clothes and Addie had a blue ribbon in her hair. In addition to their finery, both children wore big grins on their small faces.

"Mister Hugh! You're back. Mama said you were leaving," Addie said.

"I am shortly, but I didn't want to go without saying goodbye. I wanted your mama and both of you to know that I'll be nearby when you get to Baker City. All you have to do is to ask where the Rocking M ranch is. Okay?"

"Alright," answered Andy, "The Rocking M."

"Now, I won't know where you will be, but I expect you to visit when you can. Okay?"

"I'm gonna miss you, Mister Hugh," said Addie, who still clenched her doll tightly.

"And you know I'll miss you, too. I need to talk to your mama before I go. Okay?"

"Okay. Bye, Mister Hugh," said a sad Andy.

Hugh felt a stab of pain in his chest as he watched the children disappear into the wagon.

He then turned his eyes to their mother, sighed and said, "I have to admit that this really hurts, Rebecca. I wish I didn't have to do it, but it wouldn't be right not to."

"I understand, Hugh. I really am happy you stopped by, though."

"Rebecca, I wanted you to understand something. If circumstances had been different. If there hadn't been one insurmountable obstacle, things would be very different. I think you understand, don't you?"

"Hugh, I more than understand. I share those same feelings. I know they can't be overcome, so we'll have to live with them. I'll remember that you're at the Rocking M ranch outside of Baker City to the southeast."

Hugh smiled and looked into her eyes one last time.

"Rebecca, before I go, I'd like you to have something to remember me."

"Hugh, I don't need anything. I won't forget you. Ever."

"I know. But there's a reason I want you to have this. No one else can."

He reached into his saddlebag and pulled out Blue Flower's necklace and held it out to Rebecca.

She had never seen it before but knew of its significance to Hugh and Blue Flower.

Rebecca took the necklace in her trembling fingers and said, "Hugh, this is incredibly beautiful. This was Blue Flower's, wasn't it?"

"It was. Now, it's yours. Treasure it always, Rebecca, as I will treasure my memories of you."

With that, and before he could say another word, Hugh tapped the black stallion, and he trotted forward, leaving a stunned and misting Rebecca behind.

She clutched the necklace to her breast and then as she watched Hugh leave her life, she lifted the necklace and then lowered it over her head, then pulled her hair over the necklace and she knew. She was 'the other person' that should hear what Blue Flower said to him but knew that she would never hear what it was.

Betty had heard the entire conversation and was almost as upset as Rebecca. She saw how much they cared for each other and only that selfish bastard up in Ella Murphy's wagon was keeping them apart. If she had been a man, she'd go and shoot him.

———

That selfish bastard was driving Ella's wagon as Ella was clinging, rubbing him and saying soft things to him, and he hated it. He was already tired of Ella, but he had found out that she had almost seven hundred dollars in the community wagon. That, plus his three hundred and twenty would put him in very good shape. He could put up with Ella for a few more days to get that money.

Then, even as Bob was doing his calculations, Hugh and his towed array of creatures passed the wagon.

"So, he's leaving," thought Bob.

He wondered how that fit into his plans. He could start rumors that Rebecca had an adulterous relationship with him, and he wouldn't be here to deny it. This might work.

If Bob had asked anyone, he might have seen what a ludicrous plan it was. Everyone in the wagon train, including the children, knew what he was doing to Ella Murphy. They also all respected Hugh McGinnis. In addition to tracking and killing Leroy and Cliff, they had all heard about his purchase of clothes for the entire family because Bob had never even gone to the trading post's store. But Bob never talked to anyone, so he was unaware of his precarious position. He should have been more sociable.

Hugh passed Emily's wagon and noticed that Leo was driving with two horses trailing, so he slowed down, then slid Night a bit closer as he approached the front of the wagon.

"Decided that riding a wagon was easier than riding a horse, Leo?" Hugh asked with a wide smile.

Leo blustered, "It's just that, well, Emily, I mean Mrs. Amber, was getting tired from handling the horses."

Hugh laughed and said, “You don’t need to make excuses to me, Leo. How are you, Emily?”

She leaned forward, shot a huge smile his way and answered, “Couldn’t be better, Hugh. Are you leaving us?”

“Yes, ma’am. I’m heading to my ranch. Leo, could you and Emily look out for Rebecca and the children?”

“Count on it, Hugh. You take care.”

Hugh nodded and said, “Goodbye, Leo, Emily.”

He waved and resumed his trotting pace, quickly pulling ahead of the lead wagon. Soon the wagon train was gone from his sight as he crossed the last rise before his destination. He was in Oregon now, but just because he crossed an imaginary line on a map didn’t make a big difference in the geography. While it didn’t change much where the border was, he knew that another hundred miles west of that line he’d crossed yesterday, there was a huge difference in the landscape.

He decided he’d head into Baker City and the land office to make sure everything was correct, then he’d check with the local law enforcement just to make sure that there was nothing going on with the ranch. Squatters may have moved in and he didn’t want any trouble if he could avoid it.

And then there was his father. He wondered if that would come into play sooner rather than later. He had almost limitless resources at his disposal, and Hugh would be surprised if he didn’t know about the ranch, but that was a future problem. He had to find the ranch and then decide what to do with it after that.

He didn't stop for lunch, but just had some jerky and tossed a piece to Chester. Then, just a short time later, he saw Baker City in the distance and the long ride was finally almost over.

The wagon train had finally reached the same rise that Hugh had crossed hours earlier, and as they began their descent, excitement grew among the families. They had made it. They had reached Oregon.

Hugh pulled up in front of the land office, dismounted, hitched Night to the rail and went inside.

"Good afternoon, sir. How can I help you?" asked a very cheerful land office clerk.

"Hello. My name is Hugh McGinnis. I just arrived and needed to check on the status of the Rocking M. I know my brother, Brian, had told me that he had paid taxes five years in advance, but I wanted to make sure everything is okay."

"Certainly. And how is Brian? We haven't seen him in a while."

"My brother died almost four years ago while in the army. I'm sure you know about his wife. I think he was very despondent when he lost her and the baby."

"I'm sorry to hear about his loss. He was very popular in the city."

"I was fond of him, too. He was a better man than I am."

"I'm not too sure. He used to say the same thing about you. Let me pull the records."

He turned, took two steps to a file cabinet and went through a series of folders, pulled one and stepped back to the counter.

"Here we are. Yes, he paid up through next year. You, as you know, are listed on the deed, so that makes you the sole owner."

"I wish that Brian were still here, though."

"As do we all. But, nonetheless, welcome to Baker City, Mister McGinnis."

"Call me Hugh."

"I'm James. James Callaghan."

They shook hands and Hugh stepped back outside, untied and mounted Night, then turned him down the main street. One stop down, and one to go before he rode out to the ranch, and the big question of what he would find there would be answered.

He found the sheriff's office easily, but there was a sign on the door that changed his plans: Gone hunting.

Odd, thought Hugh. *They shut the office down to go hunting?* He wondered why at least a deputy wasn't there to handle problems.

He turned Night and headed for the city marshal's office that he'd already passed after leaving the land office. He didn't have jurisdiction as far out of town as the ranch, but he should have some information about the place. He dismounted before the office, looped Night's reins around the hitchrail, opened the door and walked inside.

"Good afternoon, sir. What can we do for you?" asked a very polite deputy marshal.

Hugh guessed he couldn't be much older than twenty.

"Howdy. My name is Hugh McGinnis. I just arrived from Missouri and I'm heading out to my ranch, the Rocking M. I just wanted to check in before I went out there to make sure nothing was going on out there that might catch me by surprise."

"You own the Rocking M?" he asked, his eyebrows peaked.

"Yup. My brother bought it, put my name on the deed with his and left it to me. I just checked over at the land office and everything is correct. You seem surprised. Is there something wrong?"

"Well, yes, you might say that. There are a pair of brothers named Hanson living out there, Jed and Julip Hanson."

Hugh interrupted when he asked with raised eyebrows, "Did you say Julip?"

"Yes, sir. Everyone gets a bit taken by surprise with that. I guess his parents were fond of the drink."

"Sorry to interrupt. Go on."

"Well, it seems that the two brothers have kind of taken a liking to your place. They moved in about a year or so ago, claiming that the place was abandoned. Nobody challenged them because they're kind of hard cases. To be honest, they're both wanted men, but nobody wants to go out there. Not even the sheriff."

"They're wanted, but everyone is afraid to evict them from my house?"

"That's about the size of it. The only one with jurisdiction is the sheriff, and I know he doesn't want to go out there."

"Are they wanted dead or alive?"

"Yes, sir."

"So, if I go out there and make them dead, I won't be in any sort of trouble?"

"No, sir, not at all. In fact, folks around here would be mighty pleased. They kind of come into town now and then and make trouble."

"I see. So, I'm on my own."

"Sorry, sir, but that's the size of it."

"Are there any more bad men at the house, or just those two?"

"Just the brothers. None of the other bad sorts want to work with them either."

"Okay. Then, I guess I'll have to do some varmint hunting."

"Good luck, sir."

Hugh nodded, then turned and walked outside to his horses and mule. He may as well do this on a full stomach, so, after mounting, he turned the mini-herd around and headed for the nearest diner.

———

He had a good fried chicken dinner and then returned to his horses and mule thirty minutes later. Since talking to the young deputy marshal, he had been running different plans through his mind to evict those two with prejudice. What made it easier was the dead or alive aspect. He didn't have to be subtle in his dealings with the pair but couldn't care less about the reward. Those bastards were desecrating the house Brian had built for his wife and expected baby.

He rode out of Baker City in late afternoon, heading for the ranch. He knew the location, so he followed the only road that went that direction, and then thirty minutes later, he saw the entrance road, but passed it by and continued until he saw the edge of a pine forest just south of the house.

He turned his animals into the trees and kept going east, catching flashes of the house to his left through the tree trunks as he walked Night up a gradual climb. After he had gone far enough to see the house between the trees, he turned his four-footed parade into a deeper into the forest and began looking for a campsite. It didn't take long to find a nice clearing with a large running creek nearby. He wondered if it emptied into the river that Brian had told him ran through the ranch.

He stepped down and began stripping the horses. He got the pack mule unloaded and arranged his campsite. He had plenty of food, and water was right there, so he could stay here for longer than a week if he had to, but he had no intention of doing so. Either the brothers would be dead in a day or two or he would. He had to admit, the thought of his own demise didn't please him, but at the same time, without Rebecca and the children, it was kind of irrelevant anyway. He knew he'd never find another like her because there simply wasn't another woman like Rebecca.

Enough of these morose thoughts, he said to himself, it was time to plan how to serve his eviction notice. He pulled the Sharps and six of his remaining cartridges and began to walk back toward the edge of the forest that was closest to the house. He just followed his own tracks in the already fading light, which didn't help or hurt him. He wanted to see the makeup of the ranch more closely, but if an opportunity arose, he could take a shot.

Once he reached the edge of the trees, he studied the trees looking for an easily identified marker and spotted a large fallen branch at an odd angle. If he had to return in the dark, he wouldn't be able to find his own footprints, so the branch would be his entry point.

With his return path set, Hugh resumed his walk, left the protection of the trees and counted on just the darkness to mask his approach to the house. Once there, he'd be able to do some reconnaissance and evaluate the situation before he worked out a plan to rid the house of the two unwanted thugs.

Inside the Rocking M ranch house, Jed and Julip were sitting in the main room drinking. They may have been outlaw tough guys, but the house was amazingly neat. It wasn't that they were particularly good at housekeeping, but they had two women living with them, a minor fact that the deputy marshal had failed to relay to Hugh. They had gotten lonely after a few months at the house and gone to town and grabbed two good-looking young women. No one chased after them, either. The female additions were there primarily for entertainment, but they also cooked, cleaned the house and did the brothers' laundry. They weren't paid for their work, and they weren't even treated well, they were just allowed to live from day to day.

"Say, Julip, what's say we head into town tomorrow? We ain't visited over two weeks," Jed asked as he leaned back in his chair.

"I'm thinkin' on it, Jed. You're right about that though. It's gettin' kind of boring around here lately. We need to liven things up. Any ideas?"

"I could do Nancy tonight and you could do Susan. That's a change."

"Not much. I'm getting kind of bored with those two anyway. Maybe we should trade 'em in for some newer ones."

"Don't know about that, Julip. Pickins are pretty slim these days. Besides, they clean real good."

"We could get two more and have four of 'em. That would be fun."

"Yeah, it would, but we need some more money and supplies, too."

"All the more reason to go to town tomorrow."

As they talked, the two women were sitting in the same room, exchanging glances that revealed their disgust, shame, and above all else, their fear. The brothers talked about them like they didn't even exist, and neither was sure if she really did any longer.

As Hugh walked closer the ranch house, he was impressed with the size and design. It probably had five or six bedrooms. Plenty of room for children, he thought. Then he told himself to stop his mind from wandering, he had serious business to tend to.

Hugh hadn't seen any signs of the brothers, but he could see the light coming from the front of the house, so he figured he'd take a peek inside. He had his field glasses, so he walked toward the house and made a wide arc about a hundred yards to the west so he could look through the front windows.

He was glad to see fairly large windows, so when he was in front of the house, he sat on the grass-covered ground, pulled his field glasses to his eyes and began to scan the front room. It didn't take long to see the two brothers. They were talking, and then he saw the back of two heads sitting in chairs. He wasn't sure of their height as they were sitting, but kept his glasses trained on the pair. Suddenly, one turned, and he recognized the profile of a young woman. He assumed the other head belong to another woman, and that made things much more difficult.

Now he needed to know if they were there voluntarily or not, which would make a huge difference in how he approached the issue. They would either warn the brothers or be hurt by them if they felt threatened. Either way, they presented an obstacle just by their presence.

The problem was trying to determine if they were prisoners or girlfriends. After seeing the two brothers, he found it hard to believe they could be girlfriends.

As it turned out, Hugh didn't need much time to determine their status. As he watched, one of the brothers stood and walked to the chair with one of the women, reached down and grabbed her by the hair. She started to fight back but was struck by the other brother, then she stopped fighting and just flailed weakly as she was dragged from the room. The second brother didn't do anything so drastic. He just picked up the other woman and carried her away. Hugh noticed that she was nothing more than a limp rag and felt his anger rising. If those two weren't worthy of a bullet before, watching what they were doing now earned them a few slugs of lead.

He was going to go back and prepare for action tomorrow, but his anger was taking control, but he also recognized an opportunity. They would be vulnerable now and inattentive to an unexpected visitor with serious intent.

He'd give them a couple of minutes to allow them to be in a more vulnerable position, and then he'd just walk inside and shoot them both.

After counting to a hundred, he rose and started for the house…his house. He reached the porch, then stopped, removed his boots and quietly set down the Sharps. This was going to be a look-them-in-the-eyes fight.

He pulled his pistols and cocked them both, then walked quietly to the front door, pleased to find that it was unlocked. After swinging it open slowly and quietly, he could already hear noises from inside, and they weren't pleasant noises. He had to control his anger to stay focused on what the task at hand.

He carefully stepped inside. The house was well lit, so he continued forward, one foot placed slowly in front of the other as he crossed the large, well-appointed main room, but Hugh didn't take time to examine the room or its furnishings as he heard the noises coming from two bedrooms, both on the left side of the hallway. He'd have to be careful because of the women, but the men were both much taller than the women, so he'd go for head shots. But the fact that they were in different rooms also negated the need for both pistols, so he released the trigger to his left Colt and slid it back into the holster.

Hugh slowly worked his way down to the first bedroom, stood directly in front of the door and took a breath, brought the Colt level, then turned the door handle and pushed the door open.

Jed turned at the sound, preparing to let Julip know he wasn't happy for the interruption then a confused look drifted across his face when he momentarily saw a tall stranger with a pistol in his hand.

Hugh took advantage of his shock, and without hesitation, pulled his Colt's trigger.

Jed never got a word out, as his stunned eyes watched as Hugh's right index finger pulled the trigger back, the hammer fell, igniting the percussion cap and then the gunpowder in the chamber. The powder's almost instantaneous burn blasted the .45 caliber lead projectile through the barrel and less than a tenth of a second later, the bullet smashed through the brother's chest, almost vaporizing his heart before it exited his body and punched into the wall behind him. The brother tipped over backwards, fell from the bed and his head cracked against the same wall that had absorbed the depleted bullet, but he never felt any pain as he crumpled to the floor, a surprisingly small pool of blood spreading on the floor.

Hugh didn't wait to check the man's pulse as he wasn't a real doctor anyway. He quickly turned and left the bedroom, and as expected, as soon as he reached the hallway, the second brother came tumbling out of his room, but with no pistol in his hand and no clothes, either. Julip was just as shocked as his brother had been when he spotted Hugh standing before him, having thought his brother had shot Nancy for some reason.

His surprise didn't last long as Hugh had already cocked the hammer to his pistol and as the second brother stood in his nakedness, he lived just long enough to ask in a stunned voice, "Who…", before Hugh pulled the trigger.

His second .45 drilled through the center of his chest before his heart contracted for its last time. It wasn't exactly a display of marksmanship, not at three feet. A .45 caliber round from that distance will find a fatal point, and this one did, as it exploded his aortic arch, flooding his chest cavity with so much blood that he just went to his knees as his eyes rolled back into his head and he fell forward, smashing his nose into the floor.

Hugh replaced the pistol and went into the second room. Like the first, he found the young woman tied to the bed without a stitch of clothing.

He walked around to the head of the bed, looked into her stunned and terrified eyes and said softly, "Ma'am, I'm going to cut those ropes and you can get dressed. Okay?"

From the already horrible situation she was in and then the sudden gunshot and then a second, Susan was almost beyond terror as she looked at Hugh, half expecting him to take advantage of the situation, but then his soft voice filtered past her emotions.

"What did you say?" she asked.

"I'm going to cut your ropes and you can get dressed. I've got to go next door and help the other young lady."

"Alright," she replied, still unsure of what would happen.

Hugh slid his knife from its sheath, began slicing the ropes, and soon had her free. She began to rub her wrists as Hugh quickly left the room to give her some privacy and help the other young woman.

He entered the first bedroom and, after reaching the head of the bed, said in the same soothing voice, “Ma’am, I’m going to cut those ropes so you can get dressed. Alright?”

She didn’t reply or even open her eyes, and Hugh concluded that she must have been the one that the brother had handled like a dishrag. He had missed whatever blow he had used to render her unconscious probably because he was watching the other brother drag the first young woman out of the room.

“Ma’am?” Hugh asked, “Are you all right?”

Convinced that she couldn’t respond, he began cutting the ropes. He had them all severed, yet she still didn’t move, and Hugh wondered if she was still alive.

He looked carefully and saw she was breathing, then looked around and found a blanket and slipped it over her naked body.

He returned to the hallway where he saw the other young woman staring down at the dead brother in the hallway.

“Ma’am, I know this sounds like a stupid question, but are you all right now?”

She turned to look at Hugh, then took two slow steps towards him, threw her arms around his neck and started sobbing.

He held her in a soft hug as she shuddered and said softly, “It’s all right now. They’re both dead. They can’t hurt you anymore. You’re safe.”

“Who are you?” she finally asked between sobs as she kept her head against his chest.

"My name is Hugh McGinnis. I own the ranch and found out today that these two brothers had been living here and causing trouble. I was told by the deputy marshal that there was no one else here, but when I saw you through the window, I had to come in to help."

She sniffed once more, stepped back and looked up at Hugh as she said, "Thank you. Thank you so much. It was horrible. They just took me from my home. No one seemed to care. It was like a nightmare. That one down there is Julip. They made me and Nancy do disgusting things. I don't know if I'll be able to sleep without nightmares ever again."

Hugh felt a mix of anger and compassion rise inside him as he said, "He's paid the price for doing those things, and you're protected now. What's your name?"

"Oh, I'm sorry. I'm Susan. Susan Fremont. I just got married six months ago and then this happened. My friend is Nancy Hurst."

"Didn't your husband come and try to rescue you or get the sheriff?"

"I don't know. Nobody came until you showed up."

"Susan, can you go and check on Nancy? She's unconscious. I covered her with a blanket after I cut her ropes."

"Okay."

Susan hurried past Hugh, entered the first bedroom and gasped at the sight of Jed sprawled on the floor in an awkward position, his big feet still in the air over the bed.

Hugh grimaced as he realized that he had forgotten about Jed's body and said quickly, "Susan, I'm sorry. I forgot about that one. You go over there and check on Nancy. I'll get him out of there."

She nodded and went to the left side of the bed and sat down near her head and began talking to Nancy.

Hugh scampered out the door, retrieved his boots and quickly pulled them on, grabbed the Sharps and returned to the house. He put the Sharps in the corner and returned to the bedroom to remove Jed's body.

Hugh pushed the feet sideways, then grabbed him by the ankles and pulled out of the room. He got him into the hallway and needed to get the two bodies out of the house before rigor set in, so he kept pulling Jed until he reached the front porch and didn't care how much he bounced as he dragged him down the steps, his head thumping loudly as it hit each one. Once on the ground, Hugh pulled him out into the yard, then returned and did the same to Julip. What a stupid name, Hugh kept thinking as he pulled him out into the yard to join his brother. Now, they could enjoy rigor mortis as much as they wanted. He'd get a wagon, or the county could come and get them.

He returned to the house to check on Susan and Nancy, and when he entered the room, was gratified to see Nancy awake.

"How are you doing, Nancy?"

"I'm kind of woozy. He hit me pretty hard. Susan said you killed them both."

"They earned the privilege, ma'am. Someone should have done that long ago."

Hugh walked over to her bed and sat down beside Susan and looked at Nancy.

"Nancy, look at me. Look straight into my eyes."

She did and Hugh looked at her pupils. They seemed okay.

"Susan, could you bring me a lamp, please?" he asked.

"Sure."

She stood, left the room and returned with a lamp just seconds later and handed it to Hugh.

"Thank you," said Hugh as he took the lamp.

He turned back to Nancy and said, "Now, Nancy, keep looking at me."

Hugh watched the light from the lamp hit her eyes and watched her pupils contract equally, then put the lamp down.

"That's good, Nancy. It's not too bad. You'll have a headache in the morning, but you'll be okay. Now, Susan, could you help Nancy get dressed? She'll be a bit dizzy. I'm going out to the kitchen and get some water to start cleaning this mess up."

Susan seemed horrified at the suggestion and said, "No, sir. You can't do that. I'll do it after Nancy gets dressed. That's our job."

"No, Susan. Your job and Nancy's are to get better. After Nancy gets dressed, you and Nancy go out to the front room, relax in the sitting area and I'll be out in a few minutes. Okay?"

"Alright. I guess so."

"Good. I'll be back shortly."

Hugh smiled at Susan, then stood and walked out to the kitchen. He knew there had to be a bucket and a mop somewhere, and after a short search found them in a large closet built into the south wall. It also served as a pantry and was reasonably well stocked. He took the bucket and mop out and turned to the sink looking for a pump, but not finding one, which surprised him. In fact, the whole house surprised him. It was large, but not as exotic as he would have expected from his architect brother.

He was about to go outside when he noticed a pipe coming out above the sink, but not a pump handle. He went over and found a valve, put the bucket under the pipe and opened the valve. Water came gushing out and filled the bucket quickly.

He'd have to check and see how his brother did that later, but he had to clean first. He put the bucket down and found the coffee pot and filled it, then set it on the cookstove, started a fire going in the firebox then turned back to the sink.

He shaved some white soap into the bucket, then used the mop to agitate the soapy water until there was a good layer of suds, then carried the mop and bucket to the hallway and began mopping up the blood in the hallway and then followed the red trail into the bedroom. It wasn't as messy as he thought as the nicely varnished floor made cleanup much easier. There were holes in the walls where the bullets had entered, but he'd repair those later.

Satisfied that the blood was gone, he walked out the kitchen door and emptied the bucket past the back porch. By then, the coffee pot's water was bubbling, so he added the coffee, then found three large ceramic mugs and filled them with the steaming brew, set the coffee pot aside and put the three mugs on a tray.

He walked into the sitting room and set the tray on the table.

"Okay, ladies, have a cup of coffee and tell me what happened. I just arrived in town a little while ago from Missouri, so I'm in the dark here. I just don't understand why everyone was so afraid of those two. They didn't exactly overwhelm me with their brilliance."

Susan took a sip of coffee, closed her eyes momentarily, then opened them and said, "You have to understand. They've lived here their entire lives, they were always bullies, and they were always together. We knew them in school, and they scared everyone, including our teachers. They were always big, and they were allowed to behave that way because of their father, who was just as mean. By the time they were teenagers, everyone was terrified of them. They wore guns and they were good with them. Every once and a while, someone would try and stand up to them, but they'd just kill him."

"What about the sheriff and the marshal?"

"They were scared, too, but they never would admit it. They always had excuses, but we knew. When they finally moved out here, everybody was relieved, thinking they wouldn't return, but they'd come in a couple or three times every month and take things."

"Including you."

"Including us."

"Well, Susan and Nancy, I'm sorry this happened to you both. Now, what can I do to help?"

Nancy finally spoke, saying, “Nothing. I don’t think that my parents want to see me again.”

Hugh was at a loss for words when she said that so conversationally and asked, “How can you say that, Nancy? I should think they’d be overjoyed to have you back.”

Nancy shook her head and replied, “My father is a minister. He’s always preaching about the sins of fornication, and he and my mother will know I’m a sinner.”

“Nancy, that’s not true at all. You are no more a sinner than I am, probably a lot less. You had bad things happen to you, and deserve kindness and understanding, not condemnation. If your father won’t accept you back, then he’s the sinner, not you. You didn’t sin at all, Nancy.”

“How do you know? You weren’t here. You don’t know what I did,” Nancy said in a surprisingly combative tone.

Hugh ignored her anger, understanding what drove it, and said, “I can imagine what you went through, Nancy. Now, look into my eyes and tell me that you’ll understand what I’m going to tell you.”

She lifted her head and looked into his eyes. She had bright blue eyes that were bloodshot from crying.

“Nancy, all the things that you had to do, were forced to do, were not your fault. Those two dead bastards were the ones who are now in hell paying for what they did. When you finally pass on decades from now, you will be accepted with welcoming arms into heaven as you deserve.”

Nancy had two tears fall from her eyes, as she quietly asked, “Do you believe that?”

“Absolutely. I never lie. You and Susan did nothing wrong here. You have nothing to be ashamed for.”

“What if I told you there were times when I actually felt pleasure during fornication. Then what would you say? I’m so ashamed of myself. I’m just a god-forsaken harlot.”

“Nancy, listen to me. Sex was designed by God to make people want to have children. He made it enjoyable for a reason. If He had made it painful or even boring, no one would have children and there would be no people at all, so God made it physically enjoyable for that reason. When he told Adam and Eve to go forth and multiply, if it hurt, I doubt if any multiplication would be happening, or even addition, for that matter.

“What happened to you was that despite the cruelty and violence, there may have been times when you were just physically aroused. You couldn’t prevent that any more than you could prevent hiccups. The fact that you are ashamed of it means that you didn’t intend for any of it to happen. I want you both to understand one thing. Do not blame yourselves for any part of this. Anyone in Baker City or anywhere who does is not worth a thought. Now, tonight, you can stay here and sleep quietly without fear. I’m surprised that you both still had the will to try to fight them off after months of this. Tomorrow, I’ll take you both home and see how that goes. But neither of you needs to worry. Alright?”

“Why are you helping us?” asked Susan.

“Let’s just say that I don’t like to see good people hurt. It’s a habit.”

“Are you a preacher?” asked Nancy.

Hugh laughed, shook his head and replied, "No one has ever accused me of that. If anything, I'm a doctor. I have another year of medical school to finish, though."

"We only have Doc Adams, and he's not very good."

"Where do you both sleep? I only saw three bedrooms."

"Downstairs," answered Nancy, "They would just lock us in down there when they were asleep or not around."

"There's a basement?" Hugh asked.

"Yes, sir. It has a few bedrooms down there and other rooms they wouldn't let us see."

"Do you keep your personal things downstairs?"

"All we have is what we're wearing. We could wash them when they weren't around, but they never brought us anything else to wear," replied Susan.

Hugh sighed and said, "I'm really so sorry for this. No one should have to undergo what you two ladies have had to withstand. I only wish those two had died in a lot more pain. They earned it."

"You don't sound like a doctor," said Nancy.

"Maybe when I take the Hippocratic oath, that'll miraculously change, but I doubt it."

"What's the oath?"

"It's something that all new physicians swear to when they become doctors. It basically says what a doctor should do and shouldn't do. It's like the Ten Commandments for doctors."

Susan nodded and asked, “I know you told me, but what’s your name again?”

“Hugh. Hugh McGinnis.”

“And you own the ranch?”

“Yes, ma’am. I’ll spend the next few days exploring it before I decide what I’ll do with it, though.”

“How did you get here? No one could come down the access road without them knowing about it. They have alarms and traps.”

“I went through the trees. I have my horses, mule and my dog in there now.”

Susan brightened and asked, “You have a dog?”

“Sure. Want to meet him?”

Both young women finally smiled.

“That would be really nice,” answered Nancy.

“Just a second.”

Hugh walked to the front door, opened it wide and yelled, “Chester! Come!”

Then he turned and returned to the main room and took his seat again.

“Don’t you have to stay out there so he can find you?”

“Chester is a very smart dog. He helped us track two men who had taken two women from the wagon train just a couple of days ago.”

"What happened to them?"

"The men we shot dead, just like these two. The women were returned to the train and are fine."

There was a rush of clicking feet as Chester popped through the door, ran up to Hugh and sat in front of him.

"Susan, Nancy, I'd like you to meet Chester."

Both young women stepped over and began rubbing his head and behind the ears, and Chester was thoroughly pleased with the attention.

"Where did you find him?" Susan asked.

"In Idaho. He found us, really. I had just found two children who had fallen in their wagon down a cliff. The next day, he showed up. He's been with me ever since."

"*You found two children?*" asked Nancy with wide eyes.

Hugh blew out his breath. It was a touchy subject.

"Yes. Andy, a nine-year-old boy and his seven-year-old sister, Addie. I brought them back to their mother in the wagon train."

"She must have been very happy to see them again."

Hugh was getting tight in the chest as he replied, "Yes, she was."

"So, you really seem to be in the rescuing people business."

"No offense, but I really need to change the subject. Okay?"

"Okay," replied Susan.

"So, do you want to sleep up here tonight?"

"Alright."

"Are either of you hungry?"

"No, we're fine."

"Is there someplace I can clean up? It's been a long day."

"Sure. Follow me," said Susan.

She popped up, and Hugh was impressed with her rapid return to normal behavior. Nancy was still a little behind, but better than he had expected. Women who suffered the kind of abuse these two young women experienced usually don't return to a semblance of normalcy for months, if ever.

She led him down the hallway to the last door on the right and opened it. Hugh looked inside and saw a tub with a pipe and valve, a sink with a pipe and valve, and something that looked like it belonged in a privy, but it was in the house. There was a large box near the ceiling with a chain and handle hanging nearby.

"What's that?" he asked, pointing at the overhead contraption.

"I don't know what it's called, but you use it like a privy and when you're done, you pull that chain and water comes down and cleans it out. There's no smell, either."

Hugh walked over and pulled the chain. There was a whoosh of water and the water swirled in the metal bowl and disappeared in a hole in the bottom. He could hear running water above in the box for a minute before it stopped.

"Well, I'll be. It's a water closet. I read about these things a few years ago. Brian must have had someone make the parts. He was a pretty smart man, my brother."

"There's another one downstairs. That's the one we used."

"Well, it you don't mind, ladies, I'd like to clean up and then we'll discuss what we'll do tomorrow.

"Alright. We'll be in the main room."

They both smiled at Hugh and turned back.

Fifteen miles short of Baker City, the wagon train had pulled up for the night. They were all excited about getting to a real town again.

Rebecca was sitting on the ground with Betty, while the children were off playing.

"Betty, I'm really a mess. I know that Hugh is nearby, and we'll be riding right past his ranch as we go to Willamette Valley, and there's nothing I can do about it. But what makes it worse is that sooner or later I have to go to Ella's wagon and see Bob. I have to know what he's going to do about us. He's just as much stuck by that piece of paper as I am, but I don't even have any money."

"Rebecca, you can always stay with me. I have five hundred dollars or so. That'll last a while. I'll tell you what, though. Depending on what I see in Baker City tomorrow, I may not go on at all. What do I care about that valley now? I'm not going to farm or anything. One place is as good as another, and I'm tired of traveling."

“I wish I had that option,” Rebecca replied as she idly fingered her necklace. She hadn’t taken it off since Hugh given it to her.

“You know, Rebecca, when Hugh gave you that necklace, I was near to blubbering myself. You’re the luckiest and unluckiest woman on the face of the earth. He really loves you, Rebecca.”

“I know. And the only time I’ve even touched him was when I was holding his arm together. But when I looked into his eyes that first night, I knew. I’m sure he knew as well. After that, we just danced around the whole thing, but it kept getting worse, too. The more I was around him, the more I couldn’t stand being away from him. Then he capped it off by giving me this. I’ll never know what Blue Flower said, Betty. Somehow, that adds to my feeling of loss.”

“Don’t give up hope, Rebecca. Your Mister Hugh has a knack for making things right.”

Rebecca smiled as all those memories came back to her.

“Yes, he does, doesn’t he?”

She was still fingering her necklace when she was startled to hear her husband’s voice.

“Oh! There you are!”

She turned and looked at him, suddenly worried that he might have overheard what she had been admitting to Betty.

She had expected him to be accompanied, but he was alone. Ella must be back at the wagon.

“Hello, Bob. What do you want?”

"Where'd you get that from?" he asked, pointing at the necklace.

"Hugh McGinnis gave it to me before he left."

Rebecca wasn't about to lie. She was proud of the necklace and didn't care if he knew or not.

Bob surprised her when he smiled, but then understood why he seemed pleased when he said, "I thought there was something between you two. I just came down here to tell you we're staying here in Baker City for a week or so. You need to stay here, too. If you need to stay in the hotel, I'll give you ten dollars for a room for a week."

"How am I going to feed the children for a week on ten dollars?"

"Alright. I'll give you twenty, but not a dime more. You just stay put in Baker City," he said.

Then he tossed two gold eagles at her feet and walked away as she reached down and picked up the two coins. It was the most money she had ever held.

Flo watched Bob walk away, then said, "I don't like this, Rebecca. I don't like it a bit. He's planning something. At least you got twenty dollars out of him. We'll set up outside of town. Maybe on a ranch southeast of town."

"That would be the worst idea of all, Betty. I have no idea what he's thinking of doing, but we have to stay together. I'm going to get that shotgun. Hugh said it was really easy to use. I'll go and ask Leo to show me."

"Heck, I can show you how to use a shotgun. It's as simple as you can get. You break it open, push in a pair of shells and close it. When you want to shoot, you pull back either one or two hammers, aim and pull the trigger. I've used one before. I've never fired both barrels, and I wouldn't recommend it. It'd probably break your shoulder."

"I'll go get it and you can show me how it works."

Rebecca climbed back into the wagon and retrieved the shotgun and two shells and ten minutes later, she knew how to use the simple, but very effective weapon.

Back at the Rocking M, Hugh had washed off the days of trail dust and felt better. He walked out to the main room where the two women sat talking and took the same chair he had used before.

"Mister McGinnis, what will happen if my parents or Susan's husband won't take us back?" Nancy asked.

"Then I'll see to it that you're properly provided for. I don't want either of you to worry one bit. Trust me, nothing bad is going to happen to either of you. And please, call me Hugh. I'm not that old."

For some inexplicable reason, they both believed his promise that they would be all right.

"Thank you, Hugh. Thank you for everything," said Nancy.

"Just trying to make things right, Nancy. Now, tomorrow, I'll get up early and go and retrieve my horses and gear from the trees. Then I'll come back and make breakfast."

Susan quickly said, "No, Hugh. We'll cook. We enjoy cooking. It was the rest of the stuff that we hated."

He smiled at them and said, "Alright. You can cook. It's just as well, I think Chester can cook better than I can."

They both laughed, and Hugh smiled.

"Now, ladies, if you don't mind, I'm going to get some sleep. Who gets which room?"

Susan answered, "You should use the first one. That's the main bedroom on this floor. You're a big man and need the space. We'll each take one of the others."

"I appreciate your generosity, ladies, and accept your offer. I haven't slept in a bed in almost five months, so it'll be an adventure."

They smiled at him, then stood and left the room to go to their assigned bedrooms. Hugh entered the first bedroom, and agreed that it was a large room, and the bed was far larger than most. He'd enjoy the space, but as he looked at it, he could imagine Brian sleeping there with his beautiful wife, Louise. She had been such a sweet woman. As soon as he met her, he knew why Brian had been so smitten, and now, they were both gone. He wondered why it seemed that he was destined to rescue women and children from bad men. *Where were all the good men like Brian?* He wished he had truly rescued the best woman of them all.

He finally disrobed and climbed into bed.

CHAPTER 8

As usual, Hugh woke early in the morning. Dawn had arrived, but barely. Hugh pulled out his pocket watch and noted it was five-fifteen. Since he had started his journey, he had to keep adjusting his pocket watch to keep it reasonably accurate, and he was sure it was time to do it again. But for now, it was five-fifteen, and it was time to get moving. He put on his pants and shirt but held off pulling on his boots for the time being. He wanted to try that new water closet.

He left the bathroom ten minutes later, impressed. Brian had turned the house into an engineering marvel. He really wanted to explore, but this was not the time. He'd shave later after he got some hot water.

He returned to the bedroom and pulled on his boots, then as Hugh was walking out of the bedroom and almost bowled over Nancy.

"Excuse me, Nancy. I was trying to be quiet. I thought I'd let you both sleep for a while."

"It's alright. It's the first time I was able to sleep without dread in a long time. I feel well-rested."

"Good. I'm going to get my horses and the mule. Did you want me to leave Chester with you?"

"He'll do that?"

"Sure. If I tell him to stay here, he'll wait."

"We'll give him something to eat, too."

"That will make you his new best friend. He's always hungry. You should have seen him when I found him, he was just skin and bones."

"He seems healthy now."

"He eats a lot. I'll be right back."

Hugh waved and walked out the front door. Even in the morning light, he could see why Brian bought the ranch. It was a beautiful setting.

He stepped down the stairs, turned to the south and walked toward the forest where he could already see the fallen branch. After he entered the trees, he found his camp five minutes later. The animals were all awake and grazing, so Hugh led them to the creek and let them drink.

When they were satisfied, he put on their saddles and loaded the mule, still avoiding using his still healing arm. In a few more days, he'd take out his own stitches.

He mounted Night and he led his little parade through the trees and once beyond the last line of pines, headed for the large barn that was a good hundred yards on the other side of the house. When he arrived, he stepped down and led the animals inside. He was pleasantly surprised to find four more horses, two mules and a nice wagon. There was even a well-maintained buggy. He wondered who had cared for the animals and rolling stock. It surely wasn't the Hanson brothers.

He put the animals into the stalls which filled all of them and he was thinking of putting them into the neighboring corral, but that would be later. He added some hay and poured some oats into the feed bins. The water trough was an interesting arrangement. There was a pipe with some sort of float that shut off a valve when the water level reached a certain depth. Brian again.

"You were one hell of a man, Brian," he said aloud.

Hugh left the barn and returned to the house through the back door. In the good light, he could see steps to the basement, and really wanted to check it out, but postponed it for another time.

Nancy and Susan were preparing breakfast as he entered. They both turned and smiled at him.

"Good morning, Hugh," said Susan.

"Good morning to you, Susan. I already talked to Nancy but failed in my cordiality by not wishing her a good morning. So, good morning, Nancy."

Nancy laughed, and said, "Good morning, Hugh."

They had prepared eggs, bacon and flapjacks. There was even butter and syrup.

"Wow! That's one delicious-looking breakfast."

Susan said, "Thank you. Now, please sit down and we'll bring you some food."

"Only if you two pretty ladies join me."

"We will."

The wagon train was moving and would be in Baker City by noon, and everyone was excited except for Rebecca. She was filled with a sense of doom, and Andy and Addie could sense it in their mother. They tried to cheer her up by telling her Mister Hugh stories, which didn't help, and even made her mood worse.

They understood the significance of the necklace she was wearing probably better than anyone else except for Hugh and Rebecca because they had watched as Blue Flower had given it to Mister Hugh with tears in her eyes. They knew that Blue Flower really liked Mister Hugh, that their mama liked Mister Hugh even more and Mister Hugh liked their mama. What they didn't understand is why they all weren't with Mister Hugh on his ranch, the Rocking M, southeast of Baker City.

Hugh had the buggy pulled out of the barn and brought out a black mare that Nancy had told him was used to pull the buggy.

"Another black mare," thought Hugh, "Night was going to have a small harem before long."

He drove the buggy to the house, Susan and Nancy clambered on board, one on each side.

Before he started the buggy rolling, Hugh asked, "You said they had set up a warning system. Do you know what it was?"

"No. It never went off. But it's on the access road somewhere."

"Alright. I'll take it slow."

He set out slowly down the main access road and had gone about eighty yards when he stopped. He had Susan get out, so he could check out what had caught his attention.

He carefully walked down the road to the thin wire he had seen reflecting in the bright morning sun. The steel wire was strung across the road about a foot off the ground, and his eyes followed it to a box lying low on the southern edge of the access road, where the wire ran inside. The top of the box was covered in grass, so it was almost unnoticeable. He came from behind, opened the top of the box and looked inside, finding a shotgun pointed upward at about a ten-degree angle. The steel line was attached to the trigger, and both hammers were cocked. Hugh whistled. That would blow anyone off their horse and probably kill the horse as well. He reached into the box, lowered both hammers, then he took his knife and cut the steel wire, creating a loud twang as the wire whipped across the road. He lifted the shotgun out of its box and returned to the buggy.

Both ladies' eyes were wide as he lowered the gun to the buggy floor.

"Susan, can either you or Nancy drive the buggy?"

"I can," Susan replied.

"Go ahead and start driving slowly behind me. I'll walk the rest of the road and make sure that there aren't any more traps. Whatever you do, do not let the horse get ahead of me."

"Okay, Hugh," she replied as she took the reins.

Hugh walked along and, sure enough, found two more of the deadly traps before reaching the road. He carried the other two shotguns and returned to the buggy.

He stepped in, set the two shotguns on the floor next to the first and let Susan drive in case he had to get out again.

"You do know how stupid this was, don't you?" he asked.

"The shotguns?" asked Susan.

"Yes, ma'am. If someone were going to try to capture them or kill them, they wouldn't come down the access road anyway so they wouldn't be spotted. They should have set them up in different places, but I got three nice shotguns out of the deal."

The thought of what would have happened if he hadn't been warned of the brothers' presence and just ridden innocently down the access road. It gave him the willies.

"Let's head to town, ladies," Hugh said as he leaned back in the seat, still amazed that those two morons terrorized the town, but they had done a good job with the shotgun booby traps, even if they were put in a useless position.

Susan suggested that they take Nancy to her home first because she was driving and didn't want to go home herself.

Once Susan had said that they'd go to Nancy's home, Hugh could see Nancy immediately tense.

"It'll be okay, Nancy. I'll be right there with you," Hugh said as he leaned forward to look around Susan.

She tried to smile in response to Hugh's reassurance, but failed.

Twenty minutes later, Susan stopped the buggy in front of a nice house with a subdued brown color. Hugh could see the

Baptist church next door and knew it must be Nancy's family home. He still thought she was exaggerating her parents' reaction, though. *How could any parents blame a daughter for what had happened to her?*

He stepped out, quickly walked to the other side, and helped Nancy from the buggy, feeling her hand trembling. She stood in place for a few seconds, staring at the house, then hesitantly began to walk as Hugh stepped alongside. They walked down the short walkway and stepped up onto the porch.

Hugh knocked on the darker brown door, and then stepped back as the door was opened by a stern-looking, middle-aged woman of medium height. He assumed it was the reverend's wife, Nancy's mother.

She looked at Hugh and then at Nancy but said nothing. There were no words of welcome, no joyous celebration of her return, just dead silence, so Hugh decided to intervene.

"Ma'am, my name is Hugh McGinnis. I own the Rocking M ranch and just arrived from Missouri. I found your daughter and Susan Fremont being held captive by the Hanson brothers in my home. I killed them both and freed your daughter and Mrs. Fremont. Your daughter had been a prisoner for months, and I'm sure she'll need your love and support now."

She looked at Hugh as if he were Satan himself, and then another, equally stern face appeared behind her. It was her husband, Reverend Nicholas Hurst.

"What are you doing on my porch, sir?" he demanded.

Hugh then realized that Nancy hadn't been exaggerating at all.

"Reverend, I just rescued your daughter from a horrible situation. I think you should welcome her return with the joy that any good Christian should."

"How dare you lecture me on the duties of a Christian? I have devoted my life to Jesus Christ, our savior," snapped her father.

"Then you, above all people, should readily accept your innocent daughter into your home and your hearts again. Didn't Jesus say, 'blessed be the merciful, for they shall find mercy'?"

The reverend turned deep red and stepped onto the porch. He was seething and Nancy stepped back, obviously having seen this face before.

"You will get this harlot from my porch, or I will have God smite you where you stand!"

Hugh was livid and didn't wait for God or anyone else to smite him. He did the smiting when, without warning, reached back and with one shot from his right fist crushed the reverend's jaw, sending him flying backwards into the house.

Then he looked at his stunned wife and growled, "You two will be following the Hanson brothers into hell for what you did today, you, heartless hypocrites!"

He turned to a stunned Nancy and said, "Come on, sweetheart, let's go back to the buggy. We're not welcome here."

She was so stunned by Hugh's blow to her father's face she just turned and let Hugh guide her from the porch but kept glancing back at her reverend father as he moaned on the floor. The good missus reverend just glared at them as they stepped away from the house and down their walkway.

Hugh escorted Nancy back to the buggy, helped her in, then walked around to the other side quickly and stepped into the buggy.

"Susan, let's go see your husband. Hopefully, you'll get a better reception that Nancy received from those two."

"Hugh, I'm not sure that I will," Susan replied.

"Let's hope so," Hugh said before leaning forward so he could see past Susan and asked, "Nancy, are you all right?"

She looked at Hugh with big eyes and said softly, "You struck my father."

"Yes, I did. I'm sorry. He's lucky I wasn't really mad, or I would have shot him. No man of God, or just plain man, should ever do that. He really raised my hackles."

A smile slowly began forming on Nancy's face as she said, "You knocked him off his feet, Hugh. He's been lecturing me for my entire life and you just lectured him for ten seconds. Thank you, Hugh. I feel so liberated."

Hugh didn't know what to make of that, but he was glad she wasn't too upset about his taking the wrath of God out on her father.

Susan snapped the reins and the buggy began rolling again, and after less than a mile drive, Susan stopped in front of a much smaller and more poorly maintained residence that was in dire need of a coat of whitewash.

"Do you want me to stay here, Susan?" Hugh asked.

"I'd rather you come with me, Hugh. If that's alright."

"Of course, I will," he said before he exited the buggy.

Hugh then offered Susan his hand to help her down and noticed that her hand wasn't trembling and wasn't even cold and clammy. Susan was ready for whatever happened when that door opened.

They walked to the porch-less house, and Hugh stayed one step behind Susan as she loudly knocked on the door and waited. A few seconds later the door opened, and a young woman opened it.

"Susan?" she asked with her eyes wide open.

"Nellie, what are you doing here? Where's Frank?" she asked.

"Um. He's at work right now. I, well, we thought you were gone, see. I knew he was lonely, and you know how we always got along and everything. So, well, I kind of stayed. I'm sure he'll be happy that you're not in that place anymore. But…"

Susan didn't wait to hear another word. She quickly turned to Hugh and said, "Let's go, Hugh. There's no point in my staying."

Hugh looked down at the mousy girl and said, "Nellie, you tell Frank that if I ever see him, he'll be unhappy to make my acquaintance."

She looked up at the huge man, then just nodded and closed the door.

He escorted Susan back to the buggy, but he climbed in first, took the reins and as soon as Susan was sitting, turned the buggy back toward the center of town.

"Susan, how are you doing?" he asked.

"I'm fine. I thought he'd been hanging around with Nellie shortly after we married. Nellie had a reputation for being friendly with the boys, but she always wanted Frank. Well, she can have him."

"If you don't mind my opinion, Susan, Frank's the big loser here. That girl has nothing. I saw it in her eyes. They were dull, spiritless eyes, and there's something else. I think she's pregnant. Just a wild guess, but I'd say four or five months or so. Once she has that baby, she'll tend to fat. Frank may try to make up with you, but if I were you, I'd file for divorce for adultery and get rid of him. You can do a lot better."

She smiled at him and said, "I was going to do just that, but I don't have the money."

"Money isn't a problem. You both can stay at the ranch until we figure out what you want to do. You know, it's a funny thing. I finally meet the woman that I was meant to be with, but she was married to a no-account man who didn't care one bit for her or her children, but I loved them all. But because of that little piece of paper, I had to let her go. Your husband is married to a pretty, smart and strong woman and he doesn't do anything to protect you. Instead he tosses that same little piece of paper into the wind like it meant nothing. Different views, I guess."

Susan and Nancy both looked at him before Susan asked, "Where did the woman and the children go?"

"She's probably within ten miles of where we are right now. She's in a wagon train that's probably already in town or neaby. It just doesn't matter if she's a mile or a thousand miles away. The problem is the children. She loves her children very much, and if she's unfaithful, there would be a real chance her bastard husband would hold the threat of taking the children from her to extract something. She couldn't bear to lose her children again, and I wouldn't allow it to happen, either."

"Were those the children you rescued?"

"Yes, ma'am. A few weeks ago. Anyway, let's head over to the town marshal and let him know that the Hanson brothers are no longer a menace and need to be moved off the Rocking M."

He turned the buggy onto the main street and soon stopped in front of the marshal's office, then they all stepped outside, and the two young women following him as he walked to the office.

Hugh opened the door, finding the same deputy at the desk.

The deputy saw Susan and Nancy and popped to his feet.

"Susan! Nancy! How are you? You got out!"

Susan snapped, "Yes, we did. No thanks to you!"

He shrunk back and took his seat.

Hugh asked, "Deputy, I thought you told me no one else was out at the ranch?"

"You asked about bad men, not women."

Hugh rolled his eyes in disbelief, then said, “I’ve got the almost naked bodies of the Hanson brothers decorating my front lawn. Can we notify the undertaker to ride out there and remove them?”

“*You killed the Hansons?*” he asked with wide eyes.

“No, deputy, I walked up to the door, knocked politely and asked them sweetly if they could release their two women hostages. Being the gentlemen that they were, they obliged.”

Susan and Nancy had their hands over their mouths to try and hide their obvious amusement as Hugh continued.

“Of course, I killed them. What was the reward on those two?”

“Five hundred dollars on each.”

“Give one payment to Nancy and the second to Susan. They deserve them. After the undertaker collects the body, when can they come and get their rewards?”

Susan and Nancy exchanged surprised glances.

“Um, I don’t know. The marshal is out at the moment. Um, I think it can be the day after tomorrow.”

“I’ll tell you what. I’ll save you some time and go and notify the undertaker myself. Did you want to have him bring the bodies here, so you can identify the bodies?”

“No. That’s alright. He can do that. Everybody knows them.”

“Fine. I’ll bring Susan and Nancy by in two days for their rewards.”

Then he turned to Susan and Nancy and said, “Ladies, one more stop before we head back, I’m afraid.”

Hugh turned and both women latched onto his arms without coordinating it beforehand. It just seemed like the thing to do.

He led them outside to the buggy and let Susan drive. He had no idea where the undertaker was, so she drove to the mortuary taking less than three minutes. Hugh popped out and said, “This should only take a minute.”

He walked into the undertaker’s parlor and was met by the epitome of undertakers. His face was long and featured a straight, thin nose, had slick black hair and dark eyes. He was one of those men you could guess his profession with a quick glance.

He looked up and said, “How may I help you, sir.”

“I have two bodies that need to be picked up and buried. They don’t need any formalities, nor do they require any special treatment. They’re lying on my front yard naked.”

The undertaker looked unaffected by Hugh’s comments and asked, “And where are these bodies?”

“The Rocking M.”

That did grab his attention before he said, “Um, sir, I’m not sure that we can go out to that location. It might prove somewhat hazardous.”

“The bodies belong to Jed and Julip Hanson.”

Another transformation occurred as the mortician cracked a smile.

"*They're dead? Both of them?"* he asked excitedly.

"As a doorknob."

"Well, praise be! In that case, I'll be more than happy to have my crew go out there and retrieve them as you requested, sir. There will be nothing special, and no charge, either. It will be with great personal satisfaction to put them both into the ground."

The undertaker then reached across his desk and shook Hugh's hand as he said, "A good day for Baker City. Yes, sir, a very good day indeed. I never did catch your name, sir."

"Hugh McGinnis."

"Are you related to Brian McGinnis?"

"He was my brother."

"Was?"

"He died in the war."

"I'm sorry to hear that. His wife and child are buried in a graveyard on the property."

"I'll find it and make sure that it's well kept."

"Thank you so much, Mister McGinnis."

"You're welcome."

He left the morticians, climbed aboard the buggy, took reins from Susan, and they were soon rolling out of town. As they came to the junction of the southeastern road, he could see the first of the covered wagons in the distance. Rebecca had arrived.

He turned the buggy to the southeast road and had the horse moving at a good clip.

"Is that her wagon train, Hugh?" asked Susan.

"Yup," was all he could muster.

Nancy asked, "Hugh, why did you give me and Susan the rewards? That's a lot of money."

"Because Nancy, you and Susan need it and those bastards' deaths should have some purpose. The money will be able to help you both get started again."

"I'm not sure that it will work here, Hugh," said Susan, "You saw the reaction we got when we got back, even in the marshal's office. It's like we did this on purpose."

"A lot of people have narrow minds. Don't lump everyone into that category, Susan."

"Hugh, you seem a lot wiser than someone your age. You look like you're twenty-five, but you talk like you're fifty."

Hugh laughed and said, "I guess it's because I've seen so many bad things, but then I see some truly miraculous things that balance it out. I found out early in my life that I could either concentrate on the bad things or the miraculous things. I chose to look for life's miracles and try to eliminate the bad that was within my power to do. That's why I want to help you both. Each of you has potential for a lot of miracles."

The buggy rolled on with a quiet Hugh McGinnis and two quickly recovering young women.

The wagon train settled into a large field just outside of town that had obviously been used by other wagon trains in the past. They still had another hundred and fifty miles to go, but some already announced their intention to stay in Baker City.

The first one off the wagons and to head into town was Bob Orson, but he left Ella in the wagon this time. She was anxious because she knew what he was going to do, and she was pleased in one respect because she knew that soon she'd be able to marry Bob. Yet she felt deeply guilty because she was aware of the consequences for Rebecca and the children.

She believed Bob about the adultery charge, so most of the guilt was about the two children. She had never gotten pregnant and wanted a baby badly. That was part of the reason for her latching onto Bob. Even as she thought about that possibility, she rubbed her lower belly hoping that she was with child.

Bob reached the town and began looking for the courthouse, understanding that most law offices were nearby. He found the courthouse quickly and sure enough, there were two law offices across the street. He walked into the first and was met by a clerk who asked him his business and was then directed to the second attorney who handled divorces.

He stepped into the second office and met another clerk, explained his problem and was soon talking to the attorney. The lawyer assured Bob that he could win his divorce based on adultery by his wife. He just needed one witness, and Bob assured the lawyer that he had one and signed some paperwork. He paid the fee and left the office just thirty minutes after entering.

He already had a court date and an official piece of paper he couldn't understand that he would have to give to Rebecca.

He had believed that he could just get the divorce and give it to her, but this meant that she'd have to be there for the hearing, but it wouldn't matter. Ella would testify about the necklace and how Rebecca and Hugh McGinnis would go off into the night to his campsite, leaving the children alone.

He was almost giddy as he headed back to the wagon. Ella's seven hundred dollars were as good as his. He'd have his land now and returned to the wagon almost skipping along. What he would do with Ella wasn't on his mind.

Hugh and the women arrived back at the ranch, seeing the two pink bodies on the front yard, almost white in the bright mid-day sun. They drove past without looking and headed for the barn, and once Hugh brought the buggy to a halt, the two ladies went into the house through the back door, as Hugh unharnessed the mare and put her back into her stall, then rolled the buggy back into position.

As he headed back to the house, he saw a wagon approaching. It was driven by two big men, and Hugh stayed and watched as they rolled up the drive. Hugh unhooked his hammer loop and continued to watch, and then just before they reached the house, they turned and stopped. Both men quickly dropped from the wagon, then grabbed the two pink brothers, tossed the bodies into their wagon like bad meat, climbed back into the driver's seat and simply drove off without ever saying a word.

As he watched them leave, he noticed the low line of clouds along the western horizon. It looked like a storm was coming, but being new to the area, he had no idea what form it would take.

He went inside where Susan and Nancy were preparing lunch and asked, “What’s for lunch, ladies?”

“We’ll surprise you. Go ahead and do what you want to do. We’ll have it ready in twenty minutes.”

“Okay. Oh, by the way, the front yard is now free of any debris, and it looks like we’ll be getting rain in a few hours.”

Hugh went off to clean his pistol, now that his cleaning kit was available. He’d have to check for weapons in the house later.

Susan and Nancy were chatting as they prepared lunch.

“What do you think about all this?” asked Nancy.

“About what in particular?”

“Yesterday, we were little more than slaves, with the whole sex thing thrown in and now we’re being treated like queens and we’re going to have a lot of money. Doesn’t that seem odd to you?”

“Odd how?”

“I mean, can anyone be that nice? He hasn’t done anything but try to make us feel better. When he smashed my father in the chin, I was elated. Then everything he says is to make us feel good about ourselves. What do you think he really wants?”

“Really, Nancy? You’ve got to understand Hugh. He’s exactly what he appears to be. I don’t think he has any secret motives at all. He saw that we needed help and he’s done that. We both owe him everything, but I don’t believe he sees it that way. My only question is where do we go from here? I know he'd let us stay as long as we want to, but that wouldn't be fair to him, either. He needs to find his own life. He really loves that woman on the wagon train. Maybe we could do something to help. I don't know how. I do know one thing for sure, though."

"And that is?"

"She's the luckiest woman on the planet," Susan said.

The luckiest woman on the planet wasn't feeling that way at all. Bob had just delivered her notice of his divorce filing claiming adultery as its basis. She was devastated because she knew that courts tended to favor men in cases like this, and also knew that if the divorce was granted, there was a good chance she would lose her children.

"Rebecca, we've got to fight this," Betty said.

"How? The hearing is the day after tomorrow. Almost everyone else we know will be gone."

"I'm staying. I'll testify for you."

"I know, and I appreciate it, Betty. But they'll just say you're my friend and sticking up for me. I don't know how I can win this. And even if I win, I'll lose. He'll still be here, and I won't have anything, and maybe not even my children."

The children were in back listening to their mother's laments and understood some of it. Mister Orson was saying bad things about their mama and Mister Hugh that would hurt their mama. Andy and Addie knew that this wasn't right.

Addie slid toward the front of the wagon, looked at her mother and said, “Mama, Mister Hugh can fix it. Mister Hugh can fix anything.”

“I know, sweetie, but this doesn’t involve Mister Hugh.”

“But Mister Hugh loves you, Mama!”

“I know, Addie. I love Mister Hugh, too. But this is a fight between me and Mister Orson.”

Addie’s parting comment was, “You should go see Mister Hugh at the Rocking M ranch, southeast of Baker City.”

Betty looked at Rebecca and said, “She’s right, you know. Hugh probably could come up with something, and he’s named as your adulterer. Doesn’t he have to be there anyway?”

“I don’t know. I’m not sure about this, Betty, and bringing Hugh into this might make it worse. If I’m asked how I feel about him after swearing to tell the truth, it could be a disaster.”

“Rebecca, you really have no options at this point. You’re going to risk losing your children. Let’s go and find Hugh.”

As much as she didn’t want to bring Hugh into this, she longed to see him again and it was the deciding factor.

“Let’s go and find Mister Hugh,” she finally said.

There as a loud cheer from back of the wagon before Betty and Rebecca stepped down from the driver’s seat to harness the team. They were ready to roll in twenty minutes.

———

Hugh was enjoying a fabulous lunch. Susan and Nancy had cut some cheddar cheese and melted it over some sausages and added some mild mustard and sauerkraut.

"This is amazing, ladies. This has so much flavor. Who taught you how to make this?"

They both smiled at his praise.

"We made it up, Hugh," answered Nancy.

"What did you think of it?" he asked.

"We haven't tried it."

"What? That will never do. Here. Take a taste," he said.

He sliced off two chunks and put one on his fork. He put one in Susan's mouth and then one in Nancy's.

They nodded as they chewed.

"I see potential here, Susan and Nancy. This is extraordinary," he said as he took another bite himself.

He finished his lunch and sat back.

"Amazing. But let me ask you both something. When things are settled down, I may open a doctor's office in town. I know I haven't finished my last year yet, but all of that was field learning anyway, and I learned a lot more during the war. If I opened a doctor's office, I'd need a nurse and a receptionist/secretary. I see a lot of potential in each of you. What do you think?"

The suggestion came as a huge surprise to them both.

"You mean us?" Susan asked with arched eyebrows.

Hugh made a show of turning and looking around the room.

"No, I mean the other two pretty young ladies behind me. Yes, I mean you. I realize that not everyone is cut out for the medical field, but I really would need a nurse to help me with patients and a receptionist/secretary to handle the administrative side of the office. With as few jobs available to women that mean anything, these are two that would open up to anything you'd want."

"I'm not very fond of blood, Hugh," said Nancy.

Susan replied, "It doesn't bother me. I grew up on a farm and had to slaughter pigs and do other nasty things."

"Alright, then. Nancy could be the receptionist and Susan could be the nurse. What do you think of those options?"

"Hugh, I don't have the skills to be a nurse," replied Susan.

"As smart as you both are, I think I could train you both very quickly. As you work, you'll learn, Susan. It's the way it always has been. I'd show you the basics and then you'd watch and absorb. As you go along, you'll get better every day, and what is most important, you'll both be respected, professional women. You'll be well-paid and probably attract the attention of every available bachelor in the area."

Susan smiled, and asked, "And what makes you so sure that's an incentive?"

Hugh laughed as he replied, "You've got me there."

Then he sobered and said seriously, "I just want the best for you both. I'd have the added enjoyment of watching you both grow into your potential. It's a very selfish motive on my part."

"I'm sure it is. It sounds hideously selfish," Nancy said with a smile.

"Well, you both think about it. It'll take me a few months to get everything together. I'm debating about just opening the office here instead of in town. It's only four miles out. I'd be able to make house calls."

"Do you have to buy all that medical stuff?" asked Nancy.

"Everything but my stethoscope. I still have that with me."

Susan seemed interested and asked, "Can I listen through it?"

"Sure, let me go and get it."

Hugh rose, went to his room and had to hunt a bit to find it, but soon found the stethoscope, pulled it out of its bag and returned to the kitchen.

"What do you want to listen to, Susan?"

"Could I hear your heart?"

"Sure."

He handed the earpiece end to Susan and placed the cup over his chest.

She put the earpieces into her ears, looked at him and then at his chest. Finally, she pulled the earpieces free and smiled.

"That's amazing. I could hear the different parts of the heart. Then there was this background noise that sounded like a tunnel."

Hugh smiled, and said, “Very good, Susan. What you heard was the ventricles and atria in my heart pumping the blood and the background noise was my breathing. I purposely placed the stethoscope in a location where you could hear both.”

“I think I’d really like being your nurse, Hugh.”

“I’m glad to hear it. Nancy, are you good with being the receptionist/secretary? You’d control the flow of patients, set up appointments and keep all the records straight.”

“I’d enjoy that.”

“Good. I don’t have my office yet, but my staff is all set.”

The house suddenly shook when a violent boom rocked the area.

“Sounds like our rainstorm has arrived. I’m going to let Chester in until it blows over.”

Hugh went out to the main room, stepped onto to the porch and called Chester, who came running into the house as if he were shot out of a cannon, then gratefully sat down near the fireplace. Hugh stayed out on the porch for another minute and could see the weather approaching. Ten minutes later, the heavy rain was thrumming on the roof and lightening stroked the sky followed by the rumble and crack of thunder.

———

Two miles down the road, Betty and Rebecca were driving the oxen through the suddenly muddy mess that had been a road. The oxen plowed on with the wagon sliding sideways when the wind hit.

"How much longer, Rebecca? Do you know?" Betty asked just short of a shout to be heard over the howling wind.

Rebecca shouted back, "I think only a mile or two."

Both women were huddled against the rain but hadn't expected the sudden downpour and weren't really dressed for it. Another twenty or thirty minutes driving the tall wagon in this mess would be difficult. All they could hope for was that it didn't get any worse.

———

Hugh had returned to the sitting room with the ladies.

"You know, I never did ask how old you both were. Now, I had Susan pegged at twenty and Nancy at nineteen. How close was I?"

They looked at each other and laughed.

"You're scary, Hugh. Did you want to try for birthdates now?"

"No, I'll quit while I'm ahead."

"How old are you?" asked Susan, "I'd guess twenty-eight or twenty-nine."

"Sorry, you're a bit off. I just turned twenty-six. I just look older."

"No, I was basing that on your education. I thought to be a doctor you'd have to be at least twenty-six. Then, you said you traveled after the war, so that adds a couple of more years. But, if I saw you walking down the street, I would have guessed twenty-five."

"Good recovery," he said with a smile.

They all laughed as the storm continued to rage outside and the winds grew more savage.

Susan then asked, "How did you know that Nellie was pregnant so fast? You just looked at her for a minute or so."

"It wouldn't have been such a fast diagnosis if she hadn't been so far along, but the physical changes were all there, and I noticed that she was already showing, despite her attempts to hide it."

"Oh. You know that means that she was probably pregnant before I was taken here, don't you?" Susan asked.

"I know. I got the impression from listening to you that you weren't very surprised."

"No, I wasn't surprised at all," Susan replied before the house shook with a nearby lightning strike and an almost instant explosion of thunder.

A half mile down the road, there was no laughter or normal conversation. The wagon was stuck, and those powerful winds were threatening to push the wagon off the road into the shallow ravine.

"What do we do, Rebecca? Do we ride it out?" Betty yelled, almost in a panic.

"I don't know. We've got to be close to Hugh's ranch. I think I'll try to get there and see if he can come and get everyone. It's not that cold, and I should be able to get there in a few minutes."

"What if it's further away?"

"I'll only go a few hundred yards. If I see the entrance, I'll go on. If not, I'll come back."

"Okay. I'll watch for you."

Rebecca nodded and slid down, her new shoes sinking into the mud and started walking, wishing she had worn her new boots. She lifted her skirt to give her more mobility, but the mud still made it difficult to move and soon her dress was so soaked it didn't matter anymore. It took her almost a minute to make just fifty yards, but she kept going, and soon Betty lost sight of her in the driving rain.

As Rebecca slogged forward, each step became a difficult exercise as the mud sucked at her shoes, threatening to rip them from her feet. Between the mud and that constant wind, she began to feel her strength ebbing away.

———

Hugh left Susan and Nancy to go out to the porch and watch the storm. Something about violent weather appealed to him. He had never seen a tornado and always wanted to, but not now at the cost of the house. He stared as the rain blew almost horizontally from the east, glad to be in the lee of that wind. The lightning bolts were now mostly to the east, so at least the center of the storm had passed.

———

Rebecca was about to turn around when she barely noticed the Rocking M ranch sign through the pelting rain. She smiled and tried to pick up her pace, but what she wanted to do and what she was physically capable of doing were two totally different things. She was going as fast as she could, one struggling, sucking footstep after another. She finally reached the sign and turned into the ranch and could barely make out the lights from the ranch house in the distance and she felt renewed hope as she struggled down the access road. The house was about a quarter of a mile away, she guessed, just four hundred and forty measly yards. She began to beg her legs to cooperate and reach Hugh as she felt the last of her energy leaving her.

Hugh was preparing to turn back to the house when he saw something moving down the access road, which surprised him. It was much too small to be a rider, and no animal would be out on a day like this. He stared, as the shape was coming slowly closer. He focused and then recognized the dress. *My God! It was a woman! What was she doing out there?*

It didn't matter who she was, Hugh leapt from the porch and tried to run but slid more. He dropped down off the road into the grass. It was wet but provided better footing. He moved much quicker than the woman did, aided by his longer, stronger legs and the fact he hadn't had to fight his way through the mud and wind as long as Rebecca had.

Rebecca was exhausted and wasn't sure that she'd make it, no matter how badly she wanted to reach the house. Each time she pulled her foot out of the mud, it became harder. The mud sucked her foot back as if it wanted to swallow her. She looked up and saw the ranch house lights even closer now. She was almost there.

Then she saw someone running to her, and it looked like Hugh. No, it couldn't be. It was her imagination playing tricks on her. Hugh wouldn't be out here in the rain. She started to laugh at herself for imagining things as she tried to pull her foot out, but it wouldn't come free and she felt trapped.

Hugh got within fifty yards and realized that it was Rebecca. She still wore Blue Flower's necklace.

He shouted, "Rebecca! Rebecca! I'm coming!"

Rebecca heard his shout, and it sounded like Hugh. She lifted her head again, and when she saw Hugh twenty feet away, she started crying and laughing at the same time.

Before she knew what was happening, she was being swept up from the sticking mud and carried in Hugh's strong arms. She wrapped her arms around his neck and rested her head against his chest and didn't worry anymore. Hugh would save her and the children.

Hugh stayed on the grass and walked steadily. He didn't rush as the wind and rain continued to drive across his face.

"Rebecca! Where are the children? Are they safe?" he asked loudly.

"They're down the road with Betty in her wagon. Not far," she whispered as loudly as she could as Hugh finally reached the porch.

Hugh hurriedly opened the door and brought Rebecca inside.

"Susan! Nancy! This is Rebecca. She needs your help. I'll take her into the big bedroom. I want you to take off all her wet clothes, dry her off and cover her with a couple of blankets. I'm going to get the buggy and go down the road to get her children and her friend."

Neither woman panicked as they followed him into the bedroom, where he laid Rebecca down on the bed and said to her, "Rebecca, Susan and Nancy will help you get undressed to get you dry and under the blankets. I'm going to go and get the children and Betty."

Rebecca was drifting in and out and heard the names Susan and Nancy. *Who were they?* She felt gentle hands helping her undress, women's hands. *What were women doing here with Hugh?*

Hugh slipped his way across the yard to the barn. He was going to hitch up the horse but decided to use the mule. It was a lot stronger than the small horse, so he quickly harnessed the animal and hopped on. The mule may not have been happy with the new job, but it didn't have a choice. He pulled the buggy easily out of the barn and headed down the entrance road. Hugh was glad he used the mule and vowed to treat him with more respect.

He turned onto the road and got as much speed out of the mule as he dared.

A half mile ahead, Betty was worried. The wagon was slipping, driven by the perpendicular wind and had almost reached the edge of the roadway. There wasn't a deep chasm on the other side, but there was a steep bank of thirty feet. This was turning into a dangerous situation, so she started trying to drive the oxen to pull the wagon just a few more feet onto the roadway. They began to move but moving meant that the wheels were now free of the mud buildup that had been created as the wagon had moved sideways, creating natural chocks. Once back onto the muddy road, it began to slide even faster toward that chilling edge.

Hugh saw the wagon ahead and also saw its predicament and started to figure out a way to keep it from being blown off the road.

Betty saw the buggy approaching and knew it must be Hugh. *Rebecca had made it!* She didn't know if he'd reach her in time, though, but Hugh finally arrived, and had a plan to save the wagon.

He pulled the buggy to a sudden stop, hopped out and pulled both pistols.

Betty saw him and wondered if he had gone crazy, as he cocked the hammer to his revolver.

Hugh went to the rear wheel near the center of the road and started shooting at its spokes. First one was obliterated after three shots. The second took four, two from the first pistol and two from his second, leaving just three shots left. He fired one, then his second. As he was getting ready to fire the third, the spoke snapped, the wheel splintered, and the wagon lurched to that side and sat into the mud.

He holstered his pistols, walked to the front of the wagon and shouted, "Okay, Betty, your wagon's not going anywhere now. Let's get the children out of the wagon. Start handing them down to me."

Betty nodded, then began dropping children into Hugh's waiting arms. Andy came first. Hugh sat him on the buggy's seat and told him to slip to the right. Next came Addie and once he had her in his arms, Hugh passed her to Andy and told him to have her sit on his lap. Charles came next and Hugh sat him down next to Andy. Finally, he helped Betty out of the wagon. He climbed into the buggy and then Betty climbed in. He put Charles on her lap, and now, he had to turn this thing around, wishing he'd done it when it wasn't so heavily loaded, but it was too late now.

He snapped the reins and the mule was able to get the buggy moving. Hugh was relieved that the buggy could move at all and found a flat spot next to the roadway, turned the mule onto it and made a successful direction change. They began their journey back to his ranch as the buggy kept rocking violently in the pounding wind.

Rebecca was regaining her awareness which immediately told her that she was naked, but dry and under blankets feeling warm and snug. She looked to her left and saw two pretty young women nearby.

"Who are you?" she asked softly.

"I'm Susan and this is Nancy. Hugh told us you were Rebecca. He's gone to get your children. Are those the same children he rescued?"

Rebecca was more than mildly confused, but replied, "Yes. How did you know?"

"He told us. He said that you were the one woman he was meant to be with."

As wonderful as it was to hear that Hugh had said that, the source surprised her and she asked, "He told you that? Why?"

Susan replied, "Because I'm still married to a man that took up with another woman just after I was abducted. He commented on the difference."

"*You were kidnapped?*" Rebecca asked as the shocking revelations kept arriving.

"Nancy and I both were. We were held in this house by two rotten brothers that had the whole town terrified."

Rebecca then understood, smiled and asked, “Let me guess. Hugh came in and shot them both, didn’t he?”

Susan returned her smile and answered, “Yes, he did. And then he’s treated us both like we were queens. He’s even giving us the big reward that had been posted for them. Then he said he was going to open a medical office and I could be the nurse and Nancy the receptionist. He said we could become respected professionals and we both accepted his offer. Neither of us can believe the change in our lives in just one day. Your Hugh is an amazing man.”

“I know. But he’s not my Hugh. I’m still married. That’s why I came to see him. I need his help.”

“I have a suspicion that he’ll be able to solve your problem.”

“That’s what my daughter, Addie, said.”

The buggy had finally made it down the access road and Hugh stopped in front of the porch. He let Andy clamber out first and then Charles left from the other side. Betty then stepped out of the buggy and led Charles inside.

“That leaves us, Addie. Where’s Sophie?” he asked.

“I left her in the wagon. Will she be all right?”

“She’ll be fine. I’ll go get her tomorrow. Okay?”

Addie smiled and gave him a hug before asking, “Will you help mama, Mister Hugh?”

“Of course, I will, Addie,” Hugh replied, not understanding Rebecca’s predicament.

Addie gave him a kiss and Hugh slid across the seat then stepped out and picked up Addie. He took Andy's hand and stepped onto the porch, entered the house and headed straight to Rebecca's bedroom, passing Betty and Charles who were dripping as they stood in the room.

"I'll be right back, Betty," Hugh said as they passed.

Betty understood his priorities, smiled and just nodded.

Once past the threshold, Hugh smiled and said, "Rebecca, I thought you might have lost something."

"Mama!" Addie cried as Hugh lowered her to the floor.

"Thank you again, Hugh. Can we talk?" Rebecca asked.

"In a few minutes, I have to put the buggy away, and I also owe a mule an apology."

"I'll see you when you get back."

"I'll be back shortly," he said before he turned to Susan and said, "Susan, can you and Nancy help Betty, who's in the front room with her son? We need to get everyone dry and into something warm until I can get out to the wagon and get their things."

Susan and Nancy quickly stood and said, "We'll do all we can, Hugh."

Hugh smiled then turned, and quickly returned to the main room, and didn't have to explain to Betty because Susan and Nancy were right behind him.

Hugh went back out into the storm and just led the mule back into the barn, unharnessed the mule and put him in his stall, brushed him down and gave him extra oats. He patted him on the neck and said, "I owe you for this heroic performance and apologize for all the bad things I said about you. Maybe if I gave you a good name, so you'd feel better. How about Victor? That's a nice, dignified name."

The mule didn't reply, so Hugh just laughed and said, 'Victor it is."

He patted him one more time and returned to the storm. He was totally soaked when he entered the kitchen, so he removed his shirt and took a towel before he returned to his bedroom to get a new shirt and saw fourteen eyes looking at him. Eight belonged to mature females of the species, and they all enjoyed the show.

"Excuse me folks, I just need to get through here and grab a new shirt."

For some reason, the path was blocked, so it took another minute to retrieve his shirt and put it on.

"Alright, now that you bunch of lecherous women will let me sit down. I need to take off my boots as well. I'll leave my pants on, if you don't mind."

Betty said, "We were hoping," then she started laughing.

Hugh looked at Charles and Andy and said, "We're outnumbered, men. Wait! I can even the odds. Chester! Come."

Chester bounded into the room and sat at Hugh's feet. The three children were happy to see the dog again and rewarded him with a lot of petting and scratching.

After he had commented on the lack of males, he looked at Betty's young son and asked, "Say, Charles, do you like being called Charles?"

His eyebrows furrowed, and he replied, "No. I hate it. The other boys make fun of me and say I'm a sissy."

"I thought that might be so. Boys can be mean like that. I think you should go by one of the other names for Charles. Now, Charlie is one, but I always thought kids named Charlie were a bit goofy. It seems like every one of them grew up to be someone's odd Uncle Charlie. But, how about Chuck? Chuck is a good man's name. You know, a bunch of guys are sitting around playing poker and you walk in. All the other manly men look your way, grin and say, 'Hey, look, Chuck's here. Good old Chuck.'"

Charles eyes lit up before he turned to his mother and asked, "Can I be called Chuck now, Mama? I like it a lot. Then none of the other boys will tease me."

Betty looked at Hugh and shook her head.

"You never stop, do you?" she said, then turned to her son, "If you want it to be called that, it's fine with me."

Hugh smiled at him and said, "And Chuck, if any one of those boys try to tease you again, you remind him that you're friends with the guy who shot all them Injuns."

Chuck nodded and happily joined Andy and Addie in exploring the house as Chester trailed after them. They were all wrapped in blankets and even as they ran away, they began whooping like little Indians.

Hugh finally turned to a smiling Rebecca and asked, "Rebecca, you must have one serious trouble to be coming out here and Addie already asked if I could help you, so I can only imagine it has something to do with your husband."

Rebecca lost her smile, sighed, and said, "It does. He delivered a paper today from the county court. It was a filing for a divorce with the hearing the day after tomorrow. He's accused me of adultery and named you as my partner."

Hugh smiled at her and said, "It's kind of ironic, isn't it, Rebecca? The only time your skin has ever touched mine was in front of fifty people as you held my arm together while I sutured that wound. Meanwhile, your bastard of a husband has been enjoying Ella Murphy's favors and everyone knows it."

Susan interrupted by asking, "You sewed up your own arm?"

"I had to. No one else could do it. Rebecca was the only one who helped, too. I had only known her for a day, but it seemed like it was a lot longer after listening to her children talk about her constantly for days."

He then turned his eyes back to Rebecca, and asked, "Rebecca, aside from Betty, are there any other witnesses we can call to dispute Ella's testimony, which I'm sure she'll give to get him permanently into her bed?"

"No. Almost all of them will be gone, and I'm not that familiar with the few that will remain."

"Well, let me think about this. Let me ask you something else. The last few times I saw Bob with Ella, it seemed that she was doing all the attaching and Bob was indifferent at best. If he's already tired of her, which I think he is, what's his motive for doing this?"

"You know, you're right," Rebecca said as she thought about it, "He was all grabby when they were first together, but a few days ago, it was like he didn't want to be near her. As far as motive, the only thing I can imagine is that he wants her rig and her money. We lost everything in the crash except our oxen and the money in the community wagon, which he already has."

"How much did she have?"

"I don't know."

The blanked-shrouded Betty answered, "Over seven hundred dollars. She had the biggest single account in there."

Hugh nodded and said, "That explains that. Alright, Rebecca, don't you worry about a thing, just stay warm and recover. You have plenty of female support here. I need to think about this. A stupid plan is already worming its way through my head."

He looked down into her bright eyes, smiled and said, "Don't worry, Rebecca, not one whit. I'll make Bob wish he had never heard my name."

She smiled and kept his gaze as she said, "I know, Hugh. That's why I came. It was Addie who convinced me. She thinks you can fix anything."

"Not anything, but I think I can handle this. I just need some time alone. Now, your dress is drying in the other room. It'll be dry enough soon. Susan and Nancy both need more clothes soon, too. How about you, Betty?"

"I can always get more."

"I know you probably have five more dresses in the wagon, Rebecca. But you need to find a dress that screams 'innocent' when we go to the courtroom. I'll take the wagon over to Betty's wagon tomorrow and mount a new wheel."

"What happened to the old one?" asked Rebecca, "They were all in good shape."

Betty replied, "Because Mister Hugh unloaded his guns into the spokes."

Rebecca looked at Hugh with raised eyebrows.

"The wagon was going to be blown off the road into the ditch, so I shot out the spokes to make it sit on the ground tilted into the wind. Replacing the wheel is a lot easier than replacing the wagon and having to go down there and get the contents out of it. Right now, I'm going to head out to the sitting room for a while. Something is there in the back of my mind, but I'm missing it right now. I'll see you later when you're dressed, Rebecca."

Rebecca just nodded. She was calmer, yet still apprehensive. She didn't know what Hugh could do to help her out of this devil of a dilemma.

Inside Ella's wagon, Bob and Ella waited out the storm.

"Ella, everyone else is leaving in the morning. Even the ones that said they'd stay. It turns out Baker City isn't the paradise they hoped for, but in three days, we can get married."

"Bob, we don't have to wait another three days to enjoy ourselves. You haven't made love to me in three days now. Don't you want me anymore? I sure want you."

Bob had to be attentive, knowing that there was still a chance that he might lose her even now.

"Of course, I want you, Ella. Come here."

He began fondling her and she began making those irritating guttural moans. He gritted his teeth and continued, and it wasn't too long before he was fulfilling her requirements.

Ella knew he had taken her, but she still felt empty. She wanted more but didn't push it. He was just stressed because of the divorce, she told herself. He'd pay her more attention after they were married.

———

Hugh was still lost in his thoughts when Susan announced dinner was ready. Hugh still hadn't come up with anything and it bothered him. He walked into the kitchen and decided to eat standing up than force his way into the crowded table.

Betty looked at Hugh and knew he was stumped.

"Come up with anything, Hugh?"

"No. Not a thing. Something is running around in the back of my head, but I can't grab it."

"This would all be a lot easier if you could just give them a test and see who's lying and who's telling the truth."

That idea that Hugh had running around in the back of his head suddenly sprinted to the front and exploded.

"Betty! You're a genius!" he shouted.

Hugh walked over to Betty and kissed her on the lips, then quickly left the kitchen grinning like the Cheshire cat.

The adults all looked at each other.

"What was that all about?" asked Susan.

"I don't care what it was about," replied a rapturous Betty.

"Now, doesn't beat all," commented Rebecca.

"What?" Betty asked.

"Here I am being accused of adultery with the man and you've been kissed by him once more than I have."

Susan and Nancy exchanged smiles but wondered what Hugh had suddenly conceived.

Hugh was energized. He knew what he had to do but needed to know how to do it and that would require a visit to the chemist tomorrow.

CHAPTER 9

Hugh was the first one up in the morning, as usual. He had just lain in bed for a long time before falling asleep, running through the entire wacky scheme he had come up with and it was still in the foreground of his thoughts when he awakened.

He started the cookstove and had some hot water soon for shaving, then went into the bathroom, washed and shaved, before he returned to the kitchen and made coffee. There was stirring in the house behind him and he hoped it was Rebecca.

He turned, sought her eyes and found them focused on his.

"Good morning, fair Rebecca."

"Good morning, Hugh. You're up early as usual."

"I made some coffee. Would you like some?"

"Please."

Hugh poured them each a cup of coffee and they sat down at the kitchen table.

"Ours is such a strange relationship, Rebecca."

"That, Hugh, is the understatement of the century."

"Tomorrow, that will all change. There will be no danger of losing your children. I know that worries you more than anything, but I think I have a way to prevent that. I can't tell you about it because I need your reaction in the courtroom to be totally normal. Will you trust me, Rebecca?"

"With my life, Hugh, and more importantly, with my children's lives."

They were still staring into each other's eyes when another adult stepped into the kitchen.

"How are you this morning, Rebecca?" Susan asked.

Rebecca and Hugh broke eye contact and turned as Rebeca replied, "I'm fine, Susan. How are you?"

"Great. Never better. Would you like some breakfast, Hugh, or are you just going with coffee today?"

"I'm not sure. I need to get that wagon brought in. It's only a half mile down the road, so I think I'll just roll a replacement wheel down there rather than taking the buggy. I already looked outside, and the wind has dried out the mud already. It looks like it's a clear day and a warm one, so I think I'll head out in a minute. I may have something when I get back, though."

"We'll save something for you," Susan said.

"Thanks. I'm off, then."

He took once last glance at Rebecca before he left the house through the kitchen door. He went to the barn, found the spare wheel, greased it just in case Betty's wagon was low on grease, then he began rolling it. It was almost like a game as he spun the wheel down the access road and then turned onto the road heading toward the stricken wagon. He'd roll it and trot to catch up to it and reached the wagon in just six minutes.

He set the wheel on the ground, and looked underneath the wagon, found the jack and put it in place under the axle, loosened the holding nut one turn then began lifting the heavy wagon, surprised the jack didn't sink at all. The mud had dried as hard as rock. He finally got the wagon high enough to remove the destroyed wheel, removed the nut and slid the remains of the shattered wheel from the axle. He slipped the new wheel into place, tightened the nut and backed it off. He then replaced the pin and put the damaged wheel in the foot well, not that it was useful for anything more than kindling now.

The oxen were awake but didn't seem to care much about his being there. He knew they were probably hungry, but he'd take care of that shortly.

An hour after leaving the ranch, the wagon pulled up next to the house. He went into the kitchen where everyone was eating.

"Betty, your wagon is outside. I'm going to go let the oxen graze. Did you want to unload the whole thing and stay here? We have plenty of room."

"Hugh, you have three bedrooms," she replied.

"Susan, will you enlighten Betty while I go and take care of the oxen?"

He hopped back outside, unhitched the team of oxen and let them go into the pasture and graze and drink in the stream.

After he'd gone, Susan said, "Betty, the house has seven bedrooms and some rooms we don't even know about. There are three upstairs and four downstairs, and there's another bathroom, too. And there's one room that has a thick wooden door that's always cold. I don't know why, but you can keep milk and butter and meat in there and it doesn't go bad for a long time."

"Sounds like Hugh's brother knew what he was doing," Betty said as Hugh walked back into the kitchen.

"Ladies, today, I need to run some errands in town. Susan and Nancy need to buy some more clothes and Rebecca needs that innocent dress. Susan, I'll set up the buggy so you three can go shopping. How much do you need?"

"I think forty dollars should be enough."

"Piker. Here."

He gave Susan a hundred dollars and said, "Spend it all if you can. I won't take long and should be back a little after noon."

He trotted back outside to prepare the buggy.

―――

Susan stood there looking at the wad of cash in her hand, looked up at Rebecca and asked, "Rebecca?"

She smiled and replied, "It's him. Get used to it."

―――

Hugh saddled Night and led the buggy and Night to the back of the house, hitched the buggy to the back rail and mounted Night.

He turned the tall stallion away from the house, and soon had him in a fast trot toward Baker City.

―――

In Baker City, City Marshall Will Ambrose was questioning his deputy.

"Are you sure you got the name right?"

"Yes, sir. Hugh McGinnis."

"It wasn't Brian McGinnis?"

"No, sir. Absolutely not."

"Good. Very good."

The marshal left his office and walked down the street to the Western Union office.

He walked in and said 'Good Morning, Al" to the operator and wrote:

ARTHUR MCGINNIS MAC LUMBER SAGINAW MICH

HUGH MCGINNIS ARRIVED TWO DAYS AGO TOOK UP RESIDENCE AT ROCKING M

CITY MARSHAL WILL AMBROSE BAKER CITY ORE

The operator read the message and said, "Thirty cents, Marshal."

Will Ambrose paid the money gladly. It was a good investment and he'd make $99.70 on that telegram.

———

The subject of the telegram rode past the Western Union office ten minutes later. The marshal had already returned to his desk.

His first stop was to the Oregon State Bank. He dismounted in front of the brick building, tied off Night, then walked inside and found a clerk.

“Good morning, sir. How can I help you?”

“I’d like to open an account and transfer some funds from my current bank.”

“Very good, sir. Have a seat.”

The clerk was efficient and took out the necessary forms and created a new account in the name of Hugh McGinnis in just minutes. If the name meant anything to him, he didn’t show it.

“And how much would you like to deposit to start the account?”

“I’ll give you one hundred dollars to start it and I’d like to transfer ten thousand dollars from my account at the First National Bank in Ann Arbor, Michigan. I’ll provide you with the account information and the proper code sequence.”

The clerk almost choked, but replied, “Very good, sir. If you’ll provide that information, we’ll wire the request to Ann Arbor. It usually takes a couple of days.”

“I understand. I’ll check back on Thursday to see if it came through.”

“Will that close your Ann Arbor account, sir? They usually like a notice.”

“No. Depending on how it goes here, I may transfer the rest. I’ll let you know.”

Hugh stood, shook the man's hand, then left the bank. The cashier didn't tell him he would soon be the largest depositor in the bank.

His next stop was at the drug store. He went in and met the chemist, a man in his mid-thirties with a mildly receding hairline and a smiling face. Hugh liked him immediately because of his eyes. They were honest eyes.

"What can I do for you today?" he asked.

"I'd like some silver mercury iodide. Do you have any on hand?"

"It's not a high demand compound. Let me see," he answered, before he went back to his shelves and began rummaging.

"Ah! You are fortunate, sir. I have a bottle right here," he said as he returned and set it on the counter.

"Perfect. I also need a bottle with a dropper."

"Will that be all?"

"For today. I may become your best customer. I'm thinking of opening my medical practice here."

The druggist perked up and asked, "Are you a physician?"

"I left the University of Michigan a year early because of the war. I'm going to contact them shortly and request issuance of my degree based on my record as an army surgeon. It far exceeded the normal requirements of the final year."

"If that all works out, it would be a great boon to our city to have a degreed physician in town. Our only doctor isn't really a physician at all. He claims to be one, but sometimes I have my doubts," he said as he put the bottle and eye dropper on the counter near the silver iodide.

"Well, it's good to meet you. How much do I owe you?"

"No charge. That bottle was going to sit there for another year anyway."

"Thank you very much. You'll be the first to know when I set up my practice."

"You're welcome. Have a good day."

Hugh scooped up his purchases, dropped them into his jacket pocket and walked out the door, the first step of his plan now completed. It had been a relief to have found the compound. There was a good chance that the chemist didn't have the chemical on hand, so now he needed to experiment.

The ladies made it to the store just as Hugh was leaving the chemist. It wasn't a general store, but a clothing store which was rare in a town this size. Susan parked the buggy, then they walked in and quickly headed to the women's clothing and were astounded by the selection.

Rebecca was looking for a specific look. She didn't want to overdo it, but she needed something understated. She found something that would work. It was a very conservative, light blue dress with ivory trim. It had a high neck and full sleeves. Not the kind of dress that she'd normally choose, but for this occasion, it was perfect. She'd modify it later for normal wear. It was only two dollars and forty cents, so she was done for the day. She smiled as she watched Susan and Nancy choosing their new clothes.

On the ride into town, they had told Rebecca their story and of Hugh's sudden arrival. Nancy told her about Hugh punching her father in the face when he refused to accept her, and Rebecca had shared most of her story. Rebecca didn't elaborate about the necklace, which they had noticed and admired.

—

Hugh's morning jobs were done. He had made one more stop to buy something for a contingency, then swung by the clothing store and noticed the buggy outside. He grinned as he stepped down. He needed to buy a vest and a nice jacket, or maybe a suit. He wandered to the men's section and found a jacket that fit and two vests, one black and one gray. He finally caved in and bought the suit as well. He paid for his purchases and headed over to the women's section where he found the ladies clustered around some frilly things and wasn't about to intrude.

Rebecca then spied Hugh and smiled broadly. He saw the dress over her arm and appreciated her choice. Susan and Nancy had a lot more things draped over their arms.

He finally decided to walk into the women's clothing department and when he was near, he said, "Ladies, I see you're finding things. I would suggest that you take your partial order over to the clerk, so she can start running a total and putting it into bags for you. That way you can get more things, and don't forget things like shoes and all of those frilly things. Rebecca, did you need anything else for you or the children?"

"No, Hugh. You did a marvelous job at the trading post."

"But that selection was so limited. Isn't there anything here that really just tickles your fancy?"

"Hugh, you have to stop spoiling me."

"Never. I saw you sneaking looks at that emerald green dress over there."

"Hugh, that's eleven dollars!"

"Is it your size?"

"Yes, but that's not the point."

"I'm being very selfish, Rebecca. I would love to see you in that dress."

"That's different. I'll buy it then, or more accurately, you will buy it."

Hugh watched as Rebecca slid over and picked up the dress. He was impressed with how it shone. It must be made of silk which would explain the cost.

The women finally finished their orders. The total was a staggering $77.55. Hugh smiled at their embarrassed faces to assuage any guilt they may have had for spending that much.

"This is going to be interesting. I have my order, so I can take some more on my horse, and it will take some imaginative packing to get all of that in the buggy, but I think we can make it. I'll grab what I can and you three can take the rest."

Hugh took the only heavy bag and his and each woman took two bags as they walked outside to the buggy.

Once near the buggy, Hugh said, "Okay, everybody, get in the buggy and we'll see how this works."

The ladies all sat in the buggy as Hugh arranged the bags. There was a shelf on the back that could handle three bags and he took one and hooked it over his saddle horn with his bag. That left three. He wedged two in between Susan and her two outside riders and that left one. He finally just gave up and said he'd just hold onto the last one.

After he mounted, Hugh felt somewhat chagrined by his decision as he started Night back toward the ranch. Here he was a large, manly man with two pistols on his hips and a petticoat flouncing in front of him as he rode his big black stallion. He hoped the ladies appreciated his sacrifice. They did, and not just because of the petticoat.

They returned to the ranch house and unloaded all their purchases before Hugh drove the buggy to the barn and unharnessed the horse.

Everyone was getting ready for the big courtroom showdown with Bob Orson. Hugh spent the day experimenting with mustard powder, which he had to do in private because he didn't want any of them to know what he was doing. It might not work, and if it did, it had to be a surprise in the courtroom. It wasn't until seven o'clock that evening that he was confident that his little experiment would work.

Rebecca tried on the new demure dress and made some adjustments in the fit to minimize her curves and flatten her chest somewhat. How odd, she thought. Women spend all this time trying to enhance those very things, but here she was trying to minimize them.

The next morning was cloudless and cool. The only ones going to the hearing were Rebecca, Hugh, and Betty. They boarded the buggy before nine o'clock and rode to Baker City for the divorce hearing.

As they drove along, Hugh was still curious why he hadn't been summoned as he'd been named as the offending party. Maybe things were different in Oregon. It really didn't matter, though. He was going to be there, and if things worked out right, Bob Orson would be humiliated, and Rebecca would never have to worry about him again.

In Baker City, Ella Murphy was atwitter. She was nervous, even after Bob had gone over her testimony several times. She would get through one part and then fumble another. The more he had her do it, the more mistakes she made. Bob took the precaution of giving her a brandy to soothe her nerves. It seemed to help, so he gave her a second.

After the second brandy, he had her go through her testimony one more time and she did well, a little stilted, but with no mistakes, and Bob would settle for that, but gave her a third brandy just to be sure.

Bob was still confident. He had an attorney and he knew Rebecca couldn't afford one. This should be over quickly. He had noticed earlier that there wasn't a single Conestoga around except for Ella's. Of course, it would be his soon. Even that annoying Florence Johnson was gone. He hadn't seen Rebecca at the hotel, so he didn't know if she was even going to make it. If she didn't, he'd win by default which would make Ella's questionable testimony unnecessary. The wild card was that Hugh McGinnis. He was supposed to be around, but Bob hadn't seen him, so maybe he was laying low or even gone. Being named as a wife usurper can destroy a reputation.

He and Ella began walking to the courthouse. He was wearing the new suit he had bought the day before, it had cost too much, but he wanted to make a good impression. He'd bought the suit from the same rack where Hugh had chosen his just hours later.

They were almost there when he saw a buggy arrive with what looked like Rebecca and that Hugh character! Bob couldn't believe his luck. She must have begged him to come and this was going to make it easier for his attorney. All he had to ask was the big 'L word' and that would be the end of Rebecca's chances. He began to whistle.

"There's Bob with Ella," spat Rebecca, "Let them go in first."

Bob stared at the them as they exited the buggy, yet didn't acknowledge Rebecca, but there was something different about her and he couldn't quite put his finger on it. Then he realized she was less…curvy. He and Ella entered the courthouse and walked to room 108, Judge Horace Hampton's chambers where he met his attorney, John Simpson.

Hugh, Rebecca and Betty all followed Bob and Ella into the same room. No one paid attention to the black bag that Hugh was carrying. The clerk, noting that all interested parties were in attendance, led them into the courtroom.

The attorney directed Bob and Ella to a seat, and Hugh assumed they would sit on the opposite side, so he held the chair for Rebecca and then for Betty.

Three minutes later, Judge Hampton entered, and everyone stood, then sat after the judge assumed his position behind the bench.

The judge said, "We are here today to render judgement on the matter of a divorce request as filed by Robert Eugene

Orson against Rebecca Jane Orson based on infidelity and adultery. Mister Simpson, you may proceed."

"Your honor, this is a very simple case. Mister Orson was traveling to Oregon with his wife and their two children. There was an accident and both children were assumed lost. Mister Hugh McGinnis, on the run from Cheyenne Indians, discovered them and returned them to Mrs. Orson. Mrs. Orson was grateful to Mister McGinnis and soon began sneaking off to his camp which he would always make nearby the wagon train camp to facilitate their liaisons."

He turned to face Bob and Ella as he continued, saying, "Mrs. Ella Murphy, a grieving widow on the wagon train, had seen them embracing and engaging in lewd behavior on multiple occasions and had warned Mister Orson, whom she pitied.

"Even though Mister Orson tried to win his wife's affection back by purchasing an enormous quantity of clothing and other articles for her, she refused him and remained with Mister McGinnis.

"Your honor, there can be no other recourse from this despicable behavior on her part but to grant the petition and award custody of both children to Mister Orson, who loves them dearly."

Hugh had watched Rebecca's temper rise but had warned her before they left the ranch that the lies would be flowing like a great river and to hold back her emotions while they lied. She did better than he expected but her hands were clenched even as her face remained calm.

The judge looked at Rebecca and asked, "Mrs. Orson, would you care to respond to these allegations?"

Rebecca stood and said, “Your honor, not one word of what Mister Simpson said is true. I have touched Mister McGinnis exactly once since I have known him, and that was in front of fifty people, including Mister Orson. I held his arm after he had been stabbed protecting a woman named Emily Amber. I held the wound closed while he sewed it shut. I have never even so much as held his hand.”

“Thank you, Mrs. Orson. You may be seated.”

Simpson stood, and said, “Your honor, if I may, I’d like to ask Mrs. Orson some questions.”

“All right, go ahead.”

He turned to Rebecca and asked, “Mrs. Orson, were you grateful to Mister McGinnis for returning your children?”

“Extremely grateful. I thought they were dead, and I love my children with every fiber of my being.”

“Yes, yes. I’m sure you do. Now, where did you get the necklace you are wearing?”

“From Hugh McGinnis.”

“Why?”

“I don’t know why. It was the last time I saw him on the Trail, and he came by to say good-bye to the children who love him dearly and gave it to me. It had been given to him by a Nez Perce maiden. He had told me the story and as he left, he gave it to me as a keepsake.”

“Is that why you wear it constantly, because of your attachment to Mrs. McGinnis?”

"It's a beautiful necklace, Mister Simpson. Any woman would wear it constantly."

"Perhaps, Mrs. Orson. But, tell me one thing, and one thing only. Do you love Mister McGinnis?"

"With all my heart," she answered clearly as she looked at Hugh.

Bob couldn't believe it. Rebecca had just given away her children. He had won, and he'd make McGinnis pay to get them back for her.

Hugh's reaction was somewhat different. He felt a warm glow suffuse his being as he looked into Rebecca's eyes.

The judge was shocked by her open admission.

Simpson continued with a growing sense of victory, as he turned and asked, "Mrs. Murphy, would you rise?"

Ella stood unsteadily, the three brandies having an enormous impact on the teetotaler.

"Mister Simpson stated that you witnessed Mrs. Orson and Mister McGinnis embracing and engaging in lewd behavior on multiple occasions. Could you please describe them to the court?"

Ella nodded emphatically and replied, "Uh-uh. I saw them. They were hugging and kissing. Hoo Maginish was groping her all over and then was groping her all over. He'd take her to his camp and do things to her that I, being a good Christian, you know, a good one, can't even talk about."

Simpson was stunned by Ella's obvious affectation and said, "Thank you, Mrs. Murphy. You may be seated."

Hugh stood and asked, “Your honor, may I ask Mrs. Murphy a few questions?”

“And you are?”

“Oh, I beg your pardon, your honor, I’m the accused adulterer, Hugh McGinnis. I own the Rocking M ranch southeast of town.”

“Oh. I see. By the way, are you the same man who rid this fair city of the holy terror of those despicable Hanson brothers?”

“I am, your honor.”

“Well, I for one thank you. Things are much quieter now. Go ahead.”

“Thank you, Your Honor,” then he turned to Ella and asked, “Mrs. Murphy, could I call you Ella, by the way?”

“That’s okay.”

“Fine. Now, Ella, you testified that you had witnessed me and Mrs. Orson doing all these lewd activities. Could you be more specific? Surely you can remember dates and times. For example, was it the first night that I was camped outside the wagon train?”

“I’m not sure.”

“But I remember seeing you that night, Ella. You were standing next to Bob Orson and you were holding hands with him as I sat there bleeding. And then there was the time I came riding past the train and saw you and Bob in the front seat and your hand was rubbing his right thigh. I can give you the exact time and dates for those two events, yet you seem to have a problem with any of those so-called lascivious sightings."

"I don't remember."

Simpson jumped up and said, "Your honor, may I question this man?"

"Go ahead."

"Mister McGinnis, Rebecca Orson claims she never touched you except for that night you were stabbed. Is that correct?"

"It is, although I did carry her into my house when she arrived in that rainstorm to notify me of this legal action. There were several chaperones there to ensure that it was all that happened."

"Are you saying you've never kissed her or touched her in an inappropriate manner?"

"I am."

"Yet you gave her the necklace because you wanted her to remember you?"

"I did."

"What else did you give her?"

"I bought her six dresses and the other clothing and clothes and shoes for the children. They had nothing after that wagon tumbled into the deep ravine, Mister Simpson, and very little before that. Your client provided them with nothing. She had one dress when she came to help me as I was bleeding…just one. She ripped her only dress to keep me from bleeding to death.

"The clothing that I found in the destroyed wagon, whether it was hers or the children's, was in despicable condition. Mister Orson's, on the other hand, all looked in excellent condition. I despise any man that fails in his duty to protect and care for those he is honor bound to do so.

"When the opportunity arose for me to purchase those items of clothing and daily necessities for her and her incredible children, I did so. I didn't stay but left them at the trading post with word that she be told that the order was for her. I noticed that Mister Orson claimed responsibility for the purchase. This act was one more indication of his flawed character."

"So, now you're claiming that you bought the clothing and not Mister Orson?"

"It's simple enough to prove. Ask Mister Orson what gift he bought for his son."

Simpson knew he was trapped and said, "The question is irrelevant, your honor."

Judge Hampton said "No, I'd like to hear him answer the question. Mister Orson, what gift did you buy for your son?"

Bob was irritated and snapped, "Okay. Okay. So, maybe I didn't buy those things. I just said that to try to make Rebecca take me back."

Ella stared at Bob. *He lied to her?*

Simpson then had to quickly recover from his losses and asked, "Tell us, Mister McGinnis, what gift did you buy his son?"

"That day, I didn't. The gift I bought for Andy was the day I decided to return because I had made a promise to a little girl and I wasn't about to break it. On the day I found the children, I saw a doll being swept down the river. When I found them, Addie, that's Rebecca Orson's daughter, told me she had lost her doll, a gift from her mother, I might add.

"I told her that I'd get her a new doll and found one at the trading post and wanted to give it to her but didn't feel right about not bringing anything to Andy, her almost ten-year-old brother. So, I bought him a pocketknife."

"So, you thought by ingratiating yourself with her children, you'd win the mother's affection."

"Mister Simpson, I travelled days with those children. I grew to love them as the precious small people they are. If you saw them, you'd understand. They are incredible children."

"Let's quit beating around the bush, Mister McGinnis, let me ask you the same question I asked Mister Orson, do you love her?"

"Mister Simpson, I love Rebecca with all of my heart and soul. She is the finest human being I have ever met. But since I've openly admitted to my love for Rebecca, then perhaps we can solve this whole issue of adultery right here and right now."

At that point, Rebecca didn't care about anything else. She gazed at Hugh and felt the warmth flow through her. It was an unusual way to be told that you're loved, but it was the only way available to them.

"And how do you propose to do this, Mister McGinnis? Bring in a fortune teller?" the attorney asked with a sarcastic chuckle.

"No, Mister Simpson, I have a scientific method. I attended medical school at the University of Michigan. I was one year away from becoming a Doctor of Medicine, when I went to war. I am a scientist, Mister Simpson. Now, I have a method for determining if a woman has had coital relations in the past month and understanding the charge that Rebecca was facing, I brought the necessary tools and substances to do that experiment."

"That's impossible!" exclaimed Mister Simpson.

"Not so. When women have had relations with a man, they release a hormonal substance called estrogen. The chemical makeup of this hormone stays with the woman for thirty days and permeates their entire system. When that hormone comes in contact with silver mercury iodide, it changes color from yellow to orange when it's heated. What I propose is to have Mrs. Orson subject herself to this test to determine if she had indeed committed adultery with me in the past month."

Simpson came close to sneering as he said, "Mister McGinnis, this court is not foolish. You claim this works, yet all you do is have Mrs. Orson take the test and pass."

"I can understand your skepticism. Mister Simpson. Now, I have implied in my testimony, that Mister Orson and Mrs. Murphy had been engaged many times in adulterous behavior in the past month. Perhaps we can use Mrs. Murphy to prove whether or not the test is valid. If her sample changes to orange from yellow and Mrs. Orson's remains yellow, then we'll know who the true adulterer is."

Simpson was beginning to panic. He strongly suspected that Orson had been bedding Mrs. Murphy, but to tell him it wouldn't be allowed would be tantamount to confessing that they had. His only option was to watch him carefully for a trick.

"Very well. Conduct your little experiment."

Ella Murphy was horrified. Their secret would soon be exposed, and she began to get seriously fidgety. The admission by Bob that he had lied to her had already gotten her upset, but this would be a disaster. Her foggy state of mind didn't help either. Maybe it wouldn't work. Maybe she didn't have those hormones that he talked about at all.

Hugh opened his black bag, took out a candle and two metal plates. Then he took out a bottle labeled *silver mercury iodide*.

After setting them all on the witness table, he turned to the attorney and asked, "So, Mister Simpson, who goes first? Mrs. Murphy or Mrs. Orson?"

Simpson was about to say Mrs. Murphy when he felt a violent tug on his pants and Mrs. Murphy was pointing at Rebecca.

"Mrs. Murphy wishes to be fair, so Mrs. Orson may go first."

"Fine. First, we'll light the candle. I'll take some silver mercury iodide and put it on the metal plate."

He lit the candle, took out the dropper and squirted some yellow liquid onto the plate.

"Mrs. Orson, could you come here please?"

Rebecca walked toward Hugh. She knew she hadn't engaged in anything like that for six months but was unsure of the chemical and its reaction, but she had to trust that Hugh knew what he was doing.

"Now, if you will, Mrs. Orson, blow steadily across the yellow liquid. Any estrogen in your lungs will react with the silver mercury iodide and when it's heated, it will change to orange."

Rebecca blew steadily across the yellow liquid causing small ripples that all could see. She was nervous and didn't know why.

"Thank you, Rebecca," Hugh said as he held back a serious need to wink.

She stepped back and watched as Hugh took the plate and held it over the candle's flame.

Everyone watched intently at the yellow liquid as it began to bubble, and even after a full minute of heat, it stayed yellow. Rebecca almost sighed in relief but maintained her composure.

If Rebecca had been nervous, Ella was in agonizing mental torture. She had been praying constantly since she knew what she was going to have to do.

"Now, Mrs. Murphy. Could you please come forward?" Hugh asked.

As she walked unsteadily toward Hugh, he took the bottle and sucked up some more silver mercury iodide and then squeezed it out onto the plate.

Simpson had watched carefully. It was the same substance from the same bottle, and he couldn't see any deception. It was probably just a ploy to get Ella to break down. Unfortunately, he knew that she was close to doing just that and wanted this done quickly.

Hugh held the plate with its ominous yellow liquid in front of her lips.

Ella was shaking as Hugh said, "Go ahead, Ella, one good blow across the yellow liquid. Let's see those ripples like Rebecca made."

Ella blew, the ripples appeared, and Hugh said, "Excellent. Thank you, Ella."

She didn't return to her seat but stood frozen in place as Hugh walked to the candle. The judge, Bob, Mister Simpson, Rebecca, and especially Ella stared at the plate as he held it over the candle.

Not even ten seconds later, to Ella's horror, the yellow started to shift. *It was turning orange!*

Hugh held it there until it started to boil as everyone watched it change to a bright orange. He removed it from the heat and showed it to the judge.

"Ella, do you have something to tell Judge Hampton?" he asked quietly.

Ella's mild intoxication was shoved aside as she lost any pretense of control and almost shouted as she started to cry.

"I'm sorry, Judge, I never saw Mister McGinnis with Mrs. Orson except when she helped him fix his arm. I was so lonely. I needed a man and Bob wanted me so much. I had to do it. He said if I said those things, we could get married. I'm so sorry, Judge," then she turned to Rebecca and said, "I'm sorry, Rebecca. I always liked you. You were such a good mother and nice to me. Mister McGinnis saved your children, and then he saved Emily, and then rescued Florence and Emily again. I'm just a terrible person."

She began to sob, so Hugh went up to the snuffling Ella and wrapped his arms around her.

"No, Ella, you're not a terrible person. You were just a terribly lonely person who was taken advantage of."

He let her go and gave her a gentle push toward Rebecca who automatically reached out and held her.

The judge watched the whole scene with utter fascination, then he turned to Bob Orson.

"Mister Orson, this petition is a waste of my time. You have suborned perjury, perjured yourself and generally misled this court to suit your own selfish goals. I am not going to grant this petition."

"Your honor," interrupted Hugh.

"Yes, Mister McGinnis."

"As Mister Orson is obviously the adulterer in this case, would it be possible to grant the petition under those grounds. Although I have been completely honest with the court when I said I never have kissed Mister Orson, I would like to be able to rectify that situation, but I can't do that in her current state of legal matrimony."

Judge Hanson smiled and said, "A splendid idea. Mrs. Orson, I am granting this decree of divorce naming you as the offended party. As of this moment, you are no longer married to Bob Orson."

He banged his gavel, ending the case.

Bob Orson was livid, there was no money, no Ella. Nothing.

Mister Simpson was tugging at his sleeve trying to get him out of there, then finally succeeded to get his client's attention and he led his grumbling client away.

After he had left the chambers, Judge Hanson leaned over and asked Hugh, "How does that work, anyway? I've never heard of that test."

Hugh laughed and said, "Your Honor, I have a confession to make. This test was a sham. The chemical will always turn color when exposed to heat. I had made a liquid that matched the chemical out of water and mustard powder. I sucked it into the dropper and sealed it with a bit of wax. Then, when I used it the first time. I squeezed it out onto the plate. That sample would always stay yellow. The second sample was real silver mercury iodide which always will turn orange under heat. I needed to get the truth before the court."

Then Hugh turned to Ella Murphy and said, "Ella, I am truly sorry, but I had to get you to confess to save you from Bob. He was doing this just to take your money. Let me ask you a question. How has he treated you this past week? Has he been attentive to your needs?"

"No. He treated me like I was just a mattress and I had to beg him for that."

"It would have gotten worse, Ella. As soon as you were married, he'd use your money to buy what he wanted and then he'd move on. You're a better woman than that, Ella. Don't sell yourself short."

She nodded, but Hugh could see that she needed more convincing. He'd leave that up to Rebecca, but that would be later. Right now, he had other ideas.

"Your Honor, may I make another request?"

The judge was still in awe and said, "Why not? You're doing pretty damned well."

"I told you earlier that I've never kissed Rebecca before. I'd like to make the first one special. Now that she's no longer married, could you marry us?"

Judge Hanson started grinning and said, "Now, that's got to be an all-time record for shortest unmarried time I've ever heard. Rebecca, would you consent to this very sudden marriage?"

"I was just expecting a kiss, your honor, but it would be so much more special if it were as Mrs. Hugh McGinnis."

"Alright. We'll do this backwards. After you're married, we'll go out to the office and fill out the papers."

Hugh was almost floating as he held out his hand for Rebecca. She was so incredibly happy when just minutes ago, she thought her world would end. She stepped slowly forward, just gazing into Hugh's eyes finding so much love in them and it was all for her.

Hugh took her hand and they both turned to face the judge.

He recited the marriage rites from memory, not missing a word.

Then he reached the ring portion of the ceremony.

The judge looked at Hugh and wasn't surprised one bit when he produced a small box from his pocket. Hugh opened the box and took out the two rings and handed the large ring to Rebecca. She felt tears slowly rolling down her face as she looked at them. She had never worn a wedding ring before, but now, Hugh was sliding one across her finger. Moments later, she slipped the large band across his finger.

"By the powers vested in me by the State of Oregon, I now pronounce you man and wife. You may finally kiss your bride, Mister McGinnis."

Hugh pulled Rebecca to him tightly and kissed her softly yet so passionately that Rebecca felt her toes curl.

Betty and Ella were the only two left in the courtroom to be witnesses, and Betty was very happy for her friend. Ella was coming out of her misery and saw what her honesty had led to and felt better. She smiled as they held the kiss. Finally, they separated and looked one more time into each other's eyes. This time as husband and wife.

"Okay, folks, let's go see my clerk and get those forms completed," said the judge.

The clerk was a bit startled when the judge asked for marriage forms but handed the forms to the judge who signed them. Hugh and Rebecca then filled out the blanks, then signed where appropriate and then Ella and Betty signed. The judge gave the divorce decree to his clerk and everything was done. He shook Hugh's hand and received a peck on the cheek from Hugh's new bride.

"Your Honor, before you go, could we do one more legal item?"

Rebecca looked at him curiously.

The judge threw up his hands, and said, “Why not? What do you need?”

“I would like to formally adopt Rebecca’s children.”

Rebecca’s hands flew to her mouth and her heart skipped a beat or two as the judge smiled and said, “That would make sense.”

The clerk automatically handed him the forms.

The judge wrote down the names as Rebecca gave them and then signed it. He handed it back to the clerk who added all the other information, and Andy and Addie officially became Andy and Addie McGinnis.

“Thank you for that, Hugh. It makes the day perfect,” Rebecca said.

“I couldn’t leave that undone, Mrs. McGinnis,” Hugh replied.

Hugh took her hand and they left the judge’s offices and were ten feet down the corridor when Hugh stopped dead and turned to face Ella.

“Ella, where is your money?” he asked quickly.

As soon as he asked, she knew why he had. Her hand flew to her mouth and she answered, “In my wagon.”

“Let’s move, ladies. We need to stop Bob from taking all of her money.”

Skirts were lifted, and Hugh ran ahead to unhitch the buggy. He brought it around to the front as the women hurried down the courthouse steps as quickly as they could navigate the stairs.

"Ella, you drive. You know where your wagon is. I'll hop on back."

Hugh stepped up onto the trunk shelf as the three women piled in. Seconds later, they were moving quickly through the streets of Baker City, reached Ella's wagon three minutes later and Ella pulled to a stop.

Hugh jumped off the buggy before it stopped and ran towards the Conestoga, then stopped in back, looked inside but didn't find Bob.

He turned as Ella approached with Betty and Rebecca in her wake.

"He's not here, Ella, but is your money still here?"

"I put it in a small box in the flour chest."

Hugh jumped inside, reached the attached flour box and opened the lid. He stuck his hand inside shifted it around the flour but didn't find her cash box. He looked around the crowded wagon and right near the front seats, he saw a small empty wooden box, picked it up and climbed back out.

"Is this it, Ella?"

Ella looked at it and her stomach flipped. She had no money.

"Yes, that's it. What will I do?"

“First, don’t worry about a thing. Everything will be all right. Now, I want to go and find Bob. I think I know where to find him.”

She looked at him and asked, “Where?”

“He’s not going to stick around, so he’ll need a horse and saddle and then supplies. Let’s head over to the livery stable. I can see it from here.”

He pointed out the barn-like structure and the women got into the buggy. Hugh jumped on back again as the buggy turned and leapt forward toward the livery. Again, Hugh dismounted before it stopped and ran into the livery.

He saw the liveryman sweeping out a stall.

“Excuse me! Did a man just come in here wearing a gray suit and buy a horse and saddle?”

“Yes, sir, and in quite a hurry, too. Didn’t do much inspecting or haggling, either. Just bought one and had me saddle it. Rode out of here fast, too.”

“Which direction did he go?”

“Took the southeast road.”

Hugh thought for a second and asked, “Do you have any good horses left for sale?”

“I tried to tell him that the best horse I had was that black mare.”

“How much?”

“Thirty-five dollars.”

"Here," he said as he handed him the money, then said, "I'll be back for a bill of sale in a little while. I'll ride her bareback."

Hugh walked over and looked at the beautiful black mare, and said, "Let's go, sweetheart," then leapt onto her back and trotted her out to the buggy.

"Bob bought a horse and saddle. He's gone, but I'm afraid he's gone to the Rocking M for his supplies and gear. I'm heading that way. Follow when you can."

Hugh turned the mare and set off at a fast trot. Betty had taken the reins and followed. As soon as he cleared the town, Hugh accelerated the mare. She was a fine runner and Hugh kept her to a canter, knowing she had almost five miles to go. He wondered how Bob Orson even knew about his ranch as the mare thundered down the road.

Two miles from the Rocking M, Bob Orson was searching. He knew the ranch was in this direction and needed to get some supplies to get out of the area. He knew that they wouldn't have left the children alone but suspected they had hired some woman to keep an eye on them while they were all in town. This should be easy. He'd go into the back entrance, take what he needed and then keep going southeast for a while before heading west. He had no idea what was out there, so he'd just ride until he found a town.

Hugh was closing the gap rapidly. He was about a mile and a half behind Bob with three miles to go. The horse was handling the speed easily.

Bob saw the entrance road with the large sign proclaiming the Rocking M, and a few minutes later, turned down the road and kept the horse trotting.

Hugh was less than a mile behind, but the tree-lined eastern side kept Bob out of his view.

Andy, Addie and Chuck were playing on the front porch when Bob entered the access road. Hugh had told Andy that they should be back before lunchtime, and Susan and Nancy were making a big lunch expecting a large crowd. Andy trusted Mister Hugh would do what he needed to do and kept looking down the road hoping to see his happy mama returning.

Then he saw something coming down the road, but it wasn't a buggy. It was a man on a horse and Andy didn't waste any time. He ran inside where Mister Hugh kept his guns, found a shotgun and opened it and saw that both barrels were loaded. He closed it again then trotted back to the porch. Chuck and Addie saw him come out with the gun and stared at him, but before they could say anything, they heard hooves and turned to the sound.

Andy recognized the rider and cocked both hammers. He pointed the gun at the ground, with the stock under his arm, and stared steadily at the oncoming rider.

Hugh was close to the access road and could see a rider approaching the house and knew it must be Bob. Then he squinted and looked again. It looked like the children were on the porch, but Andy was facing Bob and had a shotgun under his arm.

Bob had seen the children and wished he had a gun. Then he saw Andy did have a gun, and a shotgun at that. *What did he think he was doing?* No kid would shoot an adult.

When Bob was close, the almost-ten-year-old said loudly, "Go away, Mister Orson. You don't belong here."

Bob laughed and said, “Kid, I just need some supplies. I aim to come in there and get them. Now, put down that gun. You look foolish holding it.”

Andy didn’t back down. He raised the shotgun and pointed it at Mister Orson.

“Mister Orson, this gun has both hammers cocked. If I pull the trigger, you get both barrels. Mister Hugh told me never to point a loaded gun at someone unless I was going to kill them. If you step down from that horse, I will kill you.”

Bob licked his lips. He could see the kid had the hammers back. If he pulled the trigger, even accidentally, he wouldn’t live long enough to feel himself hit the ground.

Hugh had stepped down fifty feet behind Bob, had heard Andy’s threat, and was proud of him.

Andy had seen Hugh ride up behind Mister Orson, then dismount and knew he wouldn’t have to shoot anyone when he had made the threat. He wanted to keep Mister Orson where he was.

Hugh walked up behind Bob, who was totally ignorant of Hugh’s presence. He had been concentrating on those two enormous bores that contained instant death. They did tend to be attention-getters. Suddenly, he felt a strong hand grab his right arm and he was soaring through the air, landing ten feet from the saddle he had vacated.

Hugh walked over to him, lifted him from the ground, holding him in front of him, so his feet dangled three inches in the air.

"Bob, you are some kind of worthless pile of horse dung. I should just beat you to within an inch of your life, but I don't want to set a bad example for the boys."

He turned to Andy and said, "Son, go ahead and release those hammers."

Andy was releasing the hammers when it dawned on him that Mister Hugh had called him son and not Andy. He had never called him that before and wondered why.

Bob growled, "I just was gonna buy some supplies. You ain't got no reason to do this. You'd better unhand me, or I'll press charges."

"Why don't you do that? We'll just head back to Baker City and see the city marshal, so you can file your complaint."

"I won't file a complaint if you just let me leave. I'm a fair man. That boy just overreacted."

"My son doesn't overreact, Bob. He's a smart, level-headed young man."

Andy definitely heard that. Mister Hugh had called him 'my son'. *How could that happen?*

Hugh finally lowered Bob to the ground, then kept his eyes on him as he asked, "Andy, let me borrow your belt, will you, please?"

"Yes, Mister Hugh," he said as he began pulling out his belt.

"And, Andy, stop calling me Mister Hugh. From now on, you and Addie call me papa."

Addie had been listening and quickly yelled, "Papa!"

Hugh smiled as Andy handed him the belt, then grabbed Bob's arms and wrapped the belt tightly around his wrists before he sat him down on the ground.

Hugh walked to the porch and Addie jumped into his arms. He held her with his right arm as she put her arms around his neck. Hugh used his left arm to hold onto Andy but couldn't lift him with his injury.

That was the sight that greeted Rebecca as the buggy approached the house. Bob on the ground with his hands bound behind him, and her new husband embracing his new children. It was an image that would be etched in her memory for the rest of her life.

As the carriage stopped, Hugh turned smiled.

Hugh and everyone else watched as Ella stormed from the buggy, then stomped close to Bob who looked hopefully up at her.

"Look what they did to me, Ella, sweetheart. Can you help me up?"

"I'll help you, alright, you, lying bastard!" she screamed.

And then Ella released her fury caused by the lies, the false affection, and finally the theft. She began with a resounding slap that hit home. The echo had barely faded when she began a woman's best physical weapon…her feet. She began kicking Bob, and without his hands to protect him, he was just a target. He rolled on his side and curled up into a ball, a football, to be more accurate.

The other adults all just watched with no intention of stopping her. Susan and Nancy had heard the noise and had been standing at the door for the past two minutes.

Finally, Hugh set down Addie, released Andy and walked up next to Ella. He put his hands on her shoulders and said quietly, “It’s alright, Ella. I think he’s had enough for now.”

Ella stopped and was drained as she turned to Hugh and held onto him then started crying. She was shaking after the release of all the frustration, and Hugh realized she would need some female support, so he looked over at Rebecca and Betty. They both came forward, took Ella under control and led her into the house.

Hugh looked down at a moaning Bob Orson, then crouched down and took off Andy’s belt. Orson wasn’t going anywhere, so he handed the belt to Andy.

“Here you are, son. I’m really proud of you, Andy. You did a great job in protecting your sister and everyone else.”

Andy felt the glow of earned praise and replied, “Thank you, Papa.”

Addie posed the obvious question when she asked, “Are you and mama married now, Papa?”

“Yes, we are, sweetheart. I’ve loved your mama since I saw her hugging you both when I brought you back, but I could never tell her that until she was free from Mister Orson. As soon as she was free by law, the same judge who set her free, married us. So, now I am your papa and always will be.”

Addie sniffed and said, “I’m really, really happy, Papa. I’m happy ‘cause you’re my papa and I’m happy ‘cause you make mama happy.”

Hugh dropped to his heels to Addie’s eye level, and said, “And I need to thank you and Andy both, too. If I hadn’t found you, then I never would have found your mama. Now, we can all be happy together."

She smiled at Hugh and wanted to be picked up again.

"I'd love to pick you up, Addie. But I need to take care of Mister Orson. He's going to go to jail, I think."

Hugh stood, reached down and pulled Bob Orson to his feet before saying, "Let's go, Bob."

He walked Bob to the barn where he found a stock of pigging strings. He tied his wrists in front this time and then tied his ankles before he sat him near the trough.

"You hang tight for a few minutes, Bob. I'll be back shortly."

Hugh walked out front and took his new black mare and Bob's horse. It wasn't great, but it wasn't bad, either, then led them to the corral behind the barn and let them loose. There was another perpetual trough nearby and plenty of hay to keep them busy.

After he was sure the horses were okay, he headed for the kitchen, and when he entered, he found Nancy, Susan, Ella, and Betty with the children, but no Rebecca.

"Where's my wife?" he asked Betty.

"She's in the bedroom, Hugh. She said she's feeling under the weather. She says it was from too much excitement, but I don't think so," replied Susan.

Hugh trotted back to their bedroom, as he already thought of it and found Rebecca stretched out in her new dress. She looked up at him and smiled weakly.

"Hello, my beloved husband."

He sat on the edge of the bed and did what anyone would do when he felt her forehead.

"Rebecca, you're feverish. It's not bad. But we need to get you out of those clothes and into something else."

She smiled again and said, "It's our wedding day, shouldn't you be getting me out of this dress anyway?"

"Rebecca, I've been wanting to get you out of your dress for some time now, but today, you're just going to have to be a patient, my most precious patient. Marital consummation will have to wait until you're better. You'll need your strength. Do you feel anything else?"

"My chest hurts."

"I think that night in the rainstorm is coming back to haunt you. I need to take Bob and Ella to the marshal's office, so he can be arrested and charged with theft. I'll get back as soon as I can. I want you to stay in bed. I'll have my new nurse, Susan, look after you."

"I'll be all right, Hugh. I'm just tired. That's all."

"Tired doesn't get you feverish."

"You do."

"Quit being a smart aleck and just rest. I'll be back as soon as I'm able."

He kissed her on her forehead and felt her warmth before he returned to the kitchen.

"Ella, we need to take Bob into Baker City and have him charged with theft. I'll bring his saddlebags after I make sure the money is in there, unless you're not going to press charges."

"I sure as hell am going to press charges," snapped Ella.

"I need to get this done quickly. Susan, Rebecca is running a low-grade fever right now with chest pain. I'm not sure which direction she's headed with this, but we need to keep the fever down. Keep a cool moist cloth on her head and keep her as cool as possible. Take off some of her bulky clothing, including that damned corset or whatever else you call it that's restricting her breathing. She needs to breathe easily. Let's go, Ella."

Susan had been nodding as Hugh gave her instructions. As soon as he left with Ella, she walked to the sink, took a towel, soaked it with cold water, then returned to what should have been Rebecca's bridal suite and not her sick room.

Outside, Ella and Hugh first walked to Bob's horse, where Hugh pulled off the saddlebags and opened up the right one first. They both peered inside and found a cloth bag, that Hugh pulled free and handed it to Ella, who pulled the top open and to neither's surprise, found her stolen life's savings.

"That no-good bastard! I hope they hang him," Ella snarled.

"They won't, but he'll get a few years in prison for it. Men like Bob don't do well in prisons. He's too weak, and the really bad ones prey on the weak ones. Bob may wish he had been given the noose after a few months."

Ella mumbled, "I'd still want to see him hanged."

"We'll need to leave the money with the marshal for evidence, but you'll get it back, Ella."

Hugh could understand her wrath, and as she clutched her bag of money, he helped her into the buggy, then handed her Bob's saddlebags. As she returned the money to the saddlebags, Hugh went around the other side, stepped into the buggy, took the reins, drove it the sixty yards to the barn and then quickly popped out.

As soon as Hugh entered the very well-built barn, he was met by a scowling Bob Orson who wasted no time in expressing his displeasure.

"I'll get you for this, McGinnis!" he growled.

Hugh looked down at his prisoner and said, "Oh, please, Bob. Get some imagination in your threats, anyway. But let me give you one word of warning, and it will be the only one I'll give you. If you come within a mile of Rebecca, the children, Ella or this house, I will personally stick the shotgun that Andy showed you three inches up your butt and let both barrels go. So, keep your idle threats to yourself. If you say one word on this trip, you'll get an elbow jab that will make you cry."

Bob Orson didn't reply, but just glared at Hugh.

Hugh considered it an improvement as he walked to the side of the barn and cut a fifteen-foot length of rope from a large coil.

Bob continued to give Hugh the evil eye but remained silent as Hugh cut his leg ties and jerked him into a standing position. He tied the rope around his chest, running it under his bound arms, then walked him to the buggy, asked Ella to exit before he shoved Bob inside, then walked around to the other side and climbed in himself to stay between the couple, then after Ella was back inside, snapped the reins.

Hugh got the buggy rolling at a fast trot after leaving the access road. He needed to get back and help Rebecca. If her fever got worse, he'd try a remedy he picked up at Fort Kearny in Nebraska. He'd never tried it before, but the Lakota Sioux shaman that gave it to him swore by it. It was made from willow bark and was good for aches and pains and, most importantly, for reducing fevers.

He knew she shouldn't be feverish already if it had been just from the rainstorm. She must have already started down the road to this infection before, probably last week, but it didn't matter. Now, he had to stop it before she developed pneumonia. She really should weigh a few more pounds, but that year with Bob Orson had probably cost her the necessary weight.

Bob never said a word the entire trip as he finally seemed to have taken Hugh's threat seriously. But if looks could kill, Ella would have committed multiple homicides on the short journey.

They pulled up in front of the marshal's office, Ella exited the buggy, then stood gripping Bob's saddlebags and waited as Hugh climbed out, then walked around the other side and assisted Bob from the buggy.

"Why don't we go and say good afternoon to the marshal, Bob? Maybe you'll be able to file your complaint," Hugh said pleasantly as if Bob had a choice.

They entered the office and the same deputy was at the desk again, and Hugh wondered if the city marshal had more than one. In a town the size of Baker City, with a county sheriff's office across the street, he doubted it. Then again, he wasn't even sure that anyone was even in the sheriff's office.

"Deputy, this is Bob Orson. This morning, he entered Ella Murphy's wagon and stole her life savings. He bought a horse and was caught on my ranch trying to steal some supplies to make his escape. Here are his saddlebags with Mrs. Murphy's money still inside. She wants to press charges."

"Alright. I can write this up. Oh, and the reward came in. The marshal said the draft had to be made out to you because you killed them. What you do with it is up to you. I need you to sign a receipt, though."

He pushed a piece of paper to Hugh who signed it. The deputy gave Hugh the bank draft for a thousand dollars which he quickly folded and slid into his vest pocket.

"Deputy, can we lock up Mister Orson? I need to get back home quickly."

"Oh. Sure."

The deputy stood, took some keys from the wall and motioned to Hugh to bring Bob back. Hugh slipped the rope over Bob's head and pushed him along until he entered the cell. Once inside, Hugh pulled his knife, then severed Bob's leather bonds and the deputy closed the door behind him.

Hugh and the deputy then returned to the desk.

"Deputy, can Ella have her money back, or do you need it for evidence?"

"We'll hang onto it for a few days until the trial, but I'll give her a receipt. I need her to write a statement, too."

Hugh nodded and said, “Ella, I’ve got to get back. After you’re finished here, can you drive your wagon out to the ranch? You can stay with us until this is done or whenever you want to leave. It’ll be your choice. Okay?”

“You mean I can stay at your ranch? But you already have so many people out there.”

“We have plenty of room. Besides, I may be doing some building shortly.”

“Okay. The team is still harnessed, so I should be out there before dinner. Is that alright?”

“Absolutely. We have plenty of food and cooks, too. We’ll see you later, Ella.”

He smiled at her to let her know that she was no longer an outsider.

She smiled back, feeling somewhat accepted.

Hugh went out to the buggy and hopped in. He hoped that the poor buggy horse wasn’t getting too much of a workout as he snapped the reins and the buggy set off.

Forty minutes later, he drove the buggy to the barn and quickly returned the horse to its stall, made sure it had everything it needed, and pushed the buggy back into position before jogging back to the house. He’d been gone almost two hours and wondered how Rebecca’s fever was.

He entered the kitchen, but the only ones there were Betty and Nancy.

“How is Rebecca doing, Betty?”

“She started coughing, Hugh. Her temperature is up, too,” she answered with a worried look.

Hugh hurried back to her room and found the children and Susan with her.

He looked down at Rebecca’s tired face, and she smiled weakly when she saw his concern.

“Did you get Bob jailed?” she asked.

“Yes, we did. Ella will drive her wagon here later. They tell me you’ve started coughing.”

“Just a little. Not too much,” she said, then immediately followed with an explosive coughing spasm. She had a cloth in her hand, and it was covered with yellow sputum.

“Okay, Andy and Addie, you go and stay with Chuck and Aunt Betty and Nancy. Susan and I are going to take care of your mama. Alright?”

He could tell that Addie was on the verge of tears and Andy wasn’t much better. They were scared to death of losing their mother after having only found her a short time ago.

He crouched down and put his arm around both children. “Now, you both know I’m your papa now, but I’m still Mister Hugh. Has Mister Hugh ever made a promise he didn’t keep?”

“No, Papa,” they answered in unison.

“I’m promising you right now that I will take care of your mama.”

“Okay, Papa.”

"Now, go and stay with Aunt Betty and Nancy. I need to examine your mama."

He looked at Susan and said, "I'll be right back."

She nodded as he turned and walked quickly to the kitchen following the children down the hallway. He half-filled a glass with water and returned.

Because he had taken out his stethoscope earlier so Susan could listen to his heart sounds, he didn't need to hunt for it this time. He had to dig for the willow root, though. He still remembered his long talk with the shaman as he and Hugh had shared medical knowledge. The shaman had been different from most medicine men in that he put little store in healing by chanting. He did put great belief in the different plants and their impact on the body. He had given Hugh some ground willow bark, and that was what he was searching for now. He knew the white man's medicine had nothing to treat fever, so he had to put his faith in Sioux medicine. He found the small leather pouch hidden away in his few remnants of medical supplies.

When he returned to her sickroom, he mixed some of the powder in the water until it dissolved, then sat on the bed beside her.

"Rebecca, I need you to drink this down, then I need you to stay sitting while I listen to your chest."

She still managed a smile and asked, "Are you sure this isn't just taking advantage of your new wife?"

"I'll take advantage of you when you're able to swat me, Rebecca, but for now, I'm going to help you into a sitting position."

She tried to sit up, but Hugh had to lift her until she was sitting. As soon as she did, she had another serious coughing spasm.

After she stopped, he handed her the glass and she drank it down quickly as the fever had made her very thirsty.

Then she made a face and asked, “Can I get some regular water, please? This tastes really bitter.”

“In a minute, Rebecca. I need to listen to your chest.”

He put the stethoscope on her back and had her take in breaths as he listened to both sides of her lungs, then beckoned Susan to come over and handed her the stethoscope. He placed it in the same spots as before and she listened. Then she removed the stethoscope from her ears and nodded.

“Susan, can you get Rebecca a glass of clean water, please? She seems to object to the medicine.”

Susan nodded, took the glass and left the bedroom.

He carefully lowered Rebecca back down to her pillows after she coughed, but only once.

She looked up at Hugh with a concerned look and asked, “It’s pneumonia, isn’t it?”, then tears filled her eyes and she said, “I’m going to lose you and the children all over again.”

Hugh sat on her bed and looked into her eyes, “Rebecca, listen to me, but listen to me as your doctor and not your husband. You don’t have pneumonia. You have bronchitis. We need to keep your temperature under control and keep you elevated more. You’re a healthy young woman. This should all clear up in a few days.”

She looked into his eyes and asked, "You're not telling your first lie, are you?"

"No, my love. I never lie. And of all the people in this world, you would be the very last one I ever would even think of lying to."

"Then I'm going to be all right?"

"I won't minimize the dangers, Rebecca. A bad case of bronchitis can lead to pneumonia, so we need to control this. You'll have to drink more of the medicine every now and then and we need to keep your fever down, but if we keep at it, you'll be fine. I already promised our children that I'd make you better."

"Say that again."

"What? The whole thing?"

"No. Just the part where you said, 'our children'."

He smiled at her and said, "I promised our children that I'd make you better."

"That makes me feel so happy all over. My husband and our children."

"Don't forget, Mrs. McGinnis, you've got to get better. You owe me a raucous wedding night, and I expect to see you in that green dress and nothing else underneath."

Rebecca managed a weak laugh before saying, "Ooh! A lascivious suggestion from my new husband. Or was that from my doctor as some form of therapy? Either way, I'll have to comply to keep him happy."

“You’d better. I’ve been looking forward to ravaging you for some time now.”

She tried to laugh but had a strong coughing fit instead.

Susan had been standing at the door with the water listening for some time and knew that Hugh was trying to take her mind off her condition. She entered the room as Rebecca finished coughing.

“Susan, can you put the water on the table and collect two more pillows, please?”

She nodded, put the water down, then left the room and returned with two more pillows in less than a minute.

Hugh lifted Rebecca again and put the pillows underneath, then he gave her the full glass of water, which she drank eagerly before he gently lowered Rebecca to the pillows.

“That feels better,” she said softly.

“Susan, what did you hear when you listened to Rebecca’s chest?”

“When she breathed, it made a wheezing sound.”

“Very good. The air comes in through a tube called the trachea. It goes through the voice box called the larynx, then it enters the lungs. Now the lungs fed air through what look like a series of shrinking pipes. The big pipes that enter the lungs are called bronchi. They branch off into a lot of smaller tubes called secondary and tertiary bronchi. When it finally gets small enough, they’re called bronchioles. The bronchioles sit there with things called alveolar sacks that take the carbon dioxide out of the blood system and put in the oxygen. That’s how we breathe. Now, those bronchi can get inflamed with infection. When they do, they swell up making the tubes smaller. Air still needs to get through, but it makes a noise. That's the wheezing you heard.

"In the case of pneumonia, there is liquid in the lungs. The air goes through the liquid causing a crackling sound. I'm telling you all this because now you know that what Rebecca has is bronchitis. It'll be our job to keep it from turning into pneumonia. That means keeping the fever down and keeping as much air in her lungs as possible. We need to give her body a chance to beat the infection in her lungs. With pneumonia, it's difficult for the body to fight because of the liquid."

"Thank you, Hugh. Or should I call you doctor now?"

He smiled at her, and replied, "Hugh is fine when we're alone. When I set up my practice and have my degree, then whenever a patient is around, you'll call me doctor and I'll call you nurse."

She smiled and said, "I understand."

Hugh turned back to Rebecca. "Did you follow all of that medical mumbo-jumbo?"

"Yes, doctor. Breathing and drinking bitter liquid."

"You're turning into a model patient, Mrs. McGinnis. I'm going to have to reward you."

He leaned over and kissed her gently on her lips, which caused her to quickly lean back.

"Hugh! You shouldn't do that!" she said.

"I know. I just wanted you to know that you're very important to me, besides I already kissed you once."

"I know, but you need to be there for our children."

"I can take care of the problem. You rest for a while. I'll check on you later."

He stood and motioned for Susan to follow.

"She is right, you know. That was a risky thing to do. Bronchitis like hers is contagious. That's why I want to keep the window open in her room to let the air circulate. I'm going to go and take a shot of whiskey and gargle with it. That'll take care of the danger of contagion. Whiskey, or any alcohol, seems to have a good effect on preventing infections."

"I'm learning, Hugh."

"That's why I'm telling you all this, Susan. Oh, by the way. I need to talk to you and Nancy for a minute in the kitchen."

"I'll go get her."

Hugh went into the kitchen and found a bottle of whiskey left by the brothers, took a swig and gargled and then spit it out. He followed it with a glass of water. The taste was still there, so he walked to the cold room, found the ham, cut a chunk off, put it in his mouth and chewed it for a while, wondering how anyone could drink that stuff.

Susan and Nancy popped into the kitchen, and Hugh said, "Have a seat, ladies."

They both sat down, and after Hugh took his seat at the table, he pulled the bank draft from his pocket.

"I picked this up from the marshal's office today. He said they had to make it out to me because I shot the two ne'er-do-wells. The next time I get a chance, I'll take Nancy to the bank and I'll deposit the draft into my account. and we'll get Nancy an account in her name and I'll transfer five hundred dollars into it."

Nancy quickly asked, "But what about Susan?"

Susan answered, "I'm going to be a nurse, Nancy. It's all right."

Hugh smiled and said, "Susan, your becoming a nurse has nothing to do with it. The money is yours, but there is a problem that has to be solved before we open an account for you."

The light came on and Susan exclaimed, "I'm married!"

"Exactly. Your husband, by law, can go and take that money before you get a chance to divorce him. Now, we'll go and file for your divorce the same day that we take Nancy down to the bank. I'm on pretty good standings with the judge, so it should be granted quickly. Once you're…what's your maiden name, anyway?"

"Gardner."

"Once you are Susan Gardner again, we open the account, transfer the money into it and you'll have some cash of your own. By the way, once you start working for me, you will both be paid. We'll discuss salary later. Okay?"

"Hugh, we need to talk a lot more about this," Susan said.

"Is something wrong, Susan? I thought you liked the idea of being a nurse."

"I do. I like it a lot. But you're being too generous, buying us clothes, giving us a place to stay, giving us all that money, setting us up for careers to be proud of, and now telling us we're going to be paid. When does it end? When do we start giving back?"

Hugh looked into her explosive blue eyes and said, "Susan, you both have been giving back from the moment I found you. I've seen you both grow from victims to confident, strong women. I feel a great sense of pride in each of you. By arming you with skills and knowledge, I know that you both will make this world a better place. When you have children, you'll raise them to be like you, so your goodness will be multiplied. So, please don't worry about any of those things. You're a joy to have around."

"You should have been a preacher, Hugh," joked Susan.

"I think Nancy might disagree, Susan," he said with a light laugh.

Nancy was smiling and nodding. Preachers weren't high on her list right now.

He rose and returned to Rebecca's room finding her asleep. Her breathing sounded regular and Hugh opened the window to the warm outside air letting a spring breeze flow into the room.

He glanced again at his precious sleeping patient, then walked out to the sitting room where the children sat with Betty and Chester.

"How is she, Hugh?" asked Betty with obvious concern.

"She has bronchitis. It's not too bad, but we need to keep it from becoming pneumonia."

"Is mama going to die?" asked Addie.

Hugh crouched down in front of her and said, "We all die, Addie. It's just when that will happen, not if. It's just a part of life. We are born, we live our lives, and then we die. Now, your mama is sick, but I'm giving her medicine and doing everything I can to make her better. But doctors aren't perfect, Addie. There are many sicknesses out there that we can't even try to fix. Yes, people have died from what your mama has. But most people do not die. Most get better. So, what you and Andy can do best is to pray for your mama. That will help the most."

"Then we will do it, Papa. We'll pray the hardest ever."

"I knew you would, Addie. I'm proud to have you for my daughter and Andy for my son. I've wanted to be your papa from the day I found you both."

"And we wanted you for our papa," said Andy.

"Okay. I skipped lunch. So, does anyone else need to grab something to eat?"

Hugh must have been the only one not to have eaten in that group, so he returned to the kitchen, slapped some ham on some bread and returned to Rebecca's room, eating the sandwich as he walked.

When he arrived, he touched her forehead and found that her temperature had lessened somewhat then mentally thanked the shaman and took a seat beside her bed as Susan entered the room with a glass of water.

"She's sleeping, Susan," Hugh whispered.

Susan whispered back, "This is for you. You need something to get that dry sandwich down."

Hugh smiled at her thoughtfulness, accepted the glass and finished his dry sandwich as Susan joined him in watching Rebecca's breathing.

After ten minutes, Hugh stood and they both quietly left the bedroom and let Rebecca sleep.

An hour late, Ella arrived at the ranch and Hugh helped her unharness the oxen and turn them out to pasture with Betty's beasts.

"How's Rebecca?" Ella asked as they removed the heavy harness.

"She's resting. Her fever is down, so now we wait for her to improve. Susan is giving her sponge baths to help with the medicine I gave her."

———

The next morning, Ella and Hugh had return to Baker City for Bob's trial, which didn't last long, but the judge only gave Bob a year, which surprised him and Ella both. Hugh wondered why it was such a light sentence, knowing that back in the Territories, Bob would have been tossed in the hoosegow for three to five years for what he had done, but at least he would be gone for a year.

After the trial, Ella was given her money back, and they stopped at the bank, so she could start her own account before returning to the ranch as quickly as possible so Hugh could care for his patient, both believing that the Bob Orson problem was behind them.

CHAPTER 10

For four more days, Hugh and Susan took care of Rebecca. Rebecca had good and bad moments, as her temperature would climb and then was brought down with the medicine and the cool sponge baths.

Hugh had her eat oatmeal to keep her strength up and had her drink a lot of water, so she didn't get dehydrated, but she was losing strength, and he knew her fever would have to leave soon. Hugh barely slept, even with Susan there to help. Susan had turned out to be a godsend. Nancy, Betty and Ella took turns minding the three children and cooking, but Susan was indispensable.

Then came the fifth day.

Hugh was sitting in his normal location, a chair next to Rebecca's bed with his chin on his chest. The sun had barely emerged from the eastern horizon when Rebecca's eyes popped open. It was like she awakened for the first time. The past five days had been a fog, but now there was early morning sun spreading across the room, and Hugh was there as she knew he would be.

She looked at him and saw the tired face and the crumpled clothes. During the time she had been deathly ill, she remembered that he or Susan was always there. Susan did all the dirty work, keeping her clean and sanitary. Hugh was always listening to her chest, taking her temperature and giving her that bitter medicine. She smiled warmly at her dozing husband knowing he was more tired than she was.

"Hugh," she said softly, then a little louder, "Hugh."

Hugh's eyes snapped open, and he could see her bright eyes and knew instantly that his Rebecca was going to be fine.

He stood, then sat on her bed and stroked her face gently with his fingers, feeling no trace of a fever.

"Rebecca, it's good to have you back," he said as he smiled gently at his wife.

"Hugh, go and get some sleep. You look terrible."

"How could I? You were in our bed."

She laughed lightly; that glorious laugh that he thought he might never hear again.

"I'll sleep in a little while. Can I get you something good to eat other than oatmeal?"

"Oh, please! Bacon and eggs and coffee sounds marvelous."

"I'll go and do that. You stay in bed. You're going to be weak for a couple of days. Good food will help to replace the weight you probably lost and you couldn't afford it in the first place."

Rebecca smiled, sighed and said, "I feel so alive, Hugh."

Hugh returned her smile, and said, "I'll send our children in to see you when they're awake. I kept them away because I didn't want them to come down with bronchitis."

"Thank you for protecting them, Hugh."

"I'm their papa. I have to protect them."

"Yes, you are."

Hugh leaned over and kissed her softly before he said, "I'll go and get those eggs and bacon going."

He walked to the kitchen feeling awfully good after averaging three hours of sleep for the past week.

He fired up the cook stove and put water in the coffee pot and had just started frying the bacon when Susan stepped into the room. He didn't even have to turn to know who was behind him. He could tell just by the sounds of her footsteps.

"How's Rebecca this morning?" she asked.

"Go and see," he said as he finally turned and smiled at her.

Susan could tell by his demeanor that she was better.

She smiled back and said, "You're a wonderful doctor, Hugh."

He said, "Susan, I'll tell you that I've never seen anyone that showed as much compassion and strength as you have this past week. I'll be eternally in your debt."

Susan blushed with the compliment and blushed even more when Hugh hugged took a long stride, wrapped her in his arms and kissed her on the forehead.

"You are a true blessing, Susan," he said as he looked into those bright blue eyes.

"I'll go see Rebecca," she said after Hugh let her go.

Hugh returned to cook as Susan walked to Rebecca's room.

"You are looking bright this morning, Rebecca," she said with a big smile as she entered.

"And it's all thanks to you, Susan. I'm happy that you're going to be Hugh's nurse. Hopefully, we'll be good friends, too."

"I'd like that."

Ten minutes later, Hugh had the coffee, eggs and bacon prepared and brought a tray into Rebecca. She and Susan were still talking when he entered.

He set the tray on Rebecca's lap and she began eating, savoring each morsel.

Thirty minutes later, the house was alive with movement. Andy and Addie could see their mother for the first time in almost a week and Rebecca was ecstatic to be with her children again.

Later that morning, Hugh helped Rebecca walk around the inside of the house. She was wearing one of the dresses that Hugh had bought for her at the trading post. She wore it almost like a night dress and Hugh prohibited the use of the corset and suggested that it was an unnecessary restriction and she didn't need the enhancement anyway.

Rebecca had accused him of having alternative reasons for the ban, and he was happy to see her humor returning.

She continued to eat well and in two more days, seemed back to her normal self.

Once Hugh was satisfied that she was fully recovered, he took Susan and Nancy into Baker City, deposited the bank draft, noting the new balance of $11,100, had an account created in Nancy's name and transferred five hundred dollars into the new account.

Then, they went to the courthouse where Susan filed for divorce for adultery, naming Nellie Crump as the second party. Neither Frank Fremont nor Nellie showed for the hearing the next day and Susan became Susan Gardner again. Once it was final, Hugh marched Susan over to the bank and created her new account and transferred the five hundred dollars.

Susan was happy about the money and becoming a nurse, but she felt enormously guilty at the same time, but not for the gift of the money and a future. It was because of the man who had given her both. She had become very fond of Rebecca, yet as she rode in the buggy on the way back to the ranch, she knew she was falling in love with Hugh but vowed that it would always be her secret. She knew how much he loved Rebecca and that it was reciprocated.

She would never be so selfish as to injure that love, but she gave in to some measure of selfishness when she decided that she would still work with Hugh as his nurse just to be close to him. She would never marry again, not with her overwhelming and still growing feelings for Hugh.

Now that Rebecca's recovery was complete, Hugh thought was time to stop being her doctor and start being her husband, which he mentioned to her privately when he returned, but both knew the magic would have to wait until the children were asleep.

Rebecca had been more than anxious for that to happen, and she thought that Hugh was being overly cautious when he told her that he didn't want to risk a chance of a relapse. But now, her lungs sounded clear, and she was herself again.

There was almost a holiday atmosphere at dinner, and they had finally used the dining room, which was adjacent to the kitchen. Despite its size, it was a tight fit as six adults and three children crowded around a table designed for eight.

As they began eating, Hugh scanned the table, put down his fork, stood and announced a remarkable revelation.

"Ladies and gentlemen, may I have your attention, please? As I prepared to partake of this wonderful roast beef dinner, I noticed something that was somewhat disturbing. I suddenly realized that I am the only adult male in this house with all these handsome, young females, which means I may have to leave."

Those handsome young females and the youngsters were all wide-eyed at the idea, but it was Susan who was the first to ask, "Why would you think that, Hugh?"

"I occurred to me that with the current configuration of the house, it is either a convent of pious nuns, in which case, I should never have been here, or it could be a commercial establishment that provides, shall we say, less pious activities. In that case, I must either depart immediately or have my reputation sullied as the operator of the aforementioned house of dubious reputation."

Laughter rolled in a wave across the room among the women and the children laughed as well, but none understood what was so funny.

Hugh just smiled, then bowed, took his seat and returned to slicing his roast beef.

After dinner, the children went off to play with Chester and the adults adjourned to the sitting room.

"So, what's the plan after this?" asked Rebecca once they were all settled.

Hugh was sitting beside her on the couch, smiled at her and replied, "Aside from the obvious short-term plan that won't be mentioned, I'll talk about the other plans that don't involve just me and you, Mrs. McGinnis."

Rebecca smiled, but didn't reply verbally.

Hugh then continued, saying, "Tomorrow, I'll write a letter to the University of Michigan requesting a waiver of my final year of training. I'll include a history of my work with the Medical Corps during the war. They've granted them in the past for just that reason. If that works out, I'll start a clinic. I'm leaning toward building here, with the clinic about halfway down the access road. What do each of you think of that idea?"

"I think it's a marvelous idea," answered Rebecca.

"So, do I," echoed Susan

They all murmured their approval.

"There are some other things that I need to do, starting tomorrow. Now that things have settled down, I really need to explore this house, especially those rooms that were locked downstairs. Then, there are some other things. The next time we go into town, I'd like to buy each of the ladies three or four riding outfits, then we'll get you some horses and saddles. I have some horses out back, and I'm not sure if you noticed, but the stallion has been paying a lot of attention to the three mares. In a few months, I think we'll have some foals. But in the interim, we still need some for you to ride. That's five horses and saddles. The reason for all of this is that I want each of you have your own horse and have a feeling of independence. If you need to go somewhere, you shouldn't have to depend on me. Until we do that, I'm planning on buying a nice carriage and a team of horses, so we can go as a group if we need to. I'll do that tomorrow, too. And there is one other thing that may sound a bit reactionary."

"And what is this reactionary item?" asked Betty.

"I'd like you all to be armed. Not with big pistols or rifles, but with Remington derringers. They're very small, easy to use, and still deadly. Now, I'm armed to the teeth with guns, but I'm also six feet four inches and two hundred and twenty pounds, and a man to boot, so I'm not usually trifled with. But you are all young and pretty women and I'd feel better if you could protect yourselves. I may be all wet about this, but it'll be your decision. If anyone wants one, I'll buy some and show you how to use it."

"I'll take one," said Susan, "I'm a bit leery about Frank. Once he gets tired of Nellie, he may try to get familiar again."

"Me, too," echoed Ella.

When they had finished only Betty and Rebecca demurred.

"Okay, I'll pick up four derringers tomorrow. I know that he has some in stock. They only came out recently, but they are a well-received weapon."

Rebecca noticed the math issue and asked, “Why four? Only three wanted them.”

“You didn’t think I’d miss the opportunity to have one, do you?”

They all laughed at his gun disease, which seemed to run rampant among the male population.

Rebecca stood, faked a big yawn and winked at Hugh before she said, “I’m a little tired. I think I’ll turn in.”

After the bedroom door closed, the other women all looked at Hugh with smiles and raised eyebrows.

“Well, Hugh?” asked Susan, “Feeling a little sleepy yourself?”

Her question created a wave of giggles.

Hugh stayed sitting and asked, “Why? It’s pretty early and I don’t want to disturb Rebecca.”

The smiles grew and Nancy asked, “So, what are you going to do then?”

“I thought that we could play a few hands of gin rummy. Is anyone up to playing?”

Betty giggled again and asked, “You should be playing, Mister McGinnis, but not with us.”

Hugh looked curiously at the four ladies, shrugged and said, “Well, I may not be that tired, but maybe if I went to bed and had some exercise, I’d be able to sleep.”

As he rose, the women were engulfed in laughter, and stayed laughing as he walked down the hallway and gently knocked on their bedroom door. Rebecca opened it slightly and waved him in, then closed it behind him. The lamp was lit, but the flame was low.

Rebecca was wearing the green silk dress, and Hugh could immediately tell she was wearing only the green silk dress. How she managed to change so quickly astonished him.

"Is this what you told me you wanted to see me in on that first night I was sick?" she asked as she put her hands behind his neck.

"You know it is, but my imagination didn't do you justice, Rebecca."

Her face was just inches from his as he whispered, "Rebecca, this has been a long wait after our marriage until now, but I'll never be able to wait so long again."

Rebecca replied in a low, husky voice, "I'm waiting for you now, Hugh. I've been waiting almost from that first day and I want you so badly that it aches."

Hugh began to disrobe, and Rebecca assisted until he stood in front of her with no cloth touching his skin and pressed against her until only the thin layer of cool, shimmering cloth stood between them. He ran his hands over her softly and slowly, sliding the silk with them, feeling every curve, every nuance of her body. Then as she still stood, he walked behind her and slid his fingers down the front of the dress caressing her body as they moved. He pulled her long brown hair away and began kissing the back of her neck as he slid his hands ever lower.

Rebecca leaned back slightly and felt him hard against her, then swayed gently feeling the electric tension between them.

Hugh's hands reached the bottom of the silk dress and slowly pulled it upward, inch by inch, revealing her glorious, mature female form. As the dress reached above her breasts, she raised her arms to the ceiling to let him take away the impediment.

Hugh tossed the dress aside and turned her to face him.

No words were spoken, and none were needed.

He began kissing her forehead and then her lips, never hard, but ever soft, ever gently. He moved down her body kissing and stroking her, watching the goosebumps blossom. He ran his fingernails up her back, barely touching her skin.

Rebecca was on fire as she felt his fingers and lips stroke her passion. She had been married twice, but nothing had prepared her for this. This was being loved as she had never experienced before, and she wanted this...she wanted him.

He lowered her gently to the bed, then pulled her close and they kissed more deeply. Rebecca ran her fingernails across his muscled body, the touching alone aroused her even more. His masculinity was simply overwhelming. She felt his strong hands on her back and slid even closer against him than she thought possible and believed that she couldn't wait much longer.

And yet, they discovered the rapture of deferred completion as they spent even more time touching and exploring as their lust and passion rose to almost unfathomable heights.

Finally, neither could bear to stay apart any longer. If Rebecca had thought she had reached the apex of pleasure minutes before, she soon found herself proven wrong. Ecstasy was too mild a word to describe what she felt resulting in many references to the deity.

Hugh was in that same extraordinary pinnacle of pleasure and passion. He had never been so completely immersed in a woman and only wanted to please her, to make her feel loved like no woman has ever been loved. Yet he discovered that by doing that, by making Rebecca reach new heights of pleasure, his own levels of desire were expanded beyond measure.

When they finally collapsed and lay comfortably fitted together in a sheen of sweat, Rebecca's hair in shambles, Hugh looked down at his wife.

"That was one hell of a consummation, my love," he said softly.

"It was worth the wait, my husband. Hugh, I've been married twice, but nothing ever came close to this. It's like comparing a puddle to an ocean. I thought I'd lose my mind a few times."

"It wouldn't have been lost. It would have met up with mine somewhere on the floor."

She giggled softly, then just curled up under his arm and sighed in contentment as Hugh stroked his wife's hair.

Despite immediately gathering the children and moving into the basement to give the newlyweds privacy, the four women couldn't help but hear the extended sounds of passion coming from the bedroom upstairs and had been impressed by the volume and duration of their passion.

Just as they were preparing to return to the main floor, they had to head back to the downstairs bedroom when the noise recommenced, which did more than just impress them, it astonished them. Naturally, they spent the time commenting on the duration and frequency.

As they sat at the breakfast table the next morning, the children were the only members of the household that were unaware of the marital bliss that had been experienced in the main bedroom. But the women not named Rebecca looked at Hugh with an enhanced level of respect, which had already reached heroic levels.

Later that morning, Hugh rode into town with Susan and Rebecca in the buggy to conduct some business that should have been done before but had been delayed just as their consummation had been put on hold.

They stopped at the bank first and Hugh had Rebecca added to his account. She was stunned to learn the balance, as he gave her some blank drafts, but didn't tell her of the account in Ann Arbor yet because he simply didn't think it mattered.

After leaving the bank, he dropped them off at the clothing store and continued to the carriage maker's shop. In addition to carriages, the firm made all sorts of wheeled conveyances, buggies, wagons and buckboards, to name a few.

They only had two carriages available when he entered and both were for two horses, not four. He chose one and asked about teams for his new carriage. They had some in the back corral, but again, not a big selection, so he added a pair of gray geldings that while not perfectly matched, would do the job and add a touch of elegance at the same time.

After paying for the carriage and horses, he went to the biggest of the three liveries in town and found a good selection of horses. The liveryman said they had just received them from a local horse ranch and that they were all saddle broken.

He and Hugh walked among the animals and found five geldings that he liked. He paid cash for the horses and had lead ropes attached to their bridles, then said he'd be back shortly. He had three saddles back at the ranch already, so he needed two more. The liveryman didn't have any for sale, so Hugh went to the leather shop and bought two new complete rigs which cost almost as much as the horses. Hugh said he'd be back for them as well.

His last stop was at the gunsmith where he bought four Remington .41 caliber derringers and two boxes of cartridges. While he was there, he and the gunsmith, Harry Wilkens, began talking about a mutually favorite subject…guns.

During the conversation, Harry asked which weapons he had and when Hugh said he carried a Henry, Harry knew he had a potential sale as he pulled a carbine from the rack behind him and handed it to Hugh, who began examining the Winchester '66, which had already been christened the Yellowboy by its users. It looked just like the Henry with some noticeable differences.

"You should buy one of these Winchesters, Hugh. They have some real advantages over the Henry. They look like the Henry because Mister Winchester bought the company. They shoot the same .44 rimfire Henry cartridge, but they made some really good improvements. The biggest was that they added a loading gate, so you don't have to open the magazine tube to put in more ammunition. I'll bet there were times that you were using that Henry and had to flip it upside down and check the open slot under the barrel to see how many rounds you had left just so you didn't run out and have to spend a minute reloading."

Hugh nodded and replied, "I have, as a matter of fact. I had to space my shots, so I didn't find myself in that situation."

"That same magazine tube had that open slot, so you had to be careful not to get it dirty and cause a jam, too. And you know how careful you had to be when you did reload the Henry, so you didn't set off one of those rimfires if you slid it in too fast. The Winchester has that forearm under the barrel, so you can keep shooting with a hot barrel and not burn your fingers. The last really big improvement was that they added a safety, so you don't accidentally blow your foot off. What do you think, Hugh?"

Hugh smiled at Harry and replied, "You had me with the loading gate, Harry, but I'm not going to buy one today."

"You're not?" asked Harry in surprise.

"No, sir. I'll buy two of them. They are fine weapons and if you can, let me have one carbine and one rifle, and give me four boxes of Henry cartridges, too."

Harry grinned and said, "You're a man after my own heart, Hugh."

Then he turned, picked a Winchester with the longer rifle barrel from the rack, set it on the counter with the derringers and the .41 caliber ammunition and then added the four boxes of .44 rimfire cartridges. Hugh still had the Winchester carbine in his hands admiring the design.

Harry put the Remington derringers and all the ammunition in a bag, and Hugh paid for his purchases. Harry added two scabbards for the Winchesters, which also served as protection for the new repeaters when he slid the two Yellowboys into a sack without damaging the new Winchesters yet still allow Hugh to carry them both with one hand and the heavy bag with the other.

They shook hands and Harry clutched both of his new Winchesters in his right hand and hefted the heavy sack with his left as Harry trotted to the door to hold it open for him.

Once outside, Hugh laid his purchases on the buggy's floor, then stepped inside, took the reins and gave them a flick to let the horse know it was time to go.

He drove the buggy back to the clothing store, finding Rebecca and Susan in the women's section, which didn't require a lot of sleuthing on his part.

Hugh approached them from behind, and said, "Now, ladies, I've bought a carriage, two saddles, five horses, four derringers, two Winchesters and a lot of ammunition. What have you bought?"

Rebecca looked at him with a grimace and silently pointed at a stack of boxes.

Hugh spied the pile and simply said, "Oh."

Then he smiled and said, "Well, Susan and Rebecca, I hope those things are at least entertaining."

Rebecca laughed, saying, "Some of them you'll find very entertaining."

"Then it was money well spent. Now, for the logistics. Tell the clerk we'll be back to pick up your order shortly. If you ladies will accompany me, we'll board the buggy and go over to the carriage shop and pick up our new carriage. Susan, did you want to drive the buggy?"

"Sure."

"Then after we get the carriage, I'll swing by and pick up the two saddles. I'll put them on the carriage roof and then we'll head over to the livery to pick up the five new horses and finally we return here, load all your clothes into the carriage and head home. By the way, you did buy some riding outfits, didn't you?"

"Yes, sir," Susan replied.

"Just wondering," he said with a small smile.

They did exactly as Hugh had planned in that order: carriage, saddles, then horses, before they returned to the clothing store. Hugh did most of the lifting as they all carried boxes of clothes out to the carriage. Hugh counted seventeen boxes and wondered what 'interesting' was.

Hugh drove the carriage with Rebecca in the driver's seat beside him and the five horses trailing, while Susan drove the buggy in front. As they turned to leave the town, Rebecca was looking to the right when Hugh glanced the other direction and thought he saw Bob Orson walking along the boardwalk. *How was that possible?*

He turned to Rebecca and said, "Rebecca, I could have sworn I saw Bob walking along the road."

She turned and looked at him as she exclaimed, *"What?"*

"Maybe I was mistaken, but I don't think so. After we get home, I'm going to ride into town right away and talk to the marshal."

"Alright," she replied, "but I don't like this one bit."

"Neither do I," Hugh replied.

They drove back to the ranch house in good time and Hugh led the five horses into the corral as soon as he could, then went into the barn and brought out Bob's horse and one of the others and put them in the corral. He led the grays into the barn and put them in the stalls, put the buggy horse in his normal slot and parked the buggy. He'd move the wagon out and the carriage in until he could make a more permanent arrangement. Maybe he'd add a carriage house when he built the clinic. He had written and mailed his letter to the University of Michigan a few days earlier, but that would take a while.

Hugh carried his ammunition bag and the two Winchesters into the house and after entering the front door, set the new weapons and ammo in the corner and stepped down the hallway to the kitchen where the women who made the purchases were opening boxes with Ella, Betty and Nancy's assistance. They all looked at him as he walked in.

"I'm going to grab a quick lunch and then go and find out why Bob Orson is on the streets and not locked up somewhere."

"Do you want me to come with you, Hugh?" asked Rebecca.

"No, sweetheart, I'm going to ride Night and make it a fast trip."

"Okay," she said as they returned to their boxes, quietly relieved that she wouldn't have to see Bob again.

He made and devoured another ham sandwich, went back to the barn, quickly saddled Night, then walked him out of the barn and set him on a fast trot to town, arriving at the marshal's office thirty minutes later.

He walked into the office and found the only deputy at the desk and wondered if the town marshal even existed.

"Afternoon, Mister McGinnis. What can I do for you?"

"I have a question about Bob Orson. I thought I saw him out walking the streets earlier today."

"You probably did. After the judge gave him the sentence, we told him we didn't have the enough room to keep anyone that long, so he suspended the sentence."

"Why didn't he send him to the state penitentiary?"

"We don't have one. The county has a jail, but it's full up, and his sentence was the shortest, so he gave him probation."

"Okay, thanks for the information."

"Sorry about all this, Mister McGinnis. I know the judge was kind of angry at having to let him walk, too."

"I understand. Sometimes we get caught in a bad situation."

"Yes, sir."

Hugh nodded, then left the office. He wasn't at the anger level, more of a severely perturbed stage. He understood what had happened, but still didn't like it. Bob hadn't really been violent, so maybe he'd find some nice, frumpy wealthy woman and become a model citizen, but somehow Hugh couldn't talk himself into believing that for even a moment.

He rode Night back to the ranch in less than thirty minutes and after getting the stallion unsaddled and returned to his harem, he returned to the house and told Rebecca and Ella of the circumstances that led to Bob Orson's freedom. Neither woman was pleased but knew it as a situation that was beyond their control.

An hour later, all the ladies were out in the corral choosing their mounts. Hugh let them have their choices, except that the small gray gelding that he had already assigned to Andy. He hadn't told him yet and knew that Rebecca would want to be there when he did.

The ladies were all pleased with their choices and Hugh set them up with saddles and adjusted the stirrups as needed. He gave the new saddles to Rebecca and Susan, and the others didn't complain.

"Now, you'll have to come up with names for your horses. And whenever you want to ride, just go and put on your new riding outfits and off you go."

"Can we go for a ride right now?" asked Nancy.

"Not in those dresses. It might prove difficult. But after you change, enjoy yourselves. Rebecca, did you want to be there when I tell Andy that he has his own horse?"

"Absolutely," she replied as she grinned, "Addie won't be happy."

"Don't you worry about Addie."

"I didn't think I'd have to. I know how much you care for them both."

"Let's go," he said as he took her hand.

They walked into the kitchen and called the children, who trotted into the room just seconds later.

"Mama! Papa!" cried Addie for no particular reason other than she still enjoyed saying it.

"Andy, I have something to tell you. Go ahead and sit down."

Andy and Addie both took seats and looked up at their new father.

"Now, today, I bought five horses for all the ladies, but I forgot that I already had a small gray gelding. Now, it just wouldn't be right if the gelding didn't get a rider, so, do you know of anyone who would like a small gray horse?"

Andy's face lit up as he asked, "Could I have him?"

"Why, I never even thought of that! That's a great idea, but I'll buy you a new saddle tomorrow. Okay?"

Andy was bouncing in his seat as he glanced at his mother, then Hugh and then Addie before looking back at Hugh.

"Thank you, Papa! I have my own horse!" he exclaimed.

"You're welcome, Andy," Hugh said with a grin of his own.

Then he looked over at Addie. She didn't say anything as she clutched Sophie but looked up at him with sad eyes. Hugh felt his heart breaking, even though he knew she'd be dancing in another few seconds.

"Addie, you look sad. Why is that?" he asked.

"I'm okay, Papa."

"I'll bet you're wondering why I didn't give you a horse."

She just nodded as her eyes began to well with tears.

"There was a reason for that, too. You are my special little girl, aren't you?"

"Yes, Papa," she said quietly.

"So, did you know that in a few months the lady horses out in the corral will have babies?"

The reason for her tears was forgotten as her blonde head tilted up to face Hugh and she shouted, *"They will?"*

"Uh-uh. And who do you think will get the first pick of whichever baby horse she wants?"

"Me?" she asked hopefully.

"No one else, sweetie. I wanted you to be able to grow up with your own horse. You won't be able to ride it for a while until it's strong enough to hold you. Is that alright?"

She hopped down from her chair and leapt into Hugh's arms.

"Thank you, Papa. I can't wait to see my baby horse."

"You have to be patient, but you'll be able to watch the horses' bellies grow big and one of them will have your foal."

He put her down and said to her, "Now you can tell Chuck that he gets the second new one. Can you do that?"

"Yes, Papa. He'll be happy, too."

She scampered off to tell Chuck with Andy running quickly behind her.

Rebecca sidled up next to him and said, “You’ve made three children very happy.”

“They’re easy to please, Rebecca. Now, let’s get working on the other things that I bought.”

Hugh and Rebecca walked into the main room and picked up the bag with the derringers and ammunition leaving the empty Winchesters leaning against the wall.

He called Ella, Susan, and Betty into the room and each took a seat as he showed them how to use the simple derringers. Nancy came along just to watch. He advised them to keep them with them always when outside the house, then loaded the small pistols and handed one to each woman.

“These are perfectly safe to keep in a pocket or your purse. They’ll only fire if the hammer is pulled back. You have those two shots available to you, just pull back the hammer, fire once and then repeat if you need to.”

Ella said, “I don’t suppose this means I can shoot Bob Orson if I see him.”

They all laughed until they realized she was serious, and Hugh said, “Ella, you can’t just shoot him. I would have done it if it was legal.”

“Hugh, if you hadn’t figured out that he was going to steal my money, he’d be gone, and I’d be left with nothing. He deserved to go to jail.”

“I agree, but that was beyond our control. Besides, I wouldn’t have let anything happen to you.”

"I know, Hugh, but it still makes me mad."

"Now, if any of you armed ladies would like to practice with your new weapons, I'll set up a target range for you. I'd recommend that you do that, so you'll know what to expect when you pull the trigger."

"We'll do that, Hugh," said Susan as she examined her Remington.

"Good. Let me know when you want to start practicing."

______

That first night after the big shopping trip, Hugh found what Rebecca had claimed would be 'very entertaining'. She had found what would have passed for a nightdress if there had been any flannel or been a trifle less translucent. It wasn't transparent, but it did little to hide what was beneath. She said it was a nightgown, but it wasn't worn for very long.

______

The next day, Hugh finally got a chance to explore the house and ranch after almost two weeks of residence. He took Rebecca and Susan with him as they went downstairs where Susan showed Hugh which three rooms had been off limits to her and Nancy.

Hugh had found a key ring with several large keys in the main bedroom, and he assumed that Brian had locked the rooms for some reason and the keys were for those three rooms that must have been important to him.

The Hanson brothers had kept the keys there to keep Susan and Nancy from finding them. Of course, they had tied Susan and Nancy when they were both gone anyway. He still shuddered at what the two young women had gone through and wished he could shoot those two bastards again.

But first, Hugh wanted to see the cold room which had fascinated him when he had been inside for brief periods. The room was the first room on the right next to the kitchen outer door, and looked like a normal room, but when the thick door was opened it was probably below forty degrees inside. Hugh could immediately see how it was done, sort of. Surrounding the room were pipes…lots of pipes. They were made of copper, which surprised Hugh because one didn't see a lot of copper pipes in houses. He felt them and found them to be even colder than the surrounding air. *How did they get that way?*

After a quick examination, he said, "This is brilliant. He's running cold water through the pipes. I just don't know where it's coming from. It must be from the river that he said runs through the ranch. That river must be on the eastern side, because I haven't seen it."

"Hugh, I'm not sure if it's big enough to be called a river, but there's a big creek that runs from the east and then enters the forest on the south," said Susan.

"How close does it get to the house?" he asked.

"I'd guess about eight hundred yards."

"That must be it, but it's a long way to run pipes. That's where he'd get the pressure for the pipes in the house as well. This is all amazing. Now let's go see the mystery rooms."

The first room Brian must have used as his design room. It had a drafting table, lots of paper and drawing instruments. He had a large window that Hugh had recalled seeing outside but didn't know where it was inside the house, and besides, without light in the room, it would be impossible to know what the room contained.

The second room was a shop of some kind. There were tools of all kinds and a large table. It was Brian's work room. He'd design it in the drafting room and build it in his shop.

"I'll bet I know what the third room is," Hugh said as they left Brian's workshop.

They opened the last room, and as Hugh expected, it was a large office and library. There was a large desk, a sink in the corner, and walls of books. Rebecca and Susan were already looking at the book titles as Hugh stood in awe of his brother's talents.

"Hugh, I think Brian knew you'd be coming," said Rebecca.

Hugh walked over and looked at the books, finding a lot of scientific and technical books and, of course, architectural books. But three of the shelves were medical books. Hugh smiled and pulled out one thick volume and handed it to Susan.

"This is Gray's Anatomy, Susan. It came out just before the war. I lost my copy, but this one is better. It shows how the human body works. I don't think this room should remain locked."

Susan's eyes sparkled as she turned the first few pages.

"Could I come down and read these sometimes, Hugh?"

"Susan, this is your home. You go anywhere you wish."

She smiled broadly as she scanned the walls and said, "There is so much to learn here."

Hugh perused the walls of books as well, then said, "There is so much to learn everywhere."

Hugh walked over to the desk, took a seat and began opening drawers. In the first drawer was a copy of Brian's will, which Hugh opened. It listed his primary assets and in the final paragraph left it all to Hugh.

"I suppose I'll have to go to the attorney's office and clear this up. I'll take care of that tomorrow," he said as he refolded the will and set it on the desktop.

He opened the middle drawer and found a cloth-wrapped rectangular object. When Hugh pulled it out, he thought it might be a mirror, but then he slid it out of the cloth bag and found it to be a daguerreotype, and even remembered standing for the image, as he'd had to remain frozen for seconds while the photographer took the picture, which was hard thing to do when you're a boy.

Hugh took a deep breath and stared at the image. It was his father, mother, Brian and a young Hugh…the McGinnis family. Two of them were no longer alive and one had been murdered by another family member in the picture.

Rebecca and Susan stood behind him as he studied the image.

Rebecca asked, "When was that taken, Hugh?"

"I was about thirteen or so. Brian was about to go off to college, so my father arranged to have the photograph taken. I wondered where it had gone. I knew after my father shot my mother that he wanted nothing around to remember her after that."

Susan hadn't heard the story and was about to ask Hugh about it, but thought the time wasn't right. Hugh needed private time.

Instead, she said, "Your mother was very beautiful, Hugh."

"She was on the outside, but she was empty inside. I don't know if she was always that way or it was because of the way she was treated by my father. She needed to be loved, as we all do. He must have provided some level of physical attention because Brian and I exist, but there wasn't that deep bond that is critical to happiness.

"When I knew her well enough to see her as a human being and not my mother, I could see the great gap in her soul. By then, she looked at us as spawn of my father, and not as her children. My father probably lavished more attention and emotional capital on his many conquests than on my mother. Now, if she had been as cold and emotionless before they wed, then maybe I could understand his behavior, but not the shooting."

"Brian looks a lot like you," Susan continued.

"He did. I always thought he was the better man, too. It wasn't the usual hero worship that younger brothers sometimes feel for older brothers, either that or they can't stand them for being bullies. With Brian, it was different. He always took time to talk to me, and he'd explain things to me that should have come from my father."

Hugh allowed himself a short chuckle before he said, "Brian was the one that told me about the facts of life when I was eleven. I remember how shocked I was, and how he told me that I'd really appreciate the differences between men and women when I got older. I told him that I thought it was yucky."

Then Hugh let out his breath and continued.

“I missed him terribly when he went off to college, and he only returned one summer. He was more outspoken about my father’s lifestyle than I was. My father still supported him financially, and he still received the same monetary gifts, but my father never forgave him for saying some of the things he did. I didn’t bother because I knew it wouldn’t make any difference.

“Brian was the reason I went to medical school. After I had helped with some of the logging injuries, he pointed out my talents in that area and said I could do a lot more good as a doctor than I could as a lumberjack. Then, after he graduated, he left to go to Oregon. Before he did, he married Louise. She was a wonderful woman, and they were so very much in love. You could close your eyes and feel it.

“They took a ship to the west coast of America, not the Oregon Trail. He’d write me letters telling me about the ranch and encouraging me to come and join him after I graduated. Then Louise died with their newborn child. They’re buried somewhere on this ranch. I’ll find that tomorrow as well. I’ve got to make sure it’s well maintained.”

“You were a handsome boy, Hugh,” said Rebecca.

Hugh didn’t reply, but just looked at the daguerreotype for a few more seconds, blew out his breath again, slid it into the cloth and slipped it back into the drawer. He put Brian’s will in his pocket and stood.

“Well, now we know where everything is on the inside of the house, maybe I should go and explore the outside today. It’s still early enough.”

“Did you want company?” asked Rebecca.

“Sure. Why don’t you both come along? Susan seems to know where that elusive creek is. I want to see how Brian did the plumbing. How I could miss a big creek just a few hundred yards away is beyond me.”

They left the basement, went out to the barn and Hugh saddled the three horses and thirty minutes later, they left the barn and travelled east. Susan said it was straight ahead.

When Hugh finally spotted the creek, he could understand why he hadn’t found it as they had ridden a steady incline, then, just as they crossed the top of the rise, the wide and deep creek flowed past. The water entered the property from the mountains, miles to the east. It had cut a gorge twenty feet deep through the earth as it cut through the farthest reaches of the ranch, but then hit an outcropping of limestone. The limestone had been a natural dam, making a large, deep pool almost forty feet across, then the water had crested the limestone eventually carving a channel in the rock and creating a fifteen-foot-high waterfall at the edge of the limestone. A smaller pool maybe twenty feet across was dug by the cascading water before it continued its way down the incline towards the ranch and then turned into the forest. At the bottom of the waterfall, about five feet from the edge Hugh saw a mesh covered pipe under the water. It was three feet below the surface of the second pool.

“Well, ladies, there’s the source of the house’s water,” he said as he pointed at the pipe, then he turned to look at the distant ranch house.

“That must be almost a half a mile. That’s a lot of pipe. The water is a good fifty feet in elevation above the house, so he wouldn’t need a pump. My brother was a genius.”

Both women followed the line from the pool to the house and agreed that it was a brilliant piece of engineering.

They walked the horses to the large pool above the falls.

"I know where I'll be in those hot summer days," Hugh said as he looked at the pool.

Rebecca declined, saying, "Not me. I know how cold that water will be. I'd freeze my behind off."

"We can't have that, can we, Rebecca? It's such a lovely behind," Hugh said as he laughed.

Susan smiled as she continued to look at the deep pool, then said, "I don't know, Rebecca. That looks mighty enticing to me."

Rebecca smiled and said, "Well, you two are welcome to it. I'll stick to nice warm baths."

They mounted to continue their tour and found the eight oxen released from Ella's and Betty's wagons munching away near a smaller creek. They turned back toward the ranch house and were about a quarter of a mile from the house when they found Louise's burial plot. There was a wrought iron fence that was twenty feet by thirty, but grass had overgrown everything.

Hugh looked down at the graveyard and said, "I've got to clean this up. I should have taken care of it the first week. Let's head back to the barn. I'm going to get some tools and come back here."

After returning to the barn, Rebecca and Susan returned to the house while Hugh unsaddled their horses, brushed them down, then released them to the corral.

Then he walked to the back of the barn where the tools were neatly stored, found a scythe, a heavy rake and a hoe.

He put them over his shoulder then walked to the gravesite with Chester tagging along behind.

When he arrived, he took off his shirt. It was warm enough and he knew he'd be working up a heavy sweat. He began with the scythe, sweeping it easily, making short work of the tall grass. An hour later, the grass was reduced to a pleasant lawn before he raked the loose grass into piles and carried them out into the pasture where he tossed them onto the ground. Then he returned with the hoe and began smoothing away the earth above Louise's gravesite. The headstone was a bit dirty, so Hugh used his shirt to wipe it clean.

As he cleared it of accumulated dirt, Hugh paused and read the inscription:

Louise Mary McGinnis
18 March 1838 ~ 10 February 1863
Cherished wife of Brian
Forever in his Heart

He took a deep breath and wiped the tear that had fallen from his left eye. What had bothered him was that he knew that Brian was buried almost two thousand miles away, but he was comforted in knowing that they had been reunited.

He'd gather rocks from the multiple creeks that ran through the property and make a stone shield over her grave to keep the grass at bay sometime in the next week.

"Hugh?"

Hugh smiled at the voice. Rebecca still had that effect on him.

He turned and accepted the glass of lemonade she had brought for him.

She smiled at him and said, “I thought you might need this.”

“Thoughtful as always,” he replied as he accepted the glass and drank it down without pause.

When he finished, he said, “Thank you, Rebecca. You know, we don’t get to spend much time alone these days.”

“I know, but things may be changing, Hugh. Betty, Ella and Nancy were talking about the café in town. They heard that the owner wants to sell and think if they pool their money, they can buy it and make it better. What do you think?”

“I think we should talk about it. I’d like to inspect the place to make sure it was in good condition, but I wouldn’t want them to spend their money to buy it. They need that cash for supplies and living expenses until they start making a profit.”

“Why am I not surprised by your answer?” she asked before walking close to him and kissing him softly, then saying, “I’d hug you but you’re a bit sweaty.”

“I seem to recall you don’t mind if I’m sweaty sometimes,” he said as he smiled.

“That’s when we’re both that way. Slippery is interesting,” she replied.

“I’m finished here. Let’s go talk to the ladies.”

Hugh handed her the empty glass, hung his shirt over his shoulder, picked up the tools, then he and Rebecca walked to the barn, Chester silently padding along behind.

After reaching the barn, Hugh dropped off the tools and put his shirt back on as most of the sweat had evaporated.

They walked into the kitchen where Ella, Betty and Nancy were still in discussion while Susan sat at the table as a spectator, not a participant.

Hugh took a seat and said, “Ladies, I hear you three want to enter the business world.”

“Hugh, we just heard about the café and wanted to ask what you thought,” said Betty, “We’re really excited about the prospect of running our own business and making all the decisions ourselves.”

“Well, I know you all cook well enough. Nancy, I still remember that cheese-covered, mustard and sauerkraut sausage you and Susan made. If you do things like that, innovative, different food in addition to the standard fare, you’ll make a good amount of money. Whatever you do, don’t undervalue your product. Compute the cost of the food, including your overhead and then add a nice twenty percent profit onto it and you’ll do well.

“Now, I want to inspect the establishment for you. I’ll examine the structure, the cookstoves, sinks, and other things. If it’s all good, then I’ll buy it for you, listing each of you on the deed. I don’t want you to spend your money on the purchase. You’ll need that for supplies and living expenses until you start earning a profit. I don’t want to hear any protests, either. You’ll just have to feed the McGinnis family from time to time, and that includes Susan. Is it a deal?”

They all looked at each other and then smiled at Hugh.

“It’s a deal,” announced Betty.

"One other thing. You can take your horses, of course, but you can do me a favor and take the buggy, too. We have the carriage and I need the room in the barn for the wagon. Ella and Betty, you can raise some money by selling your wagons and oxen teams. There's a man in town who takes the wagons and converts them to regular freight wagons. He'll buy both, I'm sure."

Hugh could see that they were excited about the idea, and it was evident as they continued a long and expanded discussion about their new venture.

The next day, Hugh took the carriage into town. Everyone was on board except Susan, who stayed at the ranch house to mind the children. They all loved Susan, probably because she loved them. She was almost as popular with them as Rebecca was. She played games with them, read to them, and, most importantly, baked them cookies.

The carriage arrived at the café, and Hugh dropped off the three women and told them he'd be back shortly after he and Rebecca visited the attorney.

They all skipped into the café to meet with the owner after the carriage pulled away.

Hugh and Rebecca drove the three hundred yards to the attorney's office, who was not Mister Simpson, which would have been awkward at the least. They walked into Mister Silas Bradford's office and told his clerk that they were there to settle Brian McGinnis' estate and were ushered into the attorney's office five minutes later.

Silas Bradford was an older man, perhaps fifty and sported large muttonchop whiskers that connected to his bushy moustache.

"Come in. Come in. Have a seat."

Hugh and Rebecca sat in the only open chairs in the office.

The clerk returned with a folder and handed it to the attorney, then left, closing the door behind him.

Silas said, "I was most troubled to hear of Brian's death. Was it in battle?"

"No, sir. He died of dysentery in a training camp."

"Terrible. War is such a waste of good men."

"I couldn't agree more."

"As you've probably already read, Brian left all of his holdings to you. That includes the ranch, a house on Mason Street, and his account at the bank. That account has been left there and has been accumulating interest pending your arrival. Here is the order releasing the funds to you, the deeds to the house on Mason Street and the ranch, as well as the keys to the house and the ranch."

"Why did he have a house?" Hugh asked.

"From what I understand, he had his architectural business on the first floor and would sometimes sleep on the second."

"Oh. Which house is it?"

"You can't miss it. Just turn onto Mason Street and it will be on your right. It has a McGinnis Architecture sign out front. Mister McGinnis arranged for a woman to clean the house in his absence, so she may even be there today. I'll just need you to sign here and here, then our business will be done."

"Thank you, Mister Bradford," Hugh replied then signed the locations indicated and five minutes later, they left the office.

The bank was directly across the street, so they just walked rather than board the carriage. They entered the bank and found an idle clerk.

"How can I help you today, sir."

"I need to transfer funds from another account to my account and close the first. It's a probate."

"I understand, sir. You have the court order?"

"Yes," Hugh replied as he handed him the order.

The clerk wrote down some numbers and walked to an office. He came out a few minutes later and stepped over to the cashier's window, took out some papers, wrote on them and then returned to his desk.

"Everything is in order, Mister McGinnis. The balance in your brother's account was $17,655.70. After transferring it to your account, your current balance is $27,145.65."

Hugh didn't bat an eyelash, but Rebecca was shocked. She thought his previous balance was beyond belief.

Hugh then stood, shook his hand before he led a still disbelieving Rebecca from the bank and back to the carriage.

After they entered the cab, Rebecca turned to Hugh.

"Hugh, why weren't you surprised by the amount of money. That's a fortune!"

"Because I knew how much my father gave me. I assumed that Brian had that much, minus the cost of the ranch and the house."

"You have more?" she asked incredulously.

"In my account in Ann Arbor. I transferred ten thousand dollars when I first got here. That left me with about twenty-two thousand dollars still in that account. Which reminds me, I need to close that account. You need to be able to get that money easily if anything happens to me."

He talked about it so casually. *He was talking about almost fifty thousand dollars!*

"Let's go and see the ladies' new café."

"Alright," she answered robotically.

Hugh got the carriage moving and parked in front of the café, helped Rebecca down, just because it was one more opportunity to hold her, then took her arm as they headed for the door.

"You know. I never get less of a thrill from just touching you. It's like I'm a schoolboy."

"I hope you never do, Hugh," she replied as they entered the café.

It was only ten o'clock, so the place was pretty empty. The three potential buyers saw Hugh and Rebecca and waved them over.

The current owner, Henry Pierce, smiled as he shook Hugh's hand.

"From what Betty tells me, you're the man I need to impress," he said.

"Not really. If they want to do this, I'm just here to make sure everything works."

"Come with me, and I'll give you the tour."

They walked into the working part of the eatery and Hugh was immediately struck by how clean and well-ordered it was. As the aroma of roasting beef filled the kitchen, he found two large cook stoves and a bakery oven, two large sinks and a large stock room that held the food stores and pots and pans. There was a large assortment of plates, cups and cutlery, and the cooking area had large counters and several heavy cutting boards with shelves full of spices overhead.

"This looks like a very well set up establishment, Mister Pierce. Why are you selling?"

"My wife died two months ago. She did most of the cooking and I lost interest in the business after she was gone, so I'm heading back to Iowa. I have a son and his family there."

"I'm sorry to hear of your loss. It must have left a terrible hole in your heart."

"It did," he replied quietly.

"What is your asking price?" Hugh asked.

"I'd like to get seventeen hundred dollars out of it."

"Does that include all the contents?"

"Yes. I already told Betty about my contracts with the butcher and the dry goods store. They'll give them a good price."

"You're a good man, Mister Pierce. Let me write you out a bank draft for the restaurant. You can sign the deed over to the women and they can take it over to the land office when they get a chance."

Mister Pierce was relieved at the quick sale. He thought it would be a long time before he sold his business.

Hugh wrote out the bank draft and handed it to Henry Pierce.

He looked at the draft, then looked back at Hugh and said, "Mister McGinnis, you made a mistake. I'm only asking seventeen hundred and this is for two thousand dollars."

"It's not a mistake, Mister Pierce. You were undervaluing the restaurant to sell it quickly. I understand that. But that is still a better than average price. Betty, Ella and Nancy are still getting a bargain for a well-established business."

Mister Pierce shook Hugh's hand and soon gave the signed deed and keys to Betty.

After he shook the three new owners' hands, Betty told Mister Pierce they'd start in three days, and he agreed to keep it running until they were ready.

They left a smiling Henry Pierce behind as they walked to the carriage.

The women were chatting extensively about their new business when Hugh said, "We need to make one more stop before we return."

"Where are we going, Hugh?" asked Nancy.

"To check on a house that my brother left me in his will."

"Oh. How far is it?" she asked.

"Just a couple of blocks," he replied.

It was almost a waste of time to drive the carriage as it was only a quarter of a mile away, but when he pulled to a stop in front of the house, he agreed with the attorney that it was obviously an architect's home.

He and Rebecca stepped down from the driver's seat as the women exited the coach.

"It's a beautiful house," Ella commented as she looked at the structure.

"It would have to be. It was owned by an architect."

Hugh pulled out the key as they walked up the steps with the women surrounding him and was about to unlock it but found the door already slightly open.

Hugh said, "The cleaning lady must be here. Come on in."

The sound of footsteps in the house came to the attention of the cleaning lady, who came bouncing down the stairs wondering who was entering the vacant house.

When Hugh saw the cleaning lady, her appearance surprised him. She couldn't have been much older than seventeen and only the poor condition of her dress marked her as the person responsible for the work of maintaining the house.

"Who are you?" she asked looking at Hugh and the women.

"I'm Hugh McGinnis. I own this house now, but I don't understand. The attorney said my brother had hired a cleaning woman to take care of the place, but that was five years ago. You must have been twelve at the time."

"He hired my mother. We took care of the house, but she died two years ago. I asked Mister Bradford if I could keep the job and he said I could. My mother didn't leave me anything, and we rented the house we were livin in, so I moved in upstairs. I'm sorry."

"Why? That was a smart thing to do. The house was empty and useless unless someone occupied the place. So, how many bedrooms are upstairs?"

"Four and a bathroom."

Hugh scanned the parlor, deciding that it would make a nice waiting room, and could see the open door to Brian's office in the corner, which would make a fine surgery.

"What's your name?" he asked the girl.

"Margaret Tilton."

"Well, Margaret, I think things are going to change around here, and do you know what the first change is going to be?"

"No, sir."

"The first change is we need to get you some better clothing. Betty, Ella and Nancy, would this be a good place for you to live with Margaret?"

Their faces lit up as they realized that they had neglected the housing part of their business venture.

"Hugh, that would be marvelous!" exclaimed Betty, "It's just a short walk from the café."

"Good. Now, Margaret, how much were you being paid to clean?"

"Ten dollars a month. My mother had two other cleaning jobs as well, but they didn't want to hire me."

"If you want to still clean, I'll double that, but I think those three ladies over there are in dire need of a good waitress. As pretty as you are, I'd imagine you'd make more than that in tips each month. You can do both, of course."

Margaret was dumbfounded. She thought she'd be out on her ear once he told her that he was the new owner and the ladies would be moving in.

"As for now, let's figure out our new logistics. Margaret, before I look, does this house have a corral or barn?"

"It has both. It's a small barn with a small corral attached."

"Perfect. So, here's the new plan. We all head back to the ranch. Margaret, you're free to join us. Tomorrow, our three new café owners will take their wagons and buggy back to Baker City. I'll load up the carriage with all your things. They can sell their wagons and Nancy can take Margaret to the clothing store and, Margaret, you buy whatever you want. You've become part of the extended family now. Betty, Ella and Nancy can set up the house. How's the food supply here, Margaret?"

Margaret was almost dizzy by the whirlwind that was Hugh McGinnis as she replied, "Low."

"Okay. After I unload the women's things in the house, I'll head over to the dry goods store and stock up on supplies. After I drop that all off, I'll get out of your hair. But I do want to warn you, I have my eye on the parlor and the office for my new in-town medical office. So, ladies, have I missed anything?"

"No, Hugh. As usual, you've thought of everything," replied a smiling Nancy.

Rebecca looked at Margaret. She was thinner than she normally would be if she ate regularly. Her light brown hair and green eyes suited her, and she was about Rebecca's height.

Rebecca said, "Margaret, when we get back, I'll give you one of my dresses. When you go shopping, you might want to get dresses that allow for some filling in. Once you've eaten enough, your figure will return."

A still stunned Margaret replied, "Thank you, ma'am."

Rebecca smiled and said, "I'm Hugh's wife. Just call me Rebecca. We have two children at home and Betty has a seven-year-old son there named Chuck. Susan Gardner is also there. I'm surprised you didn't know Nancy. You can't be three years apart."

She looked down in embarrassment and said, "I never went to school. I worked helping my mother as long as I can remember."

"We can help with that, too," Rebecca said, not realizing how much like Hugh she sounded.

Hugh then said, "Margaret, if you want to learn to read and write, I can hire a tutor to come and teach you. It won't take long."

"I'd really like that, Mister McGinnis."

"Call me Hugh. I'm not that old yet."

Hugh then clapped his hands together, and as he rubbed them, he said, "Okay, then. Let's go back to the ranch, ladies, and you can begin your transition into the commercial world."

The four women escorted a disbelieving Margaret to the carriage. Hugh locked the front door when they left.

The expanded group then piled into the carriage except for Rebecca who took her place on the driver's seat beside Hugh who took the reins, snapped them, telling the grays to do their job.

As they drove back to the ranch, Hugh had to admit that he liked the new carriage. It was smooth and made the short trip fast and pleasant.

They arrived at the ranch forty minutes later, and Hugh pulled up in front of the house to let all of the passengers and his driver's seat companion leave the carriage before he drove it to the barn.

When the women all walked into the house, Susan greeted them with the children right behind her, not surprised at all when she saw a new young woman with them. Mister Hugh had struck again.

Rebecca introduced Margaret to Susan, and Susan smiled and shook her hand. They were only three years apart, but Margaret looked like a lost child compared to the very mature, fully formed Susan. Susan may only have been twenty years old, but she was so confident she could have passed for twenty-five. Susan's sandy hair and vibrant blue eyes marked her as a poised, assured woman who radiated strength.

Rebecca updated Susan on the day's events, including the amount of money that Hugh had in his two accounts. Just as Rebecca had been, Susan was startled by the amount. Hugh had never shown any trend toward ostentation, except for indulging in his tendency to help people, especially, it seems, young women in trouble. Hugh never spent recklessly.

Rebecca and Susan had become extremely close. The two strong women were alike in so many ways. Both were compassionate, considerate, and were generous with their love. They also shared one other trait; they were both deeply in love with Hugh McGinnis.

Rebecca had known it almost from the start, but she never worried for a moment that Susan would ever share her feelings with anyone, much less with Hugh. Neither woman spoke of it and Susan wasn't aware that Rebecca knew. Rebecca simply treasured Susan as she would a dear sister. The fact that Susan loved her husband was just there, and she could understand why. Partly it was because Susan was so much like herself and the other was that she couldn't understand why any woman wouldn't fall in love with her husband.

Margaret was quickly accepted by the group and Rebecca had her dressed, her hair brushed and shining, and had her looking totally different in less than an hour.

They enjoyed a big dinner in the dining room to celebrate the café, the new house and Margaret's arrival and acceptance into the extended family.

———

The next morning, Hugh rounded up the oxen and harnessed them to their covered wagons. Then he hitched up the buggy and the carriage and drove them and the two wagons one by one to the front yard and spent some time loading the carriage with all of Ella's, Betty's and Nancy's clothing and their other possessions. Ella and Betty left some of the bulkier items in the wagons and would have the man who bought the wagons deliver them to the house later unless they didn't need them. The house was already fully furnished.

By nine o'clock, they were rolling toward Baker City, and by noon, the wagons and oxen had been sold and Hugh was in the process of moving the women into their new home. He had given Margaret eighty dollars to buy her things, which had shocked the young woman, even after the other women told her to get used to it.

Nancy took Margaret to the clothing store while Hugh, Betty and Ella put all their things into their chosen bedrooms. Chuck would sleep in Betty's room until they worked out some other arrangement. The bedrooms were all large, so it wasn't a problem now, but the question would arise when Chuck grew older.

Hugh then made his shopping trip to buy the food. When he had finished with the huge order which also included some toiletry items and some personal things for Margaret like the ubiquitous hair and comb set, he drove the overworked carriage to the back of the house and began unloading the food into the kitchen. By the time he had finished, Nancy and Margaret had returned in a loaded buggy and Hugh was pleased to see Margaret wearing a huge smile on her face as they began to unload the boxes of her new clothes and other things.

Satisfied that all was in good shape, he waved at the four women and climbed into the carriage for the return journey.

As he passed the café, he noticed good old Bob Orson coming out of the door and wondered if that would pose a problem for Ella. He stared at Orson for a few seconds and Bob glared back as Hugh rolled past.

———

Bob's growing, intense hatred for Hugh McGinnis hadn't subsided in the least. He was at the top of his hate list now, just ahead of Rebecca and Ella, whom he blamed for his current situation. It had started with Rebecca, then Ella had added to his misfortune and that tall bastard was behind it all.

As he watched the carriage recede into the distance, he reveled in his bubbling cauldron of hate.

———

Still in deep thought about Bob Orson as he drove back to the ranch, Hugh was almost surprised when the grays automatically turned down the access road to the ranch.

He stopped them outside the barn, unhitched the team and put them in their assigned stalls, then brushed them down and rolled the empty carriage into the buggy's slot, the problem of room for their modes of conveyance solved.

He went into the seemingly empty house, still troubled about Bob Orson. Rebecca and Susan were in the sitting room with Andy and Addie as he entered.

"The job's done," announced Hugh, "Everyone is settled in and seemed to be ready to begin their new venture."

"I'm happy for them, Hugh," said Rebecca.

Hugh took a seat and looked at Susan. "And how about you, Susan? Will you be leaving us now?"

"Did you want me to leave, Hugh?" asked a startled Susan.

Hugh looked at her in genuine shock as he quickly replied, "No! Never! Susan, I'm horribly sorry. I meant that as just a feeble attempt at humor. Please forgive me. I don't know what I'd do without you."

"Then I'll stay," she replied with a relieved smile.

Rebecca smiled at Hugh's reaction. He didn't understand about Susan's feelings at all. He was still so amazingly innocent after all he'd seen and done. Then she shifted her gaze to Susan. It was easy for her to read Susan's eyes. She was tortured in her heart and soul yet maintained such a calm demeanor. Susan's mental strength amazed her.

"Well, I suppose dinner is necessary," said Rebecca, before she stood.

"I must be fed! Off with you women!" said Hugh imperiously, "I shall tend to these young ones and mold them in my image."

The ladies laughed as they headed into the kitchen.

Hugh plucked up Addie and sat her on his lap. Andy sat close to him on the couch.

"Papa, when can I ride my horse?" asked Andy.

"Well, I have an old army saddle that you can use until I buy you a good one. I've already cleaned it up and it will work, so let's go."

Andy was all grins as Hugh led the two children to the kitchen. He looked at the only two women in the house and said as he passed, "We're going to ride our new horse."

Rebecca nodded with a grin as her husband and her children left the house.

Hugh took them out to the corral and brought out Andy's ride, the gray Morgan gelding.

"Andy, this horse is fully grown. He's never going to get any bigger. He's very quick and agile. When you get used to riding him, you'll be able to turn faster than anyone. Cowboys all love Morgans."

Andy just nodded vigorously. He wanted to ride.

Hugh took time to show him how to saddle his horse and finally gave him brief instructions on how to handle the horse. Andy was ready to explode when Hugh finally told him to mount his horse.

Hugh had to give him a small boost to get into the stirrup. Once in place, Hugh had him walk the horse and then turn it in both directions. He had him hold his new horse while he saddled Night, which he did quickly, then plucked Addie and climbed into the saddle with her hanging around his neck, just as he had when they'd first ridden away from their smashed Conestoga.

"Let's go for a short ride, Andy," Hugh said loudly.

He set off on a slow trot, and Andy did the same. It helped that the Morgan was used to accompanying Night and would have matched his speed, but to Andy, he was in complete control.

Hugh glanced at Andy's face and saw the look of exhilaration as he rode the horse. Hugh varied his speed eventually reaching a fast trot. He turned different directions and Andy followed, this time actually controlling his horse. He was a quick learner and he and his new mount seemed to have already formed a bond.

They returned to the barn and Hugh showed Andy how to unsaddle then brush down the horse and make sure he was fed and watered. Andy was more than eager to care for his equine friend.

When both horses were content, Hugh and his two young charges returned to the house, each one of his hands holding a smaller hand.

When they ate supper that night, it was unusual to only have five people at the table, but the five that were there were a happy group. Life was good.

The next few days were quiet. Hugh had brought them all to the café for dinner where he talked to Ella and asked if Bob had stopped in, and it turned out that he had, but hadn't seen Ella or Betty who were cooking in back. Nancy had seen him giving Margaret the once over, but that was it. He had only been there once, and Margaret had said he didn't leave a tip.

Hugh and Rebecca enjoyed the semi-privacy and enjoyed each other's company as often as possible. They were still newlyweds, after all.

Susan continued to work with the children with their lessons, ensuring that they would be ready to go to school in Baker City in the fall. Addie was already equal to students in their second year but Andy would need more of a boost to catch up to the fourth-years.

The summer was turning out to be glorious. Hugh had been a regular visitor to the pool, as had Susan, just never at the same time.

Each time they visited the café or the house, Hugh noticed that Margaret was filling out nicely. She was looking every part the healthy, teenaged young lady she should be. Hugh had hired a tutor to help Margaret with her lessons and she was proving to be a willing and excellent student.

Susan had been spending more time in the library reading medical books in her spare time, and found it fascinating, although some of the phraseology and Latin words caused some confusion. When that happened, she'd ask Hugh to clarify her questions and Hugh was more impressed with Susan every day. It seemed there was nothing she couldn't do.

———

On the 17th of July, Hugh was in the main room, explaining the facts of life to Andy who looked at him with pie eyes. Hugh, of course, kept it more medical than the normal explanation, so that helped avoid some of the 'yucky-ness' of the subject that seemed to offend young boys. He'd let Rebecca give Addie the talk. He had just about wrapped it up when there was a knock on the front door.

Hugh rose, walked to the door and swung it open.

"Got some mail for you, Mister McGinnis."

The messenger handed Hugh a large envelope.

"Thank you." Hugh replied as he glanced at the sender.

The man saluted and returned to his horse.

Hugh held his breath as he stared at the official envelope.

Susan and Rebecca entered, having heard the knock and the conversation. Andy and Addie trotted in shortly after the ladies.

He looked at them, held up the envelope and said, “It’s from the University of Michigan.”

Susan said excitedly, “Open it, Hugh! I’m sure it’s wonderful news.”

Rebecca wore a giant smile as Hugh nodded and sat down in a chair.

Hugh slid his knife from its sheath on his gun belt, then slipped it under the flap and sliced open the envelope. He knew that if they had denied his request, it would have been a simple letter, but he was still a bit anxious.

Both women approached until they were standing on opposite sides of the chair as he slid the contents from the envelope.

There was a letter with the medical school’s shield and beneath it, his diploma as Hugh Lee McGinnis, Doctor of Medicine. His eyes watered as he looked at the document. It seemed like it had been so long since he’d entered medical school, but it had only been five years.

Suddenly, he was engulfed in womanhood as Rebecca and Susan clutched him and kissed him and a big grin exploded on his face, as much from their attention as the contents of the envelope.

“Congratulations, Doctor!” said Rebecca.

"Congratulations, Doctor McGinnis!" echoed Susan.

Susan let him go quickly, thinking she may have gone too far. She hadn't, but her guilt had forced her back.

"Well, now I think I need to go to work," he said as his grin stayed in place.

"I think we need to take a ride to the café and celebrate there," Rebecca said.

"That's not a bad idea."

"You didn't read your letter yet," Susan said.

"Oh. That's right."

He read the letter. It said they had reviewed his outstanding academic record and his official documents from the army and were satisfied that his training had far exceeded that which was required for the award of the degree. Then, he noticed that they had included a printed copy of the Hippocratic Oath.

"I guess I've got to take the oath, now." Hugh said as he looked at the paper.

So, with Rebecca and Susan as witnesses, Hugh intoned the oath, knowing he was now bound by its code of ethical practices.

When he finished, he smiled, gave the letter to Rebecca, and after she read it, she handed it to Susan.

Rebecca turned to Andy and Addie and said, "Your papa is now officially a doctor."

Neither child had a clue what the difference was between being a doctor or being officially a doctor was, but they began clapping and added their joy to the room.

Hugh still gazed at his degree and said, “I’m going to have to order a lot of medical supplies and equipment. They have catalogs for that, but I have no idea where I can find one. Maybe the chemist has some. In the meantime, we can get started on getting a clinic built here. I’ll have office hours in town a few days a week and some days here. I don’t want to spend an hour and a half just traveling every day.”

So, Hugh and Rebecca and Susan returned to the kitchen, and as they shared coffee, began to plan for their bright future.

CHAPTER 11

As July was coming to a close, so were Bob Orson's funds. His original three hundred and twenty dollars had taken initial hits by buying the horse and paying for the lawyer in his failed divorce attempt. His everyday costs had kept whittling away at his bankroll, and he hadn't worked since he'd arrived. It was partly by choice and partly because of his lack of skills and his refusal to do any of the hard labor jobs that were available. He couldn't last another two weeks without an infusion of funds and desperately needed money.

One of Bob's expenses was the purchase of a gun and had to have the gunsmith load it and show him how to use the Cooper Pocket pistol. The gunsmith had told him it was a .31 caliber, double-action, five-shot revolver, but all Bob knew was that he had five shots before it needed reloading and all he had to do was pull the trigger. The gun was small enough for him to keep it in his pocket, so he didn't have to buy a holster.

An armed Bob Orson left Harry Wilkens' gun shop, with little money, but knew where he could get cash, and maybe that much-needed payback at the same time. He could walk to the Rocking M ranch where he could satisfy his hate and fill his pockets at the same time. That McGinnis character always seemed to be rolling in money, and that bitch he had married was there with those brats, too, including that little bastard who had pointed a loaded and cocked shotgun at him. They still had his horse, too.

He stopped at that café with the pretty, young waitress, then after leaving with a full stomach, started walking out of Baker City. He took the southeast road, keeping an eye out for any traffic to avoid being seen. If he saw anyone coming, he'd quickly leave the roadway and hide, but he was lucky, as no one passed by.

He walked past the ranch road to the forest to the south, the same one that Hugh had used that first day. Then, like Hugh, he turned east and entered the trees. It was one o'clock in the afternoon on a warm summer day.

The three adults and two children were in the main room after lunch.

"What are the plans for the rest of the day?" Hugh asked.

Andy quickly replied with his own question, asking, "Can I go and ride my horse?"

Hugh was about to answer, when Rebecca replied, "That sounds like fun. Susan, do you want to ride? We haven't ridden in a week."

Susan nodded and replied, "That does sound like fun."

Hugh looked at Addie and asked, "What do you want to do, Addie?"

"My tummy's too full. Can I stay here?"

"Of course, sweetie. I'll show you some magic tricks," said Hugh.

"*You will?*" Addie exclaimed.

"Absolutely."

The ladies smiled, then stood and walked to their bedrooms to change into their riding clothes. Andy stayed, hoping he could see some magic before he rode.

When Susan and Rebecca re-entered the main room five minutes later, Hugh smiled and said, “You both look very enticing, ladies.”

“Are you going to spoil all this femininity by making us saddle our own horses, sir?” asked Rebecca with a grin.

“I would never do that. I’ll be back shortly.”

Hugh cut through the kitchen and walked out to the barn, saddled both women’s horses and Andy’s horse with his new saddle, then led all three horses to the back hitchrail.

He went inside, announced that the horses were ready, and Rebecca, Susan and Andy walked out from the hallway a few seconds later.

“Where will you be going? Are you heading into town?” he asked.

“No, I think we’ll go and look at the falls. Sometimes there’s a rainbow. I think Andy would like that.”

“There’s a rainbow?” asked Andy.

“Sure. The water droplets act like little prisms and break up the sunlight,” replied Hugh.

Rebecca laughed and said, “And here I was going to talk about pixies.”

“There could be pixies and elves, not to mention leprechauns. I’m just unimaginative I guess,” said Hugh.

The riders all laughed, Rebecca gave Hugh a quick kiss and they left the kitchen to mount their horses.

Hugh watched them leave, then returned to the main room where an anxious Addie awaited the magic show, her ailing tummy forgotten.

Andy rode flanked by Susan and Rebecca as they rode east across the pastures. He had been getting very good at riding his new friend because Hugh had taken him out at least once every other day. He loved his little Morgan and had named him Rebel because he wore gray.

Hugh brought out a deck of cards and had Addie mesmerized as he began his limited number of simple tricks but ran out of magic after five minutes.

"Well, Addie. That's all the magic I have. What do we do next?"

"Can we go riding now and see mama?"

Hugh laughed and said, "Of course, we can, as your tummy seems to be doing better now. I'll go and saddle my horse. You stay right here."

Bob had seen that bitch and one of her brats go riding past. He forgot about money when he saw Rebecca and her shotgun-pointing son riding east. He wanted revenge first and without that big bastard with her, this would be his best chance. She was the one that had started this downward spiral in his life and had ruined his chances with Ella.

There was another woman with her, but that wasn't a problem because he had five shots, which should leave him two more. He watched as they stopped and dismounted and felt anxious knowing he would soon have his revenge, now it was his turn to inflict pain, and he knew that nothing would hurt that woman more than to see her kid die in front of her before she died.

Rebecca and Susan hitched their horses to a large bush. waited for Andy to tie off Rebel, then they all walked to the smaller pool so he could see the rainbow display.

Andy wasn't disappointed as he pointed and shouted, "Wow! Look at the rainbow!", then ran toward the pool and the small waterfall.

Susan looked over at Rebecca and smiled. "It's a nice day for a swim, Rebecca."

"You go right ahead," Rebecca replied as she smiled back, "You feel free to freeze anytime you want."

"It's not that cold, Rebecca, but I think Andy might object to seeing a naked lady. I saw his reaction when Hugh was explaining the birds and the bees."

"That'll change soon, I think," Rebecca said as she looked at her son.

Susan wandered toward the bigger pool and looked at the deep, cool water. She and Hugh had worked out a schedule for use of the deep, refreshing water. She was assigned even numbered days and Hugh got odd numbered ones. Today was an odd number, so even if she wanted to take a dip, she'd have to wait until tomorrow.

While Susan was looking at the pool a hundred feet away, and Andy and Rebecca were enjoying the rainbow spectacle, Bob had exited the nearby trees, pulled his revolver and cocked the hammer, even though he didn't need to. He just wanted to be sure it worked. The waterfall was drowning out the sound of his approach and had gotten to within fifty feet of them without being spotted.

———

Hugh had Night saddled and was leading him out of the barn with Chester was close to his heels.

Addie was excited as he lifted her into his arms. and she wrapped her small arms around his neck before he mounted the tall stallion.

He was half a mile away when Bob drew close behind Rebecca and Andy.

———

Bob walked another thirty feet, stopped and aimed his pistol at the whelp. He would enjoy watching Rebecca wail as he died in front of her. Then it would be her turn.

He took aim at the kid's back as the boy stared at the rainbow and pulled the trigger.

———

The sound of the shot from the direction of the waterfall ignited Hugh who had Addie on her blanket in front of him. He held onto Addie tightly as he accelerated Night across the pasture with Chester racing behind.

———

Rebecca heard the shot at close range and whirled to see Bob Orson standing there with a smoking pistol, but he wasn't aiming it at her, *he was aiming it at Andy!* She turned back quickly to see her son dropping to the ground, then screamed and ran to protect Andy from a second shot, hoping he was still alive.

Susan, as soon as she heard the gunshot, turned saw Bob preparing for a second shot, then quickly began running the hundred feet toward the shooter, pulling her derringer out of her skirt pocket as she ran.

Rebecca knew what she had to do when she saw Andy on the ground, so when she reached her son, she dove on top of him as Bob Orson prepared for the second shot, gratified to see Rebecca in a panic and coming into his gun sights.

When Rebecca landed on Andy, he moaned under his mother. *He was alive!* She turned her head, and saw her ex-husband preparing for that second shot, killing shot. It was like time had stopped as she saw his pistol blow flame and smoke from its muzzle and as she heard the report, felt an almost instantaneous punch to her upper abdomen, felt the bullet burn into her body and knew she had only minutes of life in her, but knew she had to spend those minutes to protect her son, knowing Bob would shoot again.

Orson was preparing for that third shot when Susan arrived, shouting at him to draw his attention away from Rebecca and Andy. Bob didn't really care until he glanced at her and saw she was pointing a gun at him, and knew he had a problem. He whipped his pistol to his left to try and shoot Susan, but he was too late.

Once she saw him turn to see her, Susan immediately lurched to a stop, took quick aim, cocked the small hammer with her thumb and pulled the trigger of the Remington. The

.41 caliber bullet blew out of the short barrel, crossed the twenty-three feet and found its mark, hitting Bob Orson in the right shoulder, causing him to drop his weapon before he spun away. Susan quickly cocked and fired again and hit him in the right thigh.

Bob Orson went down to the ground screaming in pain from the two hits as Susan dropped her derringer and raced to Rebecca and Andy.

She rolled Rebecca onto her back and could see the massive amounts of blood flowing from her back and knew that there was nothing she or even Hugh could do.

Andy sat up and stared at his wounded mother. He had only stumbled and fallen trying to run away from Mister Orton after he heard the gunshot.

"Mama! Mama!" he shouted as he stood behind Susan feeling lost and helpless.

Rebecca heard him cry out and smiled weakly at her son, then looked at Susan and asked quietly, "Is Andy all right?"

"Yes, Rebecca he's fine. He doesn't have any wounds at all."

She stared into Susan's blue eyes knowing there wasn't much time and had to tell her.

She was already losing her breath as her life's blood continued to flow onto the ground and whispered, "Susan…Susan, I know that you love Hugh as much as I do. Please…please, love him."

She didn't wait for Susan to answer, seeing the shock in her eyes, but paused to take a ragged breath and continued in a hurried and gasping voice.

"He'll need your love. Now more than ever, Susan. Take…take care of my children. Will you do all of that for me?"

Susan nodded, the tears falling from her eyes, as she whispered, "Yes, Rebecca. I will. I'll miss you so very much."

Hugh came thundering up on Night, quickly dismounted, dropped a stunned Addie to the ground and rushed to Rebecca's side. He looked at Susan who shook her head, stood and backed away taking Andy's hand and then Addie's, letting Hugh share Rebecca's remaining seconds of life.

Andy and Addie were watching as Hugh quickly took a knee next to his wife, and leaned close to her face, expecting that Mister Hugh could help her. He could fix anything.

As Hugh slipped his hand under Rebecca's head, Susan turned to look at Bob Orson.

Bob Orson was in pain. Susan's two shots hurt, but he knew he wouldn't die. He saw his targets right in front of him and the gun was right there on the ground before him, so he reached for the pistol, but before he could get it into his fingers, his arm was stabbed with sharp pain as Chester tore into his wrist.

Susan quickly left Andy and Addie and walked to where Bob Orson lay fighting Chester.

An intense hatred came over her, but Susan said calmly, "Chester. Heel."

Chester glared at Bob as he stepped back and stood near Susan, who took two more steps toward Bob and retrieved his pistol.

———

Hugh could see Rebecca's face growing pale. She had so little time left, and his heart was dying as Rebecca was.

She looked at Hugh and smiled as she struggled to take a breath and whispered, "Hugh, I love you so much. You…you've made me happy. Now, I need you to take care of our children."

Hugh's voice was shaking as he replied quietly, "Of course, I will. I love you with all my heart, Rebecca. I always will."

Hugh fought back the tears that were clawing at his eyes to escape as Rebecca managed with her last reserves of strength to lift her right hand and touch his face.

"Hugh," she whispered, "Susan loves you as much as I do."

She wheezed, took two short breaths and gasped, "Please, please love her as you have loved me. It…it would make me happy, so very happy, to know that you will be loved."

Hugh couldn't hold back the tears as they fell from his eyes, onto Rebecca's cheeks, as he said, "But you were the one that touched my heart, Rebecca. You are my life. There can be no one but you."

Her eyes finally closed as she shuddered, then whispered, "I…I touched it but shortly, my love. She will hold it in her hands," then she took in a short breath and continued quickly, knowing there were so few breaths left for her, "She will hold your heart in her hands for the rest of her life. Please give her your love, Hugh. She needs your love as much as you need hers."

Hugh finally nodded and whispered, "I can never deny you anything, Rebecca."

She smiled and whispered, "I know."

———

Susan looked down at Bob Orson and snarled, "You, lousy heartless bastard. You're not even going to die with those two shots."

Bob looked up at Susan as she stood over him with his pistol in her hand and said, "Too bad, girly, and your doctor boyfriend is going to have to fix me up, too."

He grimaced as he tried to laugh.

Susan raised his pistol and pointed it at him.

"You ain't gonna shoot me, girly. You're just a…"

He was wrong. Susan turned the pistol and aimed at his gut. She pointed at the right side, away from the abdominal aorta. She didn't want a quick death for Bob Orson. She pulled the trigger and then tossed the gun into the creek.

She then glared at him and said, "Die a slow and painful death, you son-of-a-bitch."

She walked away leaving a screaming Bob Orson. Chester trotted next to Susan as she returned to where Rebecca lay, her life's blood still oozing onto the ground as she talked quietly to Hugh.

The report had startled Hugh, who had to turn and as he started to reach for his pistol, he saw Susan toss Bob's pistol into the creek, say something to him, then start walking back. The pistol's report still echoed across the pasture as both children approached to see their mama, still believing that Mister Hugh would save her, but they were both frightened at seeing their mother's blood and were crying and wondering why Mister Hugh was just talking to her. *Why wasn't he saving their mama?*

As they knelt beside their beloved mother, Hugh leaned back to give them room to be close to her.

She looked into their crying faces and said softly, "I love you so much, my babies."

They both leaned down to kiss her, and she managed to touch each of them with the last bit of strength in her failing body.

She still had them in her arms when her breathing stopped, and her arms fell to her sides.

Hugh was numb. *How could this have happened?* He wanted to break down and just empty his heart and soul where he knelt, but knew he had to take care of the children now and he had to bring his Rebecca home.

He ignored the screaming coming from Bob Orson as he leaned over and pulled both children to him, then turned to Susan and without saying a word, asked her to take the children.

She understood and walked to him. She took the children's hands and led them to Andy's horse as they both kept their eyes focused on their mother and Hugh. Susan helped Andy into the saddle of his hitched Morgan where he kept looking at his mother, knowing that Bob Orson had killed her. Susan lifted Addie to Andy's saddle and sat her in front of him, then untied her horse's reins, took Night's and then untied Rebel's.

She watched as Hugh gently lifted Rebecca's body from the ground, cradling her as if she were still alive and seeing the anguish in his face.

Hugh began walking back to the ranch house with Susan leading the three horses in a solemn and tragic funeral procession.

No one paid any attention to Bob Orson's screaming as they departed the murder scene. Hugh knew the heartless bastard was dying after hearing Susan's shot, but there was nothing he could do to alleviate his pain other than shooting him again, and he couldn't do that after taking the Hippocratic Oath.

The somber funeral procession slowly crossed the pasture taking fifteen minutes to walk the half mile. As they passed the corral, Susan took Addie down, and Andy quietly dismounted before Susan just led the horses inside and closed the gate, leaving their saddles in place, then took both children's hands and they followed Hugh carrying their dead mother.

The children were still quietly crying, as was Susan. Only Hugh had stopped weeping as he held his wife's lifeless body. He was simply numb.

When they reached the house, Hugh walked down to the lower floor door and Susan opened it for him. Hugh brought Rebecca into the bottom floor of the house and asked Susan to take a blanket from one of the empty bedrooms and said he would be taking Rebecca to the cold room. She left the children, entered the closest bedroom and returned with the blanket then opened the cold room, and spread the blanket on the floor before stepping back.

Hugh gently laid his wife's body on the blanket and covered her with the blanket, kissing her gently on the lips before covering her face.

He looked at Susan, knowing what terrible task she had undertaken at the pools.

Hugh had heard the shot and known that Susan had finished off Bob, something he never could have done as a doctor. Bob Orson had just murdered his wife, but he was an unarmed human being who needed medical care. Susan had saved him from the decision that would have made him either violate his oath or care for his wife's killer.

He looked at her sorrowful face and said, "Thank you for taking care of Bob, Susan. I couldn't do it and still be a doctor."

"I know. That was one of the reasons I did it. The other reason was that he deserved to die and die in a lot of pain. I wish I had been quicker, Hugh. I should have been with them. I could have done more."

Susan lowered her head, feeling the depth of anguish as she pondered how she could have stopped him from firing that fateful and deadly second shot.

Hugh slowly rose to his feet, wrapped her in his arms and whispered, "No, Susan. Don't do this to yourself. If we start playing the 'if only' game, we'll both lose our minds. You did everything you could and more, Susan. If you hadn't been there, he would have killed Andy, too. Put that behind you. We need to be strong for the children now."

He released her, then she nodded and wiped the tears from her face.

Hugh had held back his grief longer than he thought possible, but now, he had to delay it longer as he needed to help his children with their grief.

He looked down into their incredibly sad faces and said softly, "Let's go upstairs. Okay?"

They nodded as he took their hands as they left the cold room, then went to the main floor with Susan walking beside Addie.

He led them into the main room and had them both sit in one of the chairs, then took Susan's hand and guided her to the couch and sat down next to her.

Hugh took a deep breath and looked at his children, as he said, "Andy and Addie, we are all very sad about what that evil man did. We all loved your mama very, very much. She's in heaven now with all the other angels and smiling down on you both wanting you to be happy. I know that's hard to do. It's hard for me and Susan, too. It's so very, very hard. In a little while, I have to go into town and bring back the man who will help us bury your mama in the pretty cemetery here on the ranch."

Andy looked at him and asked, "But why did mama have to die, Papa? Couldn't you save her like you saved Pale Dawn?"

Addie had the same question and waited for Mister Hugh's answer.

He had already expected that question, and replied, "I really wish I could have saved her, Andy. More than anything I ever wanted, I wished it was within my power to save your mama.

But Pale Dawn had only one thing wrong and I could fix the one thing. The bullet that hit your mama hurt her too badly inside and broke so many things that I knew it was too much for anyone to save her. It broke my heart not to be able to help her. Do you understand?"

"Yes, Papa," Andy quietly replied.

"Remember when your mama was sick, and you were worried that she might die? I told you then that everyone dies. It's just a question of when it will happen. Your mama died much too soon and so very suddenly. That makes it even worse because she was smiling one moment and gone the next.

"When someone is sick, you are almost prepared for the possibility of death, but not like this. It hurts each of us here, inside our hearts. All we can do now is to remember your mama as she was, remember her smile and her laugh. I'll always remember her when she first saw you both running to her on the Trail, how her face was shiny and happy to see her precious children again. If you will remember your mama that way, then she'll be happy."

"We'll try, Papa," said Addie as Andy nodded.

Hugh smiled at his children and said, "Now, I have to go to Baker City. Susan will take care of you now and you know that she loves you both just as much as I do."

Hugh turned to Susan and asked softly, "Are you all right, Susan?"

"You go ahead, and I'll watch after the children," she replied without really answering his question.

He knew that it was all he could have hoped for from Susan and the children so soon after the shock. He knew he wasn't any better, but they had to manage to keep living.

"I'll be back in a couple of hours," he said as he stood and patted her shoulder.

He quickly left through the kitchen, and when he looked into the corral, he saw the four saddled horses, walked inside and began unsaddling them except for Night, but left their tack on the top rail of the corral rather than carry them into the barn. He led Night from the corral, closed the gate, mounted, and turned him down the access road and headed to Baker City at a fast clip. He had noticed that the screams had stopped from the eastern pastures before he left.

———

In the house, Susan sat with the children, her children now. She remembered what Rebecca had said about loving Hugh and had been stunned by the revelation. Rebecca had known about her feelings for her husband yet had still accepted her. Her already high regard for Rebecca soared as she understood what an amazing woman she had for a friend. Now, she must push her grief to the side and do what she had to do. She had to be strong, for the children, for Hugh, and for Rebecca.

———

Hugh arrived in Baker City, stepped down at the undertaker's office and walked inside.

"Good afternoon, Mister McGinnis. How can we help you?"

"My wife was just shot and killed by Bob Orson on my ranch. I need to have her returned and prepared for burial in the gravesite on the ranch. I want Bob Orson's body returned as well, but I don't want him to be in the same conveyance with my wife's body. If you could bring a hearse for my wife and a wagon for her murderer, then I'd appreciate it."

"I am truly sorry for your loss. We'll send them out right away."

"Give me time to go to the marshal's office and to tell some friends. I'll be going back in about an hour."

"Of course, sir. Again, you have my sympathies."

"Thank you."

Hugh turned left the mortuary and walked to the marshal's office.

The deputy saw him enter and smiled. "What can I do for you today, Mister McGinnis."

Hugh was beginning to get angry but calmed himself. It wasn't their fault that Bob was free to run around.

Hugh had to get it out before his grief slammed into him, so he quickly replied, "My wife was just murdered by Bob Orson on my ranch. He shot first at my son and then my wife threw herself on him to protect him from another shot and Orson shot her fatally. He was shot twice by Susan Gardner to try to stop him from shooting again and killed him. I've arranged to have my wife buried. What happens to Orson is beyond my caring. I've arranged to have his carcass removed from my ranch. Do you need any reports?"

"No, sir. It's out of our jurisdiction."

"Fine. If you ever see the sheriff, let him know."

Hugh turned and left the office, then headed for the café, which would be the hardest part of the trip. He reached the café, dismounted, tied off Night and walked inside. Margaret was waiting tables, but there was only one table occupied.

She smiled at him, then saw the expression on his face and was stunned as she had never seen him so drawn. He motioned to her to follow as he strode quickly into the back of the restaurant.

He found Nancy, Ella and Betty all engaged in various chores as he entered the kitchen. Their eyes all turned to see him as he walked in and they universally smiled at him. As with Margaret, they couldn't help but notice his gloomy visage and their smiles vanished.

"Hugh, what's wrong?" asked Betty quickly.

He directed them to a table and sat down waiting for them to take seats. When they were all sitting and looking at him with concerned faces, he tried to speak, but couldn't. He'd open his mouth and all he could do was get out a weak huff.

"Hugh, what's wrong?" Betty asked again in deep concern.

Hugh took a deep breath and blurted, "It's Rebecca. Rebecca is dead."

Then he lost all semblance of control and just fell apart. He lowered his head onto his arms and just sobbed. His heavy volume of tears fell onto the table and began pooling.

The women all sat shocked at his announcement and at his complete breakdown having never witnessed anything but a happy, confident Hugh McGinnis.

They began to cry themselves as they waited for Hugh to recover enough to tell them what had happened. It took two minutes for Hugh to manage to control his grief before he finally sat up straight and wiped his face dry.

“I’m sorry. I’ve been holding this back and couldn’t do it anymore. Just a little while ago, Rebecca, Susan and Andy went out riding on the ranch. They stopped at the pools, and somehow, Bob Orson snuck up behind them and tried to shoot Andy. Rebecca covered him with her body to protect him and Orson shot her. Susan was at the other pool and ran to help them, but was too late to help Rebecca, but she shot Orson twice with her derringer and saved Andy’s life. I got there, but there was nothing anyone could do. She died soon after I arrived. Orson was still alive with two non-fatal injuries, so Susan finished him off with his own gun.”

Then it was the women’s turn to feel the pain of loss and the tears that had been trickles before flowed from everyone’s eyes in torrents, including Hugh’s again. After a few more minutes, they had come to that point of acceptance and had to realize that they would no longer enjoy the presence of their wonderful friend.

Hugh finally said, “I’m going to have her buried in the family cemetery on the ranch next to Louise. It’s only right.”

They nodded as they wiped their faces with napkins and handkerchiefs.

“When will she be buried?” asked Nancy.

“Tomorrow afternoon.”

“We’ll be there, Hugh. How are Susan and the children?” Betty asked.

"They're dealing with the loss. Andy and Susan were there when it happened, so I think they have more to get past, but both children were there when their mother died. She was talking to them and hugging them when she took her last breath. It's a terrible thing for a child, so it will take time."

"Hugh, will you be all right?" asked Nancy.

"I have to be. The children need me. Right now, I've got to get back to meet with the undertaker."

"Tell Susan and the children our prayers are with them and for Rebecca, of course," said Ella.

Hugh nodded and stood, then touched each woman lightly on the cheek in turn before leaving the café.

After a brief stop at the mortuary to arrange for the burial time, he rode back to the ranch at an even faster rate, letting Night loose to eat up the distance and returned in less than fifteen minutes. He unsaddled Night and brushed him down before leaving him in a stall in the barn.

He entered the house through the kitchen, finding Susan and the children at the table. Susan had made coffee and she had a cup in her hands, while the children each had an untouched glass of milk before them.

He sat down and looked at Susan.

"The undertaker will be here soon. I'll take Rebecca to him. The marshal doesn't care about Orson, but I had the undertaker send a wagon with the hearse so they could remove his carcass."

He reached across the table, took Susan's hand and asked, "How are you doing, Susan?"

She put her other hand on top of his and replied, "I'm okay, now. It may be a while before I get over this, Hugh."

"I understand completely. I'll help you as much as I can."

"I know you will. Thank you, Hugh."

He looked into her eyes and he saw the same depth of feelings that he had seen in Rebecca's eyes. He had felt strongly about Susan since he had first rescued her, and Rebecca had told him to love Susan as he had loved Rebecca. *But how was that even possible?* He could love Susan easily and probably already did. *But the level of passion he felt for Rebecca, was that ever possible again?* There could never be another Rebecca. *But did Susan have to be another Rebecca?* She was a totally different person. He finally concluded that it was too soon to worry about such things. He needed to bury his beloved wife.

Susan could almost read his mind because it was so transparent to her. He was in so much pain. She couldn't imagine such agony of the soul and hoped she never had to experience it herself. She had to keep loving him and let time work its healing magic. She had to take care of the children.

There was a knock on the door and Hugh stood up and walked to the front of the house, knowing who it would be.

He opened the door and met the undertakers.

"We'll go around the back. Just follow me."

He stepped out to the yard and the undertakers drove their hearse behind him as he went to the door leading to the bottom floor. They stepped down and Hugh said, "I'll bring her out to you."

They nodded, and Hugh opened the door, left it open, then walked inside, opened the door to the cold room and knelt on one knee as he looked at the blanketed form.

"We didn't have nearly as much time together as we should have, my love. But that time was so special, so intense to make every minute special. I'll take care of our children and I'll do as you asked, but I'm not sure if I can ever love anyone as much as I loved you."

He reached down and gently slid his hands under her inert body, lifted her easily and walked out the door. He carried her slowly to the waiting hearse, and carefully gave her to the two undertakers who placed her in a temporary coffin and with reverence slid it into the hearse.

"Mister McGinnis, did you have any specific instructions?"

"Yes, I wrote down what I would like carved on her stone. We'll be doing the burial tomorrow afternoon, is that right?"

"Yes, sir. That won't be a problem. We'll be back in a little while to remove the other body.""

"That's fine. I'll come by on the following day and pay the bill, is that all right?"

"Perfectly fine."

They mounted the hearse and drove off, then Hugh returned to the cold room and closed the door, left the lower floor, closed the door behind him then blew out his breath. He had to keep himself together.

He re-entered the kitchen and saw the children still there with their glasses of milk untouched as Susan cooked. He realized that no one had eaten since breakfast.

“Susan, I have to do some other necessary things around the ranch. Could you save me something to eat when I return?”

“I’ll keep something warm for you.”

“Thank you, Susan.”

Before he left, Hugh sat at the table and looked at the sad faces of his children.

“Andy and Addie, you’ve got to drink your milk. What would your mama say if you didn’t take care of yourselves? Now, I’ll do all I can to take care of you both like I always have from the moment I found you near that river. You are my children and I love you both very much, but I can’t make you eat or drink your milk. Right now, your mama is looking down at you and wondering why you haven’t had your milk. It’s our job to keep your mama smiling while she’s up in heaven, and to do that, we have to do what she would like us to do. Can you do that?”

Andy and Addie both nodded and Addie asked, “Papa, will I always be sad?”

Hugh looked at her and smiled before replying, “No, Addie, you won’t always be sad. You have too many wonderful memories of your mama to be sad. That’s what I am going to do. I am going to spend every day remembering how we would poke fun at each other and laugh. Always remember the happy times, Addie, because those are the only times worth remembering, and soon, we’ll all be happy again and that will make your mama happier than ever.”

Then Andy asked, “Papa, are we ever going to see our mama again?”

"Of course, you will. She's up there in heaven right now waiting for all of us. You, Addie, me and Susan. She probably met my brother, Brian and his wife, too. She loves each of us and will be just as happy to see us again as she was when she saw you running down the Oregon Trail. Think of that look of incredible joy on her face when she saw you running to her and that's what you'll see when you see her again, but it won't be for a long time. Okay?"

Andy and Addie smiled at the memory of that day, and then Andy picked up his glass of milk and began to drink before Addie did the same.

When they put their glasses back down, Hugh smiled at them and said, "Now, you've both made your mama happy. I've got to go and take care of something and I'll be back in an hour or so. Okay?"

"Okay, Papa," replied Andy.

Hugh kissed each child on the forehead, stood, smiled at Susan and left the kitchen.

He walked back out to the barn to get the pick and shovel, and after finding them took one tool in each hand and walked to the cemetery that he had kept as neat as he could. Louise's grave was covered in stones and the grass was still trimmed. As he walked, he asked himself if he Should he move Bob Orson's body away from the pool. It was too nice a setting for that bastard.

He reached the cemetery, laid down the tools and was preparing to start digging when the question of Bob Orson's body came back. He glanced in the direction of the pools and something nagged the back of his mind. There was something wrong and he couldn't figure out what it was.

He continued to stare at the pools and then it hit him. There were no buzzards in the air.

He left the cemetery and began to walk quickly to the pools, taking just four minutes to get there. When he arrived, he looked around, but he couldn't see the body. He knew he was in the right spot, but there was no body. *Where was Bob Orson's body?* He began inspecting the ground for any clues that might answer the mystery and found the dark patch of dried blood where Rebecca had died and felt his stomach heave but continued to inspect the area.

Hugh noticed a glint of metal and reached down into the thick grass and found a Remington derringer. It was Susan's derringer, the one she had used to shoot Bob Orson and save Andy. He held it in his open palm, stared at it and marveled at the courage that Susan had displayed in using it. Most women, and many men, would have cowered when hearing nearby gunfire, but not Susan. She left her place of relative safety and ran toward the danger. She ran toward a man already committed to killing. She ran knowing all she had was a very close-range weapon with only two shots. She ran risking her life to protect Rebecca and Andy.

He slipped the small gun into his pocket, but still needed to find out what happened to Bob. Surely, he hadn't lived, not after Susan's belly wound. He continued searching, walking slowly back toward what should have been Orson's final resting place. Then, he found Bob's bloody ground, but still no body. Then he saw it…paw prints. Bear paw prints and creases where it had dragged off its find. He dropped and sat on his heels to study the print and knew that this was a big bear. He didn't know if it was a big brown bear or a full-fledged grizzly, but it didn't matter. He felt a grim satisfaction in his discovery and hoped that Bob had been still alive when the bear arrived.

He looked back at the tranquil scene of the two pools connected by the rainbow-producing small waterfall, and he knew that it had no blame in the tragedy and couldn't avoid the place because of that. Rebecca would have given him one of her 'you're in trouble now, mister' looks. He smiled when he pictured her mischievous face. No, he would not abandon the pools.

He turned and retraced his steps until he reached the cemetery again. He marked the ground six feet from Louise's grave and dragged the point of the pickaxe to mark the borders for Rebecca's burial site.

He began to dig with the pickaxe first then the spade. He worked like a demon to sweat out the emotions, the grief, the anger, and the devastation of spirit. The spade pounded into the earth and his muscles torqued and released as the dirt flew. Sooner than he expected, the job was complete. Hugh was covered in sweat and dirt as he climbed out of the hole. He grabbed the pickaxe and shovel and walked back to the barn where he placed them in their proper locations. He needed to clean himself, and really wanted to dive into the deep pool, but there wasn't time, so he walked to the trough, removed his shirt and began to douse his body and hair with water from the spigot. When he felt reasonably sure he had most of the dirt off, he put his shirt back on, ran his hands through his hair to straighten it out, and walked back to the house.

When he entered the kitchen, Susan saw him and smiled.

"I have your food ready, Hugh."

"Thank you, Susan. Where are the children?"

"They are in your bedroom waiting for you. They had something they wanted to ask you."

"I'll go there in a minute. Will you join me, Susan?"

"Of course, I will."

Susan brought him a plate of reheated chicken and roasted potatoes. She also brought a big glass of lemonade, then sat down across from Hugh with a glass of lemonade.

Hugh began to eat and between bites, he said, "I was wondering about moving Orson's body away from the pools, when I noticed that there weren't any buzzards overhead, which there should have been. I walked to the pools, but when I got there, his body was gone."

Susan was startled and quickly asked, "He was gone? He couldn't have lived, could he?"

"No, he wasn't alive. I just hoped he lived long enough to feel the big bear drag him off."

"A bear? There are bears nearby?"

"Obviously. In this case, it did us a service."

"That's true, but it will make me a bit more anxious taking swims in the pool."

"I think I'll fence in that area, so we don't have to worry. Susan, later tonight, can we talk for a while? There are so many things that have changed so quickly."

"I know. We can talk after I put the children to bed. It'll be quiet."

He nodded, then said, "I'll go and see the children now."

Susan smiled as he stood, unsure if she should tell Hugh what Rebecca had asked of her. It would be difficult for both of them if she did, so she decided to wait and hear what he had to say.

Hugh went into the bedroom and saw Andy and Addie sitting on the big bed.

"Andy, Addie, Susan said you want to talk to me," he said as he took a seat on the bed with them.

He was surprised when Addie was the one to speak when she said, "Papa, we've been talking. We're really sad about mama, but she's with the angels now, so it makes it better. You told us to be happy, but we're afraid you won't be happy anymore. You were always happy with mama. Will you be happy again?"

"Yes, my precious children, I'll be happy as soon as I can. I just loved your mama so very much that it was like part of me was ripped away. That hurt will take time to go away."

"Susan can help, Papa," said Addie as Andy nodded.

Hugh was surprised and said, "I know she will. Your mama told me before she died to love Susan like I loved her. I love Susan, but the hurt from your mama is so much, it may take some time before I can love her as much as I loved your mama. Do you understand?"

"Yes, Papa. We both want Susan to be our new mama, and we know that she can't be our old mama, but we can love her like our mama."

"Your mama told me that, too. She asked me to help Susan to watch after you. So, you both give us some time and we'll try to make it happy here again."

"Okay, Papa. We can wait," said Addie.

Then, she climbed onto his lap, put her arms around him and kissed him on his cheek before she said, “I love you, Papa.”

———

Two hours later, both children were ready to be put into their beds. They said their prayers and asked the angels to give their mama a kiss for them. Susan and Hugh then tucked them in and walked to the main room.

After they sat down on the couch, Hugh began the difficult conversation as he looked into Susan’s concerned blue eyes.

“Susan, we’re in a somewhat awkward situation. I know what Rebecca has asked of me and I’m sure she made similar requests of you. Taking care of the children was the simple part. The other part is anything but simple.”

Susan was relieved that he knew and said, “Yes, it’s far from simple.”

“I believe that for the next few days or even weeks, we should just continue doing the routine, everyday things, and not even talk about those difficult promises until we are both ready.”

“I totally approve. I think doing the repetitive daily tasks will make everything seem more normal.”

“Good. Now, about the clinic. What do you think? Do you still want to be my nurse?”

Susan relaxed and eagerly entered their new, everyday life as she replied, “Absolutely. You said you wanted to have two offices?”

"One in town and one here. The one here I think we build down the road a bit. What do you think?"

"I was thinking that the clinic here should just be an addition to the ranch house. That way, you'd have easy access to food and the house. So, whenever we get a chance for a lunch break, we can make it quickly."

"Excellent. I like your idea better. Another thing, Nurse Susan, I don't want you to have to be a nurse and a cook and still have to clean the house. We'll hire a cook and a maid. We have the room, and we'd be able to find them pretty easily."

"I don't mind doing the work, Hugh."

"It's not a question of that. You'll be with me all the time during the day and night. You simply won't have time to do anything but be my nurse during office hours. Luckily, the community isn't that big, so we shouldn't be overwhelmed with work. Now that Nancy is on her own, we'll need a receptionist/secretary as well. Maybe Margaret will want the job."

"She might."

"I'll let you in on another little secret. I'm not planning on charging patients who don't have much money. The ones that are well off can pay, but I see no reasons to make people pay who can't afford it."

Susan smiled, and her big blue eyes sparkled as she said, "You'll be very popular, Hugh. How long before your clinics are set up?"

"A couple of months at least. It depends on how quickly I can get the equipment and supplies."

"Sometimes I'm a little nervous about being a nurse. I'm only twenty years old, you know."

"Susan, do you remember the day we brought Margaret home?"

"Yes."

"Well, when I saw you both together, I was stunned by the difference. I knew you were only three years older than Margaret, but she was a young woman who looked the part. You were much more of a fully mature woman and it wasn't because she was so thin. It was your eyes and your confidence. It'll be that aura that you have that will give our patients confidence in you as a nurse. After a few months of training, you'll be even more confident. There is no limit to what you can do, Susan."

Susan was enormously pleased with his reply and said, "Thank you, Hugh. It means a lot."

Now that they had agreed not to discuss the buffalo in the room, things became lighter and more normal.

———

The next morning was still a normal atmosphere until Rebecca's burial the following afternoon.

Ella, Betty, Nancy and Margaret arrived around one o'clock. They had put a sign in the window closing the diner until tomorrow. Like most gatherings of this type, the grieving spoke of memories of the recently departed. They shared the wonderful moments, the magic times when Rebecca touched them all.

At 3:45, the hearse entered the access road, followed the mourners to the cemetery plot, and the two grave diggers followed in a buggy. They soon discovered that their services wouldn't be needed until after the service. There was no minister present, so the casket was lowered into the ground soon after it was removed from the hearse, then Hugh nodded to the mortician, and the grave diggers began shoveling the dirt into the grave, filling it in just ten minutes. They erected the marker, and Hugh wondered how the stonemason could have carved it so quickly as the undertakers and gravediggers left quietly after being told there was no other body to be removed.

Susan was the first to approach the grave. She looked at the memorial stone and read:

Rebecca McGinnis
September 3, 1837 ~ July 29, 1867
Beloved Wife and Mother
She Touched Our Hearts

She said quietly, "Good-bye, my beloved sister. I will do as you asked."

Each woman came close and said something before Hugh approached the foot of the grave holding Andy and Addie's hands, then stepped back a few feet to let them have private time.

Addie said, "You are the angels' Mama now."

Andy just whispered, "I love you, Mama."

After they turned away and took Susan's hands, Hugh stepped close to the fresh earth and whispered, "Good-bye, my beloved wife. I will do as you asked."

He had not heard Susan's whispered farewell to Rebecca.

They all turned and walked slowly back to the house, holding hands.

It was difficult for them to return to normal that day and conversation was stilted and meaningless as Betty and Ella made dinner. Nancy and Susan spent some time talking, but Susan didn't mention what Rebecca had asked of her.

After dinner, the women returned to Baker City because they had to get up early. Before they left, Hugh told them truthfully how much it meant to have them as friends.

Then there were only four. After the children were in bed, Hugh and Susan walked into the main room and took their now customary seats on the couch.

"Well, Susan, now we try to return to our normal life."

"Yes."

There was a short pause before he looked at her, smiled and asked, "Susan, do you play chess?"

"No, why?"

"I think you'd be good at it. I haven't played in years. Brian had a chess board in his office downstairs, so how about if I bring it up here and I can teach you to play? I like a challenge, and with your mind, I think you'll be a great player."

Susan smiled back at Hugh and said, "Alright."

Hugh nodded, then bounced off the couch and hustled downstairs to get the game board and pieces, returning just two minutes later.

After he had set them up, he explained the rules to Susan as she asked many insightful questions. Then they played their first game which Hugh won easily. But the game served its purpose as it kept their minds from drifting into sadness or the other subject they had agreed not to discuss.

They played three games that night and Hugh could see improvement in Susan's play after each game.

They called it a night around ten o'clock and Hugh said, "Thank you, Susan, for much, much more than the game."

She understood as she replied, "You're welcome. And thank you for showing me how to play."

They retired for the night into their bedrooms which were separated by a single wall, understanding that tomorrow, the routine life would need to begin.

CHAPTER 12

The routine day started with a routine breakfast. After breakfast, the children went into the main room and saw the chess board that Hugh had left in place.

Hugh was helping Susan clean up, despite her protests, and when they finished, they followed the children into the main room.

Hugh saw them examining the chess board and smiled.

Andy asked, “What’s that?”

“It’s a game called chess. I was showing Susan how to play.”

“Can you show me?”

“It’s kind of hard for a ten-year-old, but I can do that. But I may get you a checkerboard which uses the same board but is played differently, so you and Addie can play that game.”

“When will you get it?” asked Addie.

“Today. I need to go and pay a bill in town, and I’ll bring you a checkerboard when I come back.”

“Thank you, Papa. Then you’ll show us how to play?”

“You bet. Okay, then, I’m off. I won’t be long.”

Susan smiled, then said, “While you’re gone, I’ll explain chess to Andy. Maybe he’ll beat you when he returns.”

Hugh smiled back at Susan, and said, "I won't be the least bit surprised if you don't both beat me pretty soon, and then Addie can kick my behind, too."

The children's welcoming laugh was a perfect sendoff as he left the house, went to the barn, saddled Night, and rode out of the ranch five minutes later, arriving at the undertaker in thirty minutes. He went inside, paid the bill and thanked them for a job well done, and took a few minutes explaining why the need for a second transport was unnecessary.

Then, he went to the dry goods store and found the checkerboard set. As he was leaving, he found something that might generate a few smiles and added it to the order.

Before he returned, he stopped by the drug store to ask about the possibility of ordering the equipment.

"Good morning, Mister McGinnis," said Martin Childs as he entered.

"It's Doctor McGinnis now," he said as smiled at the chemist.

"Wonderful! Congratulations. What can I do for you today, doctor?"

"I'll be setting up two clinics. One will be here in town and the second out at my ranch. I'll be needing a lot of equipment and supplies. Do you have catalogs that I can use to place the orders?"

"I do. I will confess that I get a commission on equipment."

"As you should. It'll take me two or three days to get the complete list together. I'll also be needing a stock of drugs and other medications and supplies. I'll be the best customer you'll ever have."

"It'll be a good step forward for the city to have a degreed physician. I'll get you the catalogs."

He found three thick catalogs and gave Hugh a bag to carry them in.

"Thank you, Martin. I'll get these back to you as soon as I can."

"There's no hurry. No one has ordered from them yet."

Hugh waved, mounted Night, then returned to the ranch, riding him straight into the barn, where he unsaddled and brushed the stallion down before he left the barn, then walked to the lower floor and put his surprise in the cold room, before he went into the kitchen to find his family.

"Just in time for lunch," said Susan as he entered.

"I thought I smelled something tasty when I was in Baker City."

She laughed and replied, "That was probably from the café. I hear they're doing a good business since they expanded their menu."

"Just being complimentary, ma'am."

"What do you have in the bag?"

"These, my good nurse, are catalogs for outfitting our clinics. You and I will spend some time and make up the order over the next few days."

"That should be interesting."

"But I also bought the checkerboard."

"Much more interesting."

Lunch was followed by intensive checker training, which took all of ten minutes before Andy and Addie were soon engaged in extended checker play, which was good as it kept their minds busy.

Susan and Hugh played two games of chess as Andy and Addie jumped and crowned their pieces.

"You almost got me on that second one, Susan. I knew you'd be good at this."

Hugh watched the children intently studying their checkerboard, then glanced over at Susan as they shared a smile at the sight.

Hugh held up a finger to Susan and stepped over to where the children were playing their game, and said, "I think whoever wins this game will get a special surprise."

That created a pause as they both looked up.

"What kind of surprise?" asked Addie.

"A cold surprise."

"Is it lemonade?" queried Andy.

"Nope. It's something you've never had before. I don't think Susan has ever had it before, either."

Now, Susan was intrigued and asked, "Cold and I've never had it before?"

"It doesn't have to be cold, but it's cold now."

His announcement had its desired impact as they all stared at him eagerly to know what the surprise was.

"Alright, I think you all deserve the surprise. Everyone sit right here, and I'll be right back."

He trotted outside then down to the cold room, picked up the small bag with the surprise and hurried back.

Everyone was staring at the bag as Hugh sat down.

He reached inside, then slowly, enticingly drew out with great anticipation… a chocolate bar.

"Is that what I think it is?" asked a wide-eyed Susan.

"This, ladies and Andy, is a milk chocolate bar. I was really surprised to find them here. So, without further suspense, I have one for each of you."

"Addie," he said as he handed her a bar.

"Andy."

"My lady."

As Susan took her candy, she looked at Hugh. "What about you?"

"I emptied their stock. I'm fine and have had some before back in Michigan. I'll just watch you enjoy them."

Susan's eyebrows furrowed as she said, "You will not. You and I will share."

Hugh saw the same mischievous look in Susan's face that he had in Rebecca's when she was not going to change her mind and smiled.

"If you insist, ma'am."

"Ma'am does insist," Susan replied.

The children were digging into their chocolate with a vengeance.

Susan and Hugh took their time as Susan broke off a piece and handed it to Hugh, then broke off a second piece and popped it in her mouth.

"Oh, my goodness!", she thought as she closed her eyes and let it melt on her tongue.

When she opened her eyes, she saw Hugh grinning at her and blushed.

"This is unlike anything I have ever tasted before."

"That's why I bought them. I wanted you to experience something special."

"Thank you so much."

She broke off another piece and offered it to him.

"Susan, the rest is yours. I'll get more enjoyment watching you savor the taste."

"Well, enjoy the show, then," she said as she put the piece into her mouth and felt the smooth chocolate flavor fill her senses.

Hugh did exactly as he had told Susan he would and just watched her intensely happy face.

The children finished their chocolate and were soon playing checkers again, although the pieces were shifting from red and black to brown and sticky.

After Susan had eaten her last delectable morsel, she opened her eyes and saw Hugh nodding his head toward the children. She looked over at the brown-fingered, chocolate-faced children and shook her head.

“Okay, you two. Let’s get you cleaned up.”

Hugh was smirking as she led the children into the kitchen, having witnessed her perfect slide into motherhood.

He picked up the chocolaty checkerboard and pieces and carried them into the kitchen for cleanup.

Susan was just finishing with Andy when he arrived and said, “I’ll clean the checkerboard.”

“As you should,” replied Susan.

After they were clean, the children went outside to play with Chester, who had felt neglected for the past few days.

The rest of that day and the next three days were filled with checkers, chess, and making a long list of supplies and equipment.

On the fourth night, things changed, but not dramatically or even in a bad direction.

The children were sleeping, and Hugh and Susan were playing a game of chess. Susan was studying the board while

Hugh was studying Susan. It was only a few days since Rebecca's death and Hugh was almost ashamed that he wasn't more depressed. He felt as if he was cheating on Rebecca for feeling as he did about Susan. She was so much like Rebecca, but so different, too.

She moved her remaining bishop, then looked up with a giant smile and proclaimed, "Checkmate!"

Hugh looked down at the board in stunned silence, he had lost.

He stood to shake her hand for the victory, but never got the chance.

An exultant, victorious Susan leapt from her chair, stepped around the table and quickly hugged him. Hugh wrapped his arms around her, then the big change arrived.

Susan looked up at him and he looked into her blue eyes, then without hesitation, leaned down and kissed her.

Susan hadn't really expected this so soon, but when it happened, she felt the passion and love she'd been holding back for what seemed like years, explode. She then responded, adding that passion to the kiss as she pulled him closer.

After the long, meaningful kiss, Hugh pulled back slightly and stared into her vibrant blue eyes.

"Susan, can I tell you what Rebecca said to me that day?" he asked softly.

"Yes," she whispered.

"She said I should love you as much as I loved her. I do love you, Susan, but it's not the same. Maybe because it's so soon. I don't know. But I'm asking you to be patient with me."

"Hugh, I'll wait for the rest of our lives if I need to. Rebecca knew that I loved you for almost as long as I've known you. She told me that you needed my love and it will always be there for you."

Hugh smiled at her and ran his fingers across the side of her face.

"You are a very special woman, Susan."

"I am your woman, Hugh."

"And I am yours, Susan."

He kissed her again before they gravitated to the couch where Susan curled up under his arm, contented with the incredible change and understanding that she had Rebecca's approval for what had just happened.

Hugh stroked her sandy brown hair and said, "I need to confess something to you, Susan. I feel like I'm cheating on Rebecca for having my feelings for you. I know that sounds beyond stupid, but it nags at me. She even told me to love you, yet that little annoying feeling is there."

"Don't feel bad, Hugh. I have the same thoughts. The ironic thing is that I never felt like I was doing anything wrong by loving you while I was Rebecca's friend. I was never jealous of her. I loved her like a sister, and I was pleased that you made her so happy."

"We'll just have to keep going. I do know one thing, Susan. When we both feel it's right, I want to love you with as much passion as possible. I don't ever want to give you anything less."

"No woman could ask for more," she replied with a gentle smile.

Hugh wanted to feel Susan's softness under his fingers very badly, but that nagging, annoying voice kept him from doing what the rest of his mind, heart and body were screaming at him to do. He really did want to love Susan with every bit of love and passion he could muster and didn't want some annoying thought to keep him from doing just that.

Susan was much more ready for that next step than Hugh was for many reasons, but the simplest was that she and Rebecca had shared their love for Hugh and there had never been another man in her life that she would ever love as much. She wanted him as badly as he wanted her but understood that he needed time.

Hugh smiled at Susan and said, "Tomorrow, let's take the carriage into town. We can meet with the construction company and tell them what we want done out here for the clinic and I also want to modify the back of the house. I want an addition, so we can go to the bottom floor without going outside. We can have lunch at the café and talk to everyone."

Susan was just so happy with the way the day was ending that she just nodded, and Hugh could feel her head move and understood why she didn't answer.

Neither said another word for almost thirty minutes, but after a few minutes of silence, Hugh leaned over and kissed Susan again to let her know that it wasn't a spur of the moment event.

They engaged in what most teenagers considered necking, but didn't pass the kissing and handholding stage, although Hugh did begin kissing Susan's neck, which gave Susan hope that it wouldn't be much longer before he touched her. She was already having feelings of excitement that she'd never experienced before with just his relatively innocent kisses and couldn't imagine how exhilarating it would be when they finally passed his mental barrier.

The first two weeks in August were filled with days that were very ordinary. Hugh placed his massive order. The construction company had come out and finished making the modifications for the clinic and the new mud room and stairs to the lower level as both were straightforward jobs. The children were excited about going to school for the first time and the nightly games of chess and checkers continued, although sometimes, Andy tried his hand at chess, but quickly decided that he didn't like it as much because he didn't win.

After the children were asleep, the adults sat and either played chess and talked, or just sat closely together and talked. The kissing continued and there had been times when it had almost gone further, but Hugh felt like there were ropes holding him back. He knew he totally loved Susan now, but was still unsure of the passion he wanted to bestow upon her.

Susan was beginning to get extraordinarily frustrated, but still enjoyed her private time with Hugh and knew she had to be patient.

Hugh had gone into town to check on his order and knew that the more exotic items would probably take another two weeks to get there. He had told Martin to divide the order in half, as he had ordered twice what he needed, including four nurse outfits for Susan.

The orders were further along than he expected, but still had two examining tables and the new light sets for surgery still to come and his surgical tool sets weren't in yet, either.

Martin told him that Doc Adams had gotten wind of Hugh's plans and had vowed to take his business elsewhere, which they both found amusing. Martin told him that it would be difficult for him to do so, as his nearest competitor was fifty miles away.

Then Hugh went to the bank and had them send a notice to the Ann Arbor bank, closing his account there and transferring all his funds to his account.

He returned home and then settled in for a normal, quiet time, or so he thought.

It was the 17th of August, an odd day, meaning it was Hugh's turn for the pool. It was decidedly hot, so Hugh told Susan he was heading for the pool for a while, grabbed a blanket and walked the half a mile to the pool. It was the first time he had used the pool since that day. He knew that Susan had been out there a couple of times, but it was time he put it all behind him.

He reached the pools after a ten-minute walk, spread out the blanket and felt the sun on his face as he took off his boots and then disrobed. He let the warmth soak into his skin before he took a running start and leapt forward with arms outstretched and sliced into the cold, clear water. The shock of the temperature change was exhilarating as he continued the dive until he was ten feet under and slowly rose, seeing the bright sky through the lens of rippling, clear water. He broke the surface and floated on his back, enjoying the difference between the blazing heat from the sun on his front and the chilled liquid on his back, then began alternating diving and floating. He had been in the water for twenty minutes when he surfaced from a dive and he was blinking water from his eyes when he saw someone approaching. It was Susan, and he wondered if something was wrong.

He watched as she drew closer, then when she was close enough, he shouted, “Susan, is something wrong?

She kept walking until she was close to the pool and answered, “Yes, there’s something very wrong.”

“Is it the children?”

“No, they’re fine. It’s us.”

Before he could ask what was wrong, she reached the blanket, and pulled off her boots. She kept her eyes focused on him as he watched her unbuttoning her blouse. Then she removed it and tossed it on top of his clothes. Then she unbuttoned her riding skirt and let it fall to the ground, startling Hugh as he looked at her. He knew she was well-formed, but she was beyond that, Susan was exquisite.

Susan walked to the edge and dove in as Hugh had, then swam straight toward him and treaded water just inches from him as water dripped from the tip of her nose.

She put her arms on his shoulders and said, “Hugh, we can’t go on like this. Do you love me enough to make love to me? I need you, Hugh. You’ve been torturing me with your tender kisses and your light touches. I don’t want to be so selfish, but I want you so much.”

He closed the gap and felt her body touch his, then placed his hands on the side of her face before she wrapped her arms around him and they slowly sank under the water, locked in a passionate kiss as they did.

As they descended, Hugh began to slide his hands over her smooth body, and she did the same. They were wrapped together as Hugh's feet touched the bottom, then he kicked up, angling toward the shore. They broke the surface and took deep breaths.

With their eyes still locked together, they swam the short distance to the edge of the pool. Hugh stepped out first, the cold water having no impact at all on his arousal before he helped Susan from the water. He wanted her as much as he ever wanted any woman, even his beloved Rebecca.

They took four steps to the blanket and they slowly lay on its warm surface as Hugh pulled her close to him.

He was already sliding his hand across her wet skin as he said, "Susan, thank you. I needed that nudge. Now, my love, my beloved Susan, I will show you the passionate love that you deserve."

"Please, Hugh," she said softly.

Hugh was more experienced now. Rebecca had shown him what he needed to do to bring her level of excitement into the clouds, so now, he was able to let Susan benefit from that knowledge.

He touched, caressed, and kissed her until she was almost beyond consciousness. Her limited experience was nothing as she felt nirvana. She had ridden to the pool to have him make love to her, but she had no inkling of what real lovemaking could be. But she needed it to come to its climax. She wanted him to take her and make her his woman in every way.

All she could do was moan a guttural, "Now...please!"

Hugh knew that as much as Susan believed she was ready, he knew he could send her even higher, and took his time, focusing on Susan until he knew he could last no longer.

Susan's eyelids were fluttering as he continued to take his time to make her feel every nuance of pleasure possible. She was grabbing Hugh and screaming her pleasure and demands as they writhed on the blanket under the warm August sun.

Finally, at long last, Hugh knew that he couldn't last another second and did as she asked and they joined in a chaotic, frenetic climax to their lovemaking that echoed across the fields, even drowning out the nearby waterfall.

When they finally collapsed to the blanket bathed in the perspiration that glistened over their bodies, Susan lay flat on her back with the sun baking her flawless skin. Hugh was propped on his left elbow looking down at her supremely satisfied face as he traced his fingers over her beautiful body as she lay there, leaving a trail of goosebumps as he did.

She opened her eyes and smiled with the look of total contentment.

"My love," she said, "I never knew it could be like this. I was married before, but that was nothing compared to this. You made me feel so alive, so aware of every touch. Will it be like this every time?"

"Yes, sweetheart, every time. I will never let you settle for less."

She reached for his neck, wrapped her hands behind them, then pulled herself up and kissed him deeply.

“Then,” she asked softly, “can you make me happy again so soon?”

Susan had the distinct advantage of hearing Hugh and Rebecca and knew that he had the ability to do that very thing and wanted it as much as he did.

He smiled and replied, “How could I deny you anything?”

And he didn’t deny her one bit of pleasure in their second coupling. If anything, now that she anticipated it, she was able to enjoy it even more as she hungrily waited for the next level of lust to be reached and surpassed. She was more active this time as well, wanting to give him more pleasure in their lovemaking, and now that she knew he didn’t mind her uninhibited demands and reactions, was even more demonstrative.

When they were finally satisfied the second time, they lay entwined on the blanket, just looking into each other’s eyes and breathing deeply.

“Susan, can I ask you a question that has been running through my mind every now and then when I looked at you ever since that first day?”

“Of course, you can.”

“You are a truly incredible woman. Why would someone like you marry someone who could then take up with someone like Nellie, who is almost your total opposite?”

“I was almost hoping the subject would never come up. I didn’t want you to be ashamed of me.”

"Susan, that's not possible."

"Yes, it is. I married Frank because I had to. Frank had been pursuing me for years and it was just one of those stupid moments that caused everything. I was lonely, and I had let him have his way with me, and we were caught by my father. He made Frank marry me and then never wanted to see me again. I never even liked Frank that much. He was clumsy in bed and just unkempt in all aspects of his life. I was miserable, and didn't think it could get any worse, then I was taken by the Hanson brothers. I guess Frank used that as an excuse to let Nellie take my place."

"Well, beautiful lady, no more Frank and no more Hansons. The only man in your life is with you right now."

"Then I'm happy," she said with the added relief that she had told Hugh what she had done and believed him that he had lost no respect for her.

They stayed there basking in the sun and their newfound intimacy for another two hours and interspersed it with some refreshing dips into the pool. But even extraordinary times as those they had experienced must end, so they finally dressed.

Hugh wrapped up the blanket and they walked slowly back to the house, holding hands and stealing glances along the way.

Susan walked into the kitchen and then through to the main room where she found the children playing checkers.

"Hello, Andy and Addie. Who's winning?" she asked with a contented smile.

They looked up and noticed how happy she was, and both returned her smile.

"Andy won two times in a row," complained Addie.

Susan sat down in the chair next to Addie and watched her play.

Hugh returned to the house and walked into his bedroom. He wanted it to be their bedroom now, then opened a drawer and under a green silk dress, he found Blue Flower's necklace. It was time to reach that final step in healing and knew Rebecca would want nothing less.

"Susan, can I see you for a moment, please?" he called.

Susan stood and walked to the room, and when she entered, she saw the necklace in Hugh's hand as he sat on the bed. She didn't know if it would be proper for her to wear it, but it wasn't her decision to make.

"Could you sit here, next to me, Susan?" he asked softly.

She wordlessly sat next to him, but her heart was pounding.

"Susan, you know the story behind this necklace. Or most of it, anyway. When Blue Flower gave me the necklace, she told me something. When I gave it to Rebecca, I told her that what Blue Flower had said to me could only be shared between me, Blue Flower, and one other. Yet, she never asked me what she had said, and for some reason I never got a chance to tell her. So, I have never shared what Blue Flower had told me with anyone. I don't know if Rebecca knew that the necklace was intended for another, but she never asked, so now, I will tell you what she said."

Tears were falling from Susan's eyes as she remembered Rebecca's face with the necklace across her breast.

"What Blue Flower said was, 'I will miss you because you have touched my heart. Give this to the woman that will touch yours.'"

Susan turned to him, her eyes and cheeks wet with tears.

Hugh brushed some of her tears away and looked into those incredible blue eyes, and said quietly, "On that horrible day when Rebecca left us, I whispered to Rebecca that she had touched my heart. She told me that she had just touched my heart, but you would hold it in your hands for as long as you lived.

"Susan, I love you completely. Wearing the necklace would let me express that love and honor our Rebecca. She knew as she told me that the love that we shared would be too short. But our love, Susan, our love will be just as passionate, just as fulfilling, but will last for our entire lives."

He held the necklace in front of her. She bowed her head in acceptance and he lowered it gently over her head and across her neck. He pulled her hair over it as he had when he had put it around Rebecca's neck and smiled at her. She reached across softly held him, as she sobbed quietly.

Hugh whispered, "Susan Gardner, will you marry me?"

She never raised her head, but just answered softly, "Oh, yes, Hugh. Please."

When she finally stopped crying, she leaned back and smiled at Hugh. He gazed through those sky-blue eyes into her very soul and knew that true joy filled her heart as it did his. He stood and took her hands. They rose, walked out hands locked together and saw the children still playing checkers.

Andy looked at them first as Addie studied the checkerboard, saw the necklace and knew that Susan was going to be their mama now.

He looked at his sister and said, “Addie, papa and mama are here.”

Addie whirled around and saw Susan wearing the necklace, then popped up and ran to Susan.

She put out her hands and said, “Mama!”

Susan knew that everything else would be a formality. She had been wed and recognized as a parent already. The law could follow.

That night, they slept in the same bedroom for the first time. He had put the children to bed and opened the door to find Susan wearing one of the ‘interesting’ nightgowns.

“Rebecca came back from shopping and had bought two of these for me. I didn’t understand why she would do that because I had no reason to wear them then.”

Hugh stepped close to her and kissed her gently before saying, “If you’ll give me a few minutes, then I’ll show you that you won’t have to wear it long.”

He left the lamp lit as he disrobed, and she watched in anticipation. Hugh left the nightgown on longer than he expected when he discovered that it added some new level of excitement for both of them as he felt her body with that thin silky cloth between them.

But it didn’t stay on much longer.

———

The next morning was normal for the children as they saw Hugh and Susan as their parents, and they were pleased to have everyone happy again. Hugh and Susan were still awash in the release of being unwed newlyweds.

An hour after breakfast found all four riding the carriage into town.

First, they made a quick stop at the jewelry shop. He and Susan decided on a wedding ring set and were back in the carriage in fifteen minutes. Hugh had removed his old wedding ring and had laid it on Rebecca's memorial stone before they left.

Then, he drove to the café to tell their friends. Hugh and Susan were holding hands as they entered with the children, and saw Margaret serving tables to the two customers. It was almost ten o'clock, and the lunch crowd would start drifting in soon.

"Margaret, can you join us in the back for a moment?" he asked.

She nodded, smiling at the obvious change in their relationship.

When they were in the back room, Hugh said to the curious women, "Ladies, if you have a little time, I'd like you to accompany us to the courthouse for a short wedding ceremony."

There were squeals of delight and congratulations followed by a bustling cleanup of clothing.

As they were getting ready, Hugh turned to the already clean Margaret and asked, "How is the tutoring going?"

"Very well. I'm learning so much, so quickly. I can't thank you enough, Hugh."

"The reason I'm asking is that when I set up my clinics, I'll need a receptionist/secretary. Now, I know that you're doing very well as a waitress, but I also know how tiring it can be walking around all day. So, if you want the job, let me know. I'll be opening them in about two or three weeks."

Margaret was taken by surprise and asked, "Really? You'd want me to do that?"

"If you'd like to."

"I'd love to. My feet get really sore by dinner time and I get pinched too many times, too."

Hugh laughed and said, "Well, you won't get pinched in our clinics. Susan will take care of any of those sorts."

Susan smiled and said, "I will."

Margaret was almost as happy as the couple to be married.

―――

When they entered his chambers, Judge Hampton welcomed them back like old friends. He expressed his condolences for the loss of Rebecca, then performed the marriage ceremony. Two divorces and two marriages all officiated by Judge Horace Hampton within the space of a couple of months.

After he had kissed his new bride, and everyone had signed the forms, Judge Hampton gave Susan a peck on the cheek and shook Hugh's hand. The women all had to hurry back to prepare for lunch, but before she left, Margaret told Hugh that she wanted to work in the clinics.

Susan was emotionally exhausted as they left the courthouse. It was like a whirlwind. She was now Mrs. Hugh McGinnis, and the mother to Andy and Addie McGinnis.

She turned to her new husband and said, “Hugh, I’m so very happy, but I’m a bit numb to be honest.”

“Well, my love, I’m going to make it worse. Let’s head over to the bank and get your name on our account.”

“Oh,” was her short reply.

She hated to admit that the thought of seeing that much money was titillating.

The now completely McGinnis family drove the carriage to the bank and all exited. Hugh walked to the same clerk and told them he needed to remove Rebecca from the account and add Susan. The clerk, like many others had heard of the tragedy out at the ranch, but being a good clerk, just acknowledged the request. He brought the appropriate forms and Susan signed them.

Hugh then asked if his transfer of funds had come through. The clerk made a mildly sour face and said, “Yes, Mister McGinnis. It has.”

Then he added, “I would like to explain to you that the cash we have on hand at any given time wouldn’t be enough to cover any really large withdrawals. Even your previous balance would have caused us great distress had you asked for even a significant portion in cash. I just wanted you to understand that. Most of the bank’s money is actually either out in loans or in our sister bank in San Francisco.”

Hugh had no idea what was driving the explanation, but said, “Yes, I’m fully aware of how banks work. I know there’s no profit in just keeping money in stacks in a vault. I have no intention of withdrawing any large amount of cash.”

“Excellent. Excellent. Here’s your current balance.”

He slid the sheet over to Hugh, and as he stared at the sheet of paper, Susan looked across and felt her heart skip a beat.

It read: $363,456.30.

Hugh asked, “Is this correct? I only had about twenty-two thousand dollars in that account.”

The clerk almost laughed when Hugh had said, ‘only twenty-two thousand’, but kept his poker face.

“We verified it twice. The bank in Ann Arbor confirmed its accuracy.”

“Alright. But I think I’ll have to do some investigating.”

“I understand that. You do realize, Mister McGinnis, that the interest alone on that balance will be almost sixteen hundred dollars per month.”

“Thank you. I’ll let you know if I turn up something.”

“Feel free to see me at any time.”

Hugh shook his hand, then took Susan’s hand as she looked at him with glassy eyes. She was still stunned as they walked slowly out of the bank.

They walked out to the carriage and neither Addie nor Andy could understand why their new mama was acting so differently.

Hugh had to help her onto the driver's seat of the carriage as the children clambered inside.

He turned the carriage back toward the ranch and once it was underway, he looked at her.

"Hugh, what happened?" Susan asked quietly as she held onto his arm for support.

"With the money? I have no idea. At first, I thought it was a clerical mistake. But they checked twice, as they should have. If it wasn't a mistake, and banks rarely make mistakes when dealing with that kind of money, then it has something to do with my father."

"Is he that wealthy?"

"Yes. He had large logging contracts and ran four lumber mills. It was quite an empire, really. I never did tell you the story about my family, did I? I told Rebecca and Betty, but that was a while ago. I know I said some things when I found that photograph of my parents, but to clarify, my mother was a distant, but beautiful woman. My father was a man's man, he worked hard, and he womanized. He paid little attention to my mother, but we never knew why. She eventually took a lover, one of my father's foremen. She was in bed with him while I was in my room studying. My father came home with a pistol and shot them both. Nothing happened to him and he acted as if nothing had happened. We just never spoke of her again."

"Do you think he died?"

"No, I would have been contacted by his attorney."

"Hugh, what are you going to do with all that money?"

"Nothing. I have to find out if it's really there or not. Even if it's good, there's just too much of it to spend. You can have anything you want, but then, you could have had that anyway. Did you change your mind about working as my nurse?"

"Oh, heavens, no. I can't wait. It still excites me, Hugh. I'll be with you and I'll be learning. It's just that having that much money is almost like a curse."

Hugh laughed and said, "Now you know what it's been like most of my life. Even during the bad years, we always had money available. After the big contracts started coming in and we moved to the big house, if we needed something, we got it. When I left school, I made sure that no one knew about it. I had over thirty thousand dollars in the bank and still lived on my army pay and didn't even spend half of that. I never had a reason to buy things until I met Rebecca and the children. Now I have you and the children. Material things are good and necessary, Susan, but nothing can come close to the value of the love we share."

"Amen to that," she said as she leaned against his shoulder and the carriage continued to rock as the wheels churned up the Oregon dust.

CHAPTER 13

The mystery of the money lasted for three weeks. During that time, Hugh had set up both clinics and had begun to see patients.

Margaret was having some difficulty with filing but was a star at the reception part of her duties, greeting patients with warmth and understanding. Her handwriting was improving almost daily as she spent so much time with a pencil or pen in her hand.

The clinics were proving to be very popular. Even though the population of the town was just over a thousand, Hugh was seeing up to ten patients every day. He wasn't overworked and could spend time with each patient and had yet to bill anyone, not that it mattered.

Susan proved to be priceless as a nurse. She looked and acted every bit the professional she had become and was there as Hugh examined and treated patients. Hugh would explain as he went along, letting her listen through the stethoscope or examine samples under his microscope.

Hugh had hired a mother and daughter to work in the house before the clinics opened. The mother was a widow and she and her daughter were in a bad state when Betty had told Hugh about their situation. She also told Hugh that the mother was an excellent cook. Susan told Betty to bring her and her daughter to Hugh's town clinic the next day.

Hugh being Hugh, hired forty-year-old Minnie Witherspoon and her sixteen-year-old-daughter, Carrie, on the spot and gave her forty dollars to go and buy some new clothes. He told them to return to the clinic where they could change and use the bathroom upstairs. When they were changed into their new clothes and smiling, they accompanied him and Susan on their return trip to the ranch house and settled in easily. Carrie enjoyed the children and they took to her like a big sister, one that Andy could beat in checkers.

Susan, despite her original protest, appreciated being relieved of the everyday drudgery of cooking and cleaning. Luckily, Minnie didn't think of it as drudgery at all. Especially as Hugh refused to have anyone in the house need to do that most backbreaking task of all, the laundry. Every Monday, he would load the laundry into the carriage when he went to his town clinic and returned with it on Friday. All the women thought this was the greatest of all possible gifts.

Susan's chess game had improved to play at Hugh's level, which made the matches much more intriguing. Andy had finally taken a shine to the game as well, but still played checkers with Addie.

Susan wore the necklace whenever she wasn't wearing her nurse outfit. The clinics were only open five days a week as Hugh insisted that only emergencies would interrupt his family time.

It was a Friday night, and the day's clinic at the ranch had only served three patients. Susan was wearing 'civilian' clothes and sat with Hugh on the couch. They weren't playing chess, but they were watching the children play checkers. Carrie was kibitzing while Minnie was still in the kitchen, baking some cookies for the children, although Hugh had developed quite a taste for them as well.

There was a knock on the door and Hugh started to rise, but Carrie was already on her feet, so she crossed the room and opened the door.

"May I see Hugh McGinnis please?" asked a deep, cavernous voice from the open doorway.

Before Carrie could answer, Hugh said clearly, "Come in, Father."

Susan felt her hairs on the back of her neck rise as she sat up straight.

Carrie opened the door wide and a handsome, but tired looking man entered the doorway. He had a shock of gray hair and was clean shaven. His eyes were a piercing gray and reeked of command authority.

Hugh didn't rise, but just looked at his father with a horrendously confused set of emotions. He also noticed how much weight he'd lost. He looked as if he'd dropped a good sixty pounds.

"Hello, Son," he said.

"Come in and have a seat, Father. I'm sure you'd like to talk."

"I would."

He removed his light jacket then Jessie took it from him and hung it on a peg near the door.

Arthur McGinnis took a seat opposite his son.

"I see you still play," he said as he pointed at the chess board.

Hugh smiled and replied, “Susan and I get into spirited games every night. She beats me often, too. Father, this is Susan, your daughter-in-law.”

Arthur smiled warmly at Susan and said, “I’m very pleased to meet you, Susan. Call me Arthur.”

“I’m pleased to meet you, too, Arthur,” she said, examining the man who had murdered his own wife and not seeing the malevolence in his eyes that she had expected.

Arthur noticed the two children and knew they were much too old to be Susan’s, or Hugh’s for that matter. Hugh quickly solved the mystery for him.

“Father, I’d like to introduce you to our children. This is Andy and Addie. They were the children of my first wife, Rebecca, who died a short time ago.”

“I’m sorry to hear that, Hugh. I really am.”

“The young lady who let you in is Carrie Witherspoon. She and her mother, Minnie, who is in the kitchen baking cookies, are part of our extended family.”

Arthur said hello to Carrie, then turned back to Hugh and asked, “Son, could I talk to you privately for a while?”

Hugh could tell there was a profound change in the man he had known, but couldn’t understand what had driven the change, or if he just hadn’t understood his father at all.

Hugh looked to Carrie and said, “Carrie, could you take the children into the kitchen and see how your mother is doing with those cookies.”

Addie jumped up shouted, “Cookies!” as if she hadn’t noticed the enticing aroma and ran to the kitchen with Andy trailing. Carrie smiled and followed.

“They’re beautiful children, Hugh.”

“They are. I’ll tell you the whole story later, but what can I do for you?”

“Hugh, you know that I didn’t want you to go to medical school, but I’m pleased that you did well and are a fine physician.”

“I try to be.”

“What would you diagnose if I had severe back pains and difficulty in urination?”

Hugh looked at his indomitable father and arrived at his diagnosis immediately.

“How long do you have, Father?”

Arthur smiled grimly and said, “That was a quick diagnosis.”

“It wasn’t difficult. Can I guess you’ve seen other doctors?”

“It took them weeks of tests to make the diagnosis that you made in three seconds. They said I had six months.”

“Is it inoperable?”

“Yes. I was so stubborn and so convinced of my own immortality that I put off going to the doctor. By the time the pain became strong enough, it was too late. I sold the business, lock, stock and barrel and deposited the money in your Ann Arbor account. I didn’t sell the house, though. It’s in your name now. I kept five thousand dollars and started traveling. I took trains and then stagecoaches across the gap and then trains again. I took a ship up the coast, bought a buggy and drove the rest of the way."

"Would you like to stay here with us, Father?"

His father nodded, and replied in a choking voice, "More than anything, Hugh."

Despite everything it their past, Hugh felt immense compassion for his father. He was a patient dying of prostate cancer, and guessed the six-month estimate was correct as he didn't seem to be in excruciating pain yet, but the weight loss meant it must be advanced.

"Then you'll be welcome. I'll take care of you and keep the pain to acceptable levels."

"I knew you would, but before I do anything else, I'd like to explain things that happened when you were young. You deserve to know the truth."

"It's not necessary, Father."

"I know, but it would give me some measure of peace if you knew. Can I guess that Susan knows of the basic circumstances?"

"Yes, she does, Father."

He blew out his breath and said, "Hugh, you never knew about our lives before you arrived, and that was my fault. I spent so much time making money and gaining power, I never spent time with you. I regret that every day.

"I met your mother while we were still in our teens. She was very beautiful even when she was sixteen. You may not believe it, but she was also very vivacious. Every boy wanted to be her boyfriend, but I won the competition to call on your mother. I had inherited a sawmill from my father, so I already was financially secure. I'm not sure that it played a big part in her decision or not, but it was part of it, I'm sure. We were married when I turned nineteen. She was eighteen.

"After we were married, she was everything I could have wished for in a wife. We spent days in our bed, but I had to work. Sometimes, I would work fourteen hours in a day, and it wasn't too long before I began hearing rumors that she was being unfaithful, but I didn't believe it. There was no reason for it because I thought she was happy and content.

"Then she began having headaches or cramps or something else to deny me and I grew frustrated. Then I found her with one of my workers and threw him bodily out of the house. I was very angry with your mother, but didn't say a word to her, just left the house and sought the company of a prostitute."

Arthur looked up at the ceiling momentarily, then returned his eyes to look at his son.

"A month later, I found she was pregnant, but I hadn't been with her for some time by then. The result of that pregnancy was Brian. He wasn't my son, but I acted as if he was. It was difficult, Hugh. I knew he was evidence of my wife's faithlessness, but I still loved your mother and hoped it might have been a unique, one-time dalliance.

"We moved to the big house two years later, and your mother invited me into the bedroom again. I was happy, and positively ecstatic when she became pregnant with you. You were my son, Hugh, my only legitimate son. It was very difficult to treat you and Brian the same, but I tried.

"After you were born, she began denying me again, and not just the bedroom. She denied me just the pleasure of talking to her and hearing her laugh. I suppose that I should have divorced her, but I still loved her and hoped she would return to me. We slept in different rooms in that big house, and I began seeing other women. Part of it was to spite your mother, but mostly it was because I was hungry, both physically and mentally. It lasted that way for years.

"Then I heard that she was taking lovers again. You were about twelve at the time, I think. I came home one time and found evidence of it. We had a real screaming match, and she said I was an adulterer, which I was, but she denied any adultery on her part whatsoever and threatened to divorce me and take you and Brian away. That was what really bothered me and cause me a great deal of anger because I know that she didn't even like either of you. I laid low for a while and just worked but admit that I slipped a few times and visited other women but kept it quiet.

"Then came the day you witnessed. I came home, had dinner and had to go back to work. I returned to mill #3 to check on a problem and found the foreman missing. I was angry that he wasn't doing his job, then someone dropped a hint that he was visiting my home. I grabbed the gun out of my office and returned home. I was angry, yes, but I was more concerned with her threat. If she filed for divorce first, no matter what I showed of her infidelity, I would lose. I went upstairs and found her in bed with the foreman. I fired two shots and started screaming at her. I knew you were there, but I had lost control.

"I should have explained it all to you, Hugh. I should have done so much more, but I was devastated. I had just killed the woman whom I still loved. Can you imagine what that does to you inside? I went and confessed to the sheriff, and I honestly expected to be hanged for what I did. He told me that because she was shot in flagrante, there would be no charges, and I honestly was shocked.

"The bodies were removed and buried in a common grave in the town cemetery. After that, I just worked. I enjoyed the company of other women, but it was empty, meaningless sex. Brian had gone to Oregon and you went to Ann Arbor, and all I had was that giant, empty house and nothing else. So, rather than live there alone, I worked even harder. Then, last year, the pains started, and when I finally was given a diagnosis and prognosis, I knew I had to come and explain everything to you, Hugh. I had to beg your forgiveness."

Hugh had listened to the story and finally saw the other side of the relationship and it all made sense. Every moment, every word and every single emotion all fit. His father wasn't the insensitive monster he had thought him to be, he was just a human being with human problems.

Hugh looked into his father's suddenly pleading eyes and said, "I don't have to forgive you for anything, Papa. I had thought all these years that you were nothing more than a philandering, indifferent man. I was wrong."

"No, you weren't, Hugh. That's exactly what I was, which is why I came to see you."

"Father, you weren't. You were just a man who married the wrong woman. You needed to marry a good woman who loved you, as I have," he said as he smiled and touched Susan on her knee.

She beamed back at him.

"I would have given anything for that, Hugh," his father said quietly.

“I’ve been blessed, Papa. I’ve been married to two extraordinary, loving women, but maybe it’s not too late for you.”

“Son, I only have six months to live.”

“Father, six months ago, I was on the Oregon Trail with my horse and a mule. Since then, I’ve found our children, and two women that have made my life complete. I’ve opened two clinics and started helping people. Six months can be a long time.”

Arthur smiled at him and said, “You always were an optimist.”

Hugh smiled back at his father and said, “Look at Susan and tell me that I have no reason to be that way.”

He did and said, “I can see what you mean. You are a lucky man, Hugh.”

Susan interrupted and said, “Mister McGinnis, don’t sell your son short. He’s the most incredible man I’ve ever met.”

Hugh locked into her effervescent blue eyes but didn’t say a word.

Arthur watched as they gazed into each other’s eyes and saw what he had always missed, but still thought it was too late to do anything about it, despite Hugh’s optimism.

Hugh then looked back at his father and said, “Well, Papa, let’s put your buggy away and bring your things inside. The house is a bit of an eclectic assembly. There are three bedrooms upstairs and four downstairs. We can put the two children in one room if you’d rather stay upstairs, or you can stay downstairs. Minnie and Carrie live downstairs. The library is downstairs as well. Each floor has a bathroom with a water closet, so you won't have to go outdoors to the privy. That was all Brian's work. I still don't know why he didn't put any stairs inside, though."

"I do," Arthur said, "When he was seven, he fell down the stairs and it scared him to death. He hated stairs ever since."

"Speaking of seven-year-olds, you should be introduced to your grandchildren."

Then, he turned and said, "Susan, can you ask everyone to come back now?"

"I'll be right back," Susan replied as she stood, then walked down to the kitchen.

Arthur watched her leave then turned to his son and said, "Susan is a very beautiful young woman, Hugh."

"She is. Every part of her: her mind, her soul, her heart, and are all wrapped in a magnificent package."

Before his father could respond, there were noises from the hallway.

Arthur looked at the children and smiled. Then he looked at Carrie and Minnie.

Minnie smiled at him and he smiled back. She was a very handsome woman. She no longer had her girlish figure, but she was far from matronly.

Arthur stood to meet his grandchildren.

Hugh also rose and said, "Andy and Addie, I would like you to meet my father, your grandpapa."

Andy was a little intimidated by the tall gray-haired man, even though he was smiling kindly. Addie was not.

"I have a grandpapa?" she asked.

"Yes, you do, sweetheart," answered Hugh.

Addie ran up to him and Arthur plucked her from the ground. Addie put her arms around his neck, gave him a kiss on his cheek, then said, "Hello, Grandpapa. I'm Addie."

Still holding Addie, Arthur stepped over to Andy and offered his thick, gnarled hand.

"Hello, Andy."

Andy shook his hand and said, "Hello, Grandpapa. I have a horse."

Andy's response tickled Arthur and a deep laugh rumbled through his chest.

Hugh then said, "Father, this is Minnie Witherspoon, Carrie's mother."

Arthur, with Addie still attached smiled broadly at Minnie, who smiled back in return.

"It's a pleasure, Mrs. Witherspoon," he said, offering his hand.

"Please, call me Minnie, Mister McGinnis," she replied.

"And call me Arthur. It seems we'll be sharing a floor."

"It's a wonderful place, Arthur, especially the bathroom."

"So, I've heard."

"Father, why don't you all sit down, and I'll take care of your buggy and bring your things down to your room."

Susan rose and followed him outside into the cool but pleasant night air.

Once the door was closed behind them, Hugh took advantage of their privacy and pulled her against him then kissed her. She reciprocated, and they started getting carried away until Hugh pulled back.

"Oh, you wanton, wicked woman. I find once again being drawn into your temptations. You torture me with your desirable tools of lust, but, alas, I must resist your siren's song and press on to mundane matters. If, however, your plans to seduce me persist, I may find myself more amenable to your allure at a later hour in our private chambers."

"Such an eloquent way of telling me to go away."

"Hardly that. I just have to get the buggy unloaded. Did you want to come along?"

"No, I just came out to ask if you noticed."

"That my crusty old father was smitten by Minnie?"

"Yes, that."

"It would be good for him, but maybe bad for Minnie. He may not make it to Christmas."

"What does he have?"

"Cancer of the prostate gland. His is so far advanced, any surgery would kill him. But the thing with Minnie is out of our control. I'm sure he'll tell her about his cancer. If she chooses to comfort him, then it's another mark of a compassionate woman whom I seem to surround myself."

Susan gave Hugh a quick kiss before she returned to the house.

Hugh led the buggy to the barn and unharnessed the horse, putting him in an empty stall and brushing him down. He removed the trunk and travel bag from the buggy and carried the trunk to an empty room in the lower level, choosing the closest room to the library. Then he returned and carried the travel bag into the room. He went back through the newly constructed entrance cover and into the kitchen and found everyone in the kitchen sampling Minnie's cookies.

"I hope you saved some for me. What are they? Molasses?"

"No, they're oatmeal raisin, and they're yummy!" exclaimed Andy.

"You know, if you eat too much before bedtime, you'll all have nightmares."

Addie stopped in mid-bite and then continued, mumbling, "I don't care."

Hugh swiped a cookie off the ever-decreasing stack and bit off a warm chunk.

"Minnie, these are marvelous."

"Thank you, Hugh. Are they better than the molasses?"

Hugh took another bite and looked toward the ceiling, thinking.

"I'm not sure. Maybe if you made some, I could do side-by-side comparison."

"I'm going to make you fat, Hugh," she said as she laughed.

"I'll work it off…somehow," Hugh answered looking at a reddening Susan.

Then he looked at his father and said, "Father, I put your things in the room next to the library."

"Fine. I'd like to go and rest for a while. It's been a long trip."

"I'll show you the way," said a smiling Minnie.

"Thank you, Minnie," he replied as he grinned back at her.

They went off and Susan glanced at Hugh and raised her eyebrows.

The children were put to bed twenty minutes later and Jessie noticed that her mother hadn't returned.

"I wonder where she is?" Jessie asked.

"Probably showing my father the library," answered Hugh.

"Oh. You're probably right. She was very impressed with the library."

She waved goodnight and headed down to her room.

Susan looked over at Hugh, and asked, "You don't think they're…"

"No. My father's condition would prevent that."

"Oh. I didn't know."

"Come to our room, my little vixen, and I'll demonstrate the purpose of the prostate gland and its function."

"Why do I think this isn't just some medical training?" she asked suspiciously.

"It is just that, but who says all medical training has to be dull and boring?"

"In that case, I'll join you."

The training lasted some time, and Susan passed her final examination.

The next day began with a heartier than average breakfast prepared by Minnie, and Arthur complimented her extensively.

Hugh and Susan had the day off, so they sat in the sitting room with Arthur.

"Hugh, you said that you've been married twice in six months, so I know that there's a story in there. Would it be too invasive to ask you how that came about?"

"Not at all. It's a long story, though."

Susan had never heard the entire story from start to finish and she curled up next to Hugh as he began.

"It started with my trip down the Oregon Trail. I made it to Idaho without too much of a problem. Then, I ran into a party of eight Cheyenne who wanted my supplies. I had to leave the trail and then…"

Hugh continued with the story, omitting no details. Susan listened in awe at some of the events she had never heard. Arthur was just amazed.

When he told the story of Blue Flower and the necklace, Arthur watched as Susan fingered the necklace, understanding that there was a lot of story yet to come.

The part of the return of the children to Rebecca touched everyone, including Hugh, who still had the image burned into his mind.

Whenever he spoke of Rebecca, Arthur could see the deep love and respect he had for her and noticed that Susan didn't seem the least bit upset by it. In fact, she smiled at the mention of Rebecca's name.

Then came the discovery of the Hanson brothers and of Nancy and Susan's rescue. When Hugh told of his shooting of both men, Arthur reacted with a deep, rumbling growl accompanied by a firm nod of approval.

Then came the difficult part, Rebecca's death. Hugh told the tragedy trying not to let it affect him as much as he knew it would. He told of Rebecca's instructions to him and even pulled out the derringer that Susan had used to shoot Bob Orson. He extolled her courage to accomplish the act and how it had saved Andy's life.

When he told Arthur of her shooting of Bob Orson with his own pistol, Arthur nodded his head and growled, "He deserved it."

He didn't go into some of the details, like Susan's appearance at the pool, but told his father just how much he loved his wife, and why she wore the necklace.

When he finally finished. Susan was almost an emotional wreck. She had known of his stabbing and Rebecca's holding his arm closed while he sutured his wound, but not of the fight with the Cheyenne with the children in tow, nor the chase with Chester to find and shoot the two men who had kidnapped Betty and Ella. She clutched Hugh throughout the tale, and when he reached the end, she felt exhausted.

"Hugh, you did a lot of good, but you always have. I'm glad you told me 'no' when I tried to get you to stay on in the lumber business."

"So, am I, Papa."

"So, what will we do today?" he asked.

"Would you like a tour of the ranch? We could take the buggy."

"I'd like that."

Hugh left the house, prepared the buggy, then brought it around to the front of the house. Susan and his father joined him, and they rode to the southern border, along the line of the forest.

"You really need to thin those trees, Hugh. They need the light."

"You're right, Father. I still haven't worked out the details yet."

Then, they reached the pools and they all stepped out of the buggy.

"This is beautiful, Hugh. Is this where that bastard shot Rebecca?"

"Yes, and it's where Susan made him pay for what he had done."

They walked to the lower pool and saw the rainbow. Hugh pointed to Brian's water inlet and explained the water system he had developed.

Then they returned to the buggy and the tour continued. It was a long ride. Seven more miles east. Eight north and then almost eight more miles west. Then, they arrived at the cemetery. Hugh had kept it immaculate. The two graves were covered with stones from the nearby creeks and the grass surrounding them was short.

Arthur walked slowly to the two graves and stopped at Louise's.

"I never met Louise, you know," he admitted to Hugh, "That was another of my terrible mistakes."

"It was, Papa. She was a complete person. She was pretty, warm and loving, and it must have destroyed Brian when she died. He didn't have a Susan to keep him afloat and then return him to a happy life."

His father nodded, then read Rebecca's memorial stone and noticed the wedding ring sitting on top.

"Rebecca must have been a marvelous woman, too."

"She was all that and more. Rebecca was the most generous soul I have ever known," he said, his voice beginning to shake with emotion.

Arthur saw that Susan had begun to weep softly, tears sliding across her cheeks and could only imagine how special Rebecca must have been. He remembered what Hugh had told him what she had asked of him and Susan as she lay dying, and he had an inkling of what an extraordinary person she must have been.

He looked at his son, and asked quietly, “Hugh, I know I’m asking a lot, but could I be buried here, next to Louise?”

“Yes, Papa. It’s exactly what I had planned. I just didn’t want to broach the subject.”

Arthur placed his right hand on his son’s shoulder and said, “Thank you, Hugh. It means a lot to me.”

They returned to the buggy and then to the house where Minnie had a nice lunch ready for them when they entered the kitchen.

“How did the tour go, Arthur?”

“Wonderful. Minnie, have you ever seen the waterfall?”

“No, but it sounds beautiful.”

“The buggy is still harnessed, want to go and look at it in a little while?”

“That sounds wonderful, Arthur.”

Arthur wolfed down his lunch and popped up to take Minnie to the waterfall.

Hugh and Susan looked at each other and smiled.

CHAPTER 14

The month of September brought many changes to the family, both McGinnis and extended.

It began with Nancy when she walked into the clinic one morning and told Margaret that she needed to speak to Hugh, who was with a patient. When Hugh emerged, he noticed Nancy waiting and at first thought she might be a patient.

"How can I help you, Nancy? Am I Hugh or Doctor McGinnis?" he asked.

"Neither. I need you to be Papa Hugh."

That caused a surprised reaction from Hugh and from Susan and Margaret as well.

Hugh smiled at her and asked, "And how can Papa Hugh help Daughter Nancy?"

"I want you to meet someone. Jim Cranston has asked me to marry him, and I want to be sure it'll be all right. Can you talk to him?"

"Sure. Tell me about him."

It turned out that Jim Cranston had been trying to see Nancy for years, but her father had prohibited it since he wasn't a 'true' Christian. Rejected, Jim had left the area and only recently returned. When he discovered that Nancy was no longer under her father's thumb, he immediately rekindled the relationship.

"He knows about the Hanson brothers?"

"Yes. In detail. He said that he wished he had been here. He would have done what you did."

"Could he?"

"Not really. He never owned a gun."

"What does he do for a living?"

"He's a carpenter. He's working for the City Construction Company. He's very good, Hugh."

"And how about you, Nancy. How do you feel?"

"I've always loved him, Hugh. He's so kind and gentle."

"You don't need me, Nancy. You've asked all the right questions. Where does he live?"

"He's renting a house over on Winston Street. It's not very large, but he keeps it clean."

"Nancy, you go ahead and accept his proposal, but on one condition. I want you to move. You go and find a nice house and let me know which one it is. I'll buy it for you as a wedding present. If you can't find one, buy a lot and we'll hire the City Construction Company to build it."

"Hugh, we're all right for money. The restaurant is doing well, and I never even had to spend the reward money yet."

"This is a wedding present, Nancy. Just say thank you."

Nancy smiled softly and said, "Thank you, Hugh."

Susan added, "And we'll furnish it, too," then looked at Hugh and winked.

Betty and Ella also announced engagements that first week of September. Betty surprised Hugh by telling him her beau was a chemist that Hugh might know, Martin Childs. Ella had met a rancher named Tom Blake, and both women would move into nice houses, too. Ella also said she'd give up her share of the restaurant and told Nancy and Betty that the profits she had made since they opened the place was enough compensation. Betty and Ella planned a double wedding on the 21st of September.

Later in the evening of the double announcement, Hugh and Susan were sitting in the main room with Jessie as she watched Addie and Andy play checkers and Arthur and Minnie were probably in the library. The topic of discussion was the sudden rash of marriages.

"I guess Margaret's next. She's eighteen now," Hugh said with a grin.

Jessie said, "She's not seeing anybody, but she said that some man named Peter Fremont has been following her around."

Hugh looked at his wife and asked, "Did Frank have a brother?"

"He does. He's worse than Frank, too. He thinks he's a pistol shooter and wears two guns."

Hugh looked back at Jessie and asked, "Why didn't Margaret say anything to me?"

"She was worried that you might do something and get hurt."

Hugh shook his head and said, "Thank you for telling me, Jessie. I'll take care of it."

Susan gave him one last look, but she knew his mind was set. Now he was Peter Fremont's problem.

He stood, returned to the kitchen and retrieved the derringer from the weapons cache in the huge pantry. He took two rounds of ammunition and the cleaning kit, then he sat at the table. He had just begun to clean the small gun when Arthur arrived, sat across from Hugh, who looked up and smiled at him.

"How are you doing, Papa?"

"The pain is more noticeable."

"Is that why you're here? Do you want me to get you some laudanum?"

"Not yet. I came to talk to you about Minnie."

"I can understand why you'd like Minnie. She's a warm and compassionate woman and easy on the eyes, too."

"I know. Hugh, I love Minnie. It's only been a few weeks, but I feel so comfortable with her. We talk, and I've even kissed her. Well, we've kissed a lot. I told her that is all I can do, and she understands. She knows I'm dying, but she told me that it didn't matter, and we should enjoy every minute we have together."

"She's a wise lady, Father."

"I know. Hugh, I'm going to ask her to marry me."

"That would make you both happy, I'm sure."

"I wanted to tell you this because I didn't want you to think it was going to affect your inheritance."

"Papa, do you think I worry about that at all? If you told me to write her a draft for the whole thing, it wouldn't have any impact on me whatsoever."

"I suspected as much. But I will leave her the money I have left. Will you take care of her after I'm gone?"

"Papa, I made that commitment before you arrived. Minnie will never have a worry as long as I'm alive."

"Thank you, Hugh. You're a good son."

"I've just been blessed, Papa. I feel the need to return that blessing to others."

"I think I'll ask Minnie tonight. We spend a lot of time in the library."

"Papa, just a word of caution about the library. In the second desk drawer on the left, there is a photograph, a daguerreotype."

"Is that where that went? I often wondered. I'm glad you mentioned it. I may show it to Minnie. It'll depend on how I feel."

Hugh nodded.

Arthur stood, then left and walked back to the main room as Hugh continued his cleaning job. He was pleased that his father had at last found happiness. It had come too late, but any happiness is better than none.

———

Arthur proposed that night to Minnie and was accepted behind a shower of happy tears because Minnie had never expected it. They set the wedding date for the 14th of the month.

———

The next day, Hugh and Susan set off at their normal time. They arrived at the clinic at eight o'clock, and when they arrived, Hugh parked the carriage, unharnessed the grays and put them in the corral.

They walked into the clinic and Hugh smiled when he saw Margaret already working on the files.

"Good morning, Margaret."

"Good morning, Hugh. How are you, Susan?"

"Fine," answered Susan.

"Margaret, Jessie tells me that you have some young man that seems to follow you a lot."

"It's Peter Fremont. I told him to leave me alone last week, but he just laughed and said to get used to him."

"Do you know where he lives?"

"No, but he always seems to be hanging around the saloon on Main Street. It's called The City Slicker."

"What does he look like?"

"Average height, light brown hair with a moustache. He has two guns, Hugh, and he's dangerous. You should just let it go. I'm okay."

"Don't worry, Margaret. I won't take any chances."

"He's not worth it, Hugh."

"No, he's not, but you are."

As he walked into his office, Hugh felt his anger button pushed. *What is it with some men?* This one needed to be castrated. He felt the derringer in his pocket. He was going to give it to Margaret, but if this yahoo was carrying two pistols, having a derringer might get her killed. He'd have to deal with this himself.

They saw eight patients that day. One was a serious case of gout, but Hugh finally completed his work around two in the afternoon.

"Ladies, I think I fancy a beer. I'll be back shortly."

Susan and Margaret knew where he was going and why, but they both knew there was nothing they could say or do to change his mind.

Hugh walked out of the clinic and reached Main Street in ten minutes. He found The City Slicker, entered and had expected to find it almost empty at this time of day, but it wasn't. There were eight men in the saloon, and he picked out Peter Fremont easily. He stood at the bar with his two-gun rig and Hugh gave him a quick inspection. He was maybe twenty years old and cocky, with a narrow face with the moustache trying to look older while the twin pistols were at his waist trying to make him look tougher.

Hugh walked up to the bar about four feet from Peter.

"Beer," he said to the bartender, who nodded and drew him a glass.

Hugh paid the nickel and tasted the beer, finding it surprisingly good and cold. He may not have cared for whiskey, but he liked a cold beer now and then.

Hugh knew he didn't have to say a word. He had seen Fremont's eyes recognize him as he entered the bar. There just weren't a lot of men his size around town and he was sure that Fremont would have to play his role as the big man soon, so Hugh continued to sip on his beer and didn't have to wait long.

Peter snarled, "I hear you been threatenin' my brother."

Hugh acted as if he wasn't being challenged and ignored him.

"Hey, you. Big man, I heard you was threatenin' my brother."

Hugh just turned his head and stared at Peter.

"Do I know you?" he asked.

"You will. The name's Peter Fremont. Word is that you threatened my brother."

"I never make threats. If your brother is that low-life Frank Fremont, then I just left word with his girlfriend that he wouldn't want to meet me. Now, if you perceive that as a threat, then I guess your threshold of threat evaluation might be a bit too low."

"You can talk fancy all you want, mister, but these pistols won't cotton to any more threats. Do you understand?"

"Have you ever shot anyone, Peter?" Hugh asked.

"Not yet. But you're about to be the first."

"Well, Peter, I've killed eight Cheyenne, two would-be rapists and then those Hampton boys that you were all so afraid of. I don't enjoy killing people. I'm a doctor and I'd rather help folks, but if you insist on dying today, I'll make an exception."

"You ain't even packin', mister," Fremont said as he removed his hammer loops.

It was time for Hugh to let Peter that he should have been a lot smarter.

In one quick motion, he pulled the derringer from his pocket and snapped back the hammer. Before Peter Fremont could even reach for his guns, the derringer was pressed against his forehead.

"Now, Peter, you were wrong about my not being armed. This is only a derringer. I have my two Colts, my Henry repeater, two Winchesters, my Sharps rifle, and four shotguns back at the house. I'm always armed. Now, I may not shoot you today, but let me tell you what I'm going to do. If you are ever seen near Margaret Tilton, even by accident, I will perform an orchiectomy on you. Do you know what an orchiectomy is?"

Fremont croaked, "No," as sweat was flowing around the muzzle of the derringer.

"An orchiectomy is the surgical removal of both testicles. In other words, I'd cut your balls off. I wouldn't do it crudely, mind you because I'm a surgeon. I'd take one of my scalpels and make an incision across your scrotum. Do you know what your scrotum is, Peter?"

He whispered, "No."

"That's the sack that hangs between your legs. Now, I'd just make a nice incision, or a cut if you want the simple word. You do seem to prefer the simple words. I'd make the cut right above your balls and slowly draw that razor-sharp scalpel across the sack and then just pop them out of there.

"Then, I'd just cut the blood vessels and vas deferens, those are those little tubes that let you make babies. I'd cut those off and then sew you back up. You wouldn't even hurt that much, but then, your voice would begin to change. You'd sound like a little boy, and eventually, like a little girl. Then how tough would you be? Now, you may think you can drygulch me somewhere. It's been tried before, but no one has done it yet and those that have tried are dead. So, are you going to bother Margaret anymore?"

Somehow, the vision Hugh created in Peter's mind had given him pause as he squeaked, "No, sir."

"Good. Now that wasn't so difficult, was it?"

Hugh lowered the derringer and uncocked the hammer before returning it to his pocket.

He finished his beer and said loudly, "Drinks are on me until this five-dollar gold piece is gone."

He tossed the piece to the bartender who was still grinning about the incident, but still caught the coin before he gave a salute to Hugh.

The other patrons, who had watched and heard the display, eagerly took him up on his offer. None of them liked the cocky young man and were more than pleased to see him get his comeuppance. The free drinks just added to the party atmosphere.

Hugh turned and took a few steps to the batwing doors, he was listening intently, then he heard the unmistakable click of a hammer being cocked, giving him no time. He quickly jumped to his left as Fremont's first round smashed into the door jamb.

Hugh pulled the hammer on the derringer, slid behind a table and found everyone else on the floor already.

Hugh remained crouched under the table and waited.

"Come out, you, yellow bastard! You ain't cuttin' off nothin'!" Peter shouted.

Hugh stayed under the table as Peter cocked his hammer again, fired a second round and the .44 ripped through the table over his head. As soon as the round hit the table, Hugh took advantage of the time Peter Fremont took to cock and aim, and suddenly popped to his feet.

Hugh didn't aim at all, but just pointed the derringer and squeezed the trigger. The .41 caliber round ripped across the room, and slammed into Peter Fremont's right shoulder, dropping him to the floor screaming.

Hugh quickly crossed the barroom floor, walked up to him through the cloud of gunsmoke, pulled his pistol out of his left side holster, then picked up the other one from the floor and handed them to the bartender.

"Tell the marshal what happened. I'll take him over to my clinic and fix him up."

"Yes, sir!" the smiling bartender loudly replied.

One of the other patrons raced to get the marshal as Hugh reached down and lifted Peter by his left arm.

"Let's go, you idiot. I'll take that little bullet out of you and we'll see what the marshal says."

Hugh escorted a crying Peter Fremont to his clinic where he was met by his anxious wife and receptionist.

He walked Fremont past Margaret and into the examining room before Susan quickly entered but left the door open so Margaret could listen.

"What happened, Hugh?" Susan asked looking at Fremont.

"I explained to this moron what the repercussions would be if he continued to harass Margaret. He said he wouldn't bother her anymore and as I was leaving, he took two shots at me, the first one at my back, so I shot him with the derringer. I'm going to fix him up and I'll need you to assist."

Susan reverted from concerned wife to professional nurse and nodded before she closed the door.

Margaret still sat at her desk speechless by what had happened. Then, she pulled out a blank card and began filling in the patient information.

Hugh had removed the slug and had begun to suture the wound when the marshal arrived, and Margaret opened the door to let him in.

Hugh heard him enter as he was standing over Peter Fremont putting in the last of the sutures.

"Good afternoon, Marshal."

"What happened in the saloon, Doctor McGinnis?"

"I went in to have a beer, and young Mister Fremont here decided to pick a fight with me. I pulled my derringer as he was going for his right-hand pistol, stuck my derringer against his forehead and suggested that he no longer follow and harass my receptionist. I explained what I would do to him as a surgeon and he agreed not to bother her anymore. I turned to leave, and our young friend unloaded two rounds at me, the first at my back. After the second shot, I knew he had to cock his hammer again, so I jumped up and shot him in the shoulder to keep him from firing again. Now, I'm just about finished."

"That's the story I got from the other patrons in the bar. Are you pressing charges?"

"Is there any point, Marshal?" Hugh asked.

"What do you mean?"

"The last man that we had arrested was out on the streets the next day and killed my wife. Now, if we have him arrested, will there be any difference?"

The marshal knew about Bob Orson and it had been a sore point ever since.

"Oh, and my father said to thank you for telling him I was here," Hugh added as he twisted the knife.

That threw the marshal, making the need for a hasty departure more immediate.

"If you aren't going to press charges, then there's no point in my being here."

"No, I guess there isn't. Peter here won't be shooting anyone ever again, unless he learns to use his left hand."

The marshal turned and left.

Hugh then said, "Okay, Peter. That does it for you. You're all fixed, but you'll need to have those sutures removed in two weeks. That shoulder won't work quite right ever again, but those are the consequences when you try to shoot someone who knows how guns work and you don't."

Peter sat up and scowled.

Hugh noticed the attitude and said, "Peter, let me remind you. My promise still holds, and anyone who knows me will tell you that I never break a promise. So, on your way out you will apologize to Margaret and promise her that you'll leave her alone."

As he reminded Peter of his promise, he picked up a scalpel in his hand, and showed Peter the flashing, sharp blade.

The scowl disappeared before he stood, then walked out of the surgery and approached Margaret.

"Ma'am, I'm sorry. I won't bother you no more."

Then, not even waiting for Margaret to accept his apology, he turned and without looking back at Hugh, quickly left the office.

"What happened, Hugh?" asked Margaret.

"Well, Mister Fremont won't be bothering you again, Margaret. If you ever see him again, just tell him that you're going to tell the doctor. That should send him running."

Susan wanted details and asked carefully, "Hugh McGinnis, what did you do?"

"Well, I went to the bar and had a beer. It was quite good, by the way. Young Mister Hampton was standing there, about four feet to my right, wearing his two guns. He made a few comments and then threatened to shoot me. When he removed his hammer loops, I stuck the derringer with its hammer cocked against his forehead."

"And that scared him away?" asked Margaret.

"Not really. That was meant to get his attention. What I told him scared him away. I described what I would do to him if he bothered you again. I told him I'd perform an orchiectomy, and then I described the procedure to him in vivid detail."

"What's an orchiectomy?" she asked.

Susan leaned over and began whispering in her ear as Hugh sat with a smug expression on his face.

The more Susan explained, the bigger Margaret's eyes grew. When Susan leaned back, Margaret's expression changed from amazement to contentment to amusement as her lips went from the letter O and slowly transformed to a gentle U.

"Then after I thought I had him convinced, he shot at my back as I was leaving."

"He shot at you?"

"I was expecting him to. He had been emasculated in front of other men. I listened intently for the sound of a hammer being pulled back. If he'd been any good, it would have been too late, but there were a lot of indicators that he was a novice when it came to guns. After the second shot, as soon as the slug hit the table, I popped up and shot him in the shoulder, then I brought him here."

Susan walked up behind him and said, "I don't know what I'm going to do with you."

"You could reward me later," he replied as he grinned.

"That would be like rewarding myself," she said.

"Thank you, Hugh. I think that will keep him away," Margaret said before she released a long sigh.

Hugh nodded, then they closed the clinic and Margaret went upstairs to her room.

Hugh and Susan headed back to the ranch, and as the carriage moved along, Hugh, his eyes still focused ahead as Susan snuggled under his arm, asked, "Susan, do we want to keep the hours the same? We can just keep the clinic open for three hours in the morning and come back to the ranch at lunchtime."

"I noticed that we don't have a lot of patients. I think the most we've had on any one day is nine. It would give us more time."

"It would also let you get off your feet more, Susan. You need to start slowing down just a bit. Our baby needs your attention."

Susan looked up at him in surprise and said, "I was going to surprise you, Hugh."

"I know. I'm sorry. I just am so happy about it, Susan. I'd guess that your due date is sometime at the end of May."

"That's what I thought. Hugh, can I ask you a medical question?"

"That's what I'm here for."

"Does this mean that we can't, you know."

"Absolutely not. We've enjoyed ourselves quite a few times since you've been pregnant already and will do so until you are uncomfortable. We can't hurt the baby."

Suddenly she began to cry lightly and said, "I'm going to get fat, Hugh."

Hugh laughed softly and said, "No, my love. You're not going to get fat. Your body shape doesn't lend itself to fat. You'll get a big tummy just like those mares in the corral are getting, but instead of producing a little horse, you, my sweet wife, will have a beautiful baby that we can love. But on the positive side, at least as far as I'm concerned, these will grow," he said as he massaged her breast.

She sniffled, then laughed and asked, "What is it with men and breasts?"

"I have no scientific explanation. But I like them a lot and I really like yours. But if you are still worried about getting fat after the baby, remember Rebecca. She had two, and she still had a beautiful figure. You'll get a little rounder and softer. You have an exquisite young woman's body now, but after the baby is born, you'll have an even more wonderful, mature woman's body. Trust me, my love. I'm your doctor. I'm also your lecherous husband."

Susan alternated between laughing and tears, then asked, "Why is this happening?"

"Hormones. Yours are going a bit insane right now. You'll also start eating a lot more, too. It's Mother Nature's way of getting more nutrition to the baby. But the good news is that you haven't had any morning sickness. Most women have some, and some have it every day, so you're lucky."

"Then how did you know I was pregnant?"

"Aside from the fact that we have been making love two or three times a day when we had the opportunity, I noticed subtle changes in your body, including the one I already mentioned."

"You noticed that? I barely noticed."

"I pay closer attention to them than you do."

She laughed and said, "You are a lecherous husband, but I wouldn't have it any other way."

They reached the ranch access road, turned east, and after pulling to a stop before the house, Hugh let his pregnant wife off at the front door and drove the carriage to the barn. He unhitched the grays and brushed them down before settling them into their stalls.

He stepped into the kitchen and found the women huddled and Hugh guessed that Susan had told them the news.

Arthur looked at Hugh and gave him a questioning look. Hugh waved him to the main room and Andy and Addie followed the men.

Arthur took a seat and Hugh sat down across from him, before Addie hopped onto his lap.

"What's going on with the women?" Arthur asked.

"I think Susan just told them that she's going to have a baby."

Addie squealed and shouted, "I'm gonna have a baby!"

Arthur and Hugh bent over they were laughing so hard, and even women in the kitchen heard Addie's exclamation and erupted in laughter.

Addie and Chuck didn't get the joke, but Andy did, and he joined the laughter, but not as hard as the grownups.

The women filtered back into the room, still giggling.

Hugh smiled at Susan as she took her seat next to her husband.

Addie looked at Susan and asked, "Am I gonna be a brother or a sister?"

It just couldn't get any better.

That night as Susan and Hugh lay snuggled together under the blankets, Susan asked, "Hugh, I don't understand something, and if anyone can answer it, you can."

"You want to know why you became pregnant now, but not before. Is that right?"

"Yes."

Hugh kissed the top of her head and said, "I have no medical reason whatsoever. To be honest, I was a bit surprised that neither you nor Nancy became pregnant because of the Fremont brothers. I was pleased about it, but a bit surprised. All I can tell you, Susan, is that you are going to have our baby and I couldn't be happier."

Susan sighed and said, "I guess Nancy and I had a guardian angel watching over us while they kept us here, but I don't have to guess who the guardian angel who saved us is, do I?"

"You know, Susan, when I was talking to Red Owl and told him about the children, he said I was their guardian warrior. I never gave it much thought, but now I believe that it would be a good thing for me to be for you and our children, including the one you hold inside you."

Susan looked at Hugh and said, "I've always felt that way about you, my husband. Almost from that first moment I saw you, I knew you would protect me and keep me safe."

"And I always will, my love."

CHAPTER 15

On the 14th of September, Arthur McGinnis married Minnie Witherspoon. Judge Hampton commented on the frequency of McGinnis weddings before he performed the ceremony.

Hugh could tell that his father was experiencing more pain even as he stood before the judge but knew he didn't want to use the laudanum until he absolutely needed its mind-numbing relief.

He saw the joy on his father's face as he kissed his bride, and was happy for him, and forever grateful for the peace that Minnie would give him in his final days.

Hugh had arranged for a photographer, and he took four images: one of Arthur and Minnie, one of Hugh and Susan, one of both couples with the children, and one of Hugh and Susan with the children.

As they were leaving, Hugh hugged Minnie then asked her if she wanted him to call her mama and she laughingly waved off the suggestion.

Two days later, it was Nancy's turn to be married. She and Jim were wed on the 16th. He originally wanted to get married in the Methodist church, but Nancy asked if it would be okay if Judge Hampton performed the ceremony. It seemed that the Methodist pastor and her father were good friends.

They found a nice house near the restaurant and Hugh bought the house and had the names Jim and Nancy Cranston put on the deed. It was mostly furnished, but Susan insisted on going to the store and ordering a lot of new furniture and other necessities for them. Nancy was as close to a sister as Susan had now that Rebecca was gone.

Finally, the double wedding of Ella and Betty took place. That wedding was much more formal and was held in the Episcopalian Church, and they all enjoyed a big dinner afterwards at Ella's new ranch house.

So, everything was finally settled. Each of the women that called themselves 'Hugh's Ladies' were now happily married.

Arthur and Minnie spent as much time together as they could, including almost daily rides to the rainbow falls. Susan and Jessie took over a lot of the cooking to give her time to spend with her husband. There had to be lot of cooking, too, as Susan was eating everything in sight and worried about getting fat constantly, despite her husband's assurance that her weight was perfect and so was she.

It was in the middle of October that Arthur finally asked for laudanum. Hugh knew that the six-month estimate given to him originally had been optimistic and thought his father had six weeks of increasing pain before him. He felt helpless and hated the feeling.

Susan knew his father's health weighed on him, and she wished there was something she could do for him.

The children could sense the rising gloom in their parents, and Jessie was their new bright spot. She played checkers with them and kept them entertained and Chester kept the children busy as well as they constantly tried to get him to learn new tricks.

On a beautiful day in late October, Hugh was in his father's room. He had tried to make time to visit at least once a day, as his father no longer came upstairs.

Minnie was taking a much-needed nap.

"How is Susan doing, Hugh?" he asked.

"Her pregnancy is going very well. She's finally beginning to show a little, and for some reason, that seemed to push aside her concerns about gaining too much weight."

"Good. Son, can I ask a big favor?"

Hugh knew what he was going to ask but knew that he would have to deny his request.

"What is it, Papa?"

"The pain is getting really bad. I can't sleep until I'm so exhausted that I pass out. I can tell that Minnie is taking it hard and I'm just a burden to everyone now. I'd like to end this suffering for her as much as it is for me. Can you end it? Can you give me something that I could take and just go to sleep?"

"Father, I knew you'd ask eventually. I know how bad the pain must be, and I'm sure it's impossible for anyone else to fully comprehend. But if I did help you to end your life, then I could no longer practice medicine. I would have to violate an oath."

"I understand, but I'm really only asking for Minnie. I can see the pain in her eyes, Hugh, and feel like such a selfish bastard for doing this to her."

He closed his eyes and grimaced as a wave of excruciating pain swept through him and sweat formed on his brow. Hugh could only watch and agonize over the decision he was being asked to make.

He opened his eyes after almost a minute and blew out his breath.

After seeing his father's intense pain, Hugh was no longer sure that he could refuse his request and said "Papa, let me think about this. I'll give you my answer tomorrow."

"Thank you, Hugh. I would never have asked if it wasn't for Minnie."

Hugh nodded and put his hand on his father's shoulder for a few seconds before going upstairs.

For the rest of the day, Hugh was tortured by his convictions. He knew that his father was in terrible pain and had less than two weeks to live. *Would he be doing wrong to help him end his pain? But who was he to play God?* And then, there was the loss of his medical practice, which loomed as the largest factor of all. He would no longer be able to help people. He knew that many didn't care about such things as oaths and promises, but Hugh never once thought of violating either.

Susan knew he was deeply troubled by something to do with his father and correctly guessed the cause of the distress, then finally managed to catch him alone late in the afternoon so she could ask. He had walked over to the cemetery to talk to Rebecca.

Susan waited ten minutes and then followed and found him just standing by her grave looking at the marker.

She walked up behind him and gently placed her hand on his shoulder before saying quietly, “If Rebecca can’t help, Hugh, maybe I can.”

He continued to stare at her grave as he said, “Susan, if anyone could help me with this, it would be you, even more than Rebecca could. This is just such a terrible decision that no matter which I choose, there will be consequences.”

“Your father asked you to end his life.”

“Yes.”

“When do you have to make the decision?”

“By tomorrow afternoon.”

“You’ll do what’s right, Hugh. You always do. I’ll leave you now.”

“Thank you, Susan.”

Susan didn’t even look back at Hugh as she walked slowly back to the house and crossed over to the clinic side. She went to the cabinet containing all the vials and bottles of chemicals and medicines, found the bottle of potassium cyanide, measured out a quantity and poured it into a glass. She walked to the sink and added water and then mixed it until it was clear again. Then she turned and re-entered the house.

She went downstairs as Minnie was preparing dinner and Susan could see that she had been crying, which was not an unusual occurrence for her these days.

Susan knocked on Arthur’s door, then waited.

“Come in,” he answered, expecting Minnie to enter.

Susan walked in and smiled at Arthur.

"Susan, this is a pleasant surprise," he said.

He immediately shook and gritted his teeth at the surge of pain that lasted for two agonizing minutes.

Susan watched him suffering and knew that she would have to answer for what she was about to do. *What would Hugh think of her?*

When at last Arthur's pain subsided, he blew out his breath and wiped the sweat from his face.

"I'm sorry, Susan."

"Arthur, there's no reason to apologize."

She sat down in what Arthur considered 'Minnie's chair'.

"Arthur, I just talked to Hugh, and he told me of your request. He's in agony over the decision and would so much like to end your suffering, yet he would lose so much to do so. I know that Minnie's in pain watching you suffer and that gives you the additional reasons for making your appeal. Your son has come to love you and understand you as few sons have ever done with their fathers, and I believe he will toss aside his medical career to help you.

"I love him so very much, Arthur, and I know what being a doctor means to him and can't let him do that. I've grown to love you, too, and I can't begin to feel the pain you're going through. In this glass is potassium cyanide. If you drink it, you will end your life and your suffering. I will leave it with you, so it will be your decision to drink it or not. Hugh will diagnose the cause of your death and know that I provided the poison. What circumstances that may lead to, I can't predict. I only know I can't see him suffer the consequences of his decision."

She looked at his graying face and touched her fingertips to his cheek, then stood and kissed him on his forehead.

"Good night, Arthur."

Arthur looked at his beautiful daughter-in-law knowing what an incredibly difficult and courageous decision she had just made because she loved his son so much.

"Good night, Susan. Thank you and tell Minnie I love her."

Susan nodded and left the room, closing the door behind her.

She quickly walked upstairs, returned to their bedroom and closed the door, then fell to the bed on her stomach and began to cry.

Downstairs, Arthur picked up the glass and drank swiftly, and less than thirty seconds later his heart stopped.

Hugh walked back into the house and saw Minnie making dinner with her red eyes.

She turned to him and said, "Hugh, you might want to go and see Susan. She seemed very upset."

Hugh nodded, feeling guilty for spreading his morose thoughts to Susan. She had enough to worry about with the baby.

He went down the hallway and as he reached the bedroom door, he could hear Susan sobbing inside. He opened it quietly and entered before closing it just as silently.

"Susan? Sweetheart, what's the matter?" he said as he sat down on the bed next to her. He gently rolled her to onto her side, so he could see her face with its red, tear-filled eyes.

She sat and clutched him fiercely.

"Oh, Hugh! I'm so sorry! Don't hate me for what I did!"

Hugh had never seen Susan so terribly wrought with emotional stress. Even on that first night when he had found her tied to the bed in this house undergoing physical and mental torture, her inner strength had been obvious. Then he knew that only one thing could have brought her to this state.

She had done what he had decided he would do. She had let Arthur sleep in peace, and understood that she had done this for him, as much as for Arthur. He couldn't believe the amount of courage and pure love it had taken for her to make and carry out this decision.

He pulled her closer and put his hand behind her head, feeling her soft hair in his fingers as she shuddered.

"Susan, my dearest, my beloved Susan, I could never hate you for any reason. But if you did as I was going to do and helped my father to escape his prison of pain, then I love you so much more, even if I thought it wasn't possible. I understand why you did what you felt you needed to do, and I want you to stop feeling any guilt at all. Look at me, my love."

Susan heard his words and a rush of relief swept through her like a cooling wave of water from the pool. She looked at his kind eyes and saw the immense love deep in his soul.

"Susan, my incredibly perfect wife, thank you for lifting this burden from my shoulders. You knew that I was about to do what you have already done. It had to be done. Arthur was begging me to end his suffering and Minnie's as well. You have done nothing wrong. Nothing. I'll go and talk to Minnie and we'll arrange for father's final rest next to Louise as he asked. Please be at peace, my precious wife. I'll cherish you forever."

He kissed her warmly and laid her head back on the pillow to let her rest, knowing the strain she had put herself through.

Hugh stood and left the room, closing the door as he did.

He walked out to where Minnie and Jessie were preparing dinner. The children were outside with Chester, taking advantage of the beautiful weather.

"Minnie, Jessie, would you put dinner preparation on hold and sit down, please?"

They did, sensing that something was wrong. Minnie thought it had to do with Susan's pregnancy.

"Minnie, a few hours ago, my father asked me a question."

"I know. He told me he was going to ask," she said as the tears started to flow, and she dabbed at them with a towel.

"I understand why he wanted to end his pain. It was so terrible, Hugh. He placed a cruel burden on you, but he was in so much pain."

"I know. I felt powerless. All I could do was give him laudanum, but that would make his mind lost to the world when it took over."

"He told me he'd rather endure the pain and be able to talk to me, but it was so painful to see him in agony. I wanted so badly to help, but I was useless."

"No, Minnie, you were far from useless. You provided him with more comfort in these past few months than I ever could have. I had made up my mind to do as he asked. It would mean giving up my medical practice, but I was willing to do that. But Susan knew what I would do and took it on herself to provide Arthur with the means to end his suffering. She did it for Arthur, and she did it for me and you, Minnie.

"My courageous, caring wife loved us all so much that she made this terrible decision. I'm going to go downstairs now and make sure Arthur is at peace then I'll arrange for his funeral and burial. He asked me a while ago if he could be buried next to Louise in the family cemetery and I'll honor his request."

"Hugh, can you tell Susan for me that I'll always be grateful for what she did? And one other thing, Hugh. I know it's a family cemetery, but when the time comes, can I rest beside Arthur?"

"You are family, Minnie. Yes, I'll honor your request, too, but it won't be for some time."

She nodded, the tears still coming from her eyes. Hugh patted her hands and nodded to a teary Jessie as he went downstairs.

He found his father lying flat on his back, finally at peace.

He sat on his bed, rested his hand on his father's unmoving chest and said, "What an unusual relationship we've had, Papa. So many years of indifference and then total separation followed by less than three months of friendship and love. These last few weeks have balanced out the previous decades, I believe."

He kissed his father on his forehead and left the room, taking the empty glass with him.

He went upstairs and returned to their bedroom. Susan was awake but still resting. She saw him come inside and smiled at him.

"Hello, sweetheart. How are you doing?" he asked.

"Better. How did Minnie take the news?"

"Arthur had told her of his request, and she understood its consequences. She said to thank you for what you did. I'm going to go to the undertaker now and arrange for his burial. Will you be all right?"

"Yes, I'll be fine now."

"Let's go and see Minnie," he said as he held out his hand.

Susan took his hand, rose from the bed and walked with him to the kitchen.

Minnie saw Susan, stopped stirring whatever she was cooking, then walked to her and embraced her.

"Thank you for ending his terrible pain, Susan."

Susan looked into Minnie's eyes and said, "The last thing he told me was to tell you that he loved you."

Minnie began to cry again, as she clung to Susan.

Susan put her hand on Minnie's head and let her grief run its course.

Hugh signed to Susan that he needed to go. She nodded, and Hugh left via the kitchen door.

He saddled Night and rode into town to see the undertaker yet again. He arranged for them to pick up Arthur's body and for the burial the following afternoon and paid the bill. He'd let the gravediggers do their job and specified the location for the grave and the inscription for the stone.

The undertakers arrived at the house shortly after Hugh returned, and he brought them to his father's room. They wrapped him in a cloth and took his body to a temporary coffin by the door. He was placed in the hearse and returned to their mortuary. They would return the following day.

The next morning, Hugh took Night into town and told Nancy and Betty of his father's death. He didn't explain the circumstances or tell them of the burial that afternoon. He rode to his clinic and told Margaret and had her place a closed sign on the window and returned to the ranch house.

Everyone seemed to accept the death as not necessarily a somber event. Even the children knew how much pain their grandfather had been in. Unlike Rebecca's unexpected, premature and tragic death, Arthur McGinnis' passing was just the opposite.

At the appointed time, the hearse arrived, and the gravediggers had already done their work and the hole was ready. The family and friends walked to the cemetery and witnessed Arthur's casket being lowered into the ground and covered with dirt.

The undertakers had gone leaving only the mourners, as they had just three months earlier.

Arthur's memorial stone read:

Arthur McGinnis
May 11, 1810 ~ October 24, 1867
Beloved Husband and Father
Peace Came in Twilight
From Those He Touched

There were no tears. Not because they didn't care for Arthur, but because they all knew he had gained his much-sought peace for having come to Oregon where he regained his son and met Minnie.

———

In November, there was another change in the McGinnis household.

Jessie moved into the clinic-house with Margaret and took a job waitressing for Betty and Nancy. She made the decision with Hugh's and her mother's blessing, so she could meet more people. She had told Hugh and Minnie that she wanted nothing more in life than to marry and have children.

Hugh delivered his first baby in Baker City on the 7th of the month. Ironically, it was Nellie's baby and there was a bit of a row between the two Fremont brothers when Hugh started to write Frank's name on the birth certificate as the father. It seems that both brothers were enjoying Nellie's attention.

———

Susan's pregnancy was progressing smoothly. The children were enjoying school, and their teacher, Miss Draper had been surprised that neither child had been able to read or write just six months earlier.

Hugh would take Addie out to the corral and show her the fattening tummies on four of the mares. Addie was excited knowing that one of them held her new baby horse.

Hugh's practice was suddenly busier as more residents became aware of his presence and skills. That, and they discovered he rarely billed. He made more house calls and treated more trauma cases. He had a special medical set of saddlebags made for Night that allowed him to go to places even the carriage couldn't go. He had a carriage house built to house the buggy that Arthur had brought and the carriage. The burgeoning horse population required a larger corral, despite the additional eight stalls in the new carriage house.

In early December, Hugh had two special patients arrive in his clinic. Both Betty and Ella were pregnant which surprised them both. Ella was especially happy being with child as she had been afraid that she would never have a baby to call her own. Susan realized then how fortunate she had been when both women told her of their morning sickness. Not surprisingly, they were joined in that condition by Nancy the week before Christmas.

———

1868 arrived with minimal fanfare, and by February, Susan was wearing her pregnancy well and cried from happiness when Hugh let her listen to their baby's heartbeat for the first time.

Hugh seemed to be gone a lot of those dark winter nights. He was off delivering other women's babies and treating injuries. Hugh had relegated Susan to non-nursing duties, as he didn't want her exposing herself and the baby to unnecessary contagion. Margaret stepped up doing double duty.

Spring arrived, and Hugh lost Margaret. She had met a young man named Oliver Brewster when he had come to the clinic. After showing up several more times for undetectable maladies, Hugh told him just to see Margaret and not bother him. They were married on April 27th, and Hugh and Susan bought them a house, then Margaret and Susan had a good time picking out new furniture and kitchenware.

At 7:30 in the evening on May 9th, Susan went into labor.

Hugh expected an easy delivery with no surprises but was soon proven wrong.

Hugh had set aside a room in the clinic specifically for childbirth, having made the decision solely because of Susan, and she was the first one to use the new room. All previous deliveries Hugh had performed were in the mother's homes.

Minnie helped as Susan's contractions grew more intense and as the calendar turned over to May 10th, she continued in labor as her husband stayed with her into the wee hours of the morning.

Susan looked up at her husband and with a smile on her sweat-glistened face as the predawn arrived.

"I'm being a difficult patient, aren't I?" she asked.

"No, my love, you're just taking your time. You're getting close and I think we can expect to meet our baby in another hour, I think."

"Is the baby all right?" she asked with a worried look.

"The baby's fine."

Hugh wasn't lying, but he had been hearing something in his stethoscope that had him a bit confused, and confusion at this point left him uncomfortable.

Susan was exhausted by the time that Hugh told her that it was time, and that all she needed was one or two more big pushes.

She grunted and pushed.

Hugh saw the head and then the chest of his new baby, then a few seconds later, he was able to clarify the baby as their new daughter. She looked perfect and he was confused even more by his earlier confusion. Their new baby girl began to cry as Hugh cut the umbilical and was prepared to deliver the afterbirth when Susan began grunting again.

Hugh looked and saw a second head. *Susan was having twins! No wonder he had been confused!*

"Susan! You're giving us two children!" he exclaimed as he stooped back down to deliver their second child.

She laughed, despite the pain of delivery as the second baby was pushed into Hugh's waiting hands.

It was a boy this time, and after Hugh started to work on his son, Minnie carried their daughter to Susan.

Hugh took the little boy and walked to Susan's other side. She had their daughter in her left arm as he placed their son in her right. She looked at him with a tired, but ecstatic face.

"We have two children, Hugh," she said softly as she looked at her babies.

"Yes, sweetheart, two beautiful babies, so I'd better go into town tomorrow and get a second crib."

She laughed lightly, then kissed each baby's forehead.

Minnie was watching the scene and dabbing her eyes.

"Can the children come in now?" asked Susan.

"I'll go get them. I won't tell them until they see for themselves," he replied.

Hugh went out to the clinic waiting room where the children and Chester waited. They had been playing checkers while their mama had their baby brother or sister.

"Andy and Addie, you can come in now."

"Is it a brother or sister?" asked Addie, not falling into the trap of exuberance again.

"You'll find out," he replied as he smiled.

The two children walked into the room and saw their mama sitting in the elevated bed with two babies.

"Mama had twins!" shouted Andy.

"Quieter please, Andy. Your new brother and sister need to rest."

Addie looked at Hugh and said, "I have one of each?"

"Yes, sweetie."

"What are their names?" asked Andy.

Susan looked at the children and replied softly, “We had both a boy and a girl name picked out very early. Your brother is named Arthur and your sister is named Rebecca.”

Minnie hadn’t expected that, but maybe she should have as she wiped back more tears.

“Thank you, Mama,” said Addie.

Both children walked next to Susan and examined their squirming siblings.

After another two minutes of inspection, Minnie escorted the children from the room with promises of cookies, leaving Hugh alone with his wife and their babies.

“Looks like they’re hungry, sweetheart. Now, aren’t you glad that you can provide for both of them?”

“Leave it to you to notice something like that,” she said as she laughed.

“Trust me, I’ve noticed it for quite some time now. But they are perfect little humans, aren’t they?”

“Yes, my wonderful husband. They’re more beautiful than I could have imagined.”

After the babies finished their first feeding, Hugh rolled a crib nearby and set each baby inside and covered them each with a blanket.

“You get some sleep now, Susan. You need to get your rest.”

“Thank you, Hugh. For everything. For your love and now for those two miracles.”

Hugh leaned over and kissed Susan softly, then lowered the lamplight in the room and laid down on the cot he had brought into the room and soon, both adults joined their babies in slumber.

Two days later, Addie celebrated her birthday and Minnie made her a nice cake and she received real presents, but no money. Hugh had insisted.

Two weeks later, Susan and the babies were in their bedroom. The twins were gaining weight rapidly when another birth was announced, only one that didn't require Hugh's assistance. It was a natural birth.

Hugh found Addie in the kitchen and told her that one of the mares was having her foal.

"My horse!" she squealed, then grabbed Hugh's hand, pulling him out the back door.

By the time they arrived, the foal was on the ground and trying to stand. She was a pretty little filly, all black with four white stockings and a star on her forehead. Her mother was cleaning her as they watched.

"Is that one mine?" asked the eight-year-old Addie.

"If you'd like her to be. There are three more on the way, you know. But honestly, I can't imagine any that would be prettier than she is. It's a girl pony. They're called foals right now but when she's older she'll be a filly."

"I like her."

"Then, she's yours."

"Thank you, Papa!" she cried, and Hugh picked her up.

He noticed how much heavier she was then when he had first picked her up on the Oregon Trail a year before.

A year. It had been just about a year ago that he had found them. A year ago, that he had met Blue Flower and been given the necklace. A year ago, that he had first seen Rebecca. Twelve extraordinary months. He had found Rebecca and then lost her but found Susan. Now he had four children. Two children from each of his great loves. Hugh felt truly blessed.

He and Addie returned to the house and went to the bedroom to make the announcement to her mama.

Susan had laid the babies down for a nap and followed them outside to look at the foal.

"She is a beautiful foal," said Susan. "Do you have a name for her yet?"

"I'm going to call her Maggie," replied Addie.

Hugh smiled and said, "That sounds familiar, Addie. Hopefully, this Maggie won't take any long swims."

"No, Papa, my new Maggie is going to stay," she said firmly.

Susan looked at Hugh with her eyebrows raised.

"Maggie was the name of her doll that I saw floating down the river. That doll told me there were children involved in that wagon crash."

"That's a good name, Addie," said Susan.

"Thank you, Mama."

The next day Susan asked Hugh if she could resign from being his nurse to being just his wife and mother to the twins. Hugh was delighted. He found he really didn't need a nurse, or a receptionist either, obviously.

Hugh was spending most of his time away from his clinics now but decided to keep the clinics open for one day a week each. He rode more than using the carriage or the buggy.

It was mid-summer and the twins were healthy and growing rapidly.

Andy and Addie were at the newly enlarged corral admiring all the new colts and fillies. Maggie was still the prettiest of the four, a fact Addie liked to remind everyone. Chuck was visiting and had chosen one of the colts, a handsome copper colt with a white slash down his forehead. Not surprisingly, Chuck called him Red.

Susan and Hugh were relaxing for a change. It was a rare occurrence with the twins.

"Hugh, I don't know how some women do it. I have two children and don't have to cook or do housework and I'm tired. How can these women who have babies, older children and still have to run a household manage to live?"

"A lot of them don't. They're so worn out that they die before their time. Two weeks ago, Mrs. Anderson died at forty-seven. She had six children and had been working for almost thirty years without a single break. It's sad, really. Women get asked to do so much and thanked so little."

"At least I know I'm appreciated. Thank you for being such a considerate husband, Hugh."

"Susan, do you think we could introduce Rebecca and Arthur to their namesakes?"

"I was wondering when you would ask. Let's get the babies."

Hugh picked up Rebecca, her golden head of hair contrasting with little Arthur's dark crop of curls.

They walked out of the kitchen and headed for the cemetery, stepping slowly through the pasture's long grass.

As they walked through the gates to the cemetery, they felt all the memories of Rebecca and Arthur flood over them. Susan was wearing Blue Flower's necklace as she had every day, even when she was in labor.

After they stopped at the foot of the graves, Hugh said, "Father, Rebecca, I'd like you to meet our children. Your grandchildren, Papa. Your children, Rebecca. This is Rebecca, our daughter, and this is Arthur, our son. They were named after you, and like you, they have already touched our hearts."

Susan could add nothing to that simple introduction. They remained standing in silence for a few more minutes before returning to the house and laid the babies down in their cribs.

"It was getting pretty warm out there," said Susan.

"Yes, it was. Let's have Minnie mind the babies for a little while," suggested Hugh.

Susan smiled at her husband as he took her hand, picked up a blanket and said, "I think it's time for a swim."

EPILOGUE

Pale Dawn sat with her daughter on her knee talking to her sister. Blue Flower was pregnant and was due to have her child in another month.

“Sister,” she said, “you seem saddened. I thought you’d be happy that you were going to soon have a child. I know your husband is excited about having a son.”

“Yes,” answered Blue Flower, “I know he is. But he will be disappointed if I give him a daughter. I worry about this sometimes. That, and other things.”

Pale Dawn looked at her older sister and said, “I believe that you think of Hugh McGinnis too often, Sister. That is what is troubling you.”

“I know. I shouldn’t. It is a silly thing. I love my husband. He is a good man.”

“Do you believe that Hugh ever found the one to touch his heart?”

“Long Wolf told me that he said he had, but I have different dreams about him.”

“What do you mean?”

“I believe he found one that touched his heart, but something took her away.”

“And now he is alone?”

"Oh, no. When he lost the one who touched his heart, another wears the necklace now. One that does much more. She holds his heart in her hands."

BAKER CITY

1	Rock Creek	12/26/2016
2	North of Denton	01/02/2017
3	Fort Selden	01/07/2017
4	Scotts Bluff	01/14/2017
5	South of Denver	01/22/2017
6	Miles City	01/28/2017
7	Hopewell	02/04/2017
8	Nueva Luz	02/12/2017
9	The Witch of Dakota	02/19/2017
10	Baker City	03/13/2017
11	The Gun Smith	03/21/2017
12	Gus	03/24/2017
13	Wilmore	04/06/2017
14	Mister Thor	04/20/2017
15	Nora	04/26/2017
16	Max	05/09/2017
17	Hunting Pearl	05/14/2017
18	Bessie	05/25/2017
19	The Last Four	05/29/2017
20	Zack	06/12/2017
21	Finding Bucky	06/21/2017
22	The Debt	06/30/2017
23	The Scalawags	07/11/2017
24	The Stampede	07/20/2017
25	The Wake of the Bertrand	07/31/2017
26	Cole	08/09/2017
27	Luke	09/05/2017
28	The Eclipse	09/21/2017
29	A.J. Smith	10/03/2017
30	Slow John	11/05/2017
31	The Second Star	11/15/2017
32	Tate	12/03/2017
33	Virgil's Herd	12/14/2017
34	Marsh's Valley	01/01/2018
35	Alex Paine	01/18/2018
36	Ben Gray	02/05/2018

37	War Adams	03/05/2018
38	Mac's Cabin	03/21/2018
39	Will Scott	04/13/2018
40	Sheriff Joe	04/22/2018
41	Chance	05/17/2018
42	Doc Holt	06/17/2018
43	Ted Shepard	07/13/2018
44	Haven	07/30/2018
45	Sam's County	08/15/2018
46	Matt Dunne	09/10/2018
47	Conn Jackson	10/05/2018
48	Gabe Owens	10/27/2018
49	Abandoned	11/19/2018
50	Retribution	12/21/2018
51	Inevitable	02/04/2019
52	Scandal in Topeka	03/18/2019
53	Return to Hardeman County	04/10/2019
54	Deception	06/02/2019
55	The Silver Widows	06/27/2019
56	Hitch	08/21/2019
57	Dylan's Journey	09/10/2019
58	Bryn's War	11/06/2019
59	Huw's Legacy	11/30/2019
60	Lynn's Search	12/22/2019
61	Bethan's Choice	02/10/2020
62	Rhody Jones	03/11/2020